The Grass Is Singing
This Was the Old Chief's Country (*stories*)
The Habit of Loving (*stories*)
In Pursuit of the English
Going Home
Fourteen Poems
The Golden Notebook
A Man and Two Women (*stories*)
African Stories
Particularly Cats
Briefing for a Descent into Hell
The Temptation of Jack Orkney and Other Stories
The Summer Before the Dark
A Small Personal Voice
Memoirs of a Survivor
Stories

CHILDREN OF VIOLENCE:

Martha Quest
A Proper Marriage
A Ripple from the Storm
Landlocked
The Four-Gated City

CANOPUS IN ARGOS: ARCHIVES

Re: COLONISED PLANET 5

SHIKASTA

DORIS LESSING

Re: COLONISED PLANET 5

SHIKASTA

Personal, Psychological, Historical Documents
Relating to Visit by **JOHOR** (George Sherban)

EMISSARY (Grade 9)
87th of the Period of the Last Days

ALFRED A. KNOPF   NEW YORK   1979

Library of Congress Cataloging in Publication Data

Lessing, Doris May, [date]

Shikasta: re, colonised planet 5.

(Canopus in argos: archives)

I.   Title.

PZ3.L56684sh 1979   [PR6023.E833]   823'.9'14   79–11295

ISBN 0-394-50732-0

For my father, who used to sit,
hour after hour, night after night,
outside our house in Africa, watching
the stars. "Well," he would say,
"if we blow ourselves up, there's plenty
more where we came from!"

Shikasta is the first of a series of novels
with the overall title *Canopus in Argos: Archives.*
The second will be *The Marriages Between Zones Three,
Four, and Five.* The third will be *The Sirian Experiments.*

SOME REMARKS

Shikasta was started in the belief that it would be a single self-contained book, and that when it was finished I would be done with the subject. But as I wrote I was invaded with ideas for other books, other stories, and the exhilaration that comes from being set free into a larger scope, with more capacious possibilities and themes. It was clear I had made—or found—a new world for myself, a realm where the petty fates of planets, let alone individuals, are only aspects of cosmic evolution expressed in the rivalries and interactions of great galactic Empires: Canopus, Sirius, and their enemy, the Empire Puttiora, with its criminal planet Shammat. I feel as if I have been set free both to be as experimental as I like, and as traditional: the next volume in this series, *The Marriages Between Zones Three, Four, and Five*, has turned out to be a fable, or myth. Also, oddly enough, to be more realistic.

It is by now commonplace to say that novelists everywhere are breaking the bonds of the realistic novel because what we all see around us becomes daily wilder, more fantastic, incredible. Once, and not so long ago, novelists might have been accused of exaggerating, or dealing overmuch in coincidence or the improbable: now novelists themselves can be heard complaining that fact can be counted on to match our wildest inventions.

As an example, in *The Memoirs of a Survivor* I "invented" an animal that was half-cat and half-dog, and then read that scientists were experimenting on this hybrid.

Yes, I do believe that it is possible, and not only for novelists, to "plug in" to an overmind, or Ur-mind, or unconscious, or what you will, and that this accounts for a great many improbabilities and "coincidences."

The old "realistic" novel is being changed, too, because of influences from that genre loosely described as space fiction. Some people regret this. I was in the States, giving a talk, and the professor who was acting as chairwoman, and whose only fault was that perhaps she had fed too long on the pieties of academia, interrupted me with: "If I had you in my class you'd never get away with that!" (Of course it is not everyone who finds this funny.) I had been saying that space fiction, with science fiction, makes up the most original branch of literature now; it is inventive and witty; it has already enlivened all kinds of writing;

and that literary academics and pundits are much to blame for patronising or ignoring it—while of course by their nature they can be expected to do no other. This view shows signs of becoming the stuff of orthodoxy.

I do think there is something very wrong with an attitude that puts a "serious" novel on one shelf and, let's say, *First and Last Men* on another.

What a phenomenon it has been—science fiction, space fiction— exploding out of nowhere, unexpectedly of course, as always happens when the human mind is being forced to expand: this time starwards, galaxy-wise, and who knows where next. These dazzlers have mapped our world, or worlds, for us, have told us what is going on and in ways no one else has done, have described our nasty present long ago, when it was still the future and the official scientific spokesmen were saying that all manner of things now happening were impossible—who have played the indispensible and (at least at the start) thankless role of the despised illegitimate son who can afford to tell truths the respectable siblings either do not dare, or, more likely, do not notice because of their respectability. They have also explored the sacred literatures of the world in the same bold way they take scientific and social pos- sibilities to their logical conclusions so that we may examine them. How very much we do all owe them!

Shikasta has as its starting point, like many others of the genre, the Old Testament. It is our habit to dismiss the Old Testament altogether because Jehovah, or Jahve, does not think or behave like a social worker. H. G. Wells said that when man cries out his little "gimme, gimme, gimme" to God, it is as if a leveret were to snuggle up to a lion on a dark night. Or something to that effect.

The sacred literatures of all races and nations have many things in common. Almost as if they can be regarded as the products of a single mind. It is possible we make a mistake when we dismiss them as quaint fossils from a dead past.

Leaving aside the Popol Vuh, or the religious traditions of the Dogon, or the story of Gilgamesh, or any others of the now plentifully and easily available records (I sometimes wonder if the young realise how extraordinary a time this is, and one that may not last, when any book one may think of is there to be bought on a near shelf) and sticking to our local tradition and heritage, it is an exercise not without interest to read the Old Testament—which of course includes the Torah of the Jews—and the Apocrypha, together with any other works

Some Remarks

of the kind you may come on which have at various times and places been cursed or banished or pronounced non-books; and after that the New Testament, and then the Koran. There are even those who have come to believe that there has never been more than one Book in the Middle East.

7 November 1978   —Doris Lessing

CANOPUS IN ARGOS: ARCHIVES

Re: COLONISED PLANET 5
SHIKASTA

Johor has been chosen as suitable
to represent our emissaries to Shikasta—
of whom there were many, carrying out a
multiplicity of functions—in this
compilation of documents selected to
offer a very general picture of Shikasta
for the use of first-year students
of Canopean Colonial Rule.

JOHOR *reports:*

I have been sent on errands to our Colonies on many planets. Crises of all kinds are familiar to me. I have been involved in emergencies that threaten species, or carefully planned local programmes. I have known more than once what it is to accept the failure, final and irreversible, of an effort or experiment to do with creatures who have within themselves the potential of development dreamed of, planned for . . . and then—Finis! The end! The drum pattering out into silence . . .

But the ability to cut losses demands a different type of determination from the stubborn patience needed to withstand attrition, the leaking away of substance through centuries, then millennia—and with such a lowly glimmering of light at the end of it all.

Dismay has its degrees and qualities. I suggest that not all are without uses. The set of mind of a servant should be recorded.

I am a small member of the Workforce, and as such do as I must. That is not to say I do not have the right, as we all have, to say, Enough! Invisible, unwritten, uncoded rules forbid. What these rules amount to, I would say, is Love. Or so I feel, and many others, too. There are those in our Colonial Service who, we all know, hold a different view. One of my aims in setting down thoughts that perhaps fall outside the scope of the strictly necessary is to justify what is still, after all, the majority view on Canopus about Shikasta. Which is that it *is* worth so much of our time and trouble.

In these notes I shall be trying to make things clear. There will be others, after me, and they will study this record as I have studied, so often, the records of those who came before. It is not always possible to know, when you make a note of an event, or a state of mind, how this may strike someone perhaps ten thousand years later.

Things change. That is all we may be sure of.

Of all my embassies, that first one to Shikasta was the worst. I can say truthfully that I have scarcely thought of it between that time and this. I did not want to. To dwell on unavoidable wrong—no, it does no good.

This is a catastrophic universe, always; and subject to sudden reversals, upheavals, changes, cataclysms, with joy never anything but the song of substance under pressure forced into new forms and shapes. But poor Shikasta—no, I have not wanted to think about it more than

I had to. I did not make attempts to meet those of the personnel who were being sent (oh, many thousands of them, and over and over again, for no one could accuse Canopus of neglect of that unfortunate, Shikasta, no one could feel that we have evaded responsibilities), who were sent, and returned, and who filed their reports as we all did. Shikasta was always there, it is on our agenda—the cosmic agenda. It is not a place one could choose to forget altogether, for it was often in the news. But I, for one, did not "keep myself in touch," "informed"—no. Once I had filed my report that was that. And when I was sent again, on my second visit, at the Time of the Destruction of the Cities, to report on the results of such a long slow atrophy, I kept my thoughts well within the limits of my task.

And so, returning again after an interval—but is it really so many thousands of years?—I am deliberately reviving memories, re-creating memories, and these attempts will take their place in this record where they may be appropriate.

From: NOTES on PLANET SHIKASTA for GUIDANCE of COLONIAL SERVANTS

Of all the planets we have colonised totally or in part this is the richest. Specifically: with the greatest potential for variety and range and profusion of its forms of life. This has always been so, throughout the very many changes it has—the accurate word, we are afraid—suffered. Shikasta tends towards extremes in all things. For instance, it has seen phases of enormousness: gigantic life-forms and in a wide variety. It has seen phases of the minuscule. Sometimes these epochs have overlapped. More than once the inhabitants of Shikasta have included creatures so large that one of them could consume the food and living space of hundreds of their co-inhabitants in a single meal. This example is on the scale of the visible (one might even say the dramatic), for the economy of the planet is such that every life-form preys on another, is supported by another, and in its turn is preyed upon, down to the most minute, the subatomic level. This is not always evident to the creatures themselves, who tend to become obsessed with what they consume, and to forget what in turn consumes them.

Over and over again, a shock or a strain in the peculiarly precarious balance of this planet has called forth an accident, and Shikasta has been virtually denuded of life. Again and again it has been jostling-full with genera, and diseased because of it.

This planet is above all one of contrasts and contradictions, because of its in-built stresses. Tension is its essential nature. This is its strength. This is its weakness.

Envoys are requested to remember at all times that they cannot find on Shikasta what they will have become familiar with in other parts of our dominion and which therefore they will have become disposed to expect: very long periods of stasis, epochs of almost unchanging harmonious balance.

Envoys are requested to equip themselves by thorough preparation. It is left to them to make mental adjustments suggested by what they will find in Section 5 of the Planetary Demonstration Building.

For instance. They may care to stand in front of the Model of Shikasta, Scale 3—scaled, that is, to roughly present sizes. (Dominant species half of Canopean size.) This sphere, which you will see as they see it on their mapping and cartographic devices, has the diameter of their average predominant-species size. You will observe over the larger part of the sphere a smear of liquid. It is on this film of liquid that the profusion of life depends. (This planet knows nothing of the little scum of life on its surface: the planet has other ideas of itself, as we know; but that is not our concern here.) The point of the exercise is this: to understand that the proliferation of organic possibilities, the harvest of potentiality which is Shikasta, depends, from one point of view, on a scrape of liquid that could be drunk in a moment by a rogue star, or shaken off like puddle-mud from a child's ball during a game if a comet came in from elsewhere. Which event would be, after all, not without its precedents!

For instance. Adjust yourself to the various levels of being which lie in concentric shells around the planet, six of them in all, and none requiring much effort from you, since you will be entering and leaving them so quickly—none save the last Shell, or Circle, or Zone, Zone Six, which you must study in detail, since you will have to remain there for as long as it takes you to complete the various tasks you have been given: those which *can* be undertaken only through Zone Six. This is a hard place, full of dangers, but these can easily be dealt with, as is shown by the fact that not once have we ever lost one of our by now many hundreds of emissaries there, not even the most junior and inexperienced. Zone Six can present to the unprepared every sort of check, delay, and exhaustion. This is because the nature of this place is a strong emotion—"nostalgia" is their word for it—which means a longing for what has never been, or at least not in the form and shape imagined. Chimeras, ghosts, phantoms, the half-created and the unful-filled throng there, but if you are on your guard and vigilant, there will be nothing you cannot deal with.

For instance. It is suggested that you take time to acquaint yourself with the different focusses available for viewing the creatures of Shikasta. You will find every dimension possible to Shikasta in rooms 1–100 in Section 31, from the electron all the way up to the Dominant Animal. The fascinations of these different perspectives are real dangers. On the scale of the electron Shikasta appears as empty space where tinily vibrate shaped mists—the faintest possible smears of substance, the minutest impulses separated by vast spaces. (The largest building on Shikasta would collapse if the spaces that hold its electrons apart were withdrawn, into a piece of substance the size of a Shikastan fingernail.) Shikastan experience in the range of *sound* is not something to submit yourself to, if you have not become practised. Shikasta in *colour* is an assault you will not survive without preparation.

In short, none of the planets familiar to us is on as strong and as crude levels of vibration as is Shikasta, and too long a submission of one's being to any of these may pervert and suborn judgement.

JOHOR *reports:*

When I was asked to undertake this mission, my third, it was not expected that I would spend much time in Zone Six, but that I would move through it fast, perhaps stopping only as long as I would need for a task or two. But it was not known then that Taufiq had been captured and that others would have to do his work, myself in particular. And do it quickly, for there would not be time for me to incarnate and grow to adulthood before attending to the various urgencies that had developed because of Taufiq's misfortune. Our personnel on Shikasta are stretched to capacity as it is, and there is no one equipped to replace Taufiq. It is not always realised that we are not interchangeable. Our experiences, some chosen, some involuntary, mature us differently. We may have all begun on one of the planets, and some of us even on Shikasta in the same way, and with not much more to choose between us than between puppies of the same litter, but after even some hundreds of years, let alone thousands, we have been fused, baked out, crystallised, into forms as different as snowflakes are to each other. When one of us is chosen to "go down" to Shikasta or any other planet, it is only after deliberation: Johor is fitted for this or that task, Nasar for that one, and Taufiq for a specific, difficult long-term job that it seemed he and only he could do—and in parentheses and without emphasis I confess here that there is a weight of self-doubt on me. Taufiq and I have more than once been considered as very like: not equivalents, never that, but we have often headed a short list, we have been friends for . . . But how many times, and in how many planets have we worked together! And if so alike, brothers, life-and-death partners, friends on that level where there is nothing that may not be said, and no aspect of each other for which both may not take on absolute responsibility; if we are so close, and he is lost to us, temporarily of course, but nevertheless lost and part of the enemy forces, then—what may I not expect for myself? I record here that as I prepare for this trip, one of whose main tasks it is to take over Taufiq's undone work, that I spend many units of energy reinforcing my own purpose: No, no, I shall *not* (I tell myself), I shall *not* go the way of Taufiq, my brother. And again: I *shall* withstand what I know I must . . . and this is why I reacted badly to the news that I must spend so much time in Zone Six. I know well from last time that it is a place that weakens, undermines, fills one's mind with dreams, softness, hungers that one had hoped—one always does hope!—had been left behind forever. But it is our lot, our task, over and over again to submit ourselves to hazards and dangers and temptations. There is no other way. But I do not want to be in Zone Six! I was there twice before, once as a junior member of the Task Force of the First Time, then as Emissary in the Penultimate Time. Of course it will have changed, as Shikasta has.

I passed through Zones One to Five with all my inputs held to a minimum. I have visited them at various times, and they are lively and for the most part agreeable places, since their inhabitants are those who have worked their way out of and well past the Shikastan drag and pull, and are out of the reach of the miasmas of Zone Six. But they are not my concern now; and traversing them I experienced no more than rapid flickers of forms, sensations, changes from heat to cold, exhilaration. Soon I knew I was close to the environs of Zone Six by what I felt, and without being told I could have said, Ah, yes, Shikasta, there you are again—and with an inward sigh, a summoning of forces.

A twilight of grief, mists of hungry longing, a sucking drag of all the emotions—and I had to force each step, and it was as if my ankles were being held by hands I could not see, as if I walked weighted by beings I could not see. Out of the mists I came at last and there, where last time I was here I had seen grasslands, streams, grazing beasts, now was only a vast dry plain. Two flat black stones marked the Eastern Gate, and assembled there were throngs of poor souls yearning out and away from Shikasta, which lay behind them on the other side of the dusty plains of Zone Six. Feeling me there, for they could not then see me, they came jostling forward like blind people, their faces turning and searching, and they groaned, a deep yearning groan, and as I still did not show myself, they began a keening chant, or hymn, which I remembered hearing in Zone Six all those thousands of years before.

Save me, God,
Save me, Lord,
I love you,
You love me.

Eye of God,
Watching me,
Pay my fee,
Set me free. . . .

Meanwhile, my eyes were at work on those faces! How many of them were familiar to me, unchanged except for the ravages of grief, how many of them I had known, even in the First Time, when they were handsome, wholesome, sturdy animals, all self-reliance and competence. Among them I saw my old friend Ben, descendant of David and his daughter Sais, and he sensed me so strongly that he was standing close against me, tears running down his face, his hands held out as if waiting for mine. I manifested myself in the shape he had seen me last, and put my hands in his, and he flung himself into my arms and stood weeping. "At last, at last," he wept, "have you come for me now? May I come now?"—and all the others pressed in about us, clutching and holding, and I nearly lost myself into the gulf of their longing. I stood there feeling myself sway, feeling my substance dragged out from me, and I stepped back from them, making them release me, and Ben, too, took away his hands, but stood close, moaning, "It's been so long, so long . . ."

"Tell me why you are still here?" I insisted, and they became silent while Ben spoke. But it was no different from what he had told me before, and as he finished and the others stood crying out their stories one after another, I knew I was caught and bound by the necessities of Zone Six, and my whole being was fermenting with impatience and even fear, for all my work was ahead of me, my work was calling me— and I could not get myself free. What they told was always the same, had always been the same—and I wondered if they remembered how I had stood here, they had stood here, so long ago, saying the same things, . . . they had made themselves leave this gate, and they had turned themselves around and crossed the plain, and had entered Shikasta—some of them recently, some of them not for centuries or millennia—and all had succumbed to Shikasta, had suffered some failure of purpose and will, and had been expelled back to this place, clustering around the Eastern Gate. They had tried again, some of them, had succumbed again, again found themselves here—on and on, for some, while others had given up all hope of ever being strong enough to enter Shikasta and win its prize, which was, by enduring it, to be free of it forever; and hung and drifted, thin miserable ghosts, yearning and hungering for "Them" who would come for them, would lift them out and away from this terrible place as a mother cat takes its kittens to safety. The idea of rescue, of succour, was evidenced here always, at this gate, as strongly as I have known it anywhere, and the clutch and cling of it was maddening me.

"Ben," I said, and I was speaking to them all, through him, "Ben, you have to try again, there is no other way."

But he was weeping and clasping me, begging, pleading—I was in a storm of sighs and tears.

He had not given up, I could not accuse him of that! Again and again he had hovered waiting at Shikasta's "gates," and when his turn came he had gone down full of purpose and determination that *this* time at last . . . but then, it was not until he had left Shikasta, after months or years or a full life-span (whatever it was at that time) that he remembered, back in Zone Six, what he had set out to do. He had meant to save himself by the use of the terrors and hazards of Shikasta so that he would crystallise into a substance that could survive and withstand, but when he came to himself he realised he had spent his life *again* in self-indulgence and weakness and a falling away into forgetfulness. Again and again . . . so that now he regarded the place with such horror that he could not force himself to line up with the crowds of souls waiting at the Shikastan entrances for a chance of rebirth. No, he had given up. He was doomed, like all the rest here, to wait and to wait until "They" came to take him away. Until *I* came . . . and he held me and would not let go.

I said what I had said to them before, to him before: "You must all make your way across the plain to the other side, and you must patiently wait your turn—but it will not be so long a wait now, for Shikasta is being crowded with souls, they are being born in droves, more and more. Go, and wait and try again."

A great clamour and a complaint went up all around me.

Ben cried, "But it is worse now, they say. It gets worse and harder. If I could not succeed then, why should I now? I can't . . ."

"You must," I said, and began to force my way through them.

And now Ben let out a roaring raucous laugh, an accusation. "There you go," he shouted, "*you're* all right, you can come and go as you please, but what of us?"

I had passed through. Well away from them, I looked back. The crowd there wailed and lamented and swayed about under the force of their grief. But Ben took a step forward from them. And another. I pointed across the plain, and watched him take a painful step forward. He was going to try. He was on his way over that vast, painful plain.

I heard them singing as I went on:

Eye of God,
Watching me,
Pay my fee,
Set me free,

Here I am,
Waiting here,
Save me, God,
Save me, Lord. . . . on, and on, and on.

Already depleted by grief, that emotion which of all others is the most useless, I ran across the plain, feeling the dust thick and soft underfoot. I remembered the grasses and bushes and rivers of my last visit, while I stepped across dry channels and used dry riverbeds as roads. Crickets and cicadas, the shimmer of hot light on rock—this would be desert very soon. And I thought of what I must face when I at last was able to enter Shikasta.

Sitting on an outcrop of low stone I saw a figure that was familiar, and I approached a female shape drooping in sorrow and lassitude so deep she did not move as I approached. I stood over her and saw it was Rilla, who on my last visit had been with the crowds at the Eastern Gate.

I greeted her, she lifted her face, and I saw it set in dry, obdurate woe.

"I know what you are going to say," said she.

"Ben is trying again," I said. But when I looked back I could not see him: only the dust hanging reddish in the air, and the dry broken grasses. She looked with me, passively.

"He is there," I said. "Believe me."

"It is no use," she said. "I have tried so often."

"Are you going to sit here for the rest of time?"

She did not answer, but resumed her post, looking down, motionless. She seemed to herself a static weight, empty; to me she was like a whirlpool of danger. I could see myself, thinned and part transparent, could feel myself sway and lean—towards her, into her locked violences.

"Rilla," I said, "I have work to do."

"Of course," said she. "When do you ever say anything different?"

"Go and find Ben," I said.

I walked on. Long afterwards I looked around—I did not dare before, for fear I would turn and run back to her. Oh, I had known her, I had known her well. I knew what qualities were shut up there, prisoners of her despair. She was not looking at me. She had turned her head and was gazing out into the hazy plains where Ben was.

I left her.

I had lost my way. Memories of the last time were not helping me, could not—everything had changed. I was looking for the abode of the Giants. I did not want to see them, because of the degeneration I knew I would find. But they were the quickest way to Taufiq. Taufiq's condition, as captive of the Enemy, must be—could be no other—an excess of self-esteem, pride, *silliness*. I could contact Taufiq through the equivalent qualities here. The Giants, then . . . I had to!

Far away across the deserts were towering peaks of rock, bare black rock, like clusters of fists held into a blood-red sky. Purple clouds, unmoving, thick, heavy. Beneath them drifts of sand hanging in the air like armies of locusts. A still, moribund world. My long spidery shadow lay behind me almost to the horizon, following me black and menacing, an enemy. Shadows lay across the sands to my feet from the peaks. Deep tormenting shadows, full of memories . . . one of them bulged, moved, separated itself . . . out came a troop of Giants, and at the first sight of them I felt the movement of the heart like a leaking of strength that means sorrow.

This was the magnificence I remembered? These?

They were tall, their forms were something of what they had been, but they had lost strength and substance. A company of lean, lean-to, shambling ghosts, their movements awkward, their faces empty and full of shadows, they came towards me across the blowing sands, which kept rising and obscuring them and then billowed away behind them, so that they appeared again on a background of suddenly darkened sky, which was a blackish grey on red, grey making turbid the purple clouds, grey heavying and dragging everything, and rising in mists around their feet. They waded towards me through the eddying sands, wraiths, shadows . . . this was the great race I had come to warn on my first visit, came to warn and sustain, and—it was no use, I could not help it, I heard a wail of mourning come from my lips, and this was echoed by a wail from them, but in them it was a battle cry, or so they meant it. A sad mourning cry, and every gesture, every movement, was stiff with ridiculous hauteur, this company of wraiths was sick with pride of a falsely remembered past, and they would have struck me down with the bones of their arms and hands if I had not held out to them the Signature. They recognised it. Not at once or easily: but they were pulled up short, and stood on the sands in front of me, about two hundred of them, uncertain, half remembering, looking at me, at each other, at the glinting gleaming Thing I was confronting them with . . . and I was looking from one worn attenuated face to another and yes, I could recognise in those faces the kingly beings I had known.

After a while, at a loss as to what else to do, they turned about, enclosing me in their company, and walked, or stalked, or shambled towards the great rocks. Among these they had built a rough castle, or association of towers. These clumsy structures had nothing in common with what these Giants had built for themselves, in the First Time, but were expressions of pathetic grandiosity. I wanted to say, "Do you really imagine that this savage place is anything like what you created to live in when you were yourselves?"

They took me into a long hall of crudely dressed stone. Around the hall were set great chairs and thrones, and in these they placed themselves. At least they did have some inkling that they had been equal, a company of free companions. They sat in poses that said "power," in heavy robes that said "pomp," holding baubles and toys of all kinds, crowns and coronets, sceptres, globes, swords. Where had they found such rubbishy stuff? A trip must have been dared into Shikasta to fetch it!

I looked at these shadows and again was tormented with the need quite simply to keen out my mourning for the loss of all that the First Time had meant, but I was reminding myself not to waste my forces in this way, for I could not afford to let loose what I felt.

I held the Signature out before them, and asked them how they had fared since I had seen them last. A silence, a stirring, and the great hollow faces turned to each other in the shadows of the hall. . . . . I noticed I was finding difficulty in distinguishing their features, and peered closely at them. Shining black faces, the various hues of brown, of yellow, ivory, cream . . . but it was hard to see them. Over a hundred had trooped with me into the hall and filled the chairs and thrones, but it seemed as if there were fewer now. Some chairs stood empty. As I glanced around, chairs that had held occupants stood empty, as forms vanish in a deepening twilight. Only the Signature held light, and life, the Giants were so thin and grey and *gone* that they were almost transparent—yes, on a shift of pose they seemed to disappear, so that an enormous brown man in his gaudy robes would become a cloak folded over the back of a throne, and strong peering eyes searching my face for clues to memories only just out of mind would dwindle to the dull glitter of paste jewels in a broken tiara slung over the knob of a chairback. They were all dissipating and disappearing even as I sat there and watched.

I said to them, "Will you not take your chances on Shikasta? Will you not try to win through that way?"—but a hiss ran through the company, they moved their limbs and heads restlessly, they checked gestures of aggression, and would have killed me if it had not been for the Signature.

"Shikasta, Shikasta, Shikasta . . ." was the murmuring whisper all around me, and the sound was the hissing of a snake, was hatred, loathing—and a dreadful fear.

They were remembering a little of what they had been: the Signature induced this in them. Nothing much, but they did remember something splendid and right. And they knew what their descendants had become. That was what their faces stated: that even the *word* Shikasta confronted them with filth and ordure.

"I need to sit with you here," I said, "for as long as it takes me to make a visit to Shikasta."

Again the stirring rearing movement, like threatened horses.

I said, as it was my duty to do, even knowing that they would not listen (not *could* not, for otherwise I would not have wasted my energies, already depleting), I said, "Come with me, I'll help you, I'll do everything I can to help you win your way through and out."

They sat there frozen, this company of half-ghosts. They were unable to move. "Very well, then," I said. "You must sit where you are, till I come back. It is through you I can make this journey."

And surrounded by these hosts of the dead, sustained by their awful arrogance, I was able to part the mists that divided me from the realities of Shikasta, and search for my friend Taufiq.

But first I shall set down my recovered memories of my visit to Shikasta, then Rohanda, in the First Time, when this race was a glory and a hope of Canopus. I am also making use of records of other visits to Shikasta in the Time of the Giants.

The planet was for millions of years one of a category of hundreds that we kept a watch on. It was regarded as having potential because its history has always been one of sudden changes, rapid developments, as rapid degradations, periods of stagnation. Anything could be expected of it. But a period of stagnation had held for millennia when the planet was subjected to a prolonged radiation from an exploding star in Andar, and a mission was sent down to report. It was fertile, but mostly swamp. There was vegetation, but it was uniform and stable. There were varieties of lizard in the swamps, and small rodents and marsupials and monkeys on the limited areas of dry land. The drawback to this planet was the short expectation of life. Our rival Sirius had planted some of their species there, and they did not become extinct, but at once their life-spans, previously normal—some thousands of years—adapted, and individuals could expect to live no more than a few years. (I am using Shikastan time measurement.) There had been conferences between specialists on Canopus and Sirius to discuss the possibilities of these short-lived species, and if it was worthwhile to allocate the landmasses between us. Since the Great War between Sirius and Canopus that had ended all war between us, there had been regular conferences to avoid overlapping, or interfering with each other's experiments. And this practice continues to this time.

The conference was inconclusive. It was not known what to expect from the burst of radiation. Sirius and Canopus agreed to wait and see. Meanwhile, Shammat had also made an inspection—but we did not know about this until later.

Almost at once our envoys reported startling changes in the species. The whole steamy swampy fertile place was sizzling with change. The monkeys in particular were breeding all sorts of variations, some freaks and monsters, but also dramatic variations that showed the greatest promise. And so with all life: vegetation, insects, fish. We saw that the planet was on its way to becoming one of the most fruitful of its class, and it was at this time that it was named Rohanda, which means fruitful, thriving.

Meanwhile, it was still a place of mists, swamps, and dismal wetness. (There are no more depressing places than these planets that are all warm water, cloud, fen, bog, dampness—and no one likes visiting them.) But there was a change in the climate. Water was steaming off the marshes and the swamps and hung in vast lowering clouds. More dry land appeared, though approaching the planet, nothing could be seen but the rolling, seething cloud masses. There was another, completely unexpected, blast of radiation, and the poles froze, holding masses of ice. Rohanda was on its way to becoming the most desirable kind of planet, one with large landmasses and water held in defined areas, or running in channels and streams.

Long before we had planned it, Sirius and Canopus conferred again. Sirius wanted the southern hemisphere for experiments that would complement others they were making in temperate and southerly areas in another of their colonies. We wanted the northern hemisphere, because it was chiefly here that a subgroup of the former "monkeys" had established themselves and were developing. They were already three and four times the height of the little creatures who were their ancestors. They were showing tendencies to walk upright. They showed rapid increases in intelligence. Our experts told us that these creatures would continue a fast evolution and could be expected to become a Grade A species in, probably, fifty thousand years. (Provided of course there were no more accidents of the cosmic type.) And their life-span was already several times what it had been: this was considered the most important factor of all.

Canopus decided to subject Rohanda to an all-out booster, Top-Level Priority, Forced-Growth Plan. This was partly because another of our colonies, unstable, like Rohanda, was known to have only a short life ahead of it. A comet was expected to shift it off course in twenty thousand years. This would upset the so carefully maintained balances of our System. (See Maps and Charts Nos. 67M to 93M, Area 7 D3, Planetary Demonstration Building.) If Rohanda could be brought up to operational levels by then, it could take the place in our cosmic scheme of that unfortunate one—whose future alas was exactly as forecast: knocked off balance, it lost all life, and very quickly, and is now dead.

What we needed, to be precise, was to progress Rohanda up to the appropriate level in twenty thousand, not fifty thousand, years.

As is customary, we put out tenders among our colonies for volunteers, and we chose a species from Colony 10, which has been remarkably successful in symbiotic development.

Of course, a species has to be of a certain mental set even to consider such conditions: let us say that they must be adventurers! While the main outlines of a probable development are known, it is never possible to forecast exactly what will happen when two species are put into symbiosis: there are too many unforeseens. And it was not kept from them that Rohanda was by nature unpredictable, unusually subject to chance and change. Above all, it was not known how their life-spans would adjust: if badly, down to the Rohandan current norm, then this volunteering of theirs could be regarded as not far from racial suicide.

But it is enough to say that at that stage and at that time these were a strong and healthy species; they were alert and mentally adaptable; they had the genetic memory of experience in similar experiments.

Small groups of Colony 10 volunteers were introduced successfully onto Rohanda, in various parts of the northern hemisphere. There were a thousand in all, male and female, and almost at once—that is to say, within five hundred years—it was obvious that this was going to be a most successful experiment.

The interaction between the two species was admirable, both being well affected. There were no instinctive aggressions due to genetic incompatibility. We on Canopus were congratulating ourselves.

Well within the twenty thousand years, the younger (ex-monkey) race would have attained the required level; and the fast-developing Colony 10 people would have advanced themselves to a stage where they could be said to have taken an evolutionary step forward that in usual conditions might take ten times as long.

I shall describe the situation as it was about a thousand years after the introduction of the Colony 10 species.

First, the indigenous race. Nothing remarkable here: we have all seen this before, since it is a pattern that has shown itself on many planets.

The creatures were now on their hind legs, and their arms and hands were well adapted for manifold tasks and the use of tools. They had a strong sense of their own worth—that is, as creatures able to manipulate their environment and survive. They hunted, and were at the beginnings of an agriculture. They were about the size of an average Shikastan now, and were enlarging rapidly. They had thick long head hair, and short thick body fur. They lived in small groups, widely scattered, with little contact between them. They did not fight each other. They had a life expectation of about one hundred and fifty years.

A good proportion of the first Colony 10 people died early—but this was to be expected. There is never any explanation for this type of death. The infants were the size of their parents before they were out of childhood: the species was increasing in size so rapidly they called themselves Giants almost from the start. This was not without unease: no species observes itself in such rapid change without misgivings. They were a tall, strong race from the beginning, but a thousand years of Rohanda had already made them a third as tall again. They were well built. They were dark brown or black in colour, with a particularly attractive glossy healthy skin. They had no body hair, and very little head hair. The nails of their hands and feet were vestigial, no more than a thickening of the skin at toes and fingertips. It was too soon to know how their life-spans would be affected. Some of the individuals who had been introduced onto the planet were still in full vigour, and as for the young ones it was too soon to say. Colony 10 has a mild climate of very little variation. Clothes are not worn except for cere-monial occasions. But on Rohanda the Giants had to develop clothes, which they did at once, very soon being able to dispense with the shipments from warehouses on Canopus for materials made from the barks and plants of Rohanda.

They had established with the Natives a tutelary relation which gave the liveliest of interest and satisfaction to both sides. It was the Giants who taught the Natives the beginnings of plant culture. They taught them, too, how to use animals without harming the species. They were developing language in them. It was still only the basis of many talents—arts, sciences—that the Giants were laying, for it was not yet time for the establishment of the Lock between Canopus and Rohanda that would begin the Forced-Growth Phase.

Conditions continued appropriate, and about seven thousand years after the matching of the two species, a special mission was sent from Canopus to see if it was time to establish the Lock.

Here are extracts from their Report. (No. 1300, Rohanda.)

THE GIANTS

LIFE-SPAN: On Colony 10 they lived to be twelve thousand, fifteen thousand years. Fears that immersion in Rohandan conditions would drastically reduce their life-span have proved right. At the start expectancy was reduced to about two thousand years. Almost at once this began to improve, and now they live four thousand or five thousand years. The trend is upwards. We observe the usual anomalies. A minority die, without any apparent reason, very young. These are not the types that might be considered degenerate (see Size, below), the thin attenuated ones, who in fact live as long as the robust. Nor is there a way to forecast who will die at two hundred years or five hundred years.

SIZE: They are twice the size they were on leaving Colony 10. They are strong and well built, with great physical endurance. Variants are extremely thin, spindly, comparatively awkward in movement; and very stout and powerful, so that seeing examples of the two extremes together it would be easy to believe them of different species.

COLOUR: Previously dark brown and black skin tones are varied to shades of light brown and even cream.

MENTAL POWERS: These are generally improved by the symbiosis. The level of *practical* intelligence is not different from those on Colony 10, but the higher levels have been stimulated quite remarkably, and it is this fact which makes the experiment the success it undoubtedly is.

THE NATIVES

LIFE-SPAN: Increasing. But not as fast as with the Giants. They live about five hundred years, unless they are subject to accidents. They die, like the Giants, of attacks of minuscule organisms, some locally evolved, some from space. We see no sign of the Degenerative Disease.

SIZE: Half the size of the Giants, at about eight or nine feet. They have refined remarkably. Their body hair is much less. Their head hair is profuse however, with strongly marked eyebrows. Build, features, general character are broad, solid, strong. Their animal origin remains marked. They are mostly brown-eyed. From settlement to settlement across the northern hemisphere, these creatures are remarkably uniform.

COLOUR: Their skin tones range from cream to brown, but the majority are a warm light brown.

Re: Colonised Planet 5, Shikasta

MENTAL POWERS: No trace at all of Higher Powers, but their practical intelligence is developing even better than expected, and this is a sound and healthy basis for what we plan when we establish the Lock.

GENERAL

Relations between Giants and Natives are good. A steady but slight contact is maintained. The Giants make visits only when it is felt that the Natives will benefit from advice or redirection. The Giants live never more than one hundred miles from their protégés. Their settlements are comfortable, but of course not considered as more than temporary, and used as experiments for the phase to come. That is, *all* buildings, plantings, irrigation are experimental, with a view to future cosmic alignments dependent on the Lock. This mission has the pleasure of reporting that there is no sign at all of the Degenerative Disease. Nowhere are there to be seen any buildings or developments that are for any other reason than that of preparing for the Lock. The settlements are all of course aligned as far as is possible at this stage with geophysical factors.

The Natives live in much cruder settlements—viewed from the angle of cosmic alignments, though from the physical aspect some dwellings have reached quite handsome levels, with aspirations far beyond the needs of warmth and comfort. It is this factor which more than any other makes us conclude that the Lock should not be delayed. Some dwellings have designs and patterns on walls, roofs, pottery, utensils, fabrics. These designs, because of the tutelage of the Giants, are well within the needs of this phase, but an imbalance is shortly inevitable.

Hunting has ceased to be the main source of food. Agriculture is well developed, with grains of all sorts, gourds, leafy plants. Husbandry is practised, with a good developing relation with the animal stocks. There is as yet no urgent need for irrigation: natural water patterns remain adequate. But the Giants' research suggests that irrigation should be established in the hotter areas of the Central part.

Our report is one of success.

It is this mission's opinion that conditions are ripe for the establishment of the Lock. The Giants are anxious for this. Without in any way complaining or wishing to hasten phases which should not be hastened, they feel excluded from the common contacts of the galaxy. While none of them, as an individual, remembers genuine contact—the free flow of thought, ideas, information, *growth* between planet and planet across our galaxy—it is not long since the oldest of the Colony 10 immigrants died, and, in any case, their genetic memory is strong, active, developing. And all their preparations for the establishment of the Lock are made.

A WARNING

There are persistent rumours—mostly formalised as tales and songs told by the Natives, who get news very fast as their groups meet in the course of hunting or other expeditions—that "down South" there are races of extremely warlike and hostile beings. The Giants have sent expeditions to the two main landmasses, and have found only that the species established by Sirius are flourishing. (These will be the subject of a subreport.) It is clear to us that the Sirian tutors have caused these rumours to spread, so as to prevent our experimentees from wandering over into their territory. The Giants, who understood this, have created new legends and stories, and are doing everything to create mental sets that will keep our bargain with Sirius.

Nothing of this is more than was to be expected, but there is something else. There are persistent rumours about "spies," both among the Natives and among the Giants. These spies do not enter Giant territory, but appear quite frequently among the Natives, and everywhere over the northern hemisphere. At first the Giants believed these to be from Sirian colonies, on ordinary fact-finding missions, but they now believe there are also spies from some other empire. They are cautious about committing themselves, but repeat that the distinguishing feature of these creatures is not in appearance, but in behaviour. In short, they show every feature of the Degenerative Disease. In our view everything we have heard can only confirm the presence of Shammat.

OUR CONCLUSIONS

1 The Lock may begin. We have optimum conditions.
2 It should not be forgotten in our plans that this planet is subject to sudden and drastic change.

3 Enquiries should be made from Sirius if spies from Shammat have been found in their territories.

4 Attention should be directed to what Shammat is likely to be wanting. On the face of it there is no place for Shammat on this planet.

Shortly after that the Lock was established, and was a success, making missions and special envoys unnecessary. The minds of the Giants—or to put it accurately, factually, the Giant-mind—had become one with the mind of the Canopean System, at first partially, and tentatively, but it was an ever-growing and sensitizing current. What came through from Rohanda was all good news. To absorb the tapes and records from that period of nearly ten thousand years is to participate in achievement, success, development. Few of our colonies have fulfilled our plans so hearteningly. The "spies" of the mission's report mentioned above seemed to fade out of the picture. It was assumed on Canopus that they were destroyed by the suddenness of the Lock— that they had not been able to stand the change to higher and finer vibrations, though we did not rule out the possibility that these creatures of Shammat had evolved, rather than died out, and possibly even in a way that might contribute to the general variety and richness of Rohanda.

We have to look at things now rather differently. In short, it is a question, if not of apportioning blame—never a very helpful process, tending always to draw the attention away from essentials, rather than focussing it—then of knowing what went wrong, so as to avoid it on other planets. But the main cause of the disaster was what that word *dis-aster* implies: a fault in the stars. That we could not foresee, beyond acknowledging that nothing on Rohanda could be taken for granted. If there had not been that shift in stellar alignments, it would not have mattered what the Shammat agents were doing, or plotting.

But how was it we did not know they were there?

The fault was partly ours—Canopus. As for Sirius, our relations continued to be formally correct: exchanges of information took place between the Colonial Services on the mother planets. At the local Rohandan or Shikastan level, they did not behave worse than we had expected, considering the much lower level of their Empire. But it *is* this lower level of the Sirian Empire which is the key to this and other problems of Rohanda/Shikasta; and my understanding of it is different now. It must be remembered that we servants of Canopus are also in the process of evolution, and our understandings of situations change as we do. [SEE *History of the Sirian Empire.*]

In short, we were not thinking much of Shammat at all. It is easy now to say we were mistaken. Puttiora itself was concerned, or so it seemed, to keep well out of our way: the alliance between the Empire of Sirius and the Canopean Empire was not to be taken lightly. No one did take it lightly! Throughout our part of the galaxy there was peace, there was harmonious development, and no one challenged us. Why should they? Seldom has the galaxy seen such a blaze of accomplishment, such a long period without any war at all.

Perhaps it is a fault of the species who thrive in peace, mutual help, aspirations for more of the same—to forget that outside these borders dwell very different types of mind, feeding on different fuel. It is not that Canopus did not guard itself from the vile Puttiora emanations, that we did not keep ourselves informed about that revolting empire, which dismayed us more because it could only remind us of our earlier less pleasant stages of development—it was not that we were negligent in that. But Puttiora did not challenge us anywhere else—so why on Rohanda?

And so we did not take Shammat enough into account. That Puttiora should allow an outpost on a planet all rock and desert had always seemed to us inexplicable, though the rumours did come that Shammat had been colonised by criminals fleeing from Puttiora, that Puttiora had ignored them until it was too late. We had no idea at all of how Shammat was sucking and draining sources of nourishment everywhere they could be found, of how it built itself up, a thief getting fat on its loot. When Shammat was already a successful pirate state, we still thought of it as a disgraceful but unimportant appendage to the terrible but fortunately far-distant Puttiora.

And what of the Giants, that alert, intelligent species who had everything on Rohanda under their control?

Again, we believe that this is a question of benign and nurturing minds not being able to credit the reality of types of mind keyed to theft and destruction. Colony 10 had never been anything but a place of fruitful co-operation, and as I have said, they are peculiarly well adapted to harmonious symbiosis with others. And on Rohanda they had not experienced setback and threat. We now believe it is a disadvantage to allow too much prosperity, ease of development—and on none of our other colonies have we again been satisfied with an easy triumphant growth. We have always inbuilt a certain amount of stress, of danger.

But suppose there had never been a dis-aster? Probably no one would ever have known that Shammat was on Rohanda . . . for Shammat can succeed only where there is disequilibrium, harm, dismay.

We had very little notice of the crisis. There was no reason to expect it. But the balances of Canopus and her System were suddenly not right. We had to find out what was wrong, and very quickly. We did. It was Rohanda. She was out of phase, and rapidly worsening. The Lock was weakening. There were shifts in the balances of the forces from inside the body of Rohanda. These answered a shift—and now we had to look outwards, away from Rohanda—in the balances of powers elsewhere, among the stars who were holding us, Canopus, in a web of interacting currents with our colonised planets. Rohanda had felt the wrong alignment first, because it is her nature to be sensitive. Rohanda was at risk, Rohanda must be urgently rescued, held in phase, adjusted—so went our early thought.

But it was soon established that this could not be. Rohanda could not hold her place in our System. It was not so much a question of jettisoning her, as of her jettisoning herself.

Very well then: we could cushion and provide . . . so went our thought in that second stage of our discovery.

Rohanda was in for a long period—but at that stage we had no idea how very long it would be—of stagnation. But we would make sure that at least there would be no serious falling away from what she had accomplished, we would maintain her until the cosmic forces changed again, which they would do, so we had ascertained.

But then something else and worse was forced in on us. We could not make our information match with what we could register coming from Rohanda! The currents from Rohanda were coming wild, shrill, cracked . . . it was clear that they were being tapped. Previously, the strong full Lock between us and Rohanda had made impossible any such leeching away, but now there was no doubt of it.

Things started happening all at once. Information from Sirius about Puttiora, its sudden increase of strength and pride. Information from our spies in the Puttiora Empire—about Shammat, in particular. Shammat was like a drunk, shameless, boastful, reeling. . . . Shammat was going from strength to strength. Shammat was taking advantage of the new weakness of Rohanda, who was unshielded, unguarded, open to her. Which meant that Shammat had been lying in wait on Rohanda, had been established there . . . had known what was going to happen? No, that was not possible; because with all our technology, so infinitely in advance of Shammat's, we had not known.

It was not a question of Rohanda being nursed through a long quiescent period, but much worse.

An envoy would have to be sent, and at once.

And now I will describe Rohanda as I found it on my first visit.

But it was Shikasta now: Shikasta the hurt, the damaged, the wounded one. The name had already been changed.

Can I say that it is "with pleasure" that I write of it? It is a retrospective emotion, going back before the bad news I carried. Rohanda had given us all so much satisfaction, it was our easiest and our best achievement. And don't forget that it was Rohanda who was to take the place of that unfortunate planet who was so soon to be destroyed and who we were already emptying of its inhabitants, taking them to other places where they might thrive and grow.

What a crisis I left behind me on Canopus that time, what a roar of effort, change, and adjustment: plans cherished and relied on for millennia were being thrown over, adapted, substituted—and from this place of turmoil, I left for Shikasta, the stricken.

At least there is something of consolation that such excellence had been. What has been good is a promise that in other places, other times, good can develop again . . . at times of shame and destruction, we may sustain ourselves with these thoughts.

At the time of the disaster there were still not more than sixty thousand Giants, and about a million and a half Natives, distributed over the northern hemisphere. The planet was amazingly fruitful and pleasant. The waters that—released—would re-create the swamps and marshes were still locked up in ice at the poles, and we could see no reason why this should change.

There were great forests over all the northern and temperate zones, and these were plentifully stocked with animals of all sorts, differing from those of my later visits mostly in size. These were not enemies of the inhabitants. There were settlements in the north, even in extremes of climate, both of Giants and of Natives, but most of the population was settled farther south, in the Middle Areas, where there was a sparkling, light, invigorating climate.

The cities were established where the patterns of stones had been set up according to the necessities of the plan, along the lines of force in the earth of that time. These patterns, lines, circles, arrangements were no different from those familiar to us on other planets, and were the basis and foundation of the transmitting systems of the Lock between Canopus and Rohanda . . . now poor Shikasta.

The arranging and alignment of the stones had been done initially entirely by the Giants, whose size and strength made the work easy for them, but by now the understanding between the Giants and the Natives was such that the Natives wished to assist in a task which they knew was—as they put it in their songs and tales and legends—their link with the Gods, with Divinity.

They did not see the Giants as Gods. They had developed beyond that. Their intelligence was so much greater, because of the Lock, that it was now not far from that of the Giants just before the Lock.

The cities had been built on the lines indicated by the experiments that had been so extensive in the long preparatory phase before the Lock.

They were of stone, and were linked with the stone patterns as part of the transmitting system.

Cities, towns, settlements of mud, wood, or any vegetable material cannot disturb the transmitting processes, or set up unsuitable oscillations. It was for this reason that during the preparatory phase, the Giants discouraged stone as building material and themselves lived in houses of whichever organic substance was most convenient and to hand. Once the Lock was established, and the stone patterns set and operative, the cities were rebuilt of stone, and the Natives were instructed in this art—so soon to be lost to the memory of Shikasta—for the plan was that when the Natives had evolved to the adequate level, the Giants would leave for another task somewhere else, themselves evolved beyond anything that could have been envisaged by the handful from Colony 10 those many thousands of years ago.

What the Natives were being taught was the science of maintaining contact at all times with Canopus; of keeping contact with their Mother, their Maintainer, their Friend, and what they called God, the Divine. If they kept the stones aligned and moving as the forces moved and waxed and waned, and if the cities were kept up according to the laws of the Necessity, then they might expect—these little inhabitants of Rohanda who had been no more than scurrying monkeys half in and half out of the trees, animals with little in them of the Canopean nature—these animals could expect to become men, would take charge of themselves and their world when the Giants left them, the work of the symbiosis complete.

The cities were all different, because of the different terrains on which they were established, and the currents and forces of those places. They might be on the open plains, or by springs, or by seashores, or on mountains or plateaux. They might be among snow and ice, or very hot, but each was exact and perfect and laid down according to the Necessity. Each was a mathematical symbol and shape, and mathematics were taught to the young ones by travel. A tutor would take a group of pupils to sojourn in, for instance, the Square City, where they would absorb by osmosis everything there is to be known about squareness. Or the Rhomboid, or the Triangle, and so on.

Of course the shape of a city was as rigidly controlled upwards as it was in area, for roundness, or the hexagonal, or the spirit of Four, or Five, was expressed as much in the upper parts as it was by what was experienced where the patterns of stone in building enmeshed with the earth.

The flow of water around and inside a city was patterned according to the Necessity, and so was the placing of fire—as distinct from heat, which was done by steam and heated water—but fire itself, which the Natives could not rid themselves of thinking as Divine, was according to Need.

Each city, then, was a perfect artefact, with nothing in it uncontrolled: considered, with its inhabitants, as a functioning whole. For it was found that some temperaments would be best suited, and would contribute most, in a Round City, or a Triangle, and so on. And there had even evolved a science of being able to distinguish, in very early childhood, where an individual needed to live. And here was the source of that "unhappiness" which must be the lot, to one extent or another, of every inhabitant of our galaxy, for it was by no means always so that every member of a family would be suitable for the same city. And even lovers—if I may use a word for a relationship which is not one present Shikastans would recognise—might find that they should part, and did so, for everybody accepted that their very existence depended on voluntary submission to the great Whole, and that this submission, this obedience, was not serfdom or slavery—states that had never existed on the planet, and which they knew nothing of—but the source of their health and their future and their progress.

By now the two races lived together, there was no separation between them in that way, though they did not intermarry. This was physically not possible. The Giants had not grown more than was reported by the last mission: they were about eighteen feet in height. And the Natives were half that. But in the meantime, the Giants had become much varied in colour and in facial and bodily type. Some were as black, a glossy shining black, as the first immigrants. Others were all shades of lively warm brown. There were some with very pale faces, and their eyes were sometimes of a blue which when it first appeared caused unease and even abhorrence. The Natives were also of all shades of colour, and their head hair could be of any colour from black to chestnut. The Giants had evolved some head hair, probably from climatic pressure, but it was sparse, and short, contrasting with the Natives' profuse locks. The blue-eyed Giants might have colourless, or light yellow hair, but this was considered a misfortune.

Sex had different intensities for the two races. The Giants, living four thousand or five thousand years, bred once, or twice, or not at all in a lifetime. (And carried their young for a long time, four or five years.) The female Giants, when not breeding or caring for children, did the same work as the males, and this was for most of their lives. The work was mostly mental, the continuous, devotional task of keeping the proper levels of transmission between the planet and Canopus. Sex with the Giants was not a strong drive as the Natives would understand it. The powers of sex, the attractions, the repulsions, the ebbs and flows, were transmuted into higher forces except when actually in use for propagation.

The Natives were being encouraged to breed. They lived now for about a thousand years, but the planet could sustain, with ease, a larger population. It was never envisaged that there would be more than about twenty million, building up slowly over the next few thousand years: nothing had ever been planned in the nature of a sudden increase. There would be a careful, controlled building of new, well-sited cities, and there was no shortage of places suitable for the Necessity. Natives who chose to, and were considered suitable by general consent, might have several progeny in the first hundred years of their lives. After that, while sex continued as a pleasure and a balancing force, the breeding mechanisms became inoperative, and they entered a long, energetic, vigorous middle age. The Degenerative Disease, as we define it, did not yet exist; degenerative diseases of the physical sort that later were common had not come into existence. Both Giants and Natives died of accidents, of course, but otherwise not unless through the very rare invasions of viruses against which they had no defence. The breeding programmes were then adjusted as necessary.

I was sent to Rohanda by one of our fastest craft, and not by means of Zone Six. I did want to inspect Zone Six, but not until after I had studied the situation on the planet itself where I needed to be quickly, and in the flesh. It had been decided that I should be in the form of a Native and not of a Giant, because I was to stay on and help the Natives after the Giants had been taken off. This decision was correct. Others were arguable. Looking back, afterwards, I knew that I should have sacrificed other considerations to getting to my task more quickly. Yet I did need to acclimatise myself. I could not appear at once in any one of the cities, with its specialised vibrations, without suffering severe effects. The difference between Canopus and Rohanda was very great, and none of us could begin work at once on arrival: time had always to be given to the process of acclimatisation. But things were worse than we had thought: and were worsening faster than expected.

The spaceship approached the extreme eastern edge of the main landmass from the northwest, coming low over the fertile and forested mountains and plateaux and plains that later were great deserts— thousands of square miles of deserts. We saw several cities, and wondered how the inhabitants who chanced to look up thought of our crystalline sphere darting past, and how they would talk of it to those who hadn't seen us.

At that time I did not know which city it would be best to approach first. On the extreme eastern shore—the mainland, not one of the islands—I made my measurements. Meanwhile, the spaceship's crew explored, but carefully, for we did not want to startle anybody, and if we were seen, it might lead to complications, for almost certainly it would be thought that a Native had been captured by alien beings. It was not easy to assess exactly what the change was, neither its nature nor extent, but I decided that the Square City would be best: we had seen it as we passed over. It was about a week's hard walking away, and that was about right for my accustoming myself to Rohanda. I had already said that the craft might leave again, when I understood that the air of the planet had altered. And very suddenly. More calculations. The Square City would not now be right. I changed orders, and we ascended again, travelling not over the same cities, but farther south, over the Great Mountains, where I knew the Shammat transmitter must be: I could already sense it. I was put down to the east of the area of the great inland seas. There I again tested—and the same thing happened: I had decided on the Oval City to the north of the most northern inland sea, when again the atmosphere changed. But by now I had sent away the spacecraft. I had weeks of walking to do, in order to reach the Round City, which was now where I had to be. But this would take too long.

The Round City was on the high plateaux to the south of the great inland seas. It was not a centre of administration or of power, for there was no such centre. But apart from the suitability of its vibratory patterns, it was geographically central, and my news would be more easily disseminated. Also the height and the sharpness of the atmosphere would preserve this city longer than others from what would shortly befall. Or so I hoped. And I hoped, too, that there would not be another shift in the alignment of the planet, which would make the Round City the wrong one for me.

First, there was the problem of time. I approached some horses grazing in a herd on a mountain side, and stood near them, looking at them intently in a silent request for their help. They were restive and uncertain, but then one approached me, and stood waiting, and I got on its back. I directed it, and we cantered off southwards. The herd came with us. Mile after mile was covered, and I was becoming concerned for the state of the foals and young horses who were keeping up with us, and who seemed to enjoy it, flinging up their heels and neighing and racing each other, when I saw another herd not far off. I was carried to this herd by the first. I dismounted. The situation was explained by my mount to a strong and vigorous beast in the new herd. She came to me and waited, and I climbed up and off we went. This was repeated several times. I rested very little, though once or twice asked my mount to stop, and slept with my head on its flanks under the shade of a tree. A week passed this way, and I saw that my problem was over. Now it was time to use my own feet, and to approach more slowly. I thanked my escorts for their most efficient relay system, and they touched my face with their muzzles, and then wheeled, and thundered back to their own grazing grounds.

And now, day after day, I walked south, through pleasant savannah country of light airy trees, aromatic bushes, glades of grass that were drying pale gold. Everywhere birds, the flocks that are entities, with minds and souls, like men, yet composed of many units, like men. Everywhere animals, all of them friendly, curious, coming to greet me, helping me by showing the way or places where I might rest. I often spent a hot midday, or a night, with a family of deer sheltering from the heat under bushes, or with tigers stretched on rocks in the moonlight. A hot, but not painfully hot, sun—this was before the Events that slightly distanced it—the closer brighter moon of that time, gentle breezes, fruit and nuts in plenty, bright, fresh streams—this paradise I traversed during those days and nights, welcome everywhere, a friend among friends, is where now lie deserts and rock, sands and shales, the niggardly plants of drought and of blasting heats. Ruins are everywhere, and each handful of bitter sand was the substance of cities whose names the present-day Shikastans have never heard, whose existence they have not suspected. The Round City, for one, which fell into emptiness and discord, so soon after.

Always I was watching, monitoring, listening; but as yet the Shammat influence was slight, though I could sense, under the deep harmonies of Rohanda, the discords of the coming time.

I did not want this journey to end. Oh, what a lovely place was the old Rohanda! Never have I found, not in all my travellings and visitings, a more pleasant land, one that greeted you so softly and easily, bringing you into itself, charming, beguiling, so that you had to succumb, as one does to the utterly amazing charm of a smile or a laugh that seems to say, "Surprised, are you? Yes, I am extra, a gift, superfluous to the necessary, a proof of the generosity concealed in everything." And yet what I was seeing would soon have gone, and each step on the crisp warm-smelling soil, and each moment under the screens of the friendly branches was a farewell—goodbye, goodbye, Rohanda, goodbye.

I heard the Round City before I saw it. The harmonies of its mathematics evidenced themselves in a soft chant or song, the music of its own particular self. This, too, welcomed and absorbed me, and the Shammat wrong was still not more than a vibration of unease. Everywhere around the city the animals had gathered, drawn and held by this music. They grazed or lay under the trees and seemed to listen, held by contentment. I stayed to rest under a large tree, my back against the trunk, looking out under lacey boughs into the glades and avenues, and I was hoping that some beasts would come to me, for it would be the last time, and they did: soon a family of lions came padding, three adults and some cubs, and they lay down around me. I might have been one of their cubs, for size, since they were very large. The adults lay with their heads on extended paws, and looked at me with their amber eyes, and the cubs bounced and played all around and over me. I slept, and when I moved on, a couple of the cubs came with me, tussling and rolling, until a call from one of the big beasts took them back.

The trees were thinning. Between them and the environs of the city were the stone patterns. I had not seen the stones for many days of walking, but now there were circles and avenues, single Stones and clusters. Around the other cities I had passed through or skirted, among their accompanying stones the animals had been thick, crowding there, for the harmonies they found, but I saw that here, outside the Round City, the stone patterns had no animals at all. The music, if that is the word for the deep harmonies of the stones, had become too strong. Looking behind, I could see how the throngs of beasts were as it were fenced, but invisibly, by where the Stones began. The birds seemed not to be affected yet by the Stones, and I was accompanied by flocks of them, and their callings and twitterings were part of the symphony.

It was not pleasant walking through the Stones. I felt the beginnings of sickness. But there was no way of avoiding them since they completely surrounded the Round City. They ended with the wide good-tempered river which flowed completely around the city, holding it in two arms that came together in a lake on the southern side before separating and flowing away east and west. Little skiffs, canoes, craft of all kinds were tied along the banks for the use of anyone who needed them, and I took myself across the river, and on the inner bank the music of the Stones ceased, and was succeeded by a silence. A complete silence, of a quality strong enough to absorb the sounds of footfalls on stone, or the tools of a builder, or voices.

Before the curving low white cliff of buildings began was a wide belt of market gardens that surrounded the city. There were gardeners there, men and women, who of course took no notice of me, since I seemed one of them. They were a handsome breed, strong brown faces and limbs exposed by light brief garments predominantly blue. Blue was the colour used most in this city for clothes and hangings and ornament, and these blues answered the nearly always cloudless skies of the plateau.

The Round City showed nothing that was not round. It was a perfect circle, and could not expand: its bounds were what had to be. The outer walls of the outer buildings made the circle, and the side walls, as I made my way through on a path that was an arc, I saw were slightly curved. The roofs were not flat, but all domes and cupolas, and their colours were delicate pastel shades, creams, light pinks and soft blues, yellows and greens, and these glowed under the sunny sky. When I had passed through the outer city, there was a road that also made a complete circle, lined with trees and gardens. There were not many people about. A group sat talking in a garden and again I was seeing strength, health, ease. They were not less sturdy than the workers in the gardens, and this suggested that there was no division here between the physical and mental. I passed close to them, greeting and being greeted, and could see the glisten of their brown skins, and their large eyes, mostly of a full bright brown. The women's head hair was long, brown or chestnut, and dressed in various ways, and decorated with flowers and leaves. They all wore loose trousers and tunics of shades of blue, with some white.

I passed through another segment of this city into another curved street, which had more people, for there were shops here, and booths and stalls. This street was a complete circle inside the outermost one, and was a market all its way—and like every market I have seen anywhere, was all animation and busyness. Another band of buildings, another street, full of cafés and restaurants and gardens. This was thronged, and a healthier friendlier crowd I have never seen. A pervasive good humour was the note of this place, amiability—and yet it was not clamorous or hectic. And I noted that despite the noise a crowd must produce, this did not impinge on the deep silence that was the ground note of this place, the music in its inner self, which held the whole city safe in its harmonies. More circles of buildings and streets: I was nearing the centre now, and was looking for grandiosities and pomps that are always a sign of the Degenerative Disease. But there was nothing of that kind: when I came out into the one central area, where the public buildings stood, made of the same golden-brown stone, all was harmony and proportion. Not in this city could it be possible for a child being brought by its parents to be introduced to the halls, towers, centres of its heritage, to feel awed and alienated, to know itself a nothing, a little frightened creature who must obey, and watch for Authority. Long sad experience had taught me to watch for this . . . but on the contrary, anyone walking here, among these welcoming warm-coloured buildings, must feel only the closeness, the match, between individual and surroundings.

I was not as acclimatised as I should be, to undertake the difficulties of my task . . . and I was sorrowful, and unable to control it. I sat for a while on the raised edge of a small lake circling a fountain, and watched children playing unafraid among the buildings, women idling in groups, men by themselves, talking, men and women in mixed groups sitting, or walking or strolling. It was all pervaded by the clear light of the plateau and the heat that was not too strong because of the many fountains and trees and flowers. And it was full of the strong quiet purpose which I have always found to be evidence, anywhere—city, farm, or groups of people and on any planet—of the Necessity, the ebbs and flows and oscillations of the Lock.

And yet it was there, just audible, the faintest of discords, the beginnings of the end.

I had not yet seen any Giants, yet they were here somewhere. I did not want to ask for them, thus revealing myself as an alien, and setting off alarms before it was necessary. I wandered about for some time, and then caught sight of two Giants at the end of an avenue, and went towards them. These were males, both of a deep glossy black colour, both in the same loose blue garments I had seen on the Natives, both concentrated on a task. They were measuring, by means of a device I was unfamiliar with, of wood and a reddish metal, the vibrations of a column of polished black stone that stood where two avenues inter-sected. The black stone, among so much of the soft honey-coloured stone everywhere, was startling, but not sombre, for its gleam mirrored the blue of the Giants' clothes, and their strong black faces as they moved beside it.

I have to confess that I was on my guard now, waiting to see how I would be greeted: I was in appearance a Native, and I was never ready to be less than wary about the relations between tutors and taught—well, it was often my official task to be suspicious and to watch for signs of the Disease. I stood quietly waiting a few paces off, looking up to the shoulders of these enormous men: they were more than twice my height, and twice my breadth. When they had finished their task, they saw me as they turned to leave, and at once smiled and nodded—and were still prepared to move off, showing that they did not expect either side to be in need of the other.

I had satisfied myself that there was no condescension in their manner towards a Native, and now said that I was Johor, from Canopus.

They stood looking down at me.

Their faces were not as easily attractive and warming as those of the amiable people I had been watching and idling among, on my way in to the centre. Of course it is not easy to feel at home with a race different from oneself: there always must be a period of adjustment, while one learns to withstand assaults on one's sense of probability. But here there was so much more! The Giants were at home in the Canopean mind, but had not seen a citizen of Canopus for thousands of years, for we had relied on the reports of these conscientious administrators. And here was Canopus announcing a physical presence, but from the mouth of a Native. As for me, I was surprised to find in myself childishness. Looking up at these immense people was to be reminded of impulses I had not consciously remembered. I wanted to reach for their hands and to be held, supported; wanted to be lifted up to the level of those benign faces, wanted all kinds of comforts and soothings that I did not *really* want at all—so that I was ashamed, and even indignant. And these conflicts of different levels of memory in me reinforced the woe I was truly feeling, which was because of what I had to say to them. And, besides, I was not well. Normally I would have spent time in Zone Six, as preparation. I was suddenly faint, and the Giants saw it. Before they could hold me up, which they were about to do, and which I did not want, for it would only feed this long-forgotten infant in me, I sat myself down on the plinth of the column, and from this even lower level looked up at these towering men behind whom the trees did not seem much taller, and made myself say, "I have news for you. Bad news."

"We were told to expect you," was the answer.

I sat absorbing this, making my faintness an excuse for silence.

What had they been told to expect? What had Canopus allowed them to know?

It was not the case that everything in the Canopean mind was instantly the property of the Giant mind—and vice versa. No, it was all more precise and specific than that.

The aim of the Pre-Lock Phase on Rohanda had been to develop the powers—for want of a better word—of the planet, through the symbiosis of the Giants and the Natives, so that the planet Rohanda, that is, the physical being of the planet itself, could be linked, through the Giant/Native match, with the Canopean System. During this phase, which was so much shorter than had been expected, there had been little *mental* flow back and forth, Canopus to Rohanda, but there had been occasional flickerings, moments of communication: nothing that could be relied upon, or taken up and developed.

When the Lock took place, the powers, vibrations (whatever word you like, since all are inaccurate and approximate) of Rohanda were fused with Canopus, and through Canopus with its subsidiaries, planets, and stars.

But it had not been that the very moment the Lock took place the Giant mind had achieved an instant, and total, and *steady* fusion with Canopus. From that time on, Rohanda was a function of the functioning of Canopus, but nothing could be considered as accomplished and to be taken for granted. The maintenance of the Lock depended on continuous care. First of all, the placing and watching and monitoring of the Stones, which had to be constantly realigned—slightly, of course, but with so many that was an arduous and demanding task. And then the building of the cities; and with each new mathematical entity created and maintained, the Lock was strengthened, and each city had to be watched, adapted, and all this with the aid of the Natives, who were being taught everything, the moment they could take it in. And above all, what was being transmitted was how to watch their own development, and constantly to feed and adjust it, so that what they did would always be in harmony, in phase, with Canopus, the "vibrations" of Canopus.

Canopean strength was beamed continually into Rohanda. Rohanda's new, always deepening strengths were beamed continually back to Canopus. Because of this precise and expert exchange of emanations, the prime object and aim of the galaxy were furthered—the creation of ever-evolving Sons and Daughters of the Purpose.

But these interchanges of substance were infinitely varied and variable. The "mind" shared between Rohanda and Canopus did not mean that every thought in every head instantly became the property of everyone at once. What was shared was a disposition, a ground, a necessary mesh, net, or grid, a pattern which was common property, and was not itself static, since it would grow and change with the strengthenings and fallings off of emanations. If one individual wished to contact another, this was done by a careful and specific "tuning in," and thereafter what was communicated was exactly what had been decided would be communicated, no more and no less. So while the Giants were a function of the "mind" of Canopus, they would not know anything that Canopus did not want them to know. Nor were conditions always perfect for exchange of "thought." For instance, there was a period of more than a hundred years when no exchange of specific information was possible, because of interference from a certain configuration in a nearby solar system, temporarily out of phase with Canopus. The interchange of fuels went on, but subtler currents were interdicted until the star in question changed its disposition in the celestial dance.

"Were you measuring the vibrations of the column for any reason?" I asked at last.

"Yes."

"You have noticed something wrong?"

"Yes."

"You have no idea of what it might be?" I was eager, as can be seen, to introduce Shammat, for on what I learned would depend so much of planning for the future, but even as I was looking for a way to talk of Shammat, I saw that this was a subject still far off and secondary. The need for haste took hold of me again, and mastered my weakness, so that I struggled up, and faced them.

"We were told that Emissary Johor would come, and that we must meantime prepare ourselves for a crisis."

"And that was all?"

"That was all."

"Then that means they were even more afraid than I knew they were when I left of information being picked up by enemies," I said. I spoke firmly, and even with desperation, looking up first at one, then the other.

They did not respond to "enemies." The word fled by them, unmarked, it did not strike home in them anywhere, and here was a weakness that was, that must be, our fault.

Even while I report in them a flaw, and a serious one, I must record for the honour and the right memories of everyone concerned, how extraordinary a race this was—the Giants, who would soon cease to be, at least in this form. Not because of their physique, their size, their strength! I had worked among large races before. Size did not always go with qualities such as these men possessed. These had something unforgettable. There was a largeness in them, a magnanimity, a scope and sweep of understanding far beyond most of the species we were fostering. There was a deep containment in them, like the deep silence that was the air of this city. They had all the quiet strength of their function—which was service to the best there was and is. Their powerful eyes were thoughtful and observant and again spoke of links and harnessings with forces far beyond, far higher than most creatures could ever dream of. It was not that the Natives were not impressive, in their way; they, too, had thought and observation and above all an abundance of easy warm good humour. But here was something so much more, so much finer. I gazed up into these majestic faces, and it was with recognition: these men gave off the same ring, or note, as the best of Canopus. I knew that with such people I could meet with nothing but Justice, Truth—it was as simple as that.

"You need to rest, perhaps?" enquired one.

"No, no, no," I cried, again trying to force into them the urgency I felt. "No, I must talk to you. I will tell you now, if you like, and you can tell the others."

I saw that it was at last coming home to them that here was something terrible. Again I watched them muster inner strengths. Understanding flowed between these two: here was no need for inferior gestures such as exchanging glances, or meaningful nods.

In front of us the avenue of trees curved away and slightly down to a cluster of tall white buildings.

"It will be better if we arrange a gathering of a Ten," said one and forthwith he departed, with strides so long that he was at the end of the avenue in a moment, his immense figure in scale with the buildings he approached, seeming to hold them in proportion.

"My name is Jarsum," said my companion, and we walked forward. He dawdled and stopped and lingered, while I walked my fastest, but there was no strain here, and I saw that Giants and Natives were in the habit of walking together, and had adapted themselves to this form of companionship.

When I was near the arrangement of the Giants' buildings, they were certainly tall, but not oppressive; but inside the one we entered, I did feel strained and stretched, for the cylinder seemed to reach up forever above my head, and the seats and chairs were almost my height. Jarsum saw this and he sent instruction through an instrument that a Native-sized chair, table, and bed should be fetched and placed inside a special room that was smaller than the others. Even so, when I came to inhabit it, I found these articles of furniture comical enough, in a Giant-sized room.

This room, or hall, was used as a meeting place. In a short time, ten Giants had arrived. They sat on the floor, ignoring their usual seating arrangements, and put me on a pile of folded rugs, adjusted so that our faces were at the same level. They sat waiting for me to begin. They looked troubled, but not more than that. I was looking around at these kingly, magnificent beings, and thought that there can be no one so armed against shock that it is not felt, when it comes. And I would have to go slowly stage by stage, even with such beings as these.

I had to tell them that their history was over. That their purpose here was over. That the long evolution they had so brilliantly conducted and which they had believed was only just beginning—was over. As individuals they had a future, for they would be taken off to other planets. But they would no longer have an existence and a function as they had been taught to see themselves.

An individual may be told she, he, is to die, and will accept it. For the species will go on. Her or his children will die, and even absurdly and arbitrarily—but the species will go on. But that a whole species, or race, will cease, or drastically change—no, that cannot be taken in, accepted, not without a total revolution of the deepest self.

To identify with ourselves as individuals—this is the very essence of the Degenerative Disease, and every one of us in the Canopean Empire is taught to value ourselves only insofar as we are in harmony with the plan, the phases of our evolution. What I had to say would strike at everything we all valued most, for it could be no comfort here to be told: You will survive as individuals.

As for the Natives, there was no message of hope for them, unless the news that there would be a remission in the long-distant future could be called that. Evolution would begin again—after long ages.

The Giants' reason for being, their function, their *use*, was the development of the Natives, who were their other halves, their own substances. But the Natives had nothing ahead of them but degeneration. . . . The Giants were in the position of the healthy, or healthier, twin who will be saved in an operation in which the other one must die.

I had to say all this.

I said it.

And waited, for this much to be taken in.

I can remember how I sat there, ridiculously perched on that heap of rugs, feeling myself a pygmy, watching their faces, and Jarsum's in particular. Now I was on a level with him, I saw that he stood out among the others. This was a man with an extraordinarily strong face, all dramatic curves and hollows, the dark eyes brilliant under the heavy brow ledges, cheekbones jutting and moulded. He was an immensely powerful man, outwardly and inwardly. But he was losing strength as I looked. They all were. It was not lack of fortitude, not that—they were not yet capable of that disobedience to the laws governing us. But as I gazed in awe from face to face I saw them, very slightly, dwindle. There was a lack of power. And I wondered if up on Canopus they were registering this moment and knew by it that I had accomplished what I had been sent for. Partly accomplished: but at least I was past the worst of it.

I waited. Time had to be allowed for the absorption of what I had said. Time passed . . . passed. . . .

We did not speak. At first I believed that this was entirely because of the pain of this news I was bringing, but soon saw that they were waiting for what was in their minds to pulse outwards into the minds first of all of the other Giants in the Round City, and from there— though this would necessarily be in a weaker, vaguer form, would transmit probably no more than feelings of warning, danger, unease— to the Giants of the other Mathematical Cities. This tall cylinder we sat in was a transmitting chamber, constructed to work if it had in it between ten or twelve Giants. Any ten of them would do, male or female, but they had to be trained, and so the very young were not used in this function.

The way this transmitting work was done mirrored the exchange between Canopus and Rohanda. There was a grid, or common ground, which made possible the transfer of exact news; but things had to be set up, ordered, arranged. It was not that everything in the mind of one, or of ten, carefully brought together, would at once, and automatically, go out and reach the minds of others in the same city, and then the others in the other cities.

As we all sat there effects were being calculated. First a basis of emotion, if this is the right word for feelings so much higher than what was understood later on Shikasta by *emotions*. And then, the ground prepared, further news would be broadcast.

Meanwhile, I was using my eyes. . . . I was interested that among these ten was a female of a type that had been, still was, by common Canopean standards, a freak. She was taller than the other Giants, by a good span of their hands, and all her bones were frail, and long, with the flesh hollowed on them. Her skin was dead white, and cold, with grey and blueish gleams. I had not seen a skin colour like it anywhere in my journeyings, and found it repulsive at first, but then was fascinated, and did not know whether I was repelled or attracted. Her eyes were amazing, a blazing bright blue, like their sky. She, like the other Giants, had very little head hair, but what she did have was the lightest fleece of pale gold. And she had long extensions of bony tissue on her finger ends, like the Natives, who once had paws and claws. The genetic ideas evoked here were many and troubling—but what must she feel about it all! She was so much an exotic, among so many brown and black and chestnut people with their black and brown and greyish eyes. She must feel herself excluded and alien. And then, too, there was her look of attenuation, even of weakness and exhaustion, and this was not just to do with this difficult and taxing occasion, but was bred into her substance. She certainly was not full, as were the other Giants, of an immediate and obvious vitality. No, for her, everything must be an effort. I noted that she was the only one here who seemed affected by what I had said to the point of evident stress. She sighed continually, and those unbelievable cerulean eyes roamed about restlessly, and she bit her thin red lips. Again these were something I had never seen before: they looked like a wound. But she made efforts to contain her feelings, straightening herself where she sat leaning against the wall, and smoothing down the soft blue cloth of her trousers. She laid her very long delicate fingers together on her knees, and seemed to resign herself.

When the feeling of the meeting seemed right, I went on to say that the cause of this crisis was an unexpected malalignment among the stars that sustained Canopus. I have to record a reaction of restlessness —checked; of protest—checked. . . .

We are all creatures of the stars and their forces, they make us, we make them, we are part of a dance from which we by no means and not ever may consider ourselves separate. But when the Gods explode, or err, or dissolve into flying clouds of gas, or shrink, or expand, or whatever else their fates might demand, then the minuscule items of their substance may in their small ways express—not protest, which of course is inappropriate to their station in life—but an acknowledgement of the existence of irony: yes, they may sometimes allow themselves—always with respect—the mildest possible grimace of irony.

To the Natives not even this was allowable, for they would not be able to take it in, they could not understand events on the level where the Giants thought and acted. No, the chief victims of this lapse in heavenly behaviour, this unforeseen calamity, a shift in the star movements, would not know even enough to be able to nod their heads resignedly, tighten their lips, and murmur, "Well, it's all right for *them*, I suppose!" Or: "Here we go again! But it's not for *us* to complain!"

It is not reasonable for the Lords of the Galaxy, moving on their star-waves, on star-time, planet-perspective, to expect of their protégés less than this small ironical smile, a sigh, at the contrast between the aeons of effort, struggle, slow up-climbing that a life may come to seem, let alone the long evolution of a culture, with that almost casual—or so it must seem—"But we did not foresee that burst of radiation, that planetary collision!" With that: "But we are, compared with the Majesties above us, of whom we are a part as you are of us, only small beings who have to submit, just as you do. . . ."

I said when I began this report that I have not remembered my first visit from that time to this. When it came near my mind and tried to enter I barred it out. This was the worst thing I have had to do in my long service as Envoy.

I do not remember if it was half a day, a day, or how long it was we all sat there, looking at each other, trying to sustain each other while we thought of the future. The sounds of the city seemed far away, swallowed up in the silence, and in the proportions of this building. A couple of Giant children did play for a while outside in a sunny court, calling out to each other and laughing, their exuberance making a painful contrast to our condition, but soon the white frail Giant made a signal to them and they went off.

At last Jarsum said that it was not possible for them to absorb further on this occasion, and that more could be taken in tomorrow. Discussions would take place between the Giants on how best to tell the Natives, or if anything should be said at all. Meanwhile, there was my room, furnished, they all hoped, to make me as comfortable as possible. If I wished to stroll abroad, I should, for I was free to do exactly as I wished. And food would be available at such a time . . . oh, all the courtesies, everything of the kindest and pleasantest. But I felt my heart was breaking. I have to say it, in all the banality of these words. That is how I felt: desolation, an unutterable blankness and emptiness, and I was absorbing these emotions from the Giants, who were feeling all this and more.

Next day I was summoned early to the transmitting room. There were ten Giants waiting, different ones, but I did not feel any strangeness with them.

When the Giants left now, how would the Natives' carefully fostered and trained expectations take the shock of it? What aberrations and perversities might be looked for? And what of the animals of the planet, of which the Natives had so recently ceased to be one variety? It had been planned that the Natives would administer and guard the animals, and see that the powers and qualities of the different genera would match and marry with the needs of the Lock. How would they view these animals now? How treat them?

As these thoughts developed in our minds that morning, I was needing, and urgently, to introduce Shammat. So strong was this current in me that I was surprised they did not introduce Shammat themselves. And I think that a strain of uneasiness, and even suspicion, did indicate that the theme was ready to surface. But it did not. Not then. I had to take my own cue from them, to wait on their signals and decisions. Soon the end of that session was decided on, and I was dismissed, again with courtesies.

This time I availed myself of the invitation to move about as I wished, and I returned to the parts of the Round City where I would find the Natives. Everything seemed flourishing and normal. I moved from group to group, and talked to anyone who had time to talk to me. At first I said I was visiting from the Crescent City, but soon found that travel was common among them, and did not want to reveal myself then. I discovered that an ovoid city very far in the north, which they spoke of as we might of the extreme edges of the galaxy, was not one they visited, and said I came from there, making up interesting histories of ice and snowstorms, and so was able to be accepted in easy conversation. I wanted to find out if these people felt anything of Shammat, if there were travellers' tales of untoward events, or even if they felt ill, or out of sorts. I found nothing that helped me, until a female who sat with two small boys on a bench in the central square, said of their quarrelling that "they were very peevish these days." This was not much to go on. I felt low and irritable, but there were good reasons for that, and so I went back to my room, with its towering walls, at the foot of which crouched so tinily my bed and my chair, and almost at once was summoned back to the transmitting room.

Jarsum was there, but the others were again new to me. We arranged ourselves as before and I was determined to bring up Shammat, and did so, at once, thus: "I have to tell you something more and worse— worse from the point of view of the Natives, if not yours. This planet has an enemy. Were you not aware of it?"

Silence. Again, the word "enemy" seemed to fade away from them, in the atmosphere of this chamber. It seemed, quite simply, to find nowhere to hook on to! It is the oddest experience, when you have yourself always thought in terms of the balancings and outwittings, the treaties and the politicking that must go on against the wicked ones of this galaxy, to find, suddenly, and so unexpectedly, that you are among people who have never, ever, thought in terms of opposition, let alone evil.

I tried humorously: "But at least you must know that enemies do, sometimes, come into being! They exist, you know! In fact they are always at work! There are evil forces at work in this galaxy of ours, and very strong ones. . . ."

For the first time, I saw their eyes engage each other, in that instinctive reflex action which is always a sign of weakness. They were wanting to find out from each other what this thing "enemy" might be. And yet their reports had said, at least at the beginning of our experiment with Rohanda, that there were rumours of spies, and surely spies implied enemies, even to the most innocent.

I saw that these were a species who, for some reason quite unforeseen, could not think in terms of enemies. I could hardly believe it. Certainly I had not experienced anything like this on any other planet.

"When you told me, Jarsum, that you were monitoring your column, that you had suspected something was wrong, then what did you mean?"

"The currents have been uneven," he said promptly, with all the responsibility and grasp he was capable of. "We noticed it a few days ago. There are always slight variations, of course. There might sometimes be intermissions. But we none of us remember this particular *quality* of variation. There is something new. And you have explained why."

"But there is more to it than I have said."

Again a general, if slight, movement of unease, the shifting of limbs, small sighs.

Against this resistance I gave them a short history of the Puttiora Empire, and its colony Shammat.

It wasn't that they were not listening, rather they seemed *unable* to listen.

I repeated and insisted. Shammat, I said, had had agents on this planet for some time. Had there been no reports of aliens? Of suspicious activity?

Jarsum's eyes wandered. Met mine. Slid away.

"Jarsum," I said, "is there no memory among you that your ancestors —your fathers even—believed there might be hostile elements here?"

"The southern territories have been co-operative for a long time."

"No, not the Sirian territories."

Again, sighs and movements.

I tried to keep it as brief as I could.

I said that this planet, under the changed influences of the relevant stars, would suddenly find itself short of—as it were—fuel. Yes, yes, I knew I had told them this. But Shammat had found out about this, and was already tapping the currents and forces.

Rohanda, now Shikasta, the broken, the hurt one, was like a rich garden, planned to be dependent on a water supply that was inexhaustible. But it turned out that it was not inexhaustible. This garden could not be maintained as it had been. But a slight, very poor supply of Canopean power would still seep through to feed Shikasta; it would not entirely starve. But even this slight flow of power was being depleted. By Shammat. No, we did not know how, and we wanted urgently to find out.

We believed that a minimum of maintenance would be possible, the "garden" would not entirely vanish. But in order to plan and to do, then we must know everything there was to be known about the nature of our enemy.

No response. Not of the kind I needed.

"For one thing," I insisted, "the more the Natives degenerate, the more they weaken and lose substance, the better that will be for Shammat. Do you see? The worse the quality of the Canopus/Shikasta flow, the better for Shammat! Like to like! Shammat cannot feed on the high, the pure, the fine. It is poison to them. The level of the Lock in the past has been far above the grasp of Shammat. They are lying in wait, for the precise moment when their nature, the Shammat nature, can fasten with all its nasty force onto the substance of the Lock! They are already withdrawing strength, they are feeding themselves and getting fat and noisy on it, but this is nothing to what will happen unless we can somehow prevent them. Do you see?"

But they did not. They could not.

They had become unable to take in the idea of theft and parasitism. It was no longer in their genetic structure, perhaps—though how such a change had come about is hard to tell. At any rate, I saw that there was nothing I could say that would get through to them. Not on this subject. I would have to make efforts myself.

My first was to spend time with Jarsum, when the transmitting sessions were over, and to try and make an impact on him. From him I got every kind of help and information on any subject but one.

The transmitting sessions went on. They were always the same. A theme would be brought forward, held in the minds of those present, a little discussion might take place, or there might be continuous silence. The theme, as translated into ideas and facets in the individual minds of the Giants, would be enriched and developed: and this complexity would go out and reach the Giants of the other cities.

I kept urging that messengers should be sent out, to confirm and add to what was being transmitted. How did we know if the strength of the currents was still as it had been? I wanted the fastest possible individuals to be sent to run all the way, if necessary! But I came up against a curious block or barrier in the Giants. They had never had to do things this way! they said.

"Yes, but things are different now."

No, they would wait.

And I could not make them listen.

Then came news from Canopus that the spacecraft for taking off the Giants would be arriving—with the precise dates and places—near the main cities.

"Jarsum, we must hurry. We can't wait any longer. . . ."

But he had become obstinate, even suspicious.

I saw then that it had begun. The Giants were affected. Already they were not as they had been.

And if they, then very likely I was affected, too. . . . I did have moments of dizziness. Yes, and sometimes I would come to myself after an interval when it was as if my mind had been full of clouds.

I had not expected to have to do this so soon, but I took out the Signature from where it was hidden, and concealed it under my tunic, tied on to my upper arm. My mind cleared then, and I understood that in fact I had been changed without knowing it. I could see that soon I would be the only individual on Shikasta with the power of judgement, of reasoned action.

And yet the Giants did not know of their state and were in control of everything.

I found that the Giants were not influenced equally—some were still sharp-minded and responsible. Alas, Jarsum was not one. He had succumbed almost at once. I did not know what to make of that, nor did I attempt to. I was concerned with practicalities, and kept urging those who would to come into the transmitting chamber where they seemed clearer-minded than they were outside.

It was at a transmitting session that I realised there had been a real and drastic change. The form of the sessions was the same, but there was more restlessness, and moments, too, when it seemed as if everyone there had lost themselves: their eyes would glaze and wander, and they spoke at random. Then, one morning, a Giant suddenly said in a hectoring voice that he, at least, would elect to stay on the planet and not go with the others. He was making a case, as in a debate, and this was so foreign to them all that they were startled back into understanding. My friend Jarsum, for instance, was shocked into himself, and I saw that he was there again, behind those magnificent eyes of his. He did not speak, but sat concentrating all his powers. Another Giant spoke, arguing against the first, but not in favour of going as much as to make a point. The first one shouted that "it was obvious" it would be stupid to leave. Jarsum was fighting, wrestling inwardly, trying to bring that assembly back to what it had been. Another voice was in argument. I could see from the stresses on Jarsum's face, the strain in his eyes, that it was too much . . . and suddenly he snapped and his voice was added to the others in a shouting babble of disagreement.

And in that way, literally "from one moment to another," things fell apart on Shikasta. Outside could be heard shouting arguing voices, could be heard children quarrelling, the sounds of dissent, debate. Inside was all excitement and agitation. They leaned forward, trying to catch each other's eyes, gesticulated, interrupted. There were two factions, a group who still tried to hold fast to their inner strength, their faces bewildered, and the ones who had been swept away, led by Jarsum, who was shouting that "they could send all the spacecraft they liked and he wouldn't budge, not he!"—like a child. And then the group that had held out, succumbed.

I intervened. To do this I closed my hand over the Signature, and used it. I said to them that those who decided to stay would be committing Disobedience. For the first time in their history they would not be in conformity with Canopean Law.

They broke in with the arguments, the logics, of the debased modes.

They said, among other things, that their staying could only make things better for the Natives because they, the Giants, "knew local conditions," whereas outsiders did not. They said that if the Natives were going to be betrayed by Canopus, then they, the Giants, would have no part in it.

I said that if the Giants stayed, even some of them, then the modified Canopean plan would be at risk. That the Giants would not be fitted "to lead and guide" the Natives, as they kept insisting they were, because their powers, too, would be depleted—were already depleted—could they not see their behaviour now was proof of a falling away? But no, they had already forgotten what they had been, dissension and enmity were already natural to them.

I said that disobedience to the Master Plan was always, everywhere, the first sign of the Degenerative Disease . . . and looked to find noble faces, and comprehending eyes that were so no longer, for on to the faces had come peevishness and self-assertion, and into the eyes, vagueness.

The next few days were all faction-fighting, argument, and raised voices.

I was everywhere I could be, with my hidden Signature. By putting forth every power I had, I managed to beam to the Canopean space-craft that they must not expect to descend and find the Giants waiting to be taken off: things had gone beyond that. They must expect to have to go into every city and argue and persuade and if necessary to capture by force. By then the resistance to my transmissions spacewards was so great I feared nothing clear would get through. But later I learned they had understood the essentials. And in most of the cities, particularly those of the central area, it had been understood at least that there was a crisis and that spacecraft were approaching. The lift-off was nothing like the smooth planned thing that had been envisaged. In every city was argument and refusal to leave, before a bewildered submission—this at best; and in some, Canopean troops had to use force.

I did not know immediately what had happened: I had to piece information together later.

Meanwhile, in the Round City, Jarsum headed a group who refused to go at all. He showed the noblest self-sacrifice in staying. He knew that his fellows, and himself, the disobedient Giants, risked their very beings, their souls—yet he would stay. The tall white Giant with her bizarre and disturbing beauty stayed, and with her others who were her progeny, all of them sports and showing the strangest combinations of physical characteristics. She said that she was a genetic freak, and could have no place on the planet where the Giants were being taken.

How did she know this? I asked, pointing out that the galaxy included varieties of creatures she had never dreamed of. But "she knew it." Bad enough that she had had to live out her life among people different from herself, always an alien, without having to start all over again.

This while we were waiting for the spacecraft's arrival.

Meanwhile, discussions went on about what to tell the Natives.

The Giants were showing a yearning, passionate, protecting concern for their erstwhile charges which contrasted absolutely with their former strength of confidence. At every moment I was confronted with Jarsum, or another Giant, all great accusing eyes, and tragic faces. How can you treat the poor things like this! was what I was meant to feel. And every practical discussion was interrupted by heavy sighs, looks of reproach, murmurs about cruelty and callousness. But in spite of this, I was able to arrange that some songs and tales should be made, and taken by suitable individuals among the Natives from city to city, which would transmit and inform at least the basics of the new situation.

And these emissaries were informed that in each city they must seek out a few representative Natives and tell them that they must prepare for crisis, for a period of hardship and deprivation, that they must wait for other messengers to come and instruct.

The Giants arranged this. They had to. The Natives knew the Giants as their mentors and could not suddenly see them otherwise.

But the Giants were leaving—went the songs.

Winging their way to the heavens,
They are gone, the Great Ones,
Our friends, our helpers.
To distant places they have flown,
We are left, their children,
And there is nothing for us but to mourn.

And so on. These were not exactly the words I would have chosen, but they adequately expressed the indignation of the Giants on their own behalf, displaced to the Natives.

Meanwhile, I was making contacts among the Natives, carefully, slowly, testing one individual and then another. An interesting fact was that at the beginning the Giants were worse and more quickly affected than the Natives, who continued *comparatively* normal for longer. The higher, more finely tuned organisms had to submit first. This gave me time to communicate what I could. But the innate difficulty or contradiction of this task is obvious: I had to tell these unfortunates that due to circumstances entirely beyond their control and for which they bore no responsibility at all, they would become less than shadows of their former selves. How could they possibly take this in! They had not been programmed for failure, disaster! They were less equipped even than the Giants for bad news. And the more detailed and factual the information, the more I could count on its being distorted. The essence of the situation was that these were minds which very shortly would have to deform what I said, begin to invent, re-process.

It was as if I had been given the task of telling someone in perfect health that he would shortly become a moron, but that he must do his best to remember some useful facts, which were   a ... b ... c. ...

One morning, a good third of the Giants had disappeared. No one knew where to. The ones that remained waited submissively by the landing place where the spacecraft would descend—which happened, shortly afterwards. Three of our largest craft came down, and several thousand Giants left. Suddenly, no Giants, none, not one.

The Natives saw the descent of the spacecraft, watched the Giants crowd in, watched the great shining machines lift off and dart away into the clouds.

> *Winging their way into the heavens,*
> *They have left, our Great Ones ...*

went the songs, and for days the Natives crowded around the landing spaces, looking up into the skies, singing. Of course they believed that their Giants would return. These rumours were soon everywhere and bred the appropriate songs.

> *When they return, our Great Ones,*
> *We will not have failed them. ...*

I could not find out where the disobedient Giants were.

The Natives now entered all the tall buildings which had previously been the Giants' homes and functional buildings, and made them their own. This was not good for the exact dispositions of the Round City. I told them this. They had accepted me as one with a certain amount of authority, though of course nothing on the same level as their Giants, but by now most were not capable of accepting information. Already, sense and straightforwardness were being met with a vague wandering stare, or restless belligerent looks that were the first sign of the Degeneration.

A storyteller and song-maker, David, had become a friend, or at least seemed to recognise me. He was still to an extent in possession of himself, and I asked him to watch what went on around him, and report to me when I returned from a journey to the nearest city. This stood on a great river near an inland sea where the tides' movements were minimal—the Crescent City. Again a river made an arm around it, but only on one side. The open side had streets and gardens laid out crossways to it, like the strings of a lyre. The music of this city was like the harmonies of lyre music, but before I reached it I could hear the discords, a grating shrillness that told me what I would find when I got there.

It was very beautiful, built of white and yellow stone, with intricate patterns everywhere on pavements, walls, roofs. The predominant colours of the clothes of the people were rust and grey, and these shone out against the green foliage, a brilliant sky. The Natives here were similar in build to those of the Round City, but they were yellow of skin, and their hair was always jetty black. I never saw these as they were, they really were, for by the time I reached them, the process of falling away was well developed. Again I sought out one who seemed more aware of what was happening than the others. The songs and tales had reached here, and these Natives, too, had watched the Giants leave in the enormous crystalline spacecraft which were already beginning to seem like dreams. . . . I asked my friend to assemble others, to persuade them to be patient, not to take hasty decisions, not to panic or be fearful. I said these things with every sense of their absurdity.

I decided to return to the Round City. If the songs and tales had reached the Crescent City, they must have spread to all the others, and that was a beginning. Meanwhile, I felt more and more a sense of urgency, of danger—I had to get back to the Round City, and quickly. I knew this, but not why until I got near it.

I walked towards it from the other side to that where I had come at first. Again it was through light open forest. As I got near where the Stones would begin, there were walnuts and almonds, apricots, pomegranates. The animals were thick here, but all seemed apprehensive, and stood looking in towards the city. They shook their heads, as if to dismiss unwelcome sound: they were already hearing what I could not, but soon did, as I reached the space where the Stones began. There was now a harshness in the harmonies that lapped out from the city, and my ears hurt. I had the beginnings of a headache, and as I entered the Stones I felt sick. The air was ominous, threatening. Whether the disposition of the Stones had ceased to fit the needs of Canopus because of the starry discordance, or whether the harmonies of the Round City had been disrupted by the Giants' leaving, and their abodes being taken over by those who had no place there, I did not know. But whatever the reasons, by the time I reached the inner side, the pain of the sounds seemed worse than when I entered, and as I looked up, I saw birds flying in towards the Stones swerve aside to get away from what rose at that place up into the sky whose deep blue seemed marred, hostile.

Everywhere in the Round City the Natives were hustling and jostling about in groups which continually formed and re-formed. They were always in movement, looking for something, someone; they moved from street to street, from one garden to another, from the outskirts in towards the centre, and when they had reached it and had run everywhere over that place, they looked around wildly, uneasily, and their eyes, which now all had the lost restless look that seemed the strongest thing in them, were never still, always searching, always dissatisfied. These groups took little notice of each other, but pushed and elbowed, as if they had all become strangers, or even enemies. I saw fights and scuffles, children squabbling and trying to hurt each other, heard voices raised in anger. Already the golden-brown walls were defaced with scribblings and dirt. Children in ones and twos and groups stood by the walls, smearing them with mud from the flowerbeds, in the most earnest, violent attempts—at what? Interrupted, they at once turned back to their—task, for that is what it obviously seemed to them. But they, too, were searching, searching, and that was the point of all their activity. If enough people rushed around, hurrying, from place to place, if children, and some adults, daubed mud over the subtle patternings of the still glowing walls, if enough of them met each other, ran around each other, pushed each other, and then gazed hungrily into each other's faces—if enough of these activities were accomplished— then what was lost would be found! That was how it seemed to me, the outsider, clutching on to the Signature for my very life.

But these poor creatures already did not know what had been lost.

The leak, the depletion, was very great by now: must be so, for look at the results!

Were there none left unaffected? Not even enough to be prepared to listen?

I looked into faces for a gleam of sense, I began conversations, but always those brown haunted eyes that so recently had been open and friendly, turned from me, as if they had not seen me, could not hear me. I looked for the storytellers and singers who had been entrusted with as much of the information as they could bear. I found one, and then another, who looked at me doubtfully, and when I asked if people liked their songs, hesitated and seemed struck as if they *nearly* remembered. Then I saw David sitting on the ledge of a fountain that had rubbish in it, and he was half singing, half talking: "Hear me now, hear this tale of the far off times, when the Great Ones were among us, and taught us all we knew. Hear me tell of the wisdom of the great days." But he was talking of no more than thirty days before.

As he spoke, groups of people did pause in their hurrying and searching, and listened a moment, as if something in them was being touched, reached—and I went forward to stand beside him, and using him as a focal point, called out, "Friends, friends, I have something to tell you . . . do you remember me? I am Johor, Emissary from Canopus . . ." They stared. They turned away. It was not that they were hostile: they were not able to take in what I said.

I sat beside David the storyteller, who had become silent, and was sitting with his strong brown arms around his knees, musing, thoughtful.

"Do you remember me, David?" I asked. "I have talked with you many times, and as recently as a month ago. I asked you to watch what happened here, and tell me when I got back. I've been in the Crescent City."

He spread his white teeth in a great smile, one every bit as warm and attractive as before, but his eyes held no recognition.

"We are friends, you and I," I said, and sat with him for a time. But he got up and wandered off, forgetting I was there.

As for me, I stayed where I was, watching the turmoil, thinking. It was clear that things were worse than had been foreseen on Canopus. My own link with Canopus was quite lost, even with the aid of the Signature. I had to make decisions on my own account, and with insufficient information. For instance, I did not know what was happening in the Sirian territories. Where had the rebellious Giants gone? I had no means of finding out. Was the degradation of the Natives complete, or was it partially reversible? What was the situation in all the other cities?

For some hours I took no action, but observed the general restlessness, which grew worse. I then moved among the poor brutes, and saw that the by now very strong vibrations of the city and its environing Stones were causing real physical damage. They clutched their heads as they ran, or let out short howls or screams of pain, but always with a look of incredulity and wonder, for pain had not often been their lot. In fact most never knew it at all. Occasionally one might break a limb; and then there was the rare epidemic; but these happened so seldom that they were talked of as distant contingencies. Headaches, toothaches, sickness, bone aches, joint aches, disorders of the eyes and ears— all the sad list of ailments of the physical body afflicted by the Degeneracy: these were unknown to them. Again and again I watched one stagger, and clutch his head, and groan; or put hands to his stomach, or heart, and always with the look of: What's this? What is happening to me?

I had to get them away. What I had to tell them would seem impossible, preposterous. They must leave this city, this beautiful home of theirs, with its perfect symmetries, and its synchronized gardens, its subtle patterns that mirrored the movements of the stars—they must all leave and at once, if they did not want to go mad. But they did not know what madness was! Yet some were already mad. One of them would shake and shake a pain-filled head, and put up both hands to it with that gesture: What is this? I don't believe it!—and then let out howls of pain and start running, rushing everywhere, howling as if pain were something he could leave behind. Or they might find a spot, or a building where the pain was less, for the intensities of the disorder of the vibrations were not the same everywhere. And then these people would stay in the comparatively comfortable place they had found and would not leave.

As for me, I had not felt like this since I had been in a similarly afflicted place, our poor colony which it had been hoped this planet would replace.

I found David. He was lying face down, on a pavement, his hands over his ears. I forced him up and told him what must be done. Without much energy or purpose, he did at last find friends, his wife, grown-up children with their children. It was a group of about fifty I addressed, and he turned my words into song as I talked. On each face were the grimaces of pain, nausea, and they felt dizzy, and they leaned against walls or lay down anywhere, and groaned. I begged them to leave the city, to leave at once, before its vibrations killed them. I said if they would leave the horrible emanations of this place and go into the surrounding savannahs and forests, these pains would leave them. But they must run quickly through the Stones. Before they went, they must each tell as many of their friends as they could, for the safety and the future of them all.

All this was to the accompaniment of cries of disbelief, refusal, while people resisted, groaned, wept. By now thousands of Natives were staggering about, or rolling on the pavements.

Suddenly, the group I had first addressed ran out of the deadly place, through the neglected gardens, and into the Stones where the pain was so much intensified that some went back and jumped into the river and drowned, willingly, eagerly, because of what they were suffering. But some, hugging themselves, holding their heads, clutching their stomachs, ran on, crouching as if keeping low to the earth would help them, and there, outside the horrid circle of radiations, they flung themselves down among the first trees of the forests and wept in relief. For the pain had left them.

They called out to those left behind. Some heard and followed. I went around among the others, telling them that many of their fellows had left and were safe. And soon everyone went. They left behind them houses, homes, furniture, food, clothing, left their culture, their civilisation, left everything they had accomplished. This small multitude, coming together among the trees and grasses, saw that they were surrounded by animals, who stood watching with their intelligent wondering eyes. They were stripped of everything, as helpless as if they were still what they had been millennia ago, poor beasts trying to raise themselves to their hind legs.

Some of them, when they had recovered from the deadliness of what they had fled from, ran back to the peripheral gardens through the Stones, and collected vegetables and fruit and seeds, working frantically, for as long as it was possible before the pains became unbearable. A few of the really hardy returned to the city itself, where, screaming and vomitting, they reeled in and out of the houses, dragging out warmth, and shelter—bedding, clothes, utensils of all kinds. In this way enough was brought to feed them, keep them warm. But these excursions back into the city had their black side, too, as will be seen: even then it was noticeable that some of those who had subjected themselves to the Stones' emanations seemed to want to feel them again.

Shelters were being made in the forest from boughs, sheaves of grass, even packed earth. Fire had been carried from the city in an earthenware pot, and was guarded day and night in the form of a great fire which was the focal point of this settlement of—savages. Ground had been marked out and was being dug for new gardens. Attempts were being made to duplicate the workshops and factories of the cities, but they could no longer remember their crafts, which in any case depended on the powers and technology of the Giants.

The animals had begun to move away. The first hunters were killing them by walking up to one and plunging in a knife: they had never learned fear, these mild intelligent creatures of the Time of the Giants —for this was the name of the time just passed, how everyone referred to what had been lost. But the animals, learning fear, were moving away, at first reluctantly, with the same wondering disbelieving look as the Natives had when they first felt the new pains. And then, being stalked and chased, troops and bands and herds of the beautiful beasts, infinitely more varied and adapted than Shikasta ever knew afterwards, began a rapid movement out and away. There would be the sounds of thundering herds, and we knew another part of the animal population had fled.

Meanwhile, I had to try to visit all the cities, where I hoped that instinct had taken the inhabitants out and to safety. Perhaps there was enough of the communal mind left to have allowed the other cities to sense what was happening at the Round City? I and David and some others went first of all to the Crescent City, where we found bands of people wandering about outside in the fertile fields of the great river delta. They told us that their city was "full of demons," but that many of the population had not left, for "there had been no one to tell them to go, they were waiting for the Giants to come." Those who had escaped were making reed huts, and the ground had been cleared for spring planting. The animals had left. We had passed through flocks of every kind moving away from the deadly environs of the Crescent City, and from the creatures moving on two legs who had become their enemies.

To shorten this part of my account: We went from city to city, splitting ourselves into several bands; from the Square City to the City of the Triangle, from the Diamond City to the Octagon, from the City of the Oval to the Rectangular City—and on, and on. It took a full term of the Shikastan journey around its sun. The bands that set forth did not remain as they had been, for some decided to stay with settlements that attracted them, some sickened and died, some, finding a particularly beautiful forest or river, could not leave there: but about a hundred or so, with those who joined, wishing to be of use, or impelled by the new restlessness which was such a feature of this Shikasta, journeyed incessantly for a year, and found that everywhere was the same. The cities were all empty. Not one was anything but a death-trap or a madhouse. Where people had stayed, they had killed themselves or were idiots.

Around each were the new settlements of Natives living in every kind of roughly contrived hut, eating meat they had hunted, wearing skins, tending gardens and fields of grain. If there were any clothes left from their city past, these were being hoarded, were already part of ritual. The storytellers were singing of the Gods who had taught them all they knew, and—for this had been fed into the tales at the beginning— would "come again."

When we got back to the Round City, meaning to walk outside the edge of the Stones, the vibrations had become so bad that we had to make a wide detour. For miles around, there was no life, no animals, no birds. And the vegetation was withering. The settlements we had left had been moved well out and away.

The biggest change was that more children were being born than before. The safeguards had been forgotten: gone was the knowledge of who should give birth, who should mate, what type of person was a proper parent. The knowledges and uses of sex had been forgotten. And whereas previously an individual who died before the natural term of a thousand years was unlucky, it was clear that the life-span was about to fluctuate. Some had died already, very young, or in middle age, and many of the new babies had died.

This was the situation all over Shikasta a year after the Lock had failed.

At least, there were enough people living well away from the old cities to continue the species. And I knew that although for a time the cities would become more and more dangerous, after three or four hundred years (inadequate information made it impossible to be more definite), when the weather and the vegetation had done their work on the buildings and in the Stones, the cities would all become heaps of ruins, with no potency left in them for good or for harm.

I come to the final phase of my mission.

First of all I had to locate the rebel Giants. I now did have an idea of where they were, for when I was in the Hexagonal City to the north of the Great Mountains, I had seen from very far off a settlement where none was expected, and there were rumours about ghosts and devils "the size of trees."

Again, it was David I decided to take with me. To say that he understood what went on was true. To say that he did *not* understand —was true. I would sit and explain, over and over again. He listened, his eyes fixed on my face, his lips moving as he repeated to himself what I was saying. He would nod: yes, he had grasped it! But a few minutes later, when I might be saying something of the same kind, he was uncomfortable, threatened. Why was I saying that? and that? his troubled eyes asked of my face: What did I mean? His questions at such moments were as if I had never taught him anything at all. He was like one drugged or in shock. Yet it seemed that he did absorb information, for sometimes he would talk as if from a basis of shared knowledge: it was as if a part of him knew and remembered all I told him, but other parts had not heard a word! I have never before or since had so strongly that experience of being with a person and knowing that all the time there was certainly a part of that person in contact with you, something real and alive and listening—yet most of the time what one said did not reach that silent and invisible being, and what *he* said was not often said by the real part of him. It was as if someone stood there bound and gagged while an inferior impersonator spoke for him.

He mentioned, when I asked him to come travelling again with me, that he did not want to leave his youngest daughter. He had not ever mentioned this daughter. Where was she? Oh—with friends, he believed. But did he not see her? Was he not responsible for her? He seemed to want to please me, by eagerly nodding his head and producing some phrases to the effect that she was a good girl, and could look after herself. This was the first time I encountered what was to become a typical Shikastan indifference to their progeny.

His daughter Sais was a large, light brown girl, with a mass of bronze tightly curled hair. Everything about her was wholesome and lively. She was not much more than a child, and indeed could look after herself—she had had to. She seemed to have no memory of having been brought up in the Round City, or of her life there with both her parents. She talked of her mother as if she had died many years before, but I discovered she had been killed hunting with a party for deer. A couple of tigers had lain in wait, and knocked her dead with blows from their great paws. Sais did not know that so recently as a year ago such a thing would have been inconceivable. Tigers were, always had been, enemies of Native-kind!

She agreed to come with us.

When the spaceship had first set me down on the planet, it was well to the north of the Great Mountains, on the east of the central landmass. I had walked and ridden west. Now we were walking back eastwards but to the south of the Great Mountains which are such a feature of Shikasta, towering over every other part. The foothills here were higher than the tallest mountains of the southern continents, and we climbed and climbed. All around the central peaks and masses, not one range, but range after range, chain after chain, peak after peak—a world of mountains, north and south, east and west. We looked down from immense heights into the dead Hexagonal City, with its surrounding settlements, which we could not see at all from there. But I did see something quite unexpected. Far below me, in a clearing on a mountainside, was a column, or a pylon—something that glittered, and must be of metal, and was extremely tall, though from here it looked so tiny. This must be something to do with Shammat. Besides, even from where we were high in that marvellous tonic air, I could feel an evil message coming from it to me. I did not want to expose David and Sais to it, and marked where it was, so that I could return to it alone.

We went on down, down, giving the Shammat thing a good distance, and then standing on the slopes of a minor peak, surveying interminable plains, I saw what I expected. We were looking down into the queerest kind of settlement. It had not been put together for shelter or for warmth or for any of the familiar purposes, but was an act of impaired memory.

A tall cylinder lacked a roof, but a couple of branches had been laid across the top. Another, square, had a ragged gap in it. A five-sided shack was leaning and crooked. Every shape and size of building were there, not one complete. The materials had been taken from the Hexagonal City. To carry great stones for several miles was not difficult for these Giants.

What had been in their minds, though? What did they remember of the old cities? How did they explain the vicious radiations they must have submitted themselves to, and how had they been affected?

As we three walked down and down through the wooded slopes of the lower mountains, I spoke of the Giants to David and Sais. We would soon be meeting very tall, very strong people, but no, these were not the Great Ones of the stories and ballads. We would have to be careful and on our guard at all times. It was possible they might harm us.

Thus I tried to prepare these two for what I feared. But how to explain to those who had never known anything like it, never even heard of such a thing, what slavery was, or serfdom? They had no means of knowing, or imagining, the contempt a degenerated and effete race may use for another, different from themselves.

We at last reached the plain, and walked towards that haphazard settlement. The Giants were all inside their buildings. We shouted greetings when we got near, and they came out, showing fear. Then, as we did not seem to threaten them, and they could see we were half their size, first one put on an act of indignation, as it were trying it out and looking at the others to see if it was making an effect, and then they all copied, behaving as if calling out to them at all was an impertinence. They took us into a sort of corral, so badly made that light showed through the stones. Jarsum was there. He was a chief, or a leader. He did not recognise me. Beside him, like a queen, sat his consort, the freakish white Giant. She stared, and then yawned, ostentatiously. Nothing could be more pathetic than their way of looking surreptitiously at each other to see if these gestures were being admired. Both Jarsum and she then tried out all sorts of tricks and gestures of ridiculous hauteur, bridling, giving us contemptuous glances, putting their noses in the air. I could see that David and his daughter were confused, for they had never seen anything like it.

I told Jarsum that I was Johor, an old friend, and he leaned forward to stare, his great face puckering and frowning, like someone presented with a conundrum too difficult. I said that my companions were David and Sais from what had been the Round City, his old home. But he did not remember, and looked in enquiry at the white Giant who lolled insolently there beside him, and around at the other Giants who stood like servants around the walls. But none remembered the Round City. Later I found that not all these Giants were from the Round City, but had come here from several of the cities, apparently guided by what remained in them of their old intuitions. They had tried to re-create what they could in these crazy sketches of buildings.

The white Giant had been studying the sturdy David, and his healthy daughter, and now she whispered to Jarsum. He examined us, directed by her, and saw three beings half the size of him and his kind, with different features and skin colour.

He announced that we would be permitted to stay and work for them.

Then I used the name Canopus. I had to.

Something did come home to them. Their eyes sought each other, first Jarsum and the white Giant, then, finding nothing there, these two leaned forward and stared at the other Giants, who stared back.

Yes, Canopus, I said, Canopus, and waited again for the word to resonate.

They might not go against the Laws of Canopus, I said, not one of us could do that, and the first Law of Canopus was that we may not make slaves and servants of others.

This reached them.

I asked for shelter for the night.

They replied that there was no building unoccupied, but the truth was, they wanted us to go, for we presented them with a challenge too great for them.

I said that we would rest for the night outside this settlement under some trees, and come to them again in the morning, to talk.

I could see that they were going to demand that we leave, and might even chase us away.

I said that Canopus ordained that travellers must be fed and given shelter. It was a Law binding on each one of us.

This did not reach them easily. They were inwardly rebellious, and angry, and would have killed us if they were not afraid. As for us three, we stood waiting, I suppressing fear, because I knew how great our danger was, but David and Sais quite calm and even eager, since they did not understand anything of what was going on. And I saw again that these Natives were better off than the Giants, simply because they stood so much nearer to stones and earth and plants and the beasts: in them was a bedrock of strength the Giants did not have. The ones who had agreed to leave into airs and climates on planets chosen for them—yes; but these, no—I could see from their inwardly shocked, empty eyes that even their physical beings were doomed. They would not live long.

They did bring us food. Animal food, so they had taken to hunting. We had not seen animals as we approached this settlement, so the herds must have already fled a long way off across the plains.

We laid ourselves down under some nearby trees, and I stayed awake while the others slept. When it was very late, the stars crowding down in a black sky, a great shadow came stooping out of the round enclosure, and it was Jarsum, striding across to us. He stood a couple of his paces away—many of ours—and peered and puzzled, but could not see us under the boughs, and came nearer, bending close. When he saw me awake, he smiled. It was an embarrassed smile. And he went away, cracking stones and twigs under his great feet that were shod in hides now.

In the morning the three of us walked the miles to the edge of the Hexagonal City, where the stone patterns began. The ugly vibrations did not seem as strong as those in other places, either because time had already weakened them, or because so many of the stones being carried away had broken the patterns, or for other reasons I could not surmise.

But we saw something astonishing. Half a dozen of the Giants had come after us from that pathetic settlement of theirs, but took no notice of us, striding straight into the middle of the Stones, where they stood, turning themselves about, and raising their arms and bending and bowing. I understood that they were *enjoying* the sensations. Yet this practice could only make them more befuddled than they were.

After some time of this, they came out of the Stones, their limbs and heads jerking, as if they were truly diseased, and they danced and twitched their way back to their home.

I noticed that both David and Sais showed signs of wanting to "try it and see"—for they had forgotten, or so it seemed, what those discords could do. I said to them, No, no, they must not—and led them back to the Giants.

There a feast was in progress, with mounds of roast meat, and they were singing and dancing. I understood that the Giants who had gone to the Stones went to fetch back, in themselves, the power of the disharmonies, which they were using like alcohol to fuel this revelry.

I reminded them of our presence and asked for fruit.

I asked Jarsum to come and talk with us, alone, under the trees. He came, but as if drunk or half asleep.

I spoke of Canopus again.

He accepted it. He listened. But nothing much was getting past the fogs and silliness of that poor brain.

I produced the Signature and held it in front of him. I had not wanted to do this, because I had noticed that its power had uneven or sometimes contradictory effects by now.

Yes, he remembered it. He remembered something. The half-dazed eyes, reddened and narrowed, as if with drink, peered close, and the great trembling hands came out to touch it. And he did something I had never seen on this noble planet, that could not have happened on Rohanda—he bent and prostrated himself and poured sand on his head. And David and Sais copied him: they did it eagerly, pleased with themselves for learning this new attractive thing.

I led the way back to the settlement, telling Jarsum that he must make everyone come. He did, but more than half had gone out to dance among the Stones, and we had to wait for them to come back.

Then I stood before them, in a space among the lean-to fragmentary buildings, and I held out the Signature, so that it shone and dazzled, and sent its gleams everywhere into their eyes, their faces.

I said that Canopus forbade them to go near the Stones. It was an order. And I made the Signature flash and shiver.

I said that Canopus forbade them to use each other or the other creatures of the planet as servants, unless these servants were treated as well as they would treat themselves, as equals at all times.

I said that Canopus forbade them to kill animals unless it was for food, and then only with care and without cruelty. They must plant crops, I said, and must harvest fruit and nuts.

I said that they might not waste the fruits of the earth, and each might take only what was needed, no more.

They must not use violence with each other.

Above all, over and above all these prohibitions, was the first one: never, never, must they go into the old cities, or use those stones for building other settlements, and they must not intoxicate themselves in these ways if they ever again came across places or things that held the capacity to intoxicate. They were destroying themselves in these practices, and Canopus was displeased.

Then I put away the Signature, and I went up to Jarsum, who was prostrate, trembling, the white Giant beside him, and I said, "Farewell. And I will come to you again. And until that time remember the Laws of Canopus."

And I and David and Sais walked away, not looking back. I had forbidden them to, for fear this might weaken an effect which I believed was weak enough, and when we were deep in the trees on the foothills of the mountains, I asked these two companions of mine what had happened.

They did not reply. They were awed.

When I pressed them David said that I had knowledge of something called Canopus.

Sais? Perhaps it would be better with her?

I made a trial. I waited until we had gone up one range of foothills and down into a pleasant valley full of trickling streams and bright plants, and I asked them again if they had understood what had happened with the Giants.

David had that look on him which was so familiar by now, a sullenness, as if he were being asked for too much. Then he turned his eyes away and pretended to be watching a bird on a branch.

Sais was looking at me attentively.

"What do you know of Canopus?" I asked.

She said that Canopus was an angry man, and he did not want anyone to dance where there were stones. He did not want hunting bands to kill more animals than they needed for meat. He did not want . . .

Well, she got through it, and I decided to concentrate on her. As we walked, I drilled her and I drilled her, and David her father ambled on, sometimes singing to amuse himself, for we bored him in our intensity, or sometimes listening, and chiming in with a phrase or two: "Canopus doesn't want . . ."

And so we went on, day after day, wandering on among the foothills and valleys of the Great Mountains, until I felt the presence of Shammat growing stronger, and knew I must make these two go away from me.

I made a solemn and fearful thing of the occasion. They were to undertake a task of the utmost importance—for me, but above all, for Canopus. They were to go from place to place over Shikasta, everywhere there were settlements, and they were to repeat everything I had said. Sais was to be the spokesman, but David was to be her protector. And I gave her the Signature, saying that they must regard this as more important than—but what? Life? They did not have that conception: the thought of death as an ever-present threat was not in them. This came from Canopus, I said. It was the very substance and being of Canopus and must be guarded at all times, even if they were to lose their lives doing it. Thus I held Death before them, using it to create in these creatures a sorrow and a vigilance where there had been none.

Sais put the Signature reverently into her belt and kept her hand there on it, as she stood in front of me, her eyes on my face, listening.

When they reached a settlement, I said, she must first of all speak of Canopus, and if the word was enough to revive old memories and associations, and if her hearers could listen because of that word alone, then she could give her message and go. Only if she could get no one to listen, or if it seemed that she and her father might be harmed, then she might show the Signature. And when they had been everywhere, and spoken with everyone, even hunting bands they met, or solitary farmers or fishermen in the forests or by rivers, then they must bring the Signature back to me.

And then I spoke to her carefully and slowly about the concept of a task, something which had to be done—for I was afraid that this might have lapsed from her mind altogether. This journey of hers, I said, the act of making it, and carrying the Signature and guarding it, would develop her, would bring out in her something that was buried and clouded over. And when I left Shikasta, I said—telling them for the first time that I was going to leave—she would be responsible for keeping the Laws, and for passing them on. I saw panic in both of them, at the idea that I would be leaving them, but I said that they would be without me now for months, longer, and would learn they could maintain themselves and the Laws without me. We separated there, and I watched them go off, and my will went with her: You can do it, you can, you can, I was whispering, then saying, then shouting, as they went out of sight and hearing among the enormous trees of that wonderful forest. I would not see them for at least a Shikastan journey around its sun.

And now for the Shammat transmitter.

If I have ever been in a paradise, it was there. Neither Natives nor Giants had ever lived in that region. The forests were as they had grown, and the trees were some of them thousands of years old. There were flowers everywhere, and little streams. And the birds and animals did not know they should be afraid of this new animal, and came wandering up to sniff me, and they lay down by me, for company. That night I lay by the bank of a stream, with animals coming down to drink, and the worst I feared was that some great deer might tread on me in the dark. Tigers, lions did not know I was prey. Herds of elephants stretched out their trunks to me and then went on.

My lingering there, taking in the sane breath of the trees, and communing with the animals was for a purpose. I was now not armed with the Signature, and I had to confront the power of Shammat.

But now I did not know how to go about finding the transmitter. The sense of it seemed to come from everywhere. High above me, stretching up into the bluest sky I can remember, was the peak I had stood on and looked down into the glade where the glittering column was. Had I then to make the wearisome climb back up there? I could not bring myself to do it, from which I knew that I was badly affected already, and I lay down to rest under a great tree that had white flowers on it, and shed an invigorating scent. When I woke, a shaggy creature was bending over me. He was the size of a Native, but heavily furred, and I understood at once that he was the descendant of a

Native who had strayed away long ago from his fellows and had not developed with the others. He was not at all hostile, but curious, and seemed to smile, and his quick brown eyes had something like consciousness in them. He brought me fruit, and we ate it together, and after a while we were able to communicate. He had the beginnings of speech in him, a good deal more than grunts and barks. Some of his gestures and his facial grimaces were the same as the Natives', and half through sounds, half through grimaces and signs, I was able to tell him that I was looking for a thing that was new to the Great Mountains, that did not belong. Already he seemed to understand, and when I said this was a bad thing, wicked, he showed fear, but overcame it, and lifted me up solicitously from where I was sitting—for his being stronger and larger than I seemed to him reason for his protecting and assisting me always—and we set off together.

I was farther from the thing than I had thought. We went up, up, always up. We reached the snow line on some peaks, and crossed these and went down again, leaving the snow line behind. I was cold, but he was not, with his heavy fell of hair. He was concerned, and made little shelters of boughs, and at night lay down close to me so that his body would warm me. And he brought me fruit and nuts, and then leaves, but saw I could not eat these, and we had little feasts together.

But I was feeling deathly ill, and wondered if I would be able to finish my task. And he, too, was beginning to feel sick and trembling. He did not want me to go on. But I told him I had to, and that he should wait for me here. He persisted with me, for a little while. Then he became fearful, and moved in a terrified way through the trees, which, I saw, had begun to be broken and damaged. Rocks had been flung about, for no reason, trees had been cut and left lying, and above all, there was a horrible smell. We kept stumbling among the bones of animals, and there were half-decayed carcasses everywhere, and birds that had been killed and left, and all this killing and smashing had been for the sake of it. Oh, yes, this was Shammat all right!

And now I ordered my friend to stay where he was and wait for me. He did not like it, and he reached out after me with his furry hands, wanting to hold me back, but I turned so that I could not see him, and be tempted, and went on.

I soon came to a high ridge. Below was a valley, and there were great peaks all around that glittered and shone with snow. The sensation of Shammat was very strong now.

Everything in the valley was broken and spoiled. I knew that this was the valley I had looked down into from above, but could not now see the column anywhere. Yet it *was* here, I could feel it. Waves and pulses of Shammat came out at me and made me reel, but I held on to a young tree that had been half cut through at its base so that it had fallen, and lay forward at my height, making a sort of handhold. I looked and looked but I simply could not see the column I knew was there. Yet the centre of the valley where it had been was not two hundred paces ahead. And still the pulses came out, throbbing, deadly, sickening me. I sent my thoughts to Canopus in a plea for help. Help me, help me, I cried silently, this is the most terrible danger I am in, danger far too strong for me—and I kept my thoughts steady, like a bridge, and soon did feel a little trickle of help coming from there. And, as I strengthened, I did see it—a glimpse only—I saw the column. There was a jet, or narrow fountain there, sometimes visible, and then not, but coming into sight again. It was as if the air itself had thickened and become a very fine and subtle liquid, a crystalline water, jetting up and falling back on itself. But now I recognised it, and I felt that I would have done so before, if the idea had not been so far from my mind. I knew this substance! I summoned every kind of strength I could and walked forward to where this glittering column was, was not—and was again.

A few paces from it I stopped, for I could not go nearer: it held me away from it.

This was a substance recently invented, or discovered, on Canopus, Effluon 3, and that was why I had not expected to find it here. And no, it was not possible for Puttiora to have made it, for their technology was so far behind ours. And Shammat certainly could not. And so they must have stolen it from Canopus.

Effluon 3 had the property of drawing in and sending out qualities as needed—as programmed. It was the most sensitive and yet the strongest of conductors, needing no machinery to set it up, for it came into existence through the skilled use of concentrations of the mind. What Shammat, or Puttiora, had had to steal from us was not a thing, but a skill. This was too much for me to puzzle out now, feeling as I did, on the edge of losing consciousness, and besides there was a more urgent question. Effluon 3, unlike Effluons 1 and 2, did not last for long: it was a booster, no more.

From above I had seen a metal column, a thing of strength and durability, because I had been expecting something of the sort. But really it was a device which by its very nature soon would not be here at all. And yet it was hardly likely that Shammat would go to all this trouble—inviting reprisals from us, from Sirius (and possibly even from Puttiora, if this was, as it might well be, an act of defiance)—for some short-term gain.

Yet I could not be mistaken. It was a colleague on Canopus who had first thought of this device, and I had seen these evanescent columns of thickened air in all the different stages of their development. This could not be anything other than Effluon 3—and it would not be here in a year's time.

I realised that I had slipped to my knees, and was swaying there a few paces from the horrible thing—which of course could be health-giving and good-making, in other places and times—but my mind kept going dark, it kept filling with swaying grey waves, a painful shrilling attacked the inside of my brain, and I could feel blood running down my neck from my afflicted ears. The snowy peaks, the sunny slopes of the valley, the smashed and splintered trees, the half-visible jet of glistening substance, all swayed and went, and I fell into a coma.

I was not there long and certainly would have died if not for my new friend who had been watching from a ridge above, holding on to a tree for support, in fear for his sanity, because his mind, like mine, was badly attacked. He saw me swaying on my feet, then on my knees, and then lying prone. He crept down from the ridge, forcing himself forward, until he was able to reach for my ankles. He turned me over on my back, so that my face might not be cut, and he dragged me away from the place and then lifted and carried me. When I came to, on the other side of the ridge, he was lying unconscious beside me. Now it was my turn to help him, by rubbing his furry hands and his shoulders, with all my strength, but he was such a big creature it was hard to believe these small ministrations could be enough to start life flowing again. As soon as he was himself, and we were both able to stand, we supported each other away and up into the mountains, to get away from the emanations we could both feel. He had a warm cave, heaped with dry leaves, and larders of dried fruits and nuts. He knew about fire, too, and soon we were warmed and strong.

But while I had been unconscious, I had had a dream or vision, and I knew now the secret of the Shammat column. I saw the old Rohanda glowing and lovely, emitting its harmonies, rather as one does in the Planets-to-Scale Room. Between it and Canopus swung the silvery cord of our love. But over it fell a shadow, and this was a hideous face, pockmarked and pallid, with staring glaucous eyes. Hands like mouths went out to grasp and grab, and at their touch the planet shivered and its note changed. The hands tore out pieces of the planet, and crammed the mouth which sucked and gobbled and never had enough. Then this eating thing faded into the half-visible jet of the transmitter, which drew off the goodness and the strength, and then, as this column in its turn dissolved, I leaned forward in my dream, frantic to learn what it all meant, could mean . . . I saw that the inhabitants of Shikasta had changed, had become of the same nature as the hungry jetting column: Shammat had fixed itself into the nature of the Shikastan breed, and it was they who were now the transmitter, feeding Shammat.

This was the dream and now I understood why Shammat needed its transmitter there only for a short time.

I stayed with my friend for some days, getting my strength back. I understood by now a good deal of what he knew and was trying to tell me. Trembling and fearful, he told me that a great Thing had come down from the sky, and set itself on the slopes of that valley, and then horrible creatures had come—and he could not speak of them without shaking and hiding his face as if from the memory—and killed everything and broken everything. They had lit fires and let them go out of control to rage over the mountain slopes, destroying and killing. They had slaughtered for pleasure. They had caught and tortured animals. . . . He sat by me, this poor creature, whimpering a little, and tears ran down over the fur of his big cheeks, as he stared into the flames of our fire, remembering.

And how many of them?

He held up his hands palm out, then again, and then, clumsily, for this was not an easy mode of thought for him, once again. There had been thirty of them.

How long had they stayed?

Oh, an awful time, a long long time—but he put up his paws, or hands, to his eyes, and sat rocking and letting out small yelps of pain. Yes, he had been caught by them, and put in a cage of boughs, and they had stood around laughing and sticking sharpened branches at him . . . he lifted the fur of his sides to show me the scars. But he had escaped, and had let out from their cages many other animals and birds and fled away—all the animals and birds had left, and as I must have noticed, had not gone back. There were none of the creatures of the forest anywhere near that valley now. And he had crept back one dark night, and gone as silently as he could to the top of the ridge and looked over—and had seen nothing, but the emanations of the column had made him ill, so he had known that something was there . . . he did not know even now what it was, for he had not been able to see it, only feel it.

And the big Thing these terrible beings had come in? Had he seen it or touched it?

No, he had been too afraid to go close enough to touch. He had never seen anything like it, he had not known that anything like this could exist. It was round—and he made his arms round. It was enormous—and he spread them till he indicated the whole interior of this very large cave. And it was—he whimpered and swayed—horrible.

I could not learn more than that.

But I did not need to.

I told him that I would have to travel very far from here. He did not understand "very far." He would come with me, he said, and he did, but as day after day passed, he became silent and apprehensive, for he was a long way from the part of the mountains he knew. He was lonely, I could see that. But perhaps he had not known that he was lonely? Had there been others like him? Yes, there had been once! Many? Again he held out hands—once, twice and again and again. . . . There had been many and they had died out, perhaps from an epidemic, and now there was only himself. If there were others now on the mountain he did not know of them. He came shambling along beside me as I walked up mountains and down them, and up them and down again, and then left them behind and went down and down, with snows behind us, and then through the marvellous untouched forests and down again through regions of flowering scented bushes—and there in front of us were the steamy southern jungles, and beyond them, but very far away, the sea. Did he know of the sea? But he could not understand anything of my attempts at explanation.

What I had to do was to walk back to the settlements of Natives who had escaped from the Round City, for there I would meet again with Sais and her father. I tried to persuade this poor animal to come with me, for I believed that the Natives would befriend him. At least Sais would. But when I reached the low foothills beyond which stretched the jungles, he became silent and morose, turning his face away from me continually, as if I had turned myself away from *him*, and then he came stumbling and running to me, and he clutched at my arms, and tried to hold my hands so fast in his I could not leave him. Great tears ran from his kind brown eyes, and disappeared into the fur of his cheeks, and streaked his chest with wet. He let out whimpers, then a roar of pain, and ran back, falling and getting up again, till he reached the shelter of the trees. He stood with the foothills at his back, and stared and peered after me, and shouted farewells that were a plea: come back, come back! Then he ran out a little way after me, but retreated again. I waved until he was no more than a little dot under trees that it was hard to believe from where I stood a couple of miles away were so tall. But I had to go on. And so I left him to his solitudes.

I had been gone half a year by the time I reached the settlement. I was concerned for Sais and David, but there was no news of them. It even seemed as if they had already been forgotten. I made myself a shelter of earth and logs, and waited. Meanwhile, I tried to teach those among the Natives who seemed intelligent what I could of Canopus and how they could live so as to limit the power of Shammat over them. But they could not take it in.

They were prepared, though, to learn anything I could teach in the realm of the practical arts, which they were in danger of forgetting. I taught them—or retaught them—gardening and husbandry. I taught them to tame a goatlike creature, which could give them milk, and I demonstrated butter- and cheese-making. I taught them how to choose plants for their fibres, and to prepare the fibres and to weave them, and to dye them. I showed them how to make bricks from the earth and fire them. All these crafts I was teaching to creatures who had known them for thousands of years and had forgotten them a few months ago. It was hard, sometimes, to believe that they were not making fun of me, as they watched me, and then their faces lit up with amazement and delight as they saw cheese, or fired pots, or the suppleness of properly cured hides.

Two years after they had left me, Sais and David came. Even as they walked into the settlement, I could see they had had a hard time. They were wary and careful, and ready to defend themselves—which they nearly had to do, for their friends, even their family, had forgotten them. They were lean and burned brown. The girl had grown into her proper height in that journey, but was still much shorter than her father, shorter than the average of the Natives, and I saw that a reduction in height was very likely beginning.

They had succeeded in reaching most of the settlements. They had walked, ridden on the backs of animals, used canoes and boats. They had not stayed in any one place more than a day. They had done exactly what I had ordered—talked of Canopus, watched for the effect, and never used the Signature unless they had to.

In two places they had been chased away, and threatened with death if they returned.

Both talked of dead people they had seen in the settlements. It was not fear they showed, or sorrow or grief: just as the death of Sais's mother had left her more puzzled than grieved, so the evidences of the nearness of death such as an unburied corpse lying in a forest, or a group going past with a dead person on a litter, excited in them efforts at understanding. My attempts to make death real for them, by linking it with the Signature, had not succeeded. They *could* not believe in death for themselves, because those robust bodies knew that hundreds of years of life lay ahead, and their bodies' knowledge was stronger than the feeble thoughts of their impaired minds. They told me as if it were an extraordinary fact I could not really be expected to believe that some corpses they had seen had been killed in quarrels: yes, people killed each other! They did! There was no doubt of it!

In many settlements it had become the practice for many or most, particularly the older Natives who were finding it hard to adjust to new conditions, to make excursions to the Stones, and subject themselves to sensations felt first as horrible, and then as attractive or at least compulsive.

Yet the repetition of my orders had made a difference. In nearly all the settlements people had memorised the words that had been brought to them by these two strangers, repeating over and over to themselves, to each other: Canopus says we must not make servants of each other, Canopus says . . . Canopus wills . . .

Yes, over and over again, in a hundred different places, Sais had said, or chanted, for the words had turned into a song, or chant:

Canopus says we must not waste or spoil,
Canopus tell us not to use violence on each other

and had heard these words being whispered or said or sung as she left.

Sais had grown in every way in those two years. Her father remained an amiable, laughing man who could not keep anything in his head, though he had guarded her everywhere they went, since "Canopus said so." While of course in no way approaching the marvellous quick-mindedness and mental development of the time of "before the Catastrophe"—as the songs and tales were now putting it—she had in fact become steadier-minded, clearer, more able to apprehend and to keep, and this was because she had carried the Signature and had guarded it. She was a brave girl—that I had known before sending her out—and a strong one. But now I could sit with her and talk, and this was real talk, a real exchange, because she could listen. It was slow, for that starved brain kept switching off, a blank look would come into her eyes, then she would shake herself and set herself to listen, to take in.

One day she handed me back the Signature, though I had not asked her for it. She was pleased with herself that she had managed to keep it safe and it was hard for her to let go of it. I took it back, only temporarily, though she did not know that, and told her that now the most important part of what she was to learn and do was just beginning. For quite soon I had to leave Shikasta, leave for Canopus, and she would remain as custodian of the truth about Shikasta, which she must learn, and guard and impart to anybody who could listen to her.

She wept. So did her father David. And I would have liked to weep. These unfortunate creatures had such a long ordeal in front of them, such a path of wandering and hazards and dangers—but these they did not seem anywhere near being able to understand.

I let them recover fully from their journey, and then I got the three of us together in a space between huts near where the central fire burned, and I laid the Signature on the earth between us, and I got them used to the idea of listening to instruction. After some days of this, while others had seen us, and some had stood listening a little way off, wondering, and even interested, I asked that all of the people of the settlement, who were not actually hunting or on guard, or in some way attending to the maintenance of the tribe—for now one had to call them that—should sit with us, every day, for an hour or so and listen. They must learn to listen again, to understand that in this way they could gain information. For they had forgotten it entirely. They remembered nothing of how the Giants had instructed them, could understand only what they could see, as when I rubbed stones over a hide to soften it, or shook sour milk to make butter. Yet at night they did listen to David, singing of "the old days," and then they sang, too. . . .

Soon, every day, at the hour when the sun went, just after the evening meal, I talked, and they listened; they would even acknowledge what I said in words that came out from the past, in a fugitive opening of memory—and then their eyes would turn aside, and wander. Suddenly they weren't there. How can I describe it? Only with difficulty, to Canopeans!

Re: Colonised Planet 5, Shikasta

What I told these Shikastans was this.

Before the Catastrophe, in the Time of the Giants, who had been their friends and mentors, and who had taught them everything, Shikasta had been an easy pleasant world, where there was little danger or threat. Canopus was able to feed Shikasta with a rich and vigorous air, which kept everyone safe and healthy, and above all, made them love each other. But because of an accident, this substance-of-life could not reach here as it had, could reach this place only in pitifully small quantities. This supply of finer air had a name. It was called SOWF— the substance-of-we-feeling—I had of course spent time and effort on working out an easily memorable syllable. The little trickle of SOWF that reached this place was the most precious thing they had, and would keep them from falling back to animal level. I said there was a gulf between them and the other animals of Shikasta, and what made them higher was their knowledge of SOWF. SOWF would protect and preserve them. They must reverence SOWF.

For they could waste it, spend it, use it in the wrong way. It was for this reason they must never pervert themselves in the ruins of the old cities or dance among the Stones. This was why they must never, if they came on sources of intoxication, allow themselves intoxication. But coming from Canopus to Shikasta was a small steady trickle of this substance, and would continue to come, always. This was a promise from Canopus to Shikasta. In due time—I did not say thousands upon thousands of years!—this trickle would become a flood. And their descendants could bathe in it as they played now in the crystal rivers. But there would not be any descendants if they did not take care to preserve themselves. If they, those who sat before me now, listening to these precious revelations, did not guard themselves they would become worse than animals. They must not spoil themselves by taking too much of the substance of Shikasta. They must not use others. They must not let themselves become animals who lived only to eat and to sleep and eat again—no, a part of their lives must be set aside for the remembrance of Canopus, memory of the substance-of-we-feeling, which was all they had.

And there was more, and worse. On Shikasta there were enemies, wicked people, enemies of Canopus, who were stealing the SOWF. These enemies enslaved Shikastans, when they could. They did this by encouraging those qualities that Canopus hated. They thrived when they hurt each other, or used each other—they delighted in any manifestation of the absence of substance-of-we-feeling. To outwit their enemies, Shikastans must love each other, help each other, always be equals with each other, and never take each other's goods or substance. . . . This is what I told them, day after day, while the Signature lay glinting there, in the light that fled from the evening sky, and the light of the flames that burned up as night came.

Meanwhile, Sais was my most devoted assistant. She chose, using faculties that seemed to revive in her, individuals that seemed to her most promising, and repeated these lessons, over and over again. She said them and she sang them, and David made new songs and stories.

When enough people in this settlement were sure of this knowledge, I said, they must travel everywhere over Shikasta and teach it. They must be sure that everyone heard this news, and above all, remembered.

And then it was time for me to leave and go to Zone Six. I put the Signature into Sais's hand before everyone, and said that she was the custodian of it.

I did not say that it was the means of keeping the flow of SOWF from Canopus to Shikasta, but I knew they would soon believe it. And I had to leave her something to strengthen her.

Then I told them that I was going to return to Canopus and that one day I would come again.

I left the tribe one morning very early, as the sun was rising over the clearing that held the settlement. I listened to the birds arguing above me in the ancient trees, and I held out my fingers to a little goat who was a pet, and who came trotting after me. I sent it back, and I went to the river where it was very wide and deep and strong, and would sweep me well away from the settlement so that no one would find my body. I let myself down into it and swam out into the current.

I now return to my visit in the Last Days.

It was necessary that Taufiq should cause himself to be born into the minority race of the planet, the white or pale-skinned peoples indigenous to the northern areas. The city he had chosen was not on the site of one of the Mathematical Cities of the Great Time, though some of the present cities were in fact built on such sites—it goes without saying, without any idea of their potentialities. This site had never been up to much. It was low, had been marshy for much of its recent history, when the climate had been wet. The soil was always damp and enervating. Nothing about the place had ever been naturally conducive to the high energies, though for certain purposes and in certain conditions it had been attuned and used, though temporarily, by us. It was the main city of a small island that had, because of its warlike and acquisitive qualities, overrun and dominated a good part of the globe, but had recently been driven back again.

Taufiq was John, a name he had used quite often in his career—Jan, Jon, John, Sean, Yahya, Khan, Ivan, and so on. He was John Brent-Oxford, and the parents he had chosen were healthy honest people, neither too high nor too low in the society, which, since it suffered the most cumbersome division into classes and castes, all suspicious of each other, was a matter of importance and of careful judgement.

Taufiq's undertaking was, in order to accomplish what he had to do, to become a person skilled in the regulations with which the various, always warring or quarrelling individuals, or sections of society, controlled themselves and each other. And he had achieved this. His youth had been spent intelligently, he had equipped himself, and was outstanding at an early age. Just as in higher spheres promising youngsters are watched by people they know nothing about, though they may wonder or guess, so in lower spheres of activity possibilities are prepared for those who prove themselves, and John was from childhood observed by "people of influence," as the Shikastan phrase goes. But the "influences" were by no means all of the same kind!

In this corrupt and ghastly age the young man could not avoid having put on him many pressures to leave the path of duty, and it was very early—he was not more than twenty-five years old—that he succumbed. Furthermore, he knew that he was doing something wrong. The young often have moments of clear thinking, which as they grow older become fewer, and muddied. He had kept alive in some part of him a knowledge that he was "destined" to do something or other. He felt this as pure and unsullied, but—more often and more deeply as he grew older—"impractical." That he did know quite well what he was doing is shown by his tendency to laugh apologetically at certain moments, with the remark that "he had been unable to resist temptation." Yet these words on the face of it had little to do with the obvious and recognised mores of his society, which was why it was essential to laugh. The laugh paid homage to these modes and mores. He was being ridiculous, the laugh said . . . yet he was never without uneasiness about what he was doing, the choices he had made.

It was necessary for him to be at a certain place at a certain time, in order to play a role that was essential to our handling of the crisis that faced Shikasta. He was to aim for a position—not only in his own country's legal system—but a leading one in the system of northern countries which unified, or attempted to, that part of the northern hemisphere which recently had conquered and despoiled a good part of the planet, and which had until very recently been continually at war among themselves. He was to become a reliable and honest person, in this sphere. At a time of corruption, personal and public, he was to become known as incorruptible, unbribable, disinterested, straight-speaking.

But he was only just out of the last of his educational establishments, an elite one, for the production of the administrative class, when he took a false turning. Instead of going into a junior position in the Councils of the aforesaid bloc of northern countries, which was the position planned for him by us (and by him, of course, as Taufiq), he took a job in a law firm which was known for the number of its members who went into politics.

World War II was just over—Shikastan terminology. [SEE *History of Shikasta*, VOLS. 2955–3015, *The Century of Destruction*.] He had fought in it, seen much ferocity, spoiling, suffering. His judgements had been affected: his whole being—just like everybody else. He saw himself in a crucial role—as indeed he should—but one of the strongest of the false ideas of that epoch, politics, had entered into him. It was not as simple as that he wanted crude power, crude authority: no, he visualized himself "influencing things for the good." He was an idealist: a word describing people who described themselves as intending good, not self-interest at the expense of others.

And in parentheses I report here that this was true of a good many of our citizens—to borrow a Shikastan word—of that time. They turned into wrong and destructive paths believing that they were better than others whose belief in self-interest was open and expressed, better because they, and they alone, knew how the practical affairs of the planet should be conducted. An emotional reaction to the sufferings of Shikasta seemed to them a sufficient qualification for curing them.

The attitudes outlined in this paragraph define "politics," "political parties," "political programmes." Nearly all political people were incapable of thinking in terms of interaction, of cross-influences, of the various sects and "parties" forming *together* a whole, wholes—let alone of groups of nations making up a whole. No, in entering the state of mind where "politics" was ruler, it was always to enter a crippling partiality, a condition of being blinded by the "correctness" of a certain viewpoint. And when one of these sects or "parties" got power, they nearly always behaved as if their viewpoint could be the only right one. The only *good* one: when John chose a sect, he was in his own mind motivated by the highest ideas and ideals. He saw himself as a saviour of some kind, dreamed of himself as leader of the nation. From the moment he joined this group of lawyers, he met with very few people who thought differently from him. On various occasions members of our staff attempted to influence him, tried to remind him, indirectly of course, but none of them succeeded: the ways of thinking and being that he had taken to the borders of Shikasta were now so buried in him that they surfaced only rarely, in dreams, or in moments of remorse and panic that he could not ascribe to their right cause.

He had temporarily been written off. If it happened—so the judgement went on Canopus—that by some at present unforeseen processes Taufiq would "come to himself"—many such revealing phrases were common on Shikasta—and very often people apparently quite lost to us, at least temporarily, did "come to themselves," "see the light," and so on, quite often due to some awful shock or trauma of the kind Shikasta was so prodigal with, then, and then only, could trouble be spent on him. We were all so pressed, so thinly spread, and the situation on the planet so desperate.

One of my tasks was to observe him, to assess his present state, and if possible, to administer a reminder.

He was in his early fifties: that is, he was well past the halfway mark in the pitifully brief life which was all that Shikastans could now expect. As it happened he was scheduled for a longer life than most: his final assignment called for him to be about seventy-five when he would represent the aged. A *respected* representative: though at the moment it was hard to see how this could be brought about.

He lived in a house in an affluent district of the city, in a style which he would have described as moderate, was not excessive contrasted with what was usual then in that geographical area, but according to how it was to be judged very soon after—by global standards—in a shameful, wasteful, and profligate way. He had two families. A first wife had four children by him, and lived in another part of the city. His present wife had two children. The children were all indulged, spoiled, unfitted for what lay ahead. The women's lives were devoted to supporting him, his ambitions. Both felt for him emotions characteristic of anyone who had ever been close to him. He was a person who had always provoked people into extremes of liking and disliking. He influenced people. He changed lives—for good and bad. A powerful inner drive (something supremely valuable which had as it were slipped out of true) had caused his life—and again this was hardly unusual in those times—to resemble where a swathe of forest fire had passed: everything extreme: blackened earth, destroyed animals and vegetation, and then stronger brilliant growth to follow, a change in the genetic patternings, potential of all kinds.

In appearance he was ordinary: dark hair, dark eyes in which even now I liked to imagine I could see traces of those far-distant ancestors, the Giants. A pale skin which possibly came from the genetic freaks among the Giants. His sturdy energetic body reminded me of the Natives. But of course by now there were so many admixtures, from the Sirian experiments, the Shammat spies, and others.

Like all people in public life at that period, he had public and private personalities. This was governed by the fact that no such person could ever tell the truth to the people he was supposed to represent. Some sort of attack in the personality was essential equipment: persuasiveness, forcefulness, charm. And it was necessary to use methods that in other times, places, planets, would have been described as deceitful, lying, and in fact criminal. The qualities prized in "public servants" on Shikasta were, almost invariably, the most superficial and irrelevant imaginable, and could only have been accepted in a time of near total debasement and falseness. This was true of all sects, groupings, "parties": for what was remarkable about this particular time was how much they all resembled each other, while they spent most of their energies in describing and denigrating differences that they imagined existed between them.

John had become a national figure by the time he was forty. This was because he was in certain positions and places: not because he was more than ordinarily competent, or had more than the usual grasp of public affairs—seen from local viewpoints, of course. He was handicapped because of his self-division. His suppressed inner qualities made him disappointed with what he was. He knew he had greater qualities than any he was using but did not know what they were. This restlessness had caused him to drink too much, indulge in bouts of self-denigration and cynicism. He was not respected in ways that matter, and he knew it. He was only another among the hundreds, the thousands, of the politicians of the globe of whom nothing much was to be expected—certainly not by the people they were supposed to represent. These might work, fight, even commit crimes to get "their"

representatives into power, but after that they did not consider they
had any responsibility for their choices. For a feature, perhaps a predominant feature of the inhabitants of this planet, was that their
broken minds allowed them to hold, and act on—even forcibly and
violently—opinions and sets of mind that a short time later—years, a
month, even a few minutes—they might utterly repudiate.

At the time when I located his dwelling, and positioned myself (of
course well ensconced in Zone Six) where I could take in as much as
was needed to make my decisions, and to influence him, if possible,
he was in a period of intense emotional activity.

He had choices to make. Inwardly he knew this was another crisis
for him. The political faction he represented had just been deprived of
power. His faction had been in and out of a governing position several
times since the Second World War (or as we put it, the Second
Intensive Phase of the Twentieth Century War) and it was not this
that was affecting him. Pressure was being put on him (indirectly by us)
to return full-time to his legal firm and become active there, for he
would be enabled to cultivate that kind of reputation which is most
solidly based: among people who work in the same sphere as oneself.
If he did this, it would still be time for him to take on a series of cases
in ways which would be useful. The other work offered to him was in
the Councils of the northerly bloc of countries. But it was a high
position, he did not have the qualities to sustain it, and we knew that
he would not be in exactly the right place to take up the defence of
the white races at the moment when they were to be threatened with
extermination. He would not have the necessary qualities. From our
point of view, his acceptance of this post would be a bad mistake.

His present wife thought so, too. She had an inkling of what could
happen. She did not like him as an impassioned sectarian. Neither had
his first wife. Both women in fact had married him because of being
attracted to his hidden unused powers or potential, which he then did
not fulfil, and this was the real reason for their dissatisfaction with
him—which fact they did not understand, and this caused in them all
kinds of bitternesses and frustrations. This second marriage was likely to
break up. Because of all this he was in mental breakdown. His home
was a seethe of emotions and conflict. [SEE *History of Shikasta*, VOL.
3012, *Mental Instability During the Century of Destruction.* SECTION
5. PUBLIC FIGURES.] He had broken down before, and had prolonged
treatment. In fact, most of the politicians of that time needed psy-
chiatric support, because of the nature of their preoccupations: an un-

reality at the very heart of their every-day decision-making, thinking, functioning.

I watched him for some days. He was in a large room at the top of his house, a place set aside for his work, and where his family did not enter. Because he was alone, the ghastly charm of his public self was not in use. He was pacing up and down, his hair dishevelled (the exact disposition of head hair was of importance in that epoch), his eyes reddened and unable to maintain a focus. He had been drinking steadily for weeks. As he paced he groaned and muttered, he would bend over and straighten himself, as if to ease inner pain; he sat and clasped himself with both arms, hands gripping his shoulders, or he flung himself down on a day-bed and slept for a few moments, starting up to resume his restless pacing. He had decided to take the position with the northern bloc. He knew this was a mistake, and yet did not know. His rational self, the one he relied on—and indeed he possessed a fine, clear reasoning mind—could see nothing but opportunities for his ambition . . . which was never described by him in terms other than "progress," "justice," and so forth. He imagined this northern bloc becoming ever more powerful, successful, satisfying to all concerned. And yet the general collapse of the world order was apparent to everybody by then. That problems were not to be solved by the ways of thinking then accepted by partisan politics was also evident: certain minorities, and some of them influential ones, were putting forth alternative ways of thought, and these could not but appeal to John, or Taufiq . . . and yet he was committed to patterns of partisan thinking, and must be for as long as he was a politician. And he did not want his marriage to break up. Nor did he want to disappoint these two children as he had the children of his first marriage—he feared his progeny, as the people then tended to do. But of that later.

But if he stayed as a member of his local parliament, he would feel even more unused and frustrated than he had been—this was not even an alternative for him.

And then, jumping up from his disordered bed in his disordered room, or flinging himself down, or rocking, or pacing, he visualised the other possibility, that he should return seriously to his law firm and watch for opportunities to use himself in ways which he could easily envisage . . . extraordinary how attractive this prospect was . . . and yet there was nothing there to feed this ambition of his . . . he would be stepping out of the limelight, the national limelight, let alone the glamour of the wider fields open to him. And yet . . . and yet . . . he could not help being drawn to what had been planned for him, and *by* him before this entrance to Shikasta.

Here I intervened.

It was the middle of the night. It was quiet, in this pleasant and sheltered street. The din of the machines they all lived with was stilled.

Not a sound in the house. There was a single source of light in the corner of this room.

His eyes kept returning to it . . . he was in a half-tranced state, from fatigue, and from alcohol.

"Taufiq," I said. "Taufiq . . . remember! Try and remember!"

This was to his mind, of course. He did not move, but he tensed, and came to himself, and sat listening. His eyes were alert. In those strong black eyes, thoughtful now, and all there, I recognised my friend, my brother.

"Taufiq," I said. "What you are thinking *now* is right. Hold on to it. Act on it. It isn't too late. You took a very wrong bad turn when you went into politics. That wasn't for you! Don't make things worse."

Still he didn't move. He was listening, with every atom of himself. He turned his head cautiously, and I knew he was wondering if he would see somebody, or something, in the shadows of his room. He was half remembering me. But he saw nothing as he turned his head this way and that, searching into the corners and dark places. He was not afraid.

But he was shocked. The intervention of my words into his swirling half-demented condition was too much for him. He suddenly got up, flung himself down and was instantly asleep.

He dreamed. I fed in the material that would shape his dream. . . .

He and I were together in the projection room of the Planetary Demonstration Building on Canopus.

We were running scenes from Shikasta, recent scenes, of the new swarming millions upon millions upon millions—poor short-lived savages now, with the precious substance-of-we-feeling so limited and being shared among so many, the tiniest allowance for each individual, their little drop of true feeling . . . we were both overwhelmed with pity for the fate of the Shikastans, who could not help themselves, while they fought and hated and stole and half starved. Both of us had known Shikasta at such different times, he much more often and more recently than I. We were there together in the projection room because he had been asked to make this journey, and to take up this task.

There was no question of his refusing: we did not refuse such requests. Or some of us did not! [SEE *History of Canopus*, VOL. 1,752,357, *Disagreement re Policy for Shikasta, Formerly Rohanda.* SUMMARY CHAPTER.] But it was as if he had been asked to allow himself to be made lunatic, mad, deranged, and then put into a den of murdering savages. He agreed at once. Just as I agreed, shortly afterwards, when it was evident that he had failed.

He was lying utterly still on his bed. This dream caused him to stir and almost come to the surface again. But he sank back, exhausted.

He dreamed of a high bare landscape, full of coloured mountains, a brilliant unkind sky, everything beautiful and compelling, but when you looked close it was all desert. Cities had died here, been blasted to poisoned sand. Famine and death and disease were denuding these deadly plains. The beauty had a sombre deathlike under-face: yet was soaked with the emotion of longing, wanting, false need, and these were coming in from Zone Six, and causing this nightmare, which made him start up, muttering and groaning, and rush for water. He drank glass after glass, and dashed water on to his face, and then resumed his pacing. As the sky outside lightened, and the night sank down he paced, and paced. He was sober now, but really very ill.

A decision would have to be made. And soon, or he would die with the stress of it.

All that day he stayed in that room high up in his house. His wife came to him with food, and he thanked her, but in a careless, uncaring way that caused her then and there to decide she would divorce him. He left the food untouched. His eyes had lost life. Were staring. Were violent. He flung himself down to sleep, and then jumped up again. He was afraid. He feared to encounter me, his friend, who was his other self, his brother.

He was being terrified to the point of lunacy by Canopus, who was his home and his deepest self.

When he did at last fall asleep, because he could not keep himself awake, I made him dream of us, a band of his fellows, his real companions. He smiled as he slept. He wept, tears soaking his face, as he walked and talked in his dream with *us*, with himself.

And he woke smiling, and went downstairs to tell his wife he had made up his mind. He was going to take up this new position, this new important job. His manner as he told her this was full of the lying affability of his public self.

But I knew that what I had fed into him as he slept would stay there and change him. I knew—I could foresee, and exactly, for there was a picture of it in my inner sight—that later in the frightful time in front of us, I, a young man, would confront him, and say to him some exact and functioning words. He would remember. An enemy—for he was to be that for a time—would become a friend again, would come to himself.

History of Shikasta, VOL. 3012, The Century of Destruction.
EXCERPT FROM SUMMARY CHAPTER.

During the previous two centuries, the narrow fringes on the northwest of the main landmass of Shikasta achieved technical superiority over the rest of the globe, and, because of this, conquered physically or dominated by other means large numbers of cultures and civilisations. The Northwest fringe people were characterised by a peculiar insensitivity to the merits of other cultures, an insensitivity quite unparalleled in previous history. An unfortunate combination of circumstances was responsible. (1) These fringe peoples had only recently themselves emerged from barbarism. (2) The upper classes enjoyed wealth, but had never developed any degree of responsibility for the lower classes, so the whole area, while immeasurably more wealthy than most of the rest of the globe, was distinguished by contrasts between extremes of wealth and poverty. This was not true for a brief period between Phases II and III of the Twentieth Century War. [SEE VOL. 3009, Economies of Affluence.] (3) The local religion was materialistic. This was again due to an unfortunate combination of circumstances: one was geographical, another the fact that it had been a tool of the wealthy classes for most of its history, another that it retained even less than most religions of what its founder had been teaching. [SEE VOLS. 998 and 2041, Religions as Tools of Ruling Castes.] For these and other causes, its practitioners did little to mitigate the cruelties, the ignorance, the stupidity, of the Northwest fringers. On the contrary, they were often the worst offenders. For a couple of centuries at least, then, a dominant feature of the Shikastan scene was that a particularly arrogant and self-satisfied breed, a minority of the minority white race, dominated most of Shikasta, a multitude of different races, cultures, and religions which, on the whole, were superior to that of the oppressors. These white Northwest fringers were like most conquerors of history in denuding what they had overrun, but they were better able than any other in their ability to persuade themselves that what they did was "for the good" of the conquered: and it is here that the above-mentioned religion is mostly answerable.

World War I—to use Shikastan nomenclature (otherwise the First Intensive Phase of the Twentieth Century War)—began as a quarrel between the Northwest fringers over colonial spoils. It was distinguished by a savagery that could not be matched by the most backward of barbarians. Also by stupidity: the waste of human life and of the earth's products was, to us onlookers, simply unbelievable, even judged by Shikastan standards. Also by the total inability of the population masses to understand what was going on: propaganda on this scale was tried for the first time, using methods of indoctrination based on the new technologies, and was successful. What the unfortunates were told who had to give up life and property—or at the best, health—for this war, bore no relation at any time to the real facts of the matter; and while of course any local group or culture engaged in war persuades itself according to the exigencies of self-interest, never in Shikastan history, or for that matter on any planet—except for the planets of the Puttioran group—has deception been used on this scale.

This war lasted for nearly five of their years. It ended in a disease that carried off six times as many people as those killed in the actual fighting. This war slaughtered, particularly in the Northwest fringes, a generation of their best young males. But—potentially the worst result—it strengthened the position of the armament industries (mechanical, chemical, and psychological) to a point where from now on it had to be said that these industries dominated the economies and therefore the governments of all the participating nations. Above all, this war barbarised and lowered the already very low level of accepted conduct in what they referred to as "the civilised world"—by which they meant, mostly, the Northwest fringes.

This war, or phase of the Twentieth Century War, laid the bases for the next.

Several areas, because of the suffering caused by the war, exploded into revolution, including a very large area, stretching from the Northwest fringes thousands of miles to the eastern ocean. This period saw the beginning of a way of looking at governments, judged "good" and "bad" not by performance, but by label, by name. The main reason was the deterioration caused by war: one cannot spend years sunk inside false and lying propaganda without one's mental faculties becoming impaired. (This is a fact that is attested to by every one of our emissaries to Shikasta!)

Their mental processes, for reasons not their fault never very impressive, were being rapidly perverted by their own usages of them.

The period between the end of World War I and the beginning of the Second Intensive Phase contained many small wars, some of them for the purpose of testing out the weapons shortly to be employed on a massive scale. As a result of the punitive suffering inflicted on one of the defeated contestants of World War I by the victors, a Dictatorship arose there—a result that might easily have been foreseen. The Isolated Northern Continent, conquered only recently by emigrants from the Northwest fringes, and conquered with the usual disgusting brutality, was on its way to becoming a major power, while the various national areas of the Northwest fringes, weakened by war, fell behind. Frenzied exploitation of the colonised areas, chiefly of Southern Continent I, was intensified to make up for the damages sustained because of the war. As a result, native populations, exploited and oppressed beyond endurance, formed resistance movements of all kinds.

The two great Dictatorships established themselves with total ruthlessness. Both spread ideologies based on the suppression and oppression of whole populations of differing sects, opinions, religions, local cultures. Both used torture on a mass scale. Both had followings all over the world, and these Dictatorships, and their followers, saw each other as enemies, as totally different, as wicked and contemptible—while they behaved in exactly the same way.

The time gap between the end of World War I and the beginning of World War II was twenty years.

Here we must emphasise that most of the inhabitants of Shikasta were not aware that they were living through what would be seen as a hundred-years' war, the century that would bring their planet to almost total destruction. We make a point of this, because it is nearly impossible for people with whole minds—those who have had the good fortune to live (and we must never forget that it is a question of our good fortune) within the full benefits of the substance-of-we-feeling—it is nearly impossible, we stress, to understand the mentation of Shikastans. With the world's cultures being ravaged and destroyed, from end to end, by viciously inappropriate technologies, with wars raging everywhere, with whole populations being wiped out, and deliberately, for the benefit of ruling castes, with the wealth of every nation being used almost entirely for war, for preparations for war, propaganda for war, research for war; with the general levels of decency and honesty visibly vanishing, with corruption everywhere—

with all this, living in a nightmare of dissolution, was it really possible, it may be asked, for these poor creatures to believe that "on the whole" all was well?

The reply is—yes. Particularly, of course, for those already possessed of wealth or comfort—a minority; but even those millions, those billions, the ever-increasing hungry and cold and unbefriended, for these, too, it was possible to live from meal to scant meal, from one moment of warmth to the next.

Those who were stirred to "do something about it" were nearly all in the toils of one of the ideologies which were the same in performance, but so different in self-description. These, the active, scurried about like my unfortunate friend Taufiq, making speeches, talking, engaged in interminable processes that involved groups sitting around exchanging information and making statements of good intent, and always in the name of the masses, those desperate, frightened, bemused populations who knew that everything was wrong but believed that somehow, somewhere, things would come right.

It is not too much to say that in a country devastated by war, lying in ruins, poisoned, in a landscape blackened and charred under skies low with smoke, a Shikastan was capable of making a shelter out of broken bricks and fragments of metal, cooking himself a rat and drinking water from a puddle that of course tasted of oil and thinking "Well, this isn't too bad after all. . . ."

World War II lasted five years, and was incomparably worse in every way than the first. All the features of the first were present in the second, developed. The waste of human life now extended to mass extermination of civilian populations. Cities were totally destroyed. Agriculture was ruined over enormous areas. Again the armament industries flourished, and this finally established them as the real rulers of every geographical area. Above all, the worst wounds were inflicted in the very substance, the deepest minds, of the people themselves. Propaganda in every area, by every group, was totally unscrupulous, vicious, lying—and self-defeating—because in the long run, people could not believe the truth when it came their way. Under the Dictatorships, lies and propaganda *were* government. The maintenance of the dominance of the colonised parts was by lies and propaganda— these more effective and important than physical force; and the retaliation of the subjugated took the form, first of all and most importantly in influence, of lies and propaganda: this is what they had been taught by their conquerors. This war covered and involved the whole globe—the first war, or phase of the war, involved only part of it: there was no part of Shikasta by the end of World War II left unsubjected to untruth, lies, propaganda.

This war saw, too, the use of weapons that could cause total global destruction: it should go without saying, to the accompaniment of words like democracy, freedom, economic progress.

The degeneration of the already degenerate was accelerated.

By the end of World War II, one of the great Dictatorships was defeated—the same land area as saw the worst defeat in the first war. The Dictatorship which covered so much of the central landmass had been weakened, almost to the point of defeat, but survived, and made a slow, staggering recovery. Another vast area of the central landmass, to the east of this Dictatorship, ended half a century of local wars, civil wars, suffering, and over a century of exploitation and invasion by the Northwest fringes by turning to Dictatorship. The Isolated Northern Continent had been strengthened by the war and was now the major world power. The Northwest fringes on the whole had been severely weakened. They had to let go their grip of their colonies. Impoverished, brutalised—while being, formally, victors—they were no longer world powers. Retreating from these colonies they left behind technology, an idea of society based entirely on physical well-being, physical satisfaction, material accumulation—to cultures who, before encounter with these all-ravaging Northwest fringers, had been infinitely more closely attuned with Canopus than the fringers had ever been.

This period can be—is by some of our scholars—designated *The Age of Ideology*. [For this viewpoint SEE VOL. 3011, SUMMARY CHAPTER.]

The political groupings were all entrenched in bitterly defended ideologies.

The local religions continued, infinitely divided and subdivided, each entrenched in their ideologies.

Science was the most recent ideology. War had immeasurably strengthened it. Its ways of thought, in its beginnings flexible and open, had hardened, as everything must on Shikasta, and scientists, as a whole—we exclude individuals in this area as in all others—were as impervious to real experience as the religionists had ever been. Science, its basic sets of mind, its prejudices, gripped the whole globe and there was no appeal. Just as individuals of our tendencies of mind, our inclinations towards the truth, our "citizens" had had to live under the power and the threat of religions who would use any brutalities to defend their dogmas, so now individuals with differing inclinations and needs from those tolerated by science had to lead silent or prudent lives, careful of offending the bigotries of the scientific global governing class: in the service of national governments and therefore of war—an invisible global ruling caste, obedient to the warmakers. The industries that made weapons, the armies, the scientists who served them—these could not be easily attacked, since the formal picture of how the globe was run did not include this, the real picture. Never has there been such a totalitarian, all-pervasive, all-powerful governing caste anywhere: and yet the citizens of Shikasta were hardly aware of it, as they mouthed slogans and waited for their deaths by holocaust. They remained unaware of what "their" governments were doing, right up to the end. Each national grouping developed industries, weapons, horrors of all kinds, that the people knew nothing about. If glimpses were caught of these weapons, then government would deny they existed. [SEE *History of Shikasta*, VOLS. 3013, 3014, and CHAPTER 9 this volume, Use of Moon as Military Base.] There were space probes, space weapons, explorations of planets, use of planets, rivalries over their moon, about which the populations were not told.

And here is the place to say that the mass of the populations, the average individual, were, was, infinitely better, more sane, than those who ruled them: most would have been appalled at what was being done by "their" representatives. It is safe to say that if even a part of what was being kept from them had came to their notice, there would have been mass risings across the globe, massacres of the rulers, riots . . . unfortunately, when peoples are helpless, betrayed, lied to, they possess no weapons but the (useless) ones of rioting, looting, mass murder, invective.

During the years following the end of World War II, there were many "small" wars, some as vicious and extensive as wars in the recent past described as major. The needs of the armament industries, as much as ideology, dictated the form and intensities of these wars. During this period savage exterminations of previously autonomous "primitive" peoples took place, mostly in the Isolated Southern Continent (otherwise known as Southern Continent II). During this period colonial risings were used by all the major powers for their own purposes. During this period psychological methods of warfare and control of civilian populations developed to an extent previously un-dreamed of.

Here we must attempt to underline another point which it is almost impossible for those with our set of mind to appreciate.

When a war was over, or a phase of war, with its submersion in the barbarous, the savage, the degrading, Shikastans were nearly all able to perform some sort of mental realignment that caused them to "for-get." This did not mean that wars were not idols, subjects for pious mental exercises of all sorts. Heroisms and escapes and braveries of local and limited kinds were raised into national preoccupations, which were in fact forms of religion. But this not only did not assist, but prevented, an understanding of how the fabric of cultures had been attacked and destroyed. After each war, a renewed descent into barbarism was sharply visible—but apparently cause and effect were not connected, in the minds of Shikastans.

After World War II, in the Northwest fringes and in the Isolated Northern Continent, corruption, the low level of public life, was ob-vious. The two "minor" wars conducted by the Isolated Northern Continent reduced its governmental agencies, even those visible and presented to the public inspection, to public scandal. Leaders of the nation were murdered. Bribery, looting, theft, from the top of the pyramids of power to the bottom, were the norm. People were taught to live for their own advancement and the acquisition of goods. Con-sumption of food, drink, every possible commodity was built into the economic structure of every society. [VOL. 3009, *Economies of Afflu-ence.*] And yet these repulsive symptoms of decay were not seen as direct consequences of the wars that ruled their lives.

During the whole of the Century of Destruction, there were sud-den reversals: treaties between nations which had been at war, so that these turned their hostilities on nations only recently allies; secret treaties between nations actually at war; enemies and allies constantly changing positions, proving that the governing factor was in the need for war, as such. During this period every major city in the northern hemisphere lived inside a ring of terror: each had anything up to thirty weapons aimed at it, every one of which could reduce it and its inhabitants to ash in seconds—pointed from artificial satellites in the skies, directed from underwater ships that ceaselessly patrolled the seas, directed from land bases perhaps halfway across the globe. These were controlled by machines which everyone knew were not infallible—and everybody knew that more than once the destruction of cities and areas had been avoided by a "miracle." But the populations were never told how often these "miracles" had taken place—near-lethal accidents between machines in the skies, collisions between machines under the oceans, weapons only *just* not unleashed from the power bases. Looking from outside at this planet it was as if at a totally crazed species.

In large parts of the northern hemisphere was a standard of living that had recently belonged only to emperors and their courts. Particularly in the Isolated Northern Continent, the wealth was a scandal, even to many of their own citizens. Poor people lived there as the rich have done in previous epochs. The continent was heaped with waste, with wreckage, with the spoils of the rest of the world. Around every city, town, even a minor settlement in a desert, rose middens full of discarded goods and food that in other less favoured parts of the globe would mean the difference between life and death to millions. Visitors to this continent marvelled—but at what people could be taught to believe was their due, and their right.

This dominant culture set the tone and standard for most of Shikasta. For regardless of the ideological label attaching to each national area, they all had in common that technology was the key to all good, and that good was always material increase, gain, comfort, pleasure. The real purposes of life—so long ago perverted, kept alive with such difficulty by us, maintained at such a cost—had been forgotten, were ridiculed by those who had ever heard of them, for distorted inklings of the truth remained in the religions. And all this time the earth was being despoiled. The minerals were being ripped out, the fuels wasted, the soils depleted by an improvident and short-sighted agriculture, the animals and plants slaughtered and destroyed, the seas being filled with filth and poison, the atmosphere was corrupted—and always, all the time, the propaganda machines thumped out: more, more, more, drink more, eat more, consume more, discard more—in a frenzy, a mania. These were maddened creatures, and the small voices that rose in protest were not enough to halt the processes that had been set in motion and were sustained by greed. By the lack of substance-of-we-feeling.

But the extreme riches of the northern hemisphere were not distributed evenly among their own populations, and the less favoured classes were increasingly in rebellion. The Isolated Northern Continent and the Northwest fringe areas also included large numbers of dark-skinned people brought in originally as cheap labour to do jobs disdained by the whites—and while these did gain, to an extent, some of the general affluence, it could be said that looking at Shikasta as a whole, it was the white-skinned that did well, the dark-skinned poorly.

And this *was* said, of course, more and more loudly by the dark-skinned, who hated the white-skinned exploiters as perhaps conquerors have never before been hated.

Inside each national area everywhere, north and south, east and west, discontent grew. This was not only because of the gap between the well off and the poor, but because their way of life, where augmenting consumption was the only criterion, increasingly saddened and depressed their real selves, their hidden selves, which were unfed, were ignored, were starved, were lied to, by almost every agency around them, by every authority they had been taught to, but could not, respect.

Increasingly the two main southern continents were torn by wars and disorders of every kind—sometimes civil wars between blacks, sometimes between blacks and remnants of the old white oppression, and between rival sects and juntas and power groups. Local dictators abounded. Vast territories were denuded of forests, species of animals destroyed, tribes murdered or dispersed. . . .

War. Civil War. Murder. Torture. Exploitation. Oppression and suppression. And always lies, lies, lies. Always in the name of progress, and equality and development and democracy.

The main ideology all over Shikasta was now variations on this theme of economic development, justice, equality, democracy.

Not for the first time in the miserable story of this terrible century, this particular ideology—economic justice, equality, democracy, and the rest—took power at a time when the economy of an area was at its most disrupted: the Northwest fringes became dominated by governments "of the left," which presided over a descent into chaos and misery.

The formerly exploited areas of the world delighted in this fall of their former persecutors, their tormentors—the race that had enslaved them, enserfed them, stolen from them, above all, despised them because of their skin colour and destroyed their indigenous cultures now at last beginning to be understood and valued . . . but too late, for they had been destroyed by the white race and its technologies.

There was no one to rescue the Northwest fringes, in the grip of grindingly repetitive, dogmatic Dictatorships, all unable to solve the problems they had inherited—the worst and chief one being that the empires that had brought wealth had not only collapsed, leaving them in a vacuum, but had left behind false and unreal ideas of what they were, their importance in the global scale. Revenge played its part, not an inconsiderable part, in what was happening.

Chaos ruled. Chaos economic, mental, spiritual—I use this word in its exact, Canopean sense—ruled while the propaganda roared and blared from loudspeaker, radio, television.

The time of the epidemics and diseases, the time of famine and mass deaths had come.

On the main landmass two great Powers were in mortal combat. The Dictatorship that had come into being at the end of World War I, in the centre, and the Dictatorship that had taken hold of the eastern areas now drew into their conflict most of Shikasta, directly or indirectly. The younger Dictatorship was stronger. The older one was already in decline, its empire fraying away, its populations more and more in revolt or sullen, its ruling class increasingly remote from its people—processes of growth and decay that had in the past taken a couple of centuries now were accomplished in a few decades. This Dictatorship was not able to withstand the advance of the eastern Dictatorship whose populations were bursting its boundaries. These masses overran a good part of the older Dictatorship, and then over-ran, too, the Northwest fringes, in the name of a superior ideology—though in fact this was but a version of the predominating ideology of the Northwest fringes. The new masters were clever, adroit, intelligent; they foresaw for themselves the dominance of all the main landmass of Shikasta, and the continuance of that dominance.

But meanwhile the armaments piled up, up, up. . . .

The war began in error. A mechanism went wrong, and major cities were blasted into death-giving dusts. That something of this kind was bound to happen had been plentifully forecast by technicians of all countries . . . but the Shammat influences were too strong.

In a short time, nearly the whole of the northern hemisphere was in ruins. Very different, these, from the ruins of the second war, cities which were rapidly rebuilt. No, these ruins were uninhabitable, the earth around them poisoned.

Weapons that had been kept secret now filled the skies, and the dying survivors, staggering and weeping and vomiting in their ruins, lifted their eyes to watch titanic battles being fought, and with their last breaths muttered of "Gods" and "Devils" and "Angels" and "Hell."

Underground were shelters, sealed against radiation, poisons, chemical influences, deadly sound impulses, death rays. They had been built for the ruling classes. In these a few did survive.

In remote areas, islands, places sheltered by chance, a few people survived.

The populations of all the southern continents and islands were also affected by pestilence, by radiations, by soil and water and contamination, and were much reduced.

Within a couple of decades, of the billions upon billions of Shikasta perhaps 1 percent remained. The substance-of-we-feeling, previously shared among these multitudes, was now enough to sustain, and keep them all sweet, and whole, and healthy.

The inhabitants of Shikasta, restored to themselves, looked about, could not believe what they saw—and wondered *why* they had been mad.

Report by Emissaries TAUFIQ, NASAR, *and* RAWSTI, MEMBERS *of the* SPECIAL INVESTIGATORY COMMISSION *into the* STATE *of* SHIKASTA, PENULTIMATE TIME.   SUMMARY. [This was the first mission sent to the planet from Canopus since Johor's visit at the Time of the Catastrophe.]

1 We have thoroughly surveyed the northern hemisphere, and have had meetings with the representatives of Sirius, both those stationed here, and visiting. We have also encountered Shammat's agents, without their knowledge.

2 We confirm reports by our visiting and indigenous agents that there is an unexpected development. All over the northern hemisphere are a race of "little people," which is how they are referred to everywhere. Blood, tissue, and bone tests suggested Sirian origin, and Sirian representatives confirmed they originated from experiments by Sirius as far back as the epoch of Johor's visit at the Time of the Malalignment. A great part of the northern hemisphere has been covered by ice. This process has locked up more of the Shikastan

waters, and water levels have sunk, and dry land has appeared where none was, making bridges between landmasses and islands, facilitating the movement of these "little people" everywhere. Sirius confirms their extensive presence on the two major southern continents and the smaller southern continent. These "little people" can be no more than a span in height, and at their tallest are not more than four spans. They are of various types, ranging from squat, heavy, and physically very powerful to slight, exquisite, and beautiful even by Canopean standards. The former extreme tends to dwell underground in caves, caverns, and subterranean places of all kinds, sometimes very far beneath ground, to the extent they may seldom or never see the surface at all. They are skilled in mining, smelting, surveying. They produce and use iron, copper, bronze, gold, silver. The more delicate types live in and with vegetation, understanding the uses of plants, or are adapted to water and its properties, or are creatures of fire. All shun the larger inhabitants of Shikasta to the point that in some parts they are already the stuff of myth and legend. But in some places a link has been established and maintained, even to the extent of exchange of information and commodities. These races have in our opinion little or no evolutionary potential. They dwindle in size and numbers and most have already transferred themselves—not to Zone Six, where they are not at home, but to Zones One and Two.

3 Because of the pressures of the polar ice masses so far south, there have been extensive movements of the two stocks we are interested in. The Giants, established mainly in the mountainous and plateau areas of the main landmass, spread out towards the east, and emigrated to the Isolated Northern Continent in large numbers, over the new ice bridges. There they flourish. They are now two-thirds of their former height. They live about two thousand years. Their lifespans and their stature both lessen fast.

The Natives, who were settled farther south and farther north than the Giants, have crowded in on areas the Giants left empty or sparsely settled and have also emigrated southwards everywhere, even to the extent of establishing themselves over the northern areas of Southern Continent I. They, too, are losing height, and are two-thirds of what they were in Johor's time. They live about eight hundred years. As with the Giants, their life-span and stature dwindle rapidly.

4 There is now mating between these two races, which produces a physically improved type, sturdy, healthy, but above all adaptable, able to withstand extremes of climate, to sustain themselves on any diet, and to fit themselves rapidly to sudden and drastic changes. For instance, they are living adequately on the very edges of the ice cap. Their mentalities are not better than either the Giant or the Native stocks, but are ingenious and—again—very adaptable, within the limits, of course, imposed by the limited ingestion of SOWF by the planet.

The new hybrid lives among or near the Natives, but the Giants are less amenable. There is always, and increasingly, disharmony on personal and intergroup levels, but this does not yet show signs of developing into war, nor is war something considered inevitable or desirable. On the contrary, enough of the substance of Johor's "Rules" remains to make all species uneasy when they fall into bellicosity, even briefly; and antagonisms remain local and short-term affairs.

These three species—for the Cross should now be considered as a new species—breed and develop animals of all kinds, for food, for transport, and for use in agriculture. The use of metals is little understood, even though rumours of the skills of the "little people" suggest all kinds of experiments and attempts. We have inspired individuals in every part of Shikasta to search out the "little people" and learn from them what they can, particularly in the realm of metals.

5 The "Laws of Canopus," as described by Johor, have to a certain extent stabilised themselves not only in the various ethical structures, but even genetically. Transgressions cause discomfort, and have to be compensated for, in sometimes unfortunate and nonproductive ways. But we have to report that, as was expected, these Laws rapidly diminish in effect. Not least because of the efforts of Shammat, whose agents are energetically at work. The psychological malaise caused by "transgressions" provide fruitful ground for Shammat's needs. For instance, they have successfully established human sacrifice as a means of "pleasing the Gods." This practice is everywhere on the increase. Shammat encourages in every place and in every way the falling away of Shikastans into animalism. As this does not differ from what we already know of Puttiora and Shammat elsewhere, there is no need to enlarge.

OUR RECOMMENDATIONS:

a A boost of Canopean genes to the new Cross. This in our opinion has the greatest evolutionary potential, showing a tendency towards frequent and varied mutation.

b More frequent visits from our representatives. We know that Shammat's theft of SOWF cannot be stopped, but their efforts towards degenerating the stock can be combatted.

ENVOY 99, TAUFIQ, reports:

I covered the designated areas. The polar ice is retreating. The level of the oceans is almost at its former height.

The populations are settled mostly in the regions of the great inland seas, because of the climatic advantages, and on the islands in the ocean that separates the Isolated Northern Continent from the central land mass. (These islands are unstable.) That is, between 20 degrees and 40 degrees north, their measurement. The Giant/Native Cross proves, as forecast, the most enduring. Purebred Giants and purebred Natives are now minorities, and tend to live by themselves. Both are seen as "Giants" by the new Cross. This breeds with every generation shorter, smaller, and very strong and vigorous. It is intellectually inferior, even within the limits imposed by the depredations of Shammat. They are belligerent, acquisitive.

There is accumulation of wealth and even land by the few at the expense of the many, who are often in the position of slaves and servants. Some of these are escaping northwards after the retreating ice, and establishing themselves in harsh conditions. They make frequent forays southwards to raid and plunder crops and livestock. There is now continual fighting and looting everywhere.

Little remains of the instruction left them by Envoy Johor and subsequent visitors.

Systems of taboos operate around objects and artefacts and animals. Human and animal sacrifice is operated mostly by "priests," self-appointed custodians of the "Divine."

MY RECOMMENDATIONS:

a I support the recommendation of the Commission that there should be a genetic boost. There is an argument that there are already too many species on Shikasta. Against this I urge that the Giant/Native

Cross will soon predominate. Its peculiarly violent and rapacious qualities must be reduced. There will otherwise be no species left at all! For instance, the "little people" are now almost extinct, except in certain mostly northern parts where the severity of the climate preserves them. They have been hunted down *for sport*. I need say no more in underlining my contention that Shammat's influences are almost overwhelming.

b Our servants have been instructed to remain unnoticed where possible. Their function has been mostly to monitor and observe. I believe we should embark on a new policy of vigorous intervention. It will be necessary to work inside the existing mental sets and tendencies. This means making use of existing "religions," and perhaps introducing new ones.

ENVOY 102, TAUFIQ, *reports:*

Our plans must be postponed. The instability of this planet has again been confirmed. Shikasta flipped over on its axis and back again. I have arranged for the relevant experts to ascertain the cause. There were floods, storms, earthquakes. Some islands submerged. There will be changes in climate. Shikasta is slightly distanced from its sun. The effect on its moon is as yet not certain. There was great loss of life, more in the northern than in the southern hemisphere. Several promising cultures, carefully monitored by us, have been wiped out. Adalanterland is one. Agent Nasar, now permanently established on Shikasta, is sending an independent report. These events however do not change the basic situation, and after an interval for the effects of the events to lessen, the recommendations of my report should be followed.

ENVOY 105, TAUFIQ, *reports:*

I picked up five males from Eastern Sector, Canopus, five from Planet 19, and five from Planet 27.

There is not now much evidence of the recent unfortunate events, but the population levels remain reduced.

The males were divided into five groups and put down as follows: To the immediate north of the Great Mountains. To the immediate south of the same. In the extreme north of Southern Continent I. Two groups south of the Great Seas, one of which I accompanied. All of these had to acclimatise themselves for several days, before allowing themselves to be noticed.

The group of three I was with was on a mountain near a flat space where our craft put down. This flat area has sacred connotations in the area.

Our problem was that only the chosen females should mate.

I approached descendants of the old Davidic strain, who because of natural superiority tend to hold positions of influence. I told each "in secret" that "sacred beings" were present, drawn down from "higher regions" because of their beauty. These selected women were led to the males and mating was accomplished. There were about fifty of them, each at first believing she was unique.

Our plan was that they should tell others "in confidence." This was to ensure the spread of rumours about Gods and so forth. But we did not wish mating to become general.

In a short time the high place on the mountain where our volunteers were ensconced was under siege from willing females and from suspicious males. The four of us made our way as unnoticeably as possible to the space vehicle, but two of the women followed us, and mating took place in spite of my remonstrances that these were not designated women. Suggest that Planet 27 is unsuitable for this work. Planet 19 less enthusiastic.

We made sure the take-off by our vehicle was observed by the two females, who will have returned to talk about celestial chariots.

ENVOY 111, TAUFIQ, *reports:*

I made preparations to carry out our first plan. This was for me to descend through Zone Six. It had been intended that I incarnate and become visible as mentor. Reports from our agents of unexpected conditions on Shikasta interdicted this plan.

I therefore again approached by spacecraft. Our agents' reports were soon confirmed. The ice caps were melting at a quite unforeseen pace. This was the more unexpected because there has been a period when they have in fact made a minor advance, conquering some of the territory they had relinquished. The sudden reversal has again swamped coastlines everywhere. It has filled the Shikastan skies with cloud that never lifts. The resulting gloom has led to a change in the Shikastan temperament. They are less volatile, are sullen, suspicious, slower to react.

I covered the indicated areas. This survey was done as quickly as possible because of the urgency felt by me.

This is what I found. The descendants of the genetic boost—Planets 19, 27, and Canopus East—are satisfactory. The general decline halted. They form a noticeably superior strain. But the others are sinking fast to a lamentable condition. Our plans for boosting this product of our genetic improvement had obviously to be postponed, but I suggest that when Shikasta has recovered from the fresh setback we should implement them.

It was clear that a general inundation from the skies was imminent. The cloud mass grew daily heavier and more dense.

I took the head of the new strain (Davidic-improved), and warned him to be ready to leave for higher ground, together with his family, and animals for breeding stock. He understood that I came from "somewhere else"—as he put it. The legend of "Gods" is well established. A measure of the new strain's improved intelligence is their response to such information. I told him to warn all the inhabitants of that area. Those who would listen must be pressed into preparations for survival. Few could hear him: their genetic equipment made it impossible. This new emergency is in fact providing an unforeseen but useful means of separating the superior from the inferior. I shall be interested to discuss this with our envoys to the other threatened areas of Shikasta. It is my suggestion that the results of these discussions, which will provide invaluable information as to the mentality of the new Shikastan strain, should form the basis of a supplementary report.

Well before the inundation the Davidic tribe was on safe ground on a mountain. The deluge began at the same time all over Shikasta, as I have gathered from informal discussion among our envoys. In the area that is the subject of this report, the rain continued for nearly two months. Except for mountain peaks everything was inundated. The onset of the deluge was so fast that there was no time for escape to higher ground by either higher or lower animals. Nothing survived. Of course, as the waters drained to the oceans, their levels rose. The great inland seas all flooded and will remain greatly enlarged.

The psychological condition of the rescued strain was pitiable. It was necessary to make a "pact" with them that this visitation of the Gods would not occur again. For their part, they must understand that the deluge was because of their falling away into wickedness and evil practices. They must always be ready to listen to instructions from us, their friends. These instructions would come, when necessary.

When the earth dried, they were told to return to their previous territories. They must live soberly, moderately, without oppressing each other, and as custodians of the animals, whom they must not harm and oppress. They might make animal sacrifices to the Gods, but not human sacrifices, and this must be done without cruelty to the animals. (It was unfortunately necessary to allow this: the Shammat perversion is too strong.) I left them with various artefacts, as instructed. I told them that these were to strengthen the bond between them and "somewhere else."

I end this report with a personal request. If it is considered not unreasonable, I would prefer not to be assigned to Shikasta again.

ENVOY 159, TAUFIQ, reports:

Since my last visit, twenty-one cities have been established in the old flood areas. Five are large, with populations of a quarter of a million or more. Trade flourishes between the cities and as far as the eastern areas of the main landmass, its Northwest fringes, the northern parts of Southern Continent I, the Isolated Northern Continent.

The living is luxurious, wasteful, higher purposes forgotten, except for a few.

There has been racial mixing with the results of experiments from both southern continents. The merits, demerits, and general peculiarities of these crosses are analysed in the accompanying Report by the Mission of Population Analysts, Envoys 153, 154, 155.

The worst of the adverse factors is that there have been matings with Shammat stock, as a deliberate policy by Shammat to counteract our improvements as a result of genetic boosts before the inundation.

Shammat is not only constantly at work persuading Shikasta into the ways of Shammat, but is now informing these unfortunates that Shikasta is being defrauded by "the Gods," who exploit them, of their rightful heritage, and that if certain practices are followed, then Shikastans will become "as Gods."

This is now a popular belief everywhere. Revolts against us are being planned. These will take the form of mass attempts to "transcend" themselves, by means suggested through Shammat spies. They congregate together for "higher practices"—the vibrations of which are channelled off to Shammat. They perform mass slaughter of animals, as a ritual. They also practice spurious versions of the Art of the Stones, suggested by Shammat.

I support the recommendation of 153, 154, 155 to disrupt their speech centres.

Representatives from every region of Shikasta known to them are to gather in the Areas of the Cities to confer about ways to "become Gods." Unknown to them, Shammat will preside.

ENVOY 160, TAUFIQ, *reports:*

The urgency of the situation again necessitated use of spacecraft. All six of us attended the conference, purporting to be the delegates from the extreme Northwest fringes. As there were so many different types present, there were no difficulties. The recommended techniques were effective. As a result their communication systems malfunctioned, and eight main languages are now established on Shikasta. These will develop into hundreds, then thousands of languages and dialects because of the Shikastan Law of inevitable division, subdivision.

I again apply for transfer from Shikastan service into any other branch of the Colonial Service.

ENVOY 192, TAUFIQ, *reports:*

As a result of reports from our local agents that the Areas of the Cities are currently unsuitable for our purposes, investigations have been made into the Northwest fringes and the Extreme-east fringes. The Northwest fringes are sparsely populated due to the harshness of conditions and the impoverished landscape after the time of the ice. We established a few local agents to create and maintain enough stone patterns to keep our current stabilised. Similarly, in the Extreme east. But there climatic conditions are good and the soil rich, and the population increasing. We have built there a few small towns to Canopean pattern, chosen inhabitants of a suitable type to live in them, and placed stone and tree patterns in appropriate areas.

I visited the Areas of the Cities myself, and confirm that Shammat influence is so strong nothing can be expected there. I investigated in depth three of the cities and found not more than a hundred individuals who could respond in any way to Canopean vibrancies.

Your envoy points out—as have former ambassadors—that races which receive genetic prods, while on the one hand being strengthened towards usefulness and Canopus-contact, on the other are more prone than the average to become corrupted.

Nevertheless, since the contacts we have established in the Northwest fringe areas and the Extreme-east fringes will fall away from contact in 950 (their) years from now, it is recommended that further genetic addition be attempted on suitable candidates of Areas of the Cities in about four hundred years. This will allow time for the development of a new strengthened strain, but not enough time for this strain to be corrupted by Shammat. This is of course our usual *optimistic* forecast. I draw this comment to the attention of eugenists.

ENVOYS 276 and 277, TAUFIQ and JOHOR, *report:* (*Joint Mission.*)

TAUFIQ:

I visited the Northwest fringes. Our staff, who set up the Stones, and instructed locals in the Art of the Stones, have all left, most to Planet 35, as instructed. A few went to the Areas of the Cities to instruct suitable candidates in maintaining contact.

In the Northwest fringes is a stable but sparse population of indigenous stock. They practise agriculture and herd-keeping, neither on a high level. Our staff decided against advanced-level instruction as this has so often in the past led to the opposite of what was intended: extremes of accumulation and the oppression of others. (See later remarks about the Extreme-east fringes.) The basic unit is the tribe. It is still a meagre and unaccommodating landscape. These are very hardy people. Limited mating took place between them and our staff: unprogrammed. Their women are attractive, in a robust way. The progeny may be expected to improve the stock unpredictably. The indigenous people are small, dark-haired, wiry. The introduced genes tend towards tall, extremely fair-skinned blue-eyed or grey-eyed types. (Planet 14.)

I visited the territories of the Extreme east. The accumulator villages have been abandoned, on instruction. They will soon be derelict. A few individuals were secretly visiting these sites for "sacred purposes," history repeating itself. They have been warned. Our resident envoy has attempted threats and promises. These practices had already resulted in a deteriorating of the mentality. These remarks apply to the areas immediately adjacent to the accumulator villages.

Otherwise this is a vast civilisation already advanced to level G. It is growing, and constantly taking in territory, including the Southeast fringe islands. There is a stable and effective agriculture. The cities are very much more than trade centres. There is an extensive ruling class, previously efficient and devoted to duty, now luxury loving and effete. The entire civilisation is shortly to be overrun by a vigorous, more primitive culture from the north, the northwest, and the desert lands where there is no trace at all of our old Mathematical Cities, nor the more recent cities that flourished before the ice. The effete culture will therefore be revitalised. A selection of individuals has been taught contact. These are all merchants and farmers; none of the enfeebled governing class had the qualities. Arrangements have been made to ensure that these instructed individuals will be absent when the invasion takes place, and will return afterwards, to take up their allotted positions.

An earthquake recently completely devastated the chief east-fringe island. Nothing is left of any of the cities. There remains enough of the agriculture to restart a low level of culture.

I met the representatives of Sirius. They report success with their experiments. Southern Continent II has been particularly useful to them. The animals introduced there in the last experiment evolved rapidly and well, and were removed, all at once, by intensive space-lift, back to Planet 3.

They report that limited unplanned mating took place between their representatives and these animals.

May your envoy take this opportunity of suggesting that when Canopean eugenists map possibilities for Shikasta, they take into account Shikastan sexual propensities. It has long been my opinion, expressed more than once, that when sexuality was emphasised to ensure survival of species, this was perhaps overdone? Your envoy discussed this with Sirian representatives. They, having spent time on Shikasta, agree. They are putting the same point to their eugenists. I would point out that there are few cases in Canopean or Sirian history of individuals or stocks being introduced, sometimes for very short periods of time, without unplanned mating taking place.

May your envoy take this opportunity of suggesting that a delegation of eugenists actually be sent to Shikasta to experience conditions for themselves?

JOHOR:

It is thirty thousand years since I was in Shikasta; 31,505, to be exact.

How dark it is here! How hard to move, pulled to the earth, pressed down, weighted.

The air we breathe is so thin and insubstantial, the supplies of SOWF so meagre.

Entering Shikasta—entering my memories—it is as if everything is dwarfed. Can these people really be the descendants of the towering and regal Giants, the magnificent Natives? So those seem to me now, as I look back from this shrunken time and these minified people who live eight hundred years, when once the expectation of life was many times that. A hurrying, and a scurrying and a frantic cramming of a life into a few starved breaths . . . scarcely born, and then adult, and then old, and then dead.

Our people here, maintaining their real life with such difficulty, all acquire a look of quiet endurance, which all too easily melts into horror at moments when the contrasts are too great. And it is only with the greatest of effort that we prevent ourselves from grasping at every sensation that seems to promise or guarantee a meaning, even use-fulness—as these creatures do, who lacking the substance, chase after shadows, after anything that seems to remind them—for the memory is still there, somewhere deep in them, of Canopean truth. They look at the sun as if they want to pull it down to them, they linger under a moon which is much farther away than I remember it—and they hunger, they yearn, holding up their arms to the sun, and wanting to bathe in moonrays or to drink them. The gleam of light on a tree, or on water, the brief heartbreaking beauty of their young, these things torture them, without knowing why, or they half know, and make songs and tales, always with the hunger behind, a hunger not one of them could define. Yet their little lives are ruled by it, they are the subjects of an invisible king, a kingdom, even while they court Shammat, who feeds their hungers with illusions.

Re: Colonised Planet 5, Shikasta

I have been in the Areas of the Cities, which is where I was for most of my time before. Where the Round City was, the Square City, the Crescent City, and all the other marvels, cities have risen and fallen and risen, over and over again. The waters from the melting ice, the batteries of the ice itself, submerged, ground, destroyed. And yet it is green again, fertile, except where the deserts grow and spread and take possession. There are forests and green plains and herds of animals. . . .
I remember the great beasts of Rohanda, the wonderful ancestors of these little animals, miniature lions and tiny deer and half-size elephants that seem to these dwindled people so enormous—yet to those who knew those vast wise beasts of former times, they are endearing, almost toys for children. The children are heartbreaking now. In those times, the children of the Giants, the Natives' children, were each one born after such deliberation, such thought, each one *chosen* and from parents known to be the best . . . each with such a long life, time to grow, time to play, time to think, time to ripen their inner selves and grow fully into themselves. Now these delightful infants are born haphazardly of any mating, any parents, treated well or ill as chance dictates, dying as easily as they are born, and dying anyway so soon after they are born—and yet each child, every one, has all the potentiality, has it still, and completely, to leap from his low half-animal state to true humanity. Each one of them with this potential, and yet so few can be reached, to make the leap.

I do not like handling their infants, their children: it is a sad business.

And their women, who give birth to these potentials but not knowing it, or half knowing it.

And before we are through with the long sad story of Shikasta, so much more, and worse, to come.

There will be a time when these little lives will seem a great memory: a time when lives of two hundred years will seem a marvellous thing.

You are generous when you allow your envoys to express subjective feelings. But I have a spring of grief in me that you will be even more generous in not judging as *complaint*. Complaint is not allowed to the children of fatality, as the great stars move in their places. . . .

I, Johor, from this dark place, Shikasta the stricken one, raise my voice, but it is not in complaint but mourning, as these poor creatures mourn their dead who have lived so briefly that once a sheep or a deer would have lived deeper and longer, breathed more fully.

Today I walked through the streets of the city that stands where the Round City once stood, an agglomeration of streets, buildings, markets, put up anyhow, anywhere, without skills or symmetry or mastery, or even an inkling of the knowledge of how such places may be built—I walked and looked at the faces of traders, brothel-keepers, dealers in money, saw how these victims treat each other, as if their fate were felt in them as a license to cheat, lie, and murder and regard every passer-by only as a possibility for gain, to live as if each were alone in enemy territory and with no hope of reprieve.

Yet there are a few who are not like this, and who know that there will be reprieve—some day, somehow.

I sat in exactly that spot where I once sat with Jarsum and the others when they heard their sentence and the sentence of Rohanda: where that building was, surrounded by the warm glowing patterns and stones of the created city, is a narrow street of hovels made with sun-baked mud, and every face was deformed, inwardly or outwardly.

There are no eyes there that can meet your own frankly, without suspicion or fear, in acknowledgement of kinship.

This is a terrible city. And our envoys say that they are the same, all these great cities, every one engaged in warring, cheating, making treaties which are dissolved in treachery, stealing each other's goods, snatching each other's flocks, capturing each other's people to make slaves.

There are the rich, but only a few; and the innumerable slaves and servants who are the owned and the used.

Women are slaves to their beauty, and they regard their children as secondary to the admiration of men.

Men treat the women according to their degree of beauty, and the children only according to how they will advance themselves, their names, their properties.

Sex in them is twisted, broken: their desperation with the little dream that is their life between birth and death feeds sex to a famine and a flame.

What is to be done with them?

What can be done?

Only what has had to be done so often before, with the children of Shammat, Shammat the disgraced and the disgraceful . . .

My friend Taufiq has gone on a journey to the Northwest fringes, and he has said it is because he does not want to be here to see again what he has seen before.

I and your permanent agent Jussel left the cities and went among the herdsmen on the plains. We travelled from herd to herd, tribe to tribe. These are simple people, with the straightforwardness of those who deal close to the necessities of nature. I found descendants of Davidic stock, and they showed honesty, hospitality, and above all a hunger for something different.

With a tribe that manifested these characteristics more than the others, we stayed as ordinary travellers, and when affinity was accepted by them, showing itself as trust and wanting us to stay on with them, we revealed ourselves as from "somewhere else," and on a mission. They spoke of us as Lords, Gods, and Masters. These terms remain in their songs and their tales.

We told them if they would maintain certain practices, which had to be done exactly, and changed as necessity required, keeping alive among themselves, their tribe, and their descendants the knowledge that these practices were required by the Lords, the Gods, then they would be saved from the degeneration of the cities (which they abhor and fear) and their children would be strong and healthy, and not become thieves and liars and murderers. This strength, this sanity, a bond with the sources of the knowledge of the Gods, would be maintained in them as long as they were prepared to do according to our wishes.

We renewed our instructions for safe and wise existence on Shikasta— moderation, abstention from luxury, plain living, care for others whom they must never exploit or oppress, the care for animals, and for the earth, and above all, a quiet attention to what is most needed from them, obedience. A readiness to hear our wishes.

And we told the most respected of the tribe, a male already old— in their terms—that in his veins ran the "blood of the Gods," and his progeny would always remain close to the Gods, if they kept up the right ways.

We caused him to have two sons, both irradiated by Canopean vibrancies.

And we went back to the cities, to see if we could find any with enough individuals in them to make it possible to redeem them. None could be saved. In each were a few people who could hear us, and these we told to leave at once with any who would listen to them.

We returned to our old man among his flocks whose sons had by then been born, and told him that apart from his family, his tribe, and certain others soon none would remain alive, for the cities would be

destroyed, because of their wickedness. They had fallen victim to the
enemies of the Lord, who at all times worked against the Lord to
capture the hearts and minds of our creatures.

He pleaded with us.

Others of the few good people in the cities pleaded with us.

I do not wish to write further of this.

Having made sure of the safety of those who could be saved, we
signalled in the space-fleet, and the cities were blasted into oblivion,
all at the same time.

Deserts lie where these cities thrived.

The fertile, rich, teeming places, with the populous corrupt cities—
all desert now, and the heat waves shimmer and sizzle, for there are no
trees, no grass, no green.

And again I have seen all the animals rushing away, great herds of
them, galloping and tossing their heads and crying out—running from
the habitations of men.

History of Shikasta, VOL. 997, *Period of the Public Cautioners*.
EXCERPTS FROM SUMMARY CHAPTER.

While we can date the end of this period exactly, to the year, it is
not so easy to mark its beginning. For instance, do we class Taufiq and
Johor as *public* warners? On every one of their visits they cautioned—
or perhaps reminded is the better word—anybody who could hear
what was being said to them. Visits of various sorts continued without
intermission almost from the time of the retreat of the ice, and while
most were "secret"—meaning that the individuals contacted were not
aware this person among them was from another star system—there
was always, somewhere on Shikasta, an envoy or agent of some class
or calibre at work quite openly, explaining, exhorting, reminding. So
it can be said that Shikasta has always been provided with public advisers, except for a very short time indeed, 1,500 (their) years at the
end.

But this volume covers that period from about a thousand years
before the first destruction, the inundation, of the cities of the
peculiarly well-favoured and advantaged area around and south of the
Great Seas, until that date 1,500 years before the end. A close reading
of the various available texts will make it clear why this time was
considered by us as worth the continuous supply of our emissaries. It
cannot be said that there had been a change of policy towards

Shikasta—that can never, could not, be possible: our long-term policies remain intact. Nor can it be said that the general degeneration of the Shikastan stock or stocks was unforeseen. The difference between this period and others is rather in emphasis, in scale. When civilisation after civilisation, culture after culture, has had to be tolerated as long as was possible because of its low level of accomplishment (according to Canopean standards) and then either allowed to run down and vanish from the weight of its corruption, or be destroyed deliberately by us as a danger to the rest of Shikasta, to us, or to other Canopean colonies, when such a state of affairs has been reached, and on a large scale, over large parts of the central landmass, then this has to be thought of as different in kind and degree from one where sparse populations are widely spread, perhaps only just self-sufficient, where a single city whose main purpose was trade and not groups of cities in an imperial bond defined an area or areas, and where one or two of our agents could reach all the inhabitants of a large part of Shikasta simply by quite modest efforts in the course of a limited stay.

Over the many thousand years of the Period of the Exhorters or Cautioners we observe this series of events, constantly repeated:

It was observed by us, or reported to us, that the link between Canopus and Shikasta was weakening beyond safe levels.

This was followed by reports that a culture, a city, a tribe, or groups of individuals vital to our interests were falling away from what had been established as a bond.

It was urgently necessary to strengthen the link, the bond, by restoring selected individuals to suitable ways of life, thus regenerating and vitalising areas, cultures, or cities.

We sent down a technician, or two, or several. It might happen that all but one or two would be working quietly, unknown to the populace.

This one would have to be born, through Zone Six, and bred in the ordinary way by suitable parents, in order that what was said by—usually—him could take effect.

A note on sexual choice. Of course developed individuals with us are androgynous, to put it into the nearest Shikastan terminology possible: we do not have emotional or physical or psychological characteristics that are considered as appertaining to one sex rather than another, as is normal on the more backward planets. There have been many of our envoys who have manifested as "female," but since the time of the falling away from the Lock, before when males and females were equal everywhere on Shikasta and neither exploited the other, the females have been in subjection, and this has led to problems which on the whole are considered by our envoys as an unnecessary added difficulty to already difficult enough tasks. [SEE CHAPTER 9, this volume, "Manifestation of Envoys as Female for Local Cultural Purposes."]

As our envoy or representative grew to maturity in the chosen culture, he, or she, would become notable for a certain level of perception and understanding demonstrated in conduct which was nearly always at odds with the local ideas and practices.

Those individuals who were drawn to our envoy, by liking, or—as often happened—first by antagonism overcome by a growth of understanding which became liking, formed a core or nucleus which could be used to strengthen and maintain the link, the bond.

In the earlier times, these individuals were often many, and could form quite strong subcultures of their own. Or, spread among whole populations, formed a strong enough yeast to raise the whole mass to standards of decent and wholesome living in conformity with the general needs of Canopus. Then, as time passed, because of the growth of populations everywhere, which meant always less of the substance-of-we-feeling to go around, and because of the always growing strength of Shammat, there were fewer and fewer individuals who *could* respond, or who—having responded initially were able to maintain this response as a living and constantly renewed contact with us, with Canopus. In a city where the mass of the population had sunk to total self-interest, it was common that there might be one, or two, of our link-individuals, no more, desperately struggling to survive. Sometimes whole civilisations had none, had never had any, of this "yeast"; or, if our efforts had been successful in seeding a few, they were quickly driven out, or destroyed, or themselves succumbed from the weight of the pressures on them. Sometimes it was only in madhouses or as outcasts in the deserts that these valuable individuals could survive at all.

It has not been unknown for some of our own envoys, not more than a few, however, to fall victim of these pressures, either temporarily or permanently. In the latter case, they were subjected to long periods of rehabilitation on their return to Canopus, or sent to a suitable colonised planet to recover.

During the entire period under review, religions of any kind flourished. Those that concern us most here took their shape from the lives or verbal formulations of our envoys. This happened more often than not, and can be taken as a rule: every one of our public cautioners left behind a religion, or cult, and many of the unknown ones did, too.

These religions had two main aspects. The positive one, at their best: a stabilisation of the culture, preventing the worst excesses of brutality, exploitation, and greed. The negative: a priesthood manipulating rules, regulations, with punitive inflexibility; sometimes allowing, or exacerbating, excesses of brutality, exploitation, and greed. These priesthoods distorted what was left of our envoys' instruction, if it was understood by them at all, and created a self-perpetuating body of individuals totally identified with their invented ethics, rules, beliefs, and who were always the worst enemies of any envoys we sent.

These religions were a main difficulty in the way of maintaining Shikasta in our system.

They have often been willing agents of Shammat.

At no time during this period was it possible for an envoy to approach any part of Shikasta without having to outwit, stave off, or in some way make harmless, these representatives of "God," "the Gods," or whatever was the current formulation. Often our emissaries have been persecuted, or murdered, or worse—for everything of their instruction, vital and necessary to that particular place and time, was distorted. Very often the grip a "religion" had on a culture, or even a whole continent, was so pervasive that our agents could make no impact there at all, but had to work elsewhere on Shikasta where conditions were less monolithic, perhaps even—according to current ideas—more primitive. Many times in the history of Shikasta our bond has been maintained by a culture or subculture considered contemptible by the ruling power, which was nearly always a combination of the military and a religion: the military using the priests, or the priests the military.

For long periods of the history of Shikasta we can sum up the real situation thus: that in such and such a place, a few hundred, or even a handful, of individuals, were able with immense difficulty to adapt their lives to Canopean requirements, and thus saved the future of Shikasta.

The longer this process continued, the harder it was for our agents to make their way through the meshes of the emotional and intellectual formulations originating from former visitors. Shikasta was an *olla podrida* of cults, beliefs, religions, creeds, convictions; there was no end to them, and each of our envoys had to take into account the fact that even before he, she, was dead, his instruction would have already taken flight into fantasy, or been hardened into dogma: each knew that this newly minted, fresh, flexible method, adapted for that particular phase, would, before he had finished his work, have been captured by the Shikastan Law, and become mechanical, useless. She, he, would be working against not only a thousand past frozen formulations, but his own. . . . An envoy put it like this: it was as if he were running a race at the top of his speed, to keep ahead of his own words and actions springing up just behind him, and turned into enemies—what had been alive and functional a few minutes ago was already dead and used by the dead. By the representatives and captives of Shammat who, in this particular epoch, brought itself to a height of beastliness, of effective destructiveness, and almost entirely on what was channelled off from Shikasta. Shammat representatives were always on Shikasta, just as ours were. Shammat captured whole cultures, civilisations, so that they were never anything but out of our reach. Shammat was, from its own point of view, an entirely successful coloniser of Shikasta. But never entirely, never totally. This was not possible.

The major religions of the last days were all founded by Grade I emissaries. The last of these religions remained somewhat less riven and sectarian than the others. It was on its popular level a simple, emotional religion, and its basis was a scripture whose lowest reach of understanding—the level on which the religion was stabilised—was all threats and promises, for this was all that Shikastans by now could respond to. By then, very few of them could respond to anything, except in terms of personal gain, or loss. Or, if such individuals by prolonged and painstaking contact and instruction did learn that what was needed from her, him, was not on the level of gain or loss, then this had to be at a later stage, for the early stages of attraction to Canopean influences were always seen as everything *was* seen on Shikasta by then: something given, bestowed.

For Duty, in that last time, was all but forgotten. What Duty was, was not known. That something was Due, by them, was strange, inconceivable news they could not take in, absorb. They were set only for taking. Or for being given. They were all open mouths and hands held out for gifts—Shammat! All grab and grasp—Shammat! Shammat!

Whereas, in the early days of the post-disaster time, it had sometimes been enough for one of us to enter a village, a settlement, and sit down and talk to them of their past, of what they had been, of what they would one day become, but only through their own efforts and diligence—that they had dues to pay to Canopus who had bred them, would sustain them through their long dark time, was protecting them against Shammat, that they had in them a substance not Shikastan, and which would one day redeem them—told this, it was often enough, and they would set themselves to adapt to the current necessities.

But this became less and less what we could expect. Towards the end one of our agents would begin work knowing that it might take not a day, or a month, or a year, but perhaps all his life to stabilise a few individuals, so that they could listen.

Records, and reports and memoirs from our messengers show always harder and more painful effort put into less and less return.

Handfuls of individuals rescued from forgetfulness were the harvest for the efforts of dozens of our missionaries, of all grades, kinds, and degrees of experience on a dozen planets. These handfuls, these few, were enough to keep the link, the bond. But at what a cost!

How much has Shikasta cost Canopus, always!

How often have our envoys returned from a term of duty on Shikasta, amazed at what the link depended on; appalled at what they had seen.

It has to be recorded that more than once discussions have been held on whether Shikasta was worth the effort. A full-scale conference, involving all Canopus and our colonies, argued the question. There grew up a body of opinion, which remained a minority, that Shikasta should be jettisoned. This is why Shikasta is in a unique position among the colonised planets: service there is voluntary, except for those individuals who have been concerned with it from the beginning.

JOHOR *reports:*

This is the requested report on individuals who, if Taufiq had not been captured, would have been in very different situations, and on events that would have been differently aligned. I shall not always amplify, or sometimes even mention, the exact role that John Brent-Oxford might have played.

To contact them I entered Shikasta from Zone Six, at various points, but making use mostly of the Giants' habitat.

INDIVIDUAL ONE

Although she was born in a country of ample skies and capacious landscapes, she was afflicted, and from her earliest years, with feelings of being confined. It seemed to her that she ought to be able to find within herself memories of some larger experience, deeper skies. But she did not possess these memories. The society around her seemed petty, piffling, to the point of caricature. As a child she could not believe that the adults were serious in the games they played. Everything done and said seemed a repetition, or a recycling, as if they were puppets in a play being staged over and over again. Afflicted by an enormous claustrophobia, she refused all the normal developments possible to her, and as soon as she was self-supporting left her family and that society. How she earned her living was of no importance to her. She went to another city in the same continent, but there everything seemed the same. Not only identical patterns of thought and behaviour, but the people she met tended to be friends or relatives of those she had left. She moved to another city, another—and then to a different continent. While there was a general conspiracy—so it seemed to her—to agree that this culture was different from the one she had left in ways meriting a thousand books and treatises political, psychological, economic, sociological, philosophical, and religious—on the contrary, to her it seemed the same. A different language, or languages. Slightly more generous in one way—how women were treated, for instance. Worse in another: children had a bad time of it. Animals respected here but not there—and so on. But the patterns of human bondage—which was how she saw it—did not seem to vary much. And, no matter where she travelled, she met no new people. This man encountered in an improbable situation—by chance in a laundrette or at a bus stop—would turn out to be a relation of an acquaintance in another city, or a friend of a family she had known as a child. She left again, choosing an "old" society—which was how Shikastans would see it—more complex, textured, various, than those she had known. Again, differences were emphasized where she could see only resemblances. She earned her living as she could, in ways that could not bind her, would not marry, and had three abortions, because the men did not seem to her to be originally enough minted from the human stock to make their progeny worthwhile. And she could not meet new, different people. She understood she was in, or on, some invisible mesh or template, envisioned by her in bad black moods as a vast spider web, where all the people and events were interconnected, and nothing she could do, ever, would free her. And never could she say anything of what she felt, for she would not be understood. What she saw, others did not. What she heard, they could not.

She was in a certain country in the Northwest fringes. It occurred to her that this move of hers, to this country, which had cost her, so she had imagined, a good deal of effort in the way of choosing right, this great self-transportation, had not been *her* will at all: it was her father's. He had always wanted, so she now recalled, to live in this particular city, this country, and in a certain way. While she had not duplicated his dreamed-of way of life—for it had become obsolete—she was living a contemporary equivalence. Shortly after this discovery, she found herself outside a door in a street she had never been in before, to visit a doctor, and remembered that the address was one an aunt had lived in: she had written letters here from her home country.

She left again, for the extreme north of the Isolated Northern Continent. She was in a small town, which for most of the year was under snow. No one came there for pleasure. It was a working town, and she had a job in a shop that sold goods to trappers and what Indians still remained. She could not have found for herself a situation more at odds with anything her parents or her background might have foreseen for her. Then into the shop came a man she knew. He was a doctor last seen in her hometown, fifteen years before. They had been linked briefly by an impersonal pairing bond typical of that time.

She fled back to the Northwest fringes. She was in the heart of a great sprawling unshaped city of several million inhabitants and, getting off a bus on an impulse and entering a little restaurant for a cup of tea, she sensed something familiar. She was greeted by a girl working as a waitress: she was the sister of the doctor.

The world had finally snapped around her like a handcuff. She screamed, leaped up, broke crockery and overturned tables.

The police came. She was taken to hospital. About whether she was mad or not, the doctors could not agree; and the restaurant brought a charge against her. But the lawyer who would have been the right one for this task was not there. If he had been, the case could have reached far beyond its beginnings, and influenced events, people. . . .

She was kept in hospital for longer than she felt was warranted, things dawdled and delayed. She was at last fined in court, which some kindly person paid for her. She was set free and felt that she was in a prison worse than any human being could devise.

If John (or Taufiq) had defended her, he would have been able to influence her to sit still at last and allow herself to see what it was that imprisoned her.

I arranged an alternative, a temporary attack of paralysis, diagnosed as hysterical.

Unable to take flight, she struggled inwardly for a time, and then, exactly as a cornered hawk sinks down among his fluffing and awkwardly extended feathers, bright eyes staring at her assailant, so she, too, learned to gaze steadily into what frightened her most.

INDIVIDUAL TWO

Standardisation of intellectual and emotional patterns had become extreme. A main mechanism for achieving this was a device that supplied identical indoctrinational material simultaneously into every living or working unit, whether that of a single person, a family, or an institution, through a whole country. These programmes were standardised, particularly for children. At best they reinforced a low level of ethic—kindness to animals, for instance—but the worst was inherent in the sheer fact of the infinite repetition.

Ventriloquism was popular. A person with a bland and conforming appearance and personality developed a subsidiary personality and presented it as ventriloquist's dummy. This other personality could be of their own species, or variations on the animal theme. A popular one was a canine, endearing in appearance, who was clever in methods of successful dishonesty. In every episode of his story this animal stole, lied, and cheated, was able always to cover up after a failure, to deceive and boast and flatter and manipulate. It was also inordinately greedy for food. This creature was no major criminal or monster, only a small-scale trickster and, if you accepted the premise, it was quite funny. Of course, it was possible to find it humorous at all only in times of almost total corruption.

Children were identified with these "unreal" figures, which could never be taken for anything but dolls, or puppets, and which were particularly useful to take as secondary selves, simply because they did not demand the levels of self-criticism which would be demanded by creatures like themselves, who were "real."

A certain group of children, much neglected by parents, who were all working, and who left them almost entirely to themselves, developed a private world in which each one of them *was* this puppet, the half-grown dog with a typically flattering name, Crafty Collie. These children lived more and more inside the world they had created, taking, like their exemplar, to small ways of trickery, cheating, and lying—this in a motivated, patterned way, for all they had to do every afternoon was to press a button in order to see a programme for their alternative selves to follow. They took to more intricate crimes. Soon they had a leader. She was female, a bright resourceful child of eleven years. She it was who kept them together, who made sure they watched the succeeding episodes of the ventriloquist's dramas, and who translated into action the messages of Crafty Collie. This went on for three years, while the children became young adults, thirteen, fourteen, fifteen. Their crimes, at this time when nearly everybody engaged in some form of cheating or stealing, were not remarkable. They stole from shops, broke into houses, kept themselves supplied with money and goods. After every escapade, the group would gather in a ritual where what they had done was played out in terms of their pattern.

In the course of breaking into a house a murder was committed, almost accidentally, certainly without any sense of it mattering.

They were caught, and details of the cult were made public. Photographs of these young criminals, and of the room they used—in an empty house, decorated with pictures and models of Crafty Collie— were reproduced everywhere. When the doctors and psychiatrists examined the youngsters, it was found that their identification with the puppet was not affecting them more than half the time, for each had an ordinary personality, with its aims, beliefs, and standards, quite different from the other personality, which was a group one.

It was the girl who pointed out that only a month before Crafty Collie had been shown as tormenting and teasing a crazy old woman before knocking her down and leaving her apparently unconscious, reproved of course by his creator or other self, who always played the— ineffective—role of conscience to this secondary personality's excesses. Or successes.

The whole gang was tried, in a way not used before at that particular time, in an exemplary way: for child crime had become so prevalent that people were becoming more afraid of children than they were of adults.

The girl was in a special position as self-confessed, or self-proclaimed leader, for she was proud of her role as mother of this gang.

If Taufiq had been where he ought to have been, his role was to defend these children as victims of indoctrination. Whether this indoctrination was deliberate on the part of the authorities, or the result of ignorance, was not, could not be—he would have argued—any concern of the children, who had to suffer the consequences. In other words Taufiq, John, would have inspired a public campaign to get an extraordinarily lax and indifferent public to recognise where, when, and how the most sophisticated indoctrinational methods ever devised were being used on a population captive to them.

Further, if Taufiq had been able to fit into these events, his particular personality would have influenced these young people in ways not otherwise attainable. All had been neglected, none had been given any exemplar of worth to identify with. He would have been able to direct them in ways that would lead to their eventually gaining enough inner freedom to make real choices about what their lives would be.

But now, what one individual could have accomplished must be spread among several. I arranged that a group of lawyers not previously inspired to work of public responsibility take this case: they could be expected to do something at least of what was needed. As for influencing the youngsters, I saw to it that each one would come into contact with those who could help them, to some extent: a child-care officer with certain characteristics, a warder—three were sent to prison—a doctor, social workers.

The task with these young people took much longer than I expected or had planned for. It was not the most successful of my endeavours. The girl was not able to recover from a sojourn in prison calculated only to harden and deform: she came out a real criminal, soon made an emotional transfer to one of the extreme political sects which flourished then, and was killed in an exploit that could be characterised as part terrorist and part for gain. She was not twenty years old. Her rehabilitation had therefore to be reserved until after her entry into Zone Six.

INDIVIDUAL THREE (*Workers' Leader*)

A common type throughout the Century of Destruction in all parts of Shikasta, but the variation I am reporting on here was produced by the Northwest fringes and played a key part in the social structure. It was a stabilising one, and that this was so was felt by many as a bitter paradox, since their ideological birth was nearly always into the philosophy of transforming society completely, quickly, and into a sort of "paradise" not uninfluenced by the local "sacred" literature.

This individual was born into the chaotic conditions intensified by World War I. There was a small class living in affluence, but the bulk of the population was in poverty. He was an infant, a child, and then a young adult, among people who never had enough to eat, were cold, ill-housed, and often out of work. Of his immediate family three died of illnesses due to malnutrition. His mother was worn out by work and ill-feeling before she was thirty.

He lived, from the moment he came to consciousness of his situation, and that was early, in a state of anguished incredulity about the hardships of the people around him. This undersized urchin would wander the streets, upheld through cold, hunger, and the bitterness of injustice by visions and dreams. Each man or woman or shrunken child he passed seemed to him to have a double, another alternate being . . . what could be, what could have been. . . . He would gaze, exalted, into the face of one, and address him silently: "You poor exhausted thing, you could be anything, it is not your fault. . . ." He would watch his sister, a girl exhausted with anaemia who had been working since she was fourteen, with no hope for anything but a future as narrow as her mother's, and he would be saying to her inwardly, "You don't know what you are, what you could be"—and it was as if he had put his arms around not only her, but the poor and the suffering everywhere. He cherished the twisted and the deformed with his gaze, he sustained the hungry and the desperate as he whispered, "You have it in you to be a marvel! Yes, you are a marvel and a wonder and you don't know it!" And he was making promises, fierce inward vows, to himself, and to them.

He simply could not believe that this extreme of deprivation was possible in a country—he saw the problem in terms of his own country, even his own town, for "the world" to him was names in newspapers—that described itself as rich, and headed a world empire.

He was informed beyond most of his fellows, because his father was a workers' representative, insofar as his hard life allowed him time and energy to be. There were books in his home, and ideas apart from those to do with the struggle to feed and clothe the family.

He was in the army five years, in World War II. His predominant emotion of marvelling incredulity that people could inflict such suffering on others, changed. He was no longer incredulous: as a soldier he travelled widely, and he saw the conditions of his upbringing everywhere. The war taught him to think in terms of Shikasta as a whole, and of interacting forces, at least to an extent: he was not able to encompass the dark-skinned in his compassion, not able to withstand the influences of his upbringing which had taught him to think of himself as superior. But he was also being affected, like everybody in or out of the army, by the general brutalising, coarsening. He accepted things as "human nature" which as a child he would have rejected. But he was full of purpose, dreaming of returning home to uplift others, rescuing, supporting, shielding them from realities which he felt himself able to withstand, though they could not.

When he got home from the army, he set himself actively to "speak for the working class," as the phrase then went, and he very soon stood out among others.

The period immediately following World War II was bitter, impoverished, grey, colourless. The nations of the Northwest fringes had shattered themselves, physically and morally. [SEE *History of Shikasta*, VOL. 3014, *Period Between World Wars II and III.* SUMMARY CHAPTER.] The Isolated Northern Continent had strengthened itself and was supporting the nations of the Northwest fringes on condition they become subservient and obedient allies in the military bloc this continent dominated. Wealth flowed from the military bloc into the Northwest fringes, and about fifteen years after the end of World War II there was a sudden brief prosperity all over the area. That was a paradoxical thing, in a paradoxical time, and deeply demoralising to populations already demoralised and lacking in purpose.

The system of economic production depended on consumption of every conceivable kind of goods by everyone—consumption of entirely unnecessary objects, food, drink, clothes, gadgets, devices. Every person in the Northwest fringes—as in the Isolated Northern Continent—was subjected, every moment of every day, through propaganda methods more powerful than any ever known before, to the need to buy, consume, waste, destroy, throw away—and this at a time when the globe as a whole was already short of goods of every kind and the majority of Shikasta's people starved and went without.

The individual under consideration here was at the age of forty an influential person in a workers' organisation.

His role was to prevent the people he represented from being paid less than they could live on decently—this as a minimum goal; otherwise to get them "as large a slice of the cake as possible"; otherwise— but this aim had long since become secondary to the others—to overturn the economic system and substitute a workers' rule. He often contrasted how he saw things now with how he had seen them when he was a child and streets, areas of streets, no, whole cities, hungered and dwindled. This spurt of quite spurious and baseless affluence so soon to end, was intoxicating. Suddenly everything seemed possible. Within reach were experiences, ways of living he had never dreamed of as available to people of his kind. Not "a decent living wage," which slogan now seemed to him mean-spirited and cowardly, but as much as could be got. And this attitude was reinforced all the time, by everything around him. It was not that the working classes got anything like what the rich still got, but that millions were getting more than had seemed possible without some shocking overturn of society, or a revolution . . . in this atmosphere where there seemed no limit to what could be expected, there seemed no reason either why the workers of the nation should not exact retribution for the poverty of their parents, their grandparents, their great-grandparents, for the humiliations of their own childhoods. Revenge was a motive, clear for everyone to see.

But it was not in the nature of things that the Age of Affluence could continue; and the reasons were not to be sought in local conditions but globally—so far our friend did understand. He was still one who examined events less narrowly than most. He remained solitary. He was referred to as "an odd man out." Where groups of people are close, kept together by forces they combat by being defensive, the characteristics of individuals become affectionately regarded, are prized, made much of.

He was admired for standing for minority points of view. For being quiet, observant, reflective, often critical.

This was his role.

He had integrity.

He was proud of this, was still proud, but now saw that such words can acquire a double edge. He noted that people were very ready to congratulate him on this integrity of his. He had seen that people are willing to compliment others in the way these want to be complimented: an exacted flattery.

"Integrity" was his perquisite.

Not the only one. Many good things came his way because of this position of his, as representative of the workers. But why not? Nothing compared to what came the way of "his betters"—as he had been expected as a child to call them, and had so stubbornly rebelled. And everyone did it. Did what? Nothing very much! Little crumbs and bits of this and that off the cake. What was the harm? For one thing, it could be said that these "perks" were not for him, personally, at all, but were an honour paid to his position and therefore to the workers. He would brood, secretly, about bribery, where it began and where it ended. About flattery as a food that sustained—and *bought?* He seemed to be spending hours of his time in definitions, self-assessments, doubts.

Nearly fifty, his life two-thirds gone, his children grown up. His children dismayed him. They cared for nothing but their own good, their pleasure, their possessions, their comfort. Criticising them, he told himself that this was no more than how parents always were with their children. (Rightly, he might mutter obstinately to himself, but not to his wife, who thought him prickly and difficult.) He was also proud of them, because by an inevitable process that he understood perfectly, they were a step up on the class ladder from him in this infinitely class-divided society; just as their children, his grandchildren, could expect to be a step higher still—but he was proud with a part of himself that he despised. He was self-divided, delighted they made demands on life that he was not able to believe even now were his due, while it was at the cost of rising in a society which he despised as much as ever he did.

But, criticising his children, he was criticising, too, the younger members of his own union—an entire generation. This was dangerous because treachery and disloyalty threatened. But he could not banish his thoughts. The incredulity that had been the strongest emotion of his childhood returned, transformed. How was it possible that people could forget as they did, taking everything that came their way as their due—thieves, snitching what they could whenever they could (and everybody knew it, including themselves), but they were even proud of it, regarding this pilfering and skyving as a sort of cleverness on their part, a way of outdoing the world—they were all careless, heedless, thoughtless, unable to see that this time of ease and even wealth was due to some transitory shift in the international economic juggling. Yet these were the sons and daughters of people so bitterly afflicted that they had gone to bed hungry more often than not, and were so stunted in growth that in looking at a crowd of working people it was a simple thing to pick out grandparents, even parents, who were often dwarves compared to their progeny. The history of the lower classes in this country had always been one of dire poverty and deprivation. Had they forgotten it? How was it possible? How could all this be happening?

Meanwhile, he was busy, in a hundred ways, sitting on committees, arguing with the employers, travelling and making speeches, attending conferences.

What exactly was it that he was doing?

Where did he stand now compared with his dreams for himself at the end of World War II?

He would find himself at a meeting, or a conference, with men, and women, whom he had known sometimes since he was a child. He would observe, hoping he was unobserved, feeling himself increasingly a stranger to them.

All his life he had polished and perfected a certain practice: that of keeping bright and close certain memories of his childhood as a conscience, or gauge, to measure present events against. After the war, beginning his work on the committees, there was a memory that was strong and alive, and kept so by what he could see around him. A cousin had sold vegetables from a barrow on a pavement. His fight to survive had been dreadful, and had worn him out early. He stood by the barrow all hours of the day and evening, and in all weathers, coughing, shivering, just holding himself together. But it was that stance of his which stuck in the mind—that of a schoolboy who has been knocked down by bullies so many times he knows the effort of getting to his feet will result only in his being knocked down again. It was a swaggering bravado, and every gesture said, You can't get *me* down, I'm a big man, I'm strong, I'm on top of circumstances . . . and so he swaggered there, the poor victim. Well, to the small boy who watched, it was terrible; and now, he was seeing all the same gestures, the bravado, in the people around him, and it was terrible again.

But came the times of ease, of "affluence."

When he was a youth, he had a clear knowledge of those opposing him, "the class enemy." Their characteristic was that they did not tell the truth. They lied. They cheated. When it was a question of defending their position, what they had, there was no trick or meanness they would not descend to. In any confrontation between them, those representatives of the "ruling classes," and the men who spoke for the struggling millions, they presented the bland calm faces of accomplished liars, who were proud of that accomplishment. He had seen himself, as a youth, a fighter armed with truth and with the facts, against these armies of thieves and liars.

And now? He would watch a good-humoured, smiling affable man, presenting a case, and remember. . . .

They were not victors, he and his kind, not in any way, they were the defeated still, for they had become like their "betters." He, his kind, had been taken captive by everything they ought to hate, and *had* hated but had forgotten to hate. They *had* looked, earlier in their history, into the faces of their oppressors, who bullied and bluffed—and tricked; and had felt themselves superior, because they were honest, and stood on the truth. And now they, too, bluffed and bullied and tricked—just like everyone else of course. Who did not? Who did not lie and steal and filch, and take what he could grab? And so why should they be any different?

What he was thinking was a sort of treason.

Thinking like this, not wanting to think like this, being ashamed of himself, and then telling himself he was right, and should hold fast to these thoughts, he had a breakdown. He was given leave for a year by concerned—and relieved—colleagues. He had been for months now sitting silently through deliberations of various kinds and then coming out with something like: "But shouldn't we get back to first principles?" Or: "Why do we tolerate so much thieving and crookedness?" Or: "Yes, but that isn't true, is it?"—and with a wrung face and the hot dry eyes of sleeplessness.

He went home to his wife, who was out all day working at a job which he thought was unnecessary and degrading to her. She worked because she said she couldn't make ends meet, but he told her that he earned enough to live in a way their respective parents would have thought luxury. Why shouldn't she make something of herself, something serious!

What, for instance?

Well, she could go to night classes. Or learn some real skill.

Like *what*? And what for?

Or she could start some association for improving the position of women?

But she continued to earn money in order to fill a house with furniture he thought of as pretentious. She could never stop replacing clothes and curtains, or stocking freezers with enough food to feed great families.

He went off on a long walking trip, by himself, visiting old friends, some of them not seen for years. They had become possessed, it seemed to him, as happened in fairy tales, by some kind of evil spirit, for he could not find anything in them of what they had been. Or what he had thought they were?

Tramping, wandering, alone, he kept returning to himself as a boy, when everyone he saw seemed to him only a shadow of what was possible, for he could see so clearly their potential self, what they ought to be, could be, *would* be . . . or had he imagined all that?

He went to visit a sister, not the one whom he had cherished, and comforted silently in his thoughts, for the dreadfulness of her life, for she had died of tuberculosis; but another, much younger than himself. He found a woman who was tired. That was her characteristic. She ministered to her husband, a pleasant enough man who seemed tired and silent, too, and who did not seem to care for her much beyond what she provided for him. They both went to bed early. She talked a good deal to her cats. The daughter had gone to Australia with her family. She was worried about a carpet she felt should be replaced, but was finding the whole thing more than she could face, the disturbance of it, the getting rid of the old one, the workmen coming in and out. She could not talk of much else. Apart from the war, which she remembered with fondness because of "everyone being so kind to each other."

When he got home from an extensive walking tour, he told his wife he was going to sue himself.

"You are going to what?"

"I am going to put myself on trial."

"You have gone crazy, you have," said she, quite accurately, of course, departing to tell friends and colleagues that he had not yet got over whatever it was that "was eating him."

He appeared at a meeting of his union and informed them that he was going to put himself on trial, "on behalf of us all," and invited their co-operation.

They indulged him.

But he could not find anyone to take his case.

At that time exemplary trials of every kind were not uncommon. A group of people would set up a trial of some process or institution that seemed to them inadequate or dishonest.

What our friend wanted was to set up a trial where his youthful self prosecuted his middle-aged self, asking what had happened to the ideals, the vision, the ability to see individuals as infinitely capable of development, the hatred of pettiness and evasion, the hatred above all of lies, and double talk, the deceits of the conference tables and committees, the public announcements, the public face.

He wanted that burning, fiery, hungry, *marvellous* young man to stand up in public and expose and shred to pieces the awful dishonest smiling tool and puppet that he had become.

He went from lawyer to lawyer. Individuals. Then organisations. There were a thousand small political groupings, with different aims, or at least formulations.

The big political parties, the big trade unions, all the organs of government had become so enormous, so cumbersome, so ridden with bureaucracy, that nothing could get done except through the continually forming and re-forming pressure groups: it was government by pressure group, administration by pressure group, for government could not initiate, it could only respond. But all these groups, sometimes admirable for their purpose, had ideologies and allegiances, and not one was prepared to take on this odd and freakish case, and not one saw that incorruptible, *truthful* young man as he did. They indulged him. Or, again and again, he saw that he was about to find himself on some platform defending partisan causes. He was going from group to group, engaged in interminable and usually acrimonious discussions, arguments, definitions: at first he was prepared to see the acrimony as a sign of inner strength, "integrity," but then could no longer. He wondered if what he admired in himself, when young, had been no more than intolerance, the energy that is the result of identification with a limited objective?

It was not long before he had a heart attack, and then another, and died.

If Taufiq had been there, the case would have been perfectly adapted to his capacities.

He would not have permitted this "trial" to be freakish, or silly, or self-advertising. It would have captured the imaginations of a generation, focussing inner questionings and doubts; have led above all to a deeper understanding by young people of the rapid shifts and changes in the recent past, which to them seemed so distant.

INDIVIDUAL FOUR *(Terrorist Type 3)*

[For a list of the different types of terrorists produced during this period, SEE *History of Shikasta*, VOL. 3014, *Period Between World Wars II and III*.]

This young woman was known to her colleagues, and to the world in her brief moment of exposure, as The Brand.

She had spent her childhood in concentration camps, where her parents died. If there were members of her family still alive, she made no attempt to trace them. She was given a home by foster parents with whom she was obedient, correct—a shadow. They were not real to her. Only people who had been in the camps were real for her. With them she maintained contact. They were her friends, because they shared a knowledge of "what the world is really like." She was part-Jewish, but did not identify particularly with any aspect of being Jewish. As soon as she was grown up, pressures came on her to be normal. To these she responded by calling herself The Brand. She had refused to remove the tattoo of the camps. Now she had shirts, sweaters, with her brand on them, in black. In bed with her "lovers"—where she challenged the world in the cold indifferent way that was her style—she would take the fingers of the man or woman (she was bisexual) and smile as she placed them on the brand on her forearm.

She sought out, more and more, people who had been in concentration camps, refugee camps, prisons. Several times she slipped through frontiers to enter camps, prisons: these exploits were "impossible." Daring the "impossible" she was alive, as she never was otherwise. She prepared more difficult exploits for herself. She even lived as a member of a corrective prison in a certain Northwest fringe country for a year. The inmates saw her as engaged in some political task, but she was testing herself. For what? But her "historical role" had not yet been "minted by history": her vocabulary consisted entirely of political slogans or clichés, mostly of the left, together with concentration camp and prison jargon. At that stage she did not see herself with a definite future. She had no home of her own, but moved from one flat to another in a dozen cities of the Northwest fringes. These were owned by people like herself, some of whom had ordinary jobs, or got money illegally in one way or another. Money did not matter to her. She always wore trousers, and a shirt or sweater, and if these did not have on them her brand, she wore it on a silver bracelet.

She was a stocky plain girl, with nothing remarkable about her; but people would find themselves watching her, uneasy because of this coldly observant presence. She was always in command of herself, and hostile, unless when with her other selves, the products of the camps. Then she was affectionate, in a clumsy childish way. But only one other person knew the full details of her exploits among the camps and prisons. This was a man called "X."

When terrorist groups sprang up everywhere, most of them of

younger people than she, The Brand was not far from a legend. People saw this as a danger, "exhibitionism," and kept clear of her; but in that network of flats, houses, where these people moved, she had always just left, or would soon be there, someone knew her, she had helped somebody. One man, respected among them, who was about to start, correctly and formally, a group of whom he would be "leader"—though the word was understood differently among them—refused to talk about her, but allowed it to be understood that she was more skilled and brave than anyone he had known. He insisted that she should be asked to be a member of his group: insisted against opposition.

He had said she was a mistress of disguise.

She came to a flat one afternoon in an industrial city in the north of the Northwest fringes. It was a bitter cold day, snowing, a freezing wind. Four people in their twenties, two men, two women, saw this woman enter: blond, sunburned, a little overfed, in a fur coat that was vulgar and expensive, with the good-humoured easy smile of the indulged and sheltered of this world. This middle-class woman sat down fussily, guarding her handbag that had cost a fortune but was a bit shabby, in the way people do who care for their possessions. Her audience burst out laughing. She became an elder sister to them, an infinitely clever comrade, who had always done, and with success, more difficult things than any of them had dreamed of. This circle of out-laws was her family, and would have to be till death, for they could never leave such a circle and return to ordinary life—a condition that was not desirable or understandable to any of them. Her self-challenges, her feats, were disclosed by her, discussed, and all kinds of practical lessons drawn from them.

This was one of the more successful of the terrorist groups. It op-erated for more than ten years before The Brand was caught, with eight others. Their goals were always the same: an extremely difficult and dangerous feat that needed resources of skill, bravery, cunning. They were all people who had to have danger to feel alive at all. They were "left-wing," socialists of a sort. But discussions of a "line," the varia-tions of dogma, were never important to them. When they exchanged the phrases of the international left-wing vocabulary, it was without passion.

They did not court, or crave, publicity, but used it.

Most of their engagements with danger were anonymous and did not reach newspapers and television.

They blackmailed an international business corporation or individual, for money. Large sums would find their way to refugee organisations, prisoners escaping or in hiding, or to the "network." Young people in refugee camps would find themselves mysteriously supported into universities or training of some kind. Flats and houses were set up in this country or that, sometimes across the world, for the use of the "network." Organisations similar to theirs, temporarily in difficulties, would be helped. They also blackmailed and kidnapped, for information. They wanted details of how this business worked, the linkages and bonds of that multinational firm. They wanted information from secret military installations—and got it. They acquired materials to make various types of bomb, weapon, and supplied other groups with them. If any one of these young people had been asked why she or he did not use these talents "for the common good" the reply would have been "But I do already!" for they saw themselves as an alternative world government.

When they were caught, it was by chance; and this is not the place to describe how.

The Brand, and her associates, were in prison, all with multiple charges against them. Murders had been committed, but not for the pleasure of murder. The *pleasure*—if that is a word that may be used for the heightened, taut, lightning shimmer of excitement they sought, or rather, manufactured—did not come from the isolated brutal act or torture of an individual, but from the exploit as a whole—its conception, the planning, the slow building of tension, the exact scrupulous attention to a thousand details.

INDIVIDUAL FIVE (*Terrorist Type 12*)

X was the son of rich parents, business people who had made a fortune through armaments and industries associated with war: World War I provided the basis of this fortune. His parents had both been married several times, he had known no family life, had been emotionally self-sufficient since a small child. He spoke many languages, could claim citizenship from several countries. Was he Italian, German, Jewish, Armenian, Egyptian? He was any one of these, at his convenience.

A man of talent and resources, he could have become an efficient part of the machinery of death that was his inheritance, but he would not, could not, be any man's heir.

He was fifteen when he brought off several coups of blackmail— emotional legerdemain—among the ramifications of his several families' businesses. These showed the capacity to analyse; a cold far-sightedness, an indifference to personal feelings. He was one of those unable to separate an individual from her, his circumstances. The man who was his real father (though he did not think of him as such, claimed a man met half a dozen times almost casually, whose conversation had illuminated his life, as "father"), this ordinary, harassed, anxious man, who died in middle age of a heart attack, one of the richest men in the world, was seen by him as a monster, because of the circumstances he had been born into. X had never questioned this attitude: could not. For him, a man or a woman *was* his, her circumstances, actions. Thus guilt was ruled out for him; it was a word he could not understand, not even by the processes of imaginative effort. He had never made the attempt to understand the people of his upbringing: they were all rotten, evil. His own milieu, the "network," was his family.

Meeting The Brand was important to him. He was twelve years younger than she was. He studied her adventures with the total absorption others might bring to "God," or some absolute.

First there had been that casually met man whose ruthless utterances seemed to him the essence of wisdom. Then there was The Brand.

When they had sexual relations—almost at once, since for her sex was an appetite to be fed, and no more—he felt confirmed in his deepest sense of himself: the cold efficiency of the business, never far from perversity, seemed to him a statement of what life was.

He had never felt warmth for any human being, only admiration, a determination to understand excellence, as he defined it.

He did not want, or claim, attention from the public or the press or any propaganda instrument: the world was contemptible to him. But when he had pulled off, with or without the "network" (he often worked alone, or with The Brand), a coup that was always inside the empire of one of his families, he would leave his mark, so that they should know whom they had to thank: an X, like that of an illiterate.

In bed with The Brand, he would trace an X over the raised pattern of the concentration camp number on her forearm, particularly in orgiastic moments.

He was never caught. Later, he joined one of the international police forces that helped to govern Shikasta in its last days.

INDIVIDUAL SIX (*Terrorist Type 8*)

The parents of this individual were in camps of various kinds throughout World War II. The father was Jewish. That they survived at all was "impossible." There are thousands of documents testifying to these "impossible" survivals, each one a history of dedication to survival, inner strength, cunning, courage—and luck. These two did not leave the domain of the camps—they were in a forced labour camp in the eastern part of the Northwest fringes for the last part of the war—until nearly five years after the war ended. There was no place for them. By then the individual who concerns us here had been born, into conditions of near starvation, and cold: *impossible* conditions. He was puny, damaged, but was able to function. There were no siblings: the parents' vitality had been exhausted by the business of setting themselves up, with the aid of official charitable organisations, as a family unit in a small town where the father became an industrial worker. They were frugal, careful, wary, husbanding every resource: people such as these understand, above all, what things cost, what life costs. Their love for the child was gratitude for continued existence: nothing unthinking, animal, instinctive, about this love. He was to them something that had been rescued—impossibly—from disaster.

The parents did not make friends easily: their experience had cut them off from the people around them, all of whom had been reduced to the edge of extinction by the war—but few had been in the camps. The parents did not often speak about their years in the camps, but when they did, what they said took hold of the child with the strength of an alternative vision. What did these two rooms they lived in, poor, but warm and safe, have to do with that nightmare his parents spoke of? Sometimes at this time of life, youngsters in the grip of glandular upheaval crystallise in opposition to their parents with a vigour that preserves opposition for the rest of their lives.

This boy looked at his parents, and was appalled. *How was it possible?* was his thought.

I digress here to the incredulity referred to in my report on Individual Three, who spent years examining the deprivations of the people around him with: *How is it possible? I simply don't believe it!* Meaning partly: Why do they put up with it? Meaning, too: That human beings should treat each other like this? I don't believe it!

In Individual Six this incredulity was wider far than that of Individual Three, who saw the streets around him, then a town, and could only with difficulty envisage the Northwest fringes, let alone the central landmass, the world: it took years of experience in the war to enlarge his boundaries.

But Individual Six felt *himself* to be the war, and the war had been a global event: had printed his vision of life as a system of interlocking, interacting processes.

From the time he first began to think for himself, he was unable to see the developments of events as the generation before his had done. There was no such thing as a "guilty nation," any more than there could be defeated or victorious nations. A single nation could not be solely responsible for what it did, since groups of nations were a whole, interacting as a whole. The geographical area called "Germany"—it had become another name for wickedness—could not be responsible entirely for the mass murders and brutalities it had perpetrated: how could it be, when one day with the facts in a library was enough to show that "World War II" was multicaused, an expression of the whole of the Northwest fringes, a development of "World War I." *How was it possible* that these old people saw things in this isolated piecemeal way, like children, or like idiots! They were simple-minded. They were stupid! Above all, *they did not seem to have any idea at all of what they were like*.

A boy of fifteen imposed on himself a regime completely distressing to his parents. He did not have a room of his own, but there was a folding bed in the kitchen, and this he covered with what they had been given in the camps: a single, thin, dirty blanket. He shaved his head, and kept it shaved. On one day a week he ate only the diet provided in the camp during the final days of the war: hot greasy water, potato peelings, scraps from rubbish bins. He was careful, not to say obsessed, in getting his "food" for himself, and put the filthy stuff on the table at mealtimes, eating reverently—a sacrament. Meanwhile, his parents ate their frugal meals; their damaged stomachs could not absorb normal amounts of food. He read to them passages from biographies, accounts of conditions in camps, the negotiations or lack of them that led to "World War II"—always stressing multicause and effect: if that nation had done that, then this would not have happened. If such and such warnings had been heeded . . . that step taken . . . that statesman listened to . . .

For these poor people it was as if a nightmare they had escaped from only by a miracle had returned and was taking over their lives. They had made for themselves a little sheltered place, where they could believe themselves kept safe, because evil was the property of that other place, or that other nation; wickedness was contained in the past, in history—terror might come again, but thank God, that would be the future, and by then with luck, they would be dead and safe . . . and now their refuge was being broken open, not by "history" or "the future," but by this precious child of theirs, who was all they had been been able to bring out from the holocaust.

The father begged him to take his truths elsewhere.

"Are they true or not?" the youngster challenged.

"Yes . . . no . . . I don't care, for *God's* sake . . ."

"You don't care!"

"Your mother . . . you don't know what she had to put up with, go easy on her!"

The boy added to his discipline by wearing, on certain days of the week, dirty rags and tatters. All over the walls of the kitchen, which after all was the only room he had, and he was entitled to consider them his, were a thousand pictures of the concentration camps, but not only those of the Northwest fringes: soon the pictured record of the atrocious treatment of man by man covered the walls.

He sat quiet at the table, his father and mother hastily eating their meal in a silence that was a prayer he would not "begin again"—and then he *would* begin again, reciting facts, figures, litanies of destruction, deaths by ill treatment and torture in communist countries, non-communist countries, any country anywhere.

[SEE *History of Shikasta*, VOL. 3011, *The Age of Ideology*, "Self-Portraits of Nations." Geographical areas, or temporary associations of peoples for the purposes of defence or aggression. Such an entity capable of believing itself different, better, more "civilised" than another, when in fact to an outside view there is nothing to choose between them. And VOL. 3010, *Psychology of the Masses*, "Self-Protective Mechanisms."]

Through a series of chances, it had become impossible for this youngster to identify himself with national myths and self-flatteries. He literally could not understand how others did. He believed that they must be pretending, or were being wilfully cowardly. He was of that generation—part of a generation—who could not see a newspaper except as a screen for lies, automatically translated any television newscast or documentary into what the truth *probably* was, reminded himself all the time, as a religious person might remind himself of the wiles of the Devil, that what was being fed to the world or nation about any event was by definition bound to be only a small part of real information, knew that at no time, anywhere, was the population of a country told the truth: facts about events trickled into general consciousness much later, if ever.

All this was good, was a step towards freedom from the miasmas of Shikasta.

But it was useless to him, for he had no kindness.

He was intolerable to his parents. The mother, still only a middle-aged woman by ordinary reckoning, seemed old to herself, became ill, had a heart attack. The father remonstrated, pleaded, even used words like: Spare her, spare us.

The stern avenging angel of righteousness remained in the meagre rooms that held the family, his eyes fixed in unbelieving dislike on his parents: How is it possible that you are like this!

At last his father said to him that if he could not treat his mother— "Yes, and me too! I admit it!"—more gently, then he must leave home.

The boy was sixteen. They are throwing me out! he exulted, for everything he knew was being confirmed.

He found himself a room in the home of a school friend, and thereafter did not see his parents.

At school he set himself to be an unsettling presence. It was an ordinary small-town school, providing nothing remarkable for its pupils in the way of teachers and teachings. He sat at the back of a class and emanated a punishing dislike, arms folded, legs stretched to one side, maintaining a steady unblinking stare first at one target, and then at another. He would rise to his feet, first having most correctly held his hand up to ask permission: "Is it not a fact that . . . ? Are you perhaps unaware . . . ? You are of course familiar with Government Report No. XYZ . . . ? I take it that such and such a book will be part of the curriculum for this subject? No? But how can that be possible?"

He was feared by the staff, and by most of the pupils, but some of these admired him. At this time, when every kind of extreme political group tormented the authorities, and "the youth" was by definition a threat, he had not reached his seventeenth year when his name was known to the police, for the headmaster had mentioned him to them with the air of one covering himself against future probabilities.

He drifted towards various groups first right-wing and unaffiliated to a political party, then fell in with a left-wing revolutionary group. But this had very specific allegiances: this country was good, that bad, this creed abhorrent, this one "correct." Again he was saying; "But surely you must be aware . . . ? Have you not read . . . ? Don't you know that . . . ?" It was clear that he would have to form his own group, but he was in no hurry. To keep himself he pilfered, and took part in various petty crimes. He was indifferent about how he came by a couple of months in a flat somewhere, or free meals for a week, or a girlfriend. He was completely, even amiably, amoral. Accused of some lie or theft he might allow himself a smile that commented unfavourably on everything around him. His reputation among the political groups was still unformed, but on the whole he was seen as clever, as skillful at surviving in ways respected by them, but careless.

When his group of a dozen young men and women crystallised out finally it was not on the basis of any particular political creed. Everyone had been formed by experiences of emotional or physical deprivation, had been directly affected by war. None could do anything but fix the world with a cold, hating eye: *This is what you are like.* They did not dream of utopias in the future: their imaginations were not tuned to the future at all, unlike those of previous revolutionaries or religionists: it was not that "next year, or in the next decade, or next century, we create paradise on earth . . . ," only, "*This* is what you are like." When this hypocritical, lying, miserably stupid system was done away with, then everyone would be able to see. . . .

It was their task to expose the system for what it was.

But they had a faith, and no programme. They had the truth—but what to do with it? They had a vocabulary, but no language.

They watched the exploits of guerrilla groups, the deeds of the terrorists.

They saw that what was needed was to highlight situations, events.

They staged the kidnapping of a certain politician who had been involved in some transaction they disapproved of, demanding the release of a man in prison who seemed to them innocent. They detailed the reasons why this imprisoned man was innocent, and when he was not released, shot their hostage and left him in the town square. *This is what you are like* was what they felt, as they murdered him, meaning, the world.

The murder had not been planned. The details of the kidnapping had been adequately worked out, but they had not expected they would kill the politician, had half believed that the authorities would hand over their "innocent." There was something careless, unthought-out about the thing, and several of the members of the group demanded a more "serious" approach, analyses, reconsideration.

Our Individual Six listened to them, with his characteristic careless smile, but his black eyes deadly. "Of course, what else can be expected from people like you?" he was communicating.

Two of the protesting individuals met with "accidents" in the next few days, and he now commanded a group that did not think of him as "careless"—or not as they had done previously.

There were nine of them, three women.

One of the women thought of herself as "his," but he refused to accept this view of the situation. They had group sex, in every sort of combination. It was violent, ingenious, employing drugs and weapons of various kinds. Sticks of gelignite, for instance. Four of the group blew themselves up in an orgy. He did not recruit others.

It was observed by the four remaining that he had enjoyed the publicity. He insisted on staging a "funeral service" which, although police did not know which group had been responsible for this minor massacre, was asking for notice and arrest. Elegies for the dead, poems, drawings of a heroic nature were left in the warehouse where the "socialist requiem" was held.

By then it had occurred to them that he was mad, but it was too late for any of them to leave the group.

They staged another kidnapping. The carelessness of it amounted to contempt, and they were caught and put on trial. It was a trial that undermined the country, because of their contempt for the law, for legal processes.

At that time, throughout the Northwest fringes, almost every person regarded the processes of the law as a frail—the frailest possible—barrier between themselves and a total brutal anarchy.

Everyone knew that "civilisation" depended on the most fragile supports. The view of the older people of what was happening in the world was no less fearful, in its way, than that of the young ones like Individual Six and his group, or of the other terrorists, but it was opposite in effect. They knew that the slightest pressure, even an accident or something unintended, could bring down the entire fabric . . . and here were these madmen, these young idiots, prepared to risk everything—more, *intending* to bring it down, *wanting* to destroy and waste. If people like Individual Six "could not believe it," then ordinary citizens "could not believe it" either: they never did understand each other.

When the five were brought to trial and stood in the dock loaded with chains, and behind barriers of extra bars, they reached their fulfilment, the apex of achievement.

"This is what you are like," they were saying to the world. "These brutal chains, these bars, the fact that you will give us sentences that will keep us behind bars for the rest of our lives—this is what *you* are like! Regard your mirror, in us!"

In prison, and in court, they were elated, victorious, singing and laughing, as if at a festival.

About a year after sentence, Individual Six and two others escaped. They went their separate ways. Individual Six got fat, wore a wig, and acquired a correct clerkly appearance. He did not contact either the escaped members of his group or those in prison. He hardly thought of them: that was the past!

He deliberately courted danger. He would stand chatting to policemen on the street. He went into police stations to report minor crimes, such as the theft of a bicycle. He was arrested for speeding. He actually appeared in court on one charge. All this with a secret glowing contempt: this is what you are like, stupid, incompetent . . .

He went back to the town he had grown up in, and got an undemanding job, and made a life for himself that lacked any concealment except for the change of name and appearance. People recognised him, and he was talked about. Knowing this gave him pleasure.

His father was now in an institution for the elderly and incapacitated, his mother having died, and, hearing his son was in town, he took to hanging about the streets in the hope of seeing him. He did, but Individual Six waved his hand in a jolly, friendly, don't-bother-me-now gesture, and walked on.

He was expecting from his inevitable rearrest a trial of the same degree of publicity as his first. He wanted that moment when he would stand chained, like a dog, behind double bars. But when he was arrested, he was sent back to jail to serve his sentence.

An elation, a lunacy—which had been carrying him up, up, up, from the moment of truth when he had first seen what the world was like, had "had his eyes opened"—suddenly dissolved, and he committed suicide.

INDIVIDUAL SEVEN *(Terrorist Type 5)*

This was a child of rich parents, manufacturers of an internationally known household commodity of no use whatsoever, contributing nothing except to the economic imperative: thou shalt consume.

She had a brother, but as they were at different schools and it was not thought important that they should meet, she had little physical or emotional contact with him after early childhood.

She was unhappy, unnurtured, without knowing what was wrong with her. When she reached adolescence she saw there was no central place in the family, no place where responsibility was taken: no father, or mother, or brother—who never had any other destiny but to be his father's heir—imposed themselves on circumstances. They were passive in the face of events, ideas, fashions, expected conduct. When she had understood it—and she could not believe how she had taken so long—she saw that she was the only one of her family who thought like this. It occurred to none that it was ever possible to say "no." She saw them and herself as bits of paper or refuse blown along streets.

She did not hate them. She did not despise them. She found them irrelevant.

She went to university for three years. There she enjoyed the double life of such young people: democratic and frugal in the university, and the luxuriousness of an indulged minority to whom everything was possible, at home.

She was not interested in what she was taught, only in whom she met. She drifted in and out of political sects, all on the left. She used in them the cult vocabulary obligatory in those circles, the same in all of them—and they might very well be enemies at various times.

What they all had in common was that "the system" was doomed. And would be replaced by people like themselves, who were different.

These groups, and there were hundreds of them in the Northwest fringes—we are not now considering other parts of the world—were free to make up their own programmes, frameworks of ideas, exactly as they liked, without reference to objective reality. (This girl never saw for instance that during her years among the groups she was as passively accepting as she had ever been in her family.) [SEE *History of Shikasta*, VOL. 3011, *The Age of Ideology*, "Pathology of Political Groups."]

From the time the dominant religions lost their grip not only in the Northwest fringes, but everywhere throughout Shikasta, there was a recurrent phenomenon among young people: as they came to young adulthood and saw their immediate predecessors with the cold unliking eye that was the result of the breakdown of the culture into barbarism, groups of them would suddenly, struck for the first time by "truth," reject everything around them and seek in political ideology (emotionally this was of course identical to the reaction of groups that continuously formed and re-formed under the religious tyrannies) solutions to their situation, always seen as new-minted with themselves. Such a group would come into existence overnight, struck by a vision of the world believed by them to be entirely original, and within days they would have framed a philosophy, a code of conduct, lists of enemies and allies, personal, intergroup, national, and international. Inside a cocoon of righteousness, for the essence of it was that they were in the right, these young people would live for weeks, months, even years. And then the group would subdivide. Exactly as a stem branches, lightning branches, cells divide. But their emotional identification with the group was such that it prohibited any examination of the dynamics which must operate in groups. While studies by psychologists, researchers of all kinds, the examiners of the mechanics of society, became every day more intelligent, comprehensive, accurate, these conclusions were never applied to political groups—any more than it had ever been possible to apply a rational eye to religious behaviour while the religions maintained tyrannies, or for religious groups to apply such ideas to themselves. Politics had joined the realm of the sacred—the tabooed. The slightest examination of history showed that every group without exception was bound to divide and subdivide like amoeba, and could not help doing this, but when it happened it was always to the accompaniment of cries of "traitor," "treachery," "sedition," and similar mindless noises. For the member of any such group to suggest that the laws known (in other areas) must be operating here, was treachery; and such a person would be instantly flung out, exactly as had happened inside religions and religious groups, with curses and violent denunciations and emotionalism—not to mention physical torture or even death. Thus it came about that in this infinitely subdivided society, where different sets of ideas could exist side by side without their affecting each other—or at least not for long periods—the mechanisms like parliaments, councils, political parties, groups championing minority ideas, could remain unexamined, tabooed from examination of a cool rational sort, while in another area of the society, psychologists and sociologists could be receiving awards and recognition for work, which were it to be applied, would destroy this structure entirely.

When Individual Seven left university, nothing she had learned there seemed of any relevance to her. Her family expected her to marry a man like her father or her brother, or to take a job of an unchallenging kind. It seemed to her, suddenly, that she was nothing at all, and nothing of interest lay ahead of her.

This was a time when "demonstrations" took place continually. The populace was always taking to the streets to shout out the demands of the hour.

She had taken part in demonstrations at university, and, looking back on them, it seemed to her that during the hours of running and chanting, of shouting and singing, in great crowds, she had been more alive and feeling than ever in her entire life.

She took to slipping away from home when there were demonstrations, for a few hours of intoxication. It did not matter what the occasion was, or the cause. Then, by chance, she found herself at the front of a crowd fighting the police, and soon she was engaged in a hand-to-hand struggle with a policeman, a young man who grabbed her, called her insulting names, and tossed her like a bundle of rags into the arms of another, who threw her back. She screamed and struggled, and she was dragged away from the police like a trophy and found herself with a young man whose name she knew as "a leader."

He was a common type of that time: narrow-minded, ill-informed, dogmatic, humourless—a fanatic who could exist only in a group. She admired him completely and without reservation, and had sex with him that night before returning home. He was indifferent to her, but made a favour of it.

She now set herself to win this youth. She wanted to be "his woman." He was flattered when it became known that this girl was the daughter of one of the city's—no, the Northwest fringes'—rich families. But he was stern, even brutal with her, making it a test of her devotion to the cause (and himself, for he saw these as the same) that she should engage herself more and more in dangerous activity. This was not the serious, well-planned type of feat, or coup planned by terrorists type 12, or 3. He demanded of her that she should be with him in the forefront of demonstrations, and fling herself at lines of police, that she should shout and scream louder than the other girls, that she should struggle in the hands of the police, who in fact enjoyed these hysterical women. He was demanding of her, in fact, an ever-increasing degree of voluntary degradation.

She enjoyed it. More and more her life was spent dealing with the police. He was always being arrested, and she was in and out of police stations standing bail, or going with him in police wagons, or handing out leaflets about him and associates. These activities came to the notice of her parents, but after consultation with other parents, they consoled themselves with the formula: young people will be young people.

She was furious at their attitude: she was not being taken seriously. Her lover took her seriously. So did the police. She allowed herself to be arrested and spent some days in jail. Once—twice—three times. And then her parents insisted on bailing her out and so she was always leaving "her man" and her comrades in police cells while she was being driven home behind a chauffeur in one of the family cars.

She changed her name, and left home, insisting that she should live with her man. Which meant, a group of twelve or so young people. She accepted everything, living in a filthy hovel that had been condemned years before. She exulted in the discomfort, the dirt. She found herself cooking and cleaning and waiting on her man and his friends. They took a certain pleasure in this, because of her background, but she felt she was taken seriously, even that she was being forgiven.

Her parents found her, came after her, and she sent them away. They insisted on opening bank accounts for her, despatching messengers with cash, food, artefacts of all kinds, clothes. They were giving her what they had always given her—*things*.

Her lover would sit, legs astraddle on a hard chair, arms folded on the back of it, watching her with a cold sarcastic smile, waiting to see what she would do.

She did not value what she knew had cost her parents nothing enough to return them: but dedicated all these things, and the money, to "the cause."

Her lover was indifferent. That they eat anything pleasant, wear anything attractive, care about being warm or comfortable, seemed to him contemptible. He and his cronies discussed her, her class position, her economic position, her psychology, at length, shuffling and reshuffling the jargon of the left-wing phrase books. She listened feeling unworthy, but taken seriously.

He demanded of her that at the next "demo" she should seriously assault a policeman. She did it without question: never had she felt so fulfilled. She was three months in prison, where her lover visited her once. He visited others more often. Why? she humbly wondered. Not all of them were of the poor and the ignorant; one of his associates was in fact quite well off, and educated. But she was very rich, yes, that must be it. They were all more worthy than she was. In prison, among the other prisoners, most of them unpolitical, she radiated a smiling unalterable conviction which manifested itself as humility. She was always doing things no one else would do. Dirty tasks and punishment were food and drink to her. The prisoners christened her, disgusted, the Saint; but she took it as a compliment. "I am trying to be worthy to become a real member of—" and she supplied the name of her political group. "To become a real socialist one has to suffer and aspire."

When she came out, her man was living with another woman. She accepted it: of course it was because she was not good enough. She served them. She waited on them. She crouched on the floor outside the room her lover and the woman were wrapped together in, comparing herself to a dog, glorying in her abasement, and she muttered, like the phrases of a rosary, I will be worthy, I will overcome, I will show them, I will . . . and so on.

She took a kitchen knife to the next "demo" and did not even look to see if it was sharpened: the gesture of carrying it was enough. Intoxicated, lifted above herself, she fought and struggled, a Valkyrie with flying dirty blond hair, reddened blue eyes, a fixed, ugly smile. (In her family she had been noticed for her "sweet gentle look.") She attacked policemen with her fists, and then took out the—as it happened—blunt knife, and hacked about her with it. But she was not being arrested. Others were. There was such a disproportion between the atmosphere, and even the purpose, of this demonstration, and her appearance and her frenzy, that the police were puzzled by her. A senior official sent the word around that she was not to be arrested: she was clearly unbalanced. Ecstatic with renewed effort, she yelled and waved the knife about, but perceived that the demonstration was ending and people streaming home. *She was not being taken seriously.* She was standing watching the arrested being piled into the police vans like a child turned away from a party, the knife held in her hand as if she were intending to chop meat or vegetables with it.

A group of people had been watching her: not only this day, but at previous demonstrations.

A girl standing like a heroic statue on the edge of the pavement with the knife at the ready in her hand, hair falling bedraggled round a swollen and reddened face, weeping tears of angry disappointment, saw in front of her a man waiting for her to notice him. He had a smile which she thought *kind.* His eyes were "stern" and "penetrating": he understood her emotional type very well.

"I think you should come with me," he suggested.

"Why?" said she, all belligerence, which nevertheless suggested a readiness to obey.

"You can be of use."

She automatically took a step towards him, but stopped herself, confused.

"What to?"

"You can be of use to socialism."

Briefly on to her face flitted the expression that means: You can't get me as easily as that! while phrases from the *vocabulary* whirled through her brain.

"Your particular capacities and qualities are just what are needed," he said.

She went with him.

This group was in a large shabby flat on the outskirts of the city, a workman's home, one of the refuges of these twelve young women and men whose leader had accosted her. While the circumstances— poverty made worse, and emphasised—of her previous living place had been of emotional necessity to the work of self-definition of her previous group, these people were indifferent to how they lived, and moved from opulence, to discomfort, to middle-class comfort in the space of a day, as necessary, without making anything of what they were surrounded by. The girl adapted herself at once. Although she had been lying, exulting in her misery, outside the door of her lover and his new woman, for days, now she hardly thought of that life— *where she had not been appreciated.* She did not immediately see what was to be asked of her, but was patient, obedient, gentle, doing any task that suggested itself.

These new comrades were engaged in planning some coup, but she was not told what. Soon she was taken to yet another flat, where she had not been before, and told that she was to strip and examine a young woman brought in for "questioning." This girl was in fact an accomplice, but just before the "examination" began, Individual Seven was told that "this one was a particularly hard case" and that "there was no point in using kid gloves on her."

Alone with her victim, who seemed dazed and demoralised, the girl felt herself uplifted by the same familiar and longed-for elation of her combats with the police, the atmosphere of danger. She "examined" the captive, who, it seemed to her, had every mark of disgusting stupidity and corruption. It was not far off torture, and she enjoyed it.

She was complimented on the job she had done by this group of severe, serious, responsible young revolutionaries. Thus they described themselves. But she had not yet heard them define their particular creed or commitment. And in fact she was never to hear it.

She was told not to go out, to keep herself hidden: she was too valuable to risk. When the group moved, she was always blindfolded. She accepted this with a humble joy: it must be necessary.

This group added to the kidnapping of rich or well-known individuals a refinement, which was the kidnapping and torture, or threat of torture, of their relatives—mistresses, sisters, wives, daughters. Always women. The girl was given the task of torturing, first in minor ways, and then comprehensively, one young woman after another.

She looked forward to it. She had accepted her situation. Moments of disquiet were silenced with: They have more experience than I have, they are better than I am, and it must be necessary.

Reflecting that she did not know their allegiances, she was comforted by the phrases she was familiar with, and had been ever since—as she put it—she had become politically mature.

At moments when sharp pleasure held her in its power either because of some encounter just over or one promised her, she wondered if perhaps she had been physically drugged: whether these new friends of hers were feeding her stimulants, so alive did she feel, so vital and full of energy.

This group lasted three years before it was taken by the police, and the girl committed suicide when it was evident she could not avoid arrest. The impulse behind this act was a continuation of their dictate that she must not ever be visible—go out, be seen, or even know where she was. She felt that under torture—she now lived in her mind in a world where torture was not merely possible but inevitable—she would "betray them." Her suicide was, therefore, in her own eyes, an act of heroism and self-sacrifice in the service of socialism.

It will have been noted that none of the individuals categorised here was among those identified with a particular injustice, such as suffering under an arbitrary or tyrannous power, or being deprived of a country, or persecuted for being one of a despised or subjugated race, or kept in poverty by the thoughtless, the careless, or the cruel.

I could not contact the next individual through the Giants, or anything like them. I had been looking for someone suitable, and during my trips in and out of Shikasta, I had seen an old friend, Ranee, waiting on the margins of Zone Six at that place where the lines form for their chance of re-entry. I had told her that I needed very soon to spend time with her, and why. Now, searching up and down the lines I could not see her, and saw, too, that they were shorter and more sparse. I heard that there were rumours of an emergency, of frightful danger, in Zone Six, and all those able to understand had left to help people escape. The souls remaining in the lines were too fixed on their hope of an early re-entry, crowding forward each time the gates opened, jostling each other, their eyes only for the gates, and I could not get anything more out of them.

I walked on past them into the scrub and thin grasses of the high plateau, quite alone, as evening came on. I felt uneasy, and thought first this was because I had been told there was danger, but soon the sense of threat was so strong that I left the scrublands and climbed a small ridge, scrambling from rock to rock upwards, in the dark. I set my back to a small cliff, and my face to where I could expect the dawn. It was silent. But not completely silent. I could hear a soft whispering, like a sea . . . a sea where no sea was, or could be. The stars were crowding bright and thick, and their dim light showed low bushes and outcrops of stone. Nothing to account for this sound, which I could not remember ever hearing before. Yet it whispered danger, danger, and I stayed where I was, turning myself about and sensing and peering, like an animal alerted to some menace it cannot understand. When the light came into the sky and the stars went, the sound was there, and stronger. I descended from the ridge, and walked on, soon coming to the desert's edge, where I could hear the steady sibilant hissing. Yet there was no wind to blow the sand. Everything was quite still, and there was a small sweetness of dew rising from around my feet as I set them down on a crunchy surface. I walked on, every step slower, for all my senses shouted warnings at me. I kept close to my right the low ridge I had used for shelter the night before. It ran on in front of me until it joined black jagged peaks far ahead that were sombre and even sinister in the cool grey dawn. The rustling voice of the sands grew louder . . . not far from me I saw wisps of sand in the air, which vanished: yet there was no wind! The lower clouds hung dark and motionless, and the higher clouds, all tinted with the dawn, were in packed unmoving masses. A windless landscape and a still sky: and yet the whispering came from everywhere. A small smudge in the air far in front of me enlarged, and close to me the sands seemed to shiver. I left them and again climbed on the ridge, where I turned to look back at where I had been standing. At first, nothing; and then, almost exactly where I had been, I saw the sands shake. They lay still again. But I had not imagined it. At various places now over the plain of sands that lay on the left of the ridge I saw smudges of sand hanging. To the right of the ridge I had not yet looked, not daring to take my eyes away from the place I had been in, for it seemed essential to watch, as if something might pounce out like an animal, if I once removed my gaze. There was no reason in it, but I had to stand fixed there, staring . . . the place where the sands had moved, quaked again. They moved, definitely, and stopped. As if an enormous invisible stick had given half a stir . . . the soft whistling filled my ears and I could hear nothing else. I waited. An area I could span with my arms stretched wide was stirred again by the invisible stick: there was the slow, halting movement of a whirlpool, which stopped. Half a mile ahead I believed I could see a spinning underneath one of the air smudges. But I kept my eyes on the birth—for now I knew that this was what I was watching—of the sand whirlpool near to me. Slowly, creakingly, with halts, and new beginnings, the vortex formed, and then at various distances around it, the sand shivered, and lay still, and began again. . . . Then the central place was in a slow regular spin, and grains of sand flung up and off to one side glittered as they fell. So the sun was up, was it? I looked, and saw all the sky in front a wild enraged red, shedding a ruddy glow down on to the gleam of the sands.

The whirlpool was now established, and steadily encompassing more and more of the sands around it, and the places near it where I had noted small movements, each were beginning to circle and subside, then start again as the new subsidiary pools formed. I saw that all the plain was covered with these spots of movement, and the air above them each showed a small cloud that hung there, enlarging but not drifting, because of the lack of wind. And now, with difficulty, I made myself look away from this dreadfully treacherous plain, and I gazed out to my right. Desert again, stretching interminably, and I could see no movement here. The wastes lay quiet and still, inflamed by the wild scarlet of the skies, but then a desert fox came towards me, its soft yellow all aglow, and it trotted into the ridge of rocks and disappeared. Another came. Suddenly I saw that there were many animals in flight from some danger behind them. Far behind them: for I could see no movement in the sands on this side of the ridge, though on the other side all the plain was shaking and quivering between the whirlpools of sand. Far over this solid and ordinary plain, I could see that the sky, now fully light in a clear morning where the reds and pinks rapidly faded, was hung with a low haze, which I now understood.

I had taken in what was happening, was going to happen, and I ran clumsily forward along the rocky ridge, which I believed, or hoped, would not succumb to the movement of the sands, was solidly rooted.

I was looking for refugees from these terrible whirlpools who might have climbed to the safety of the rocks, but believed they were more likely to be on the mountains that still seemed to be such a distance from me. And then I did see a party of five approach, a woman, a man, and two half-grown children, and these were dazed and silly with the dangers they had survived, and could not see me. They were accompanied by someone whose face I knew from the lines at the frontier, and I stopped her and asked what was happening. "Be quick," she said, "there are still people on the sands. But you must be quick"— and she went on along the ridge, calling to her charges to hurry. They were standing with their mouths hanging open, eyes fixed on the shivering and swirling sands of the plain to my left, their right, and seemed unable to hear her. She had to hustle them on, pushing them into movement. Again I ran onwards, clumsily, scrambling and falling over the rocks, and several times passed little groups, each shepherded by a person from the lines. The rescued ones shook and trembled, and stared at the liquid-seeming desert, and had to be continually reminded to move on, and to keep their eyes in front of them.

When at last I reached the beginnings of the mountain peaks, which rose straight up out of the sands, it was not too soon, for I had seen that if the great sands on my right were to dissolve into movement as they had on the other side, the ridge could not stand for long, but must be engulfed. I turned to look back from the mountain and saw that on the one side of the ridge there were no unmoving places left: all that desert was shivering, swirling, dissolving. On the other side, still, things seemed safe, yet, looking over those reaches of sands as far as I could, it was possible to see crowds of hopping, running, flying animals and birds. None looked back, none was panicky or stricken or had lost their senses, but purposefully and carefully picked their way through the dunes and hollows of the sands to the ridge, where they must all be working their way back through the rocks to the plateau I had come from. But from a certain point on that plain of sand, there was no movement of animals at all: I was seeing the last exodus of the refugees, and behind them the sands lay quiet. On the horizons, the dust clouds had risen higher into the cobalt blue of the morning sky.

I was not certain what I should do next. I had not met groups of refugees for some time now. Perhaps everyone had been rescued, there were none left? I went forward up the stony, cracked sides of the mountain, towards the right, and when I reached a small outcrop of young, harsh cracked rocks and dry bushes, I was able to see straight down into the plain where, ahead, suddenly, there were the beginnings of movement, the birth of sand whirlpools. And, at the same time, I saw down there a little bunching of black rocks, and on them two people. They had their backs to me, and they stood staring away across the plain. I seemed to know them. I ran down again towards them, with many thoughts in my mind. One, that a symptom of the shock suffered by these victims was that they were stricken into a condition where they could do nothing but stare, hypnotised, unable to move. Another, that I *could* get to them in time, but whether I could lead them out again was another matter . . . and I was thinking, too, that these were my old friend Ben and my old friend Rilla, together, and at least safe, if marooned.

As I reached the plain of the desert and ran forward I could feel the sands trembling under me. I staggered on, shouting and calling to them, but they did not hear me, or if they did, could not move. When I came up to their little outcrop, a whirlpool had formed not far away, and I jumped up onto the rock they stood on, and shouted, Rilla! Ben! They stood shivering like dogs that have got wet and cold and did not look at me, but stared at the liquefying whirling desert. I shouted, and then they turned vague eyes on me but could not recognise me. I grabbed them and shook them, and they did not resist. I slapped their cheeks and shouted, and their eyes, turned towards me, seemed to have in them the shadow of an indignant, What are you doing that for? But already they had turned to stare, transfixed.

I climbed around so that I stood immediately in front of them. "This is Johor," I said, "Johor, your friend." Ben seemed to come slightly to himself, but already he was trying to peer around me, so as to watch the sand. Rilla, it seemed, had not seen me. I took out the Signature and held it up in front of their staring eyes. Both sets of eyes followed the Signature as I stepped downwards, and they followed. They followed!—but like sleepwalkers. Holding up the Signature and walking backwards in front of them, I reached the desert floor, which was quivering everywhere now, with a singing hiss of sound, and I shouted, "Now follow me! Follow me!" continuously moving the Signature so that it flashed and gleamed. I walked as fast I could, first backwards, and then, because I could see the terrible danger we were in, with the beginnings of vortexes everywhere around us, I turned myself half sideways and so led them forward. They stumbled and they fell, and seemed all the time drawn by a need to look back, but I pulled them forward with the power of the Signature, and at last we stood on the firm slopes of the mountain. There they at once turned and stood staring, clutching each other. And I stood with them, for I was affected, too, by that hypnotising dreadfulness. Where we had come stumbling to safety was already now all movement and shifting sub-sidence: as far as we could see, the golden sands were moving. And we stood there, we stood there, for I was lost as they, and we were staring at a vast whirlpool, all the plain had become one swirling centrifuge, spinning, spinning, with its centre deep, and deeper and then out of sight. Some appalling necessity was dragging and sucking at this place, feeding on the energies, the released powers, and I could not pull my eyes away, it seemed as if my eyes themselves were being sucked out, my mind was going away, draining into the spin—and then from the sky swooped down a black screaming eagle, and it was warning us: Go . . o . . o . . . Go . . o . . o . . . Go . . o . . o . . . and the clattering rush of its wings above my head brought me back into myself. I had even dropped the Signature, and I had to scramble and search for it, and there was its gleam under some rocks. I had to shake and slap and wake Ben and Rilla, and again move the Signature back and forth in front of their eyes to charm them away from their contemplation of the sands. Above, the eagle that had saved us swung in a wide circle peering to see if we were indeed safely awake, and then, when it knew we were watching, turned its glide so that it was off towards the east, where the ground climbed from the level of the sands, up into scrub-land, grasses, low rocks, safe from the deadly plain which it was essential for us to get away from as soon as we could. Ben and Rilla were passive, almost imbecile, as I shepherded them on, the eagle showing the way. I did not try to talk to them, only wondered what to do, for we were walking in the opposite direction from the borders of Zone Six with Shikasta, which was where we all had to go. But I followed the eagle, I had to. If he had known enough to rescue me from my trance, then I must trust him . . . and after hours of stumbling heavy walk, beside my two dazed companions, the great bird screamed to attract my attention, and swung away leftwards in a deep and wide arc, and I knew that that was where we must make our way. And we travelled on all that day, until evening, trusting in the bird, for I did not know where we were. Rilla and Ben were talking a little now, but only clumsy half-phrases and random words. At night we found a sheltered place, and I made them sit quietly beside me and rest. They slept at last, and I got up and climbed to a high place where I could look back over the scrub of the plateau to the desert. Under the starlight I saw a single great vortex, which filled the whole expanse: the spine of the rocky ridge had been sucked down and had gone entirely. Nothing remained but the horizons-wide swirl, and the sound of it now was a roar, which made the earth I stood on shake. I crept back again through the dark to my friends and sat by them until the dawn, when the eagle, which was sitting on a high peak of rock, screamed a greeting to me. There was an urgency in it, and I knew we must move on. I roused Ben and Rilla, and all that day we followed the bird, through the higher lands that surrounded the sand plains, which we were working our way around. We could not see them, but we could hear, always, the roaring of the enraged and compelled earth. Towards evening I recognised where we were. And now I was thinking that I was late with my tasks on Shikasta, and that it was most urgent and necessary for me to get back to them. But I could not trust Ben and Rilla yet, to be alone. As they walked they kept turning their heads to listen to that distant roaring like a sea that keeps crashing itself again and again on shores that shake and tremble, and I knew that left alone they would drift back to the sands. I could not leave them the Signature: they were not reliable. After all, I had nearly lost it, and compared to them, my senses had been my own. I called up to the eagle that I needed its help, and as it circled above us, asked it to shepherd Ben and Rilla onwards. I held the Signature in front of them again, and said that the bird was the servant of the Signature, and they must do exactly what it told them. I said I would see them again on the borders of Shikasta, and they must not give up. Thus exhorting and pleading, I impressed on them everything I could, and then went on by myself alone, fast. I looked back later and saw them stumbling slowly forward, their eyes raised to the glide and the swerve and the balance of the eagle, who moved on, on, on, in front.

I found Ranee with a group she had saved from the whirlpools not far from the frontier. I asked if I might travel with her, so that I could make contact as I had to, and she agreed. So I went on with her. Her charges were as stunned, as lost to their selves, as poor Ben and Rilla. But they did seem slowly to improve, while Ranee talked to them in a low steady compelling voice, as a mother talks a child up out of a nightmare, soothing, and explaining.

Re: Colonised Planet 5, Shikasta

Her type and situation were endemic on Shikasta, repeating themselves over and over again, and this had been so ever since inequalities of
position, and expectation, first appeared. Because females were at risk,
needed help during the time their offspring were small (I repeat
obvious facts, since basic facts tend always to be those most easily
overlooked), because of this dependency of women, they have at all
times found themselves in positions where they had no alternative but
to become a servant.

A noble word.

A noble condition.

In Shikasta a race dominant in one epoch may be subservient in the
next. A race or people in a condition of slavery in one time or place
may within a few decades become master of others. The roles of the
females have adjusted accordingly, and whenever a people, a country,
a race, is *down*, then its females, doubly burdened, will be used as
servants in the homes of the dominating ones.

Such a female, often to the detriment of her own children, whom
she may even have to abandon, may be the prop, the stay, the support,
the nourishment of an entire family, and perhaps for all of her life.
For her *working* life, for such a servant may be turned out in old age
without any more than what she came with. Yet she may have been
the bond that held the family together.

An unregarded if not despised person, someone at least considered
inferior, and thought of not so much as an individual as a role—a
servant: but this female in fact being the centre of a family, its point
of balance—it is a situation that has been re-created over and over
again, in every time, every culture, every place. . . .

The example of it that was my concern occurred in an island at the
extreme west of the Northwest fringes. It had been, for centuries, a
poor place, much exploited by other countries.

A family priding itself on its "blood," but without much money,
employed a poor girl from the village. Because of economic conditions,
marriage was never easy on the island, but the reason this girl did not
marry, never even considered it, was that she was emotionally absorbed
into the needs of this family by the time she was fifteen. She cleaned
the house—a large one—did the cooking, and looked after the children
as they were born. She worked as hard as any slave ever did, and

accepted low wages, because she knew the family was not rich, and because she had never been taught to expect much—and because she loved them. She would spend a month's wages on a toy for a child or a dress for a loved little girl.

Several times mother and father quarrelled, and separated: then she looked after the children, held things together until the parents were united again.

The children, five of them, grew up while she grew old. They left home and the island for other countries. The two now old parents were in a large house, increasingly rickety, alone, with nothing in common but memories of having had a family. They decided to emigrate. One evening they told their servant, who had now been working for them for fifty years, that her services were no longer needed.

They took off, leaving her to clean and lock up the house, which was to be sold, and walk back to the village where she now had no tie but a widowed sister, who grumblingly offered her a home. The servant had nothing at all, only her clothes, and these were mostly cast-offs given her by the family.

It took months for her to understand what had happened to her. She had never seen herself as exploited, as badly treated. She had loved the family, collectively and as individuals, and their lives had been her life. They had not loved her, but she believed they had, "in their way." She had often thought them careless, thoughtless: but they had charmed her, delighted her! A kiss from one of the little girls, a smile from "the lady" and "I don't know what we would do without you!"— this had seemed enough.

She was numbed, low in spirits, and subject to crying fits "for no blessed reason I can see."

The sister gossiped indignantly about the treatment of her sister. A young woman in the village who had aspirations to journalism wrote up the story, and it appeared in a local newspaper, and was later reprinted in a big newspaper on the neighbouring island.

The servant was brought even lower by these events. She dreaded that the family might think her ungrateful.

She received a reproachful letter from the parents, now on an island where it was sunny, and where because of economic conditions, servants were plentiful. Her distress became known in the village. The same young woman who had written the article, and who saw a possibility that her promising career might be halted, discussed the matter with a lawyer. The sister, hearing of this, went to her own lawyer: the island was famed for its litigiousness, like all areas that have been kept poor and exploited by others.

The servant found herself being snarled and growled and wrangled over, while she remained passive, not knowing what had happened or how.

She wrote an incoherent letter to her former employers, full of phrases like "I didn't know anything about it!" "They did it without telling me."

Now they took advice from a lawyer. This ought to have been Taufiq, for, properly handled, the case would have exposed a good many areas of exploitation. He would have pointed out, for instance, that this situation, the woman working for any number of years in the most intimate service of a family, only to be dismissed with as little consideration as would be given to an animal, and less, in some cases, was at that time prevalent—and he would have been able to cite a dozen countries, bringing witnesses of several races and cultures.

A case did take place, but it was of the kind that onlookers find distasteful, embarrassing, a conflict of self-interest and dishonesties, with no real focus or point to it.

My responsibility did not go further than the servant herself: an old friend, though of course she did not know it, and two of the sisters, who were remorseful over what had happened. They had never thought of the old servant, except in sentimental terms, since they had left home, but the newspaper article and emotionally self-pitying letters from their parents made them think again. Both were open to better influences, which I supplied, and arranged their future accordingly.

As for the servant, her distress was acute. She felt in the wrong, and wronged. Her life with her sister was doing neither of them any good; she soon died.

I put her in the care of Ranee, in Zone Six, for she was already game for re-entry into Shikasta for "another try."

While engaged in these tasks, I was more and more concerned with the problems of reporting adequately: having so recently been tutor to individuals who had volunteered for service on Shikasta during its last and terrible phase, I was able to contrast their expectations and imaginings of Shikasta with the reality. *Facts* are easily written down: atmospheres and the emanations of certain mental sets are not. I knew that my notes and reports were being read by minds very far indeed from the Shikastan situation. I therefore devised certain additional material, to supplement my reports.

ILLUSTRATIONS: The Shikastan Situation

[On his return from Shikasta Johor offered the records some sketches and notes made in excess of his mandate. He believed that, as is recorded above, students of this unfortunate planet would find it helpful to have illustrations of the extremes of conduct produced by such a low concentration of SOWF. Emissary Johor tended almost to apologise for these sketches, which he admitted he had written, sometimes, for his own use, to clarify his mind, as well as to assist others. For our part, we have to point out—and we do this with Emissary Johor's full permission—that Johor had been within the Shikastan influences for some time when these sketches were made, and these are influences which conduce to emotionalism. *Archivists.*]

In the extreme western island of the Northwest fringes (mentioned already in the case of Individual Eight), which, as has been said, suffered every kind of conquest, settlement, and invasion, and this over many centuries and by many different peoples, a period of poverty intensified to starvation devastated the economy, forced millions into emigration, and intensified deprivation of every sort. A certain youth found himself without work or resources. Except for one. He had been bred in a slum, but grandparents still on the land had kept milk and potatoes supplied to the family, and he had grown tall, broad, and strong. And stupid. He did not have the wits to emigrate and make a new life for himself. Because of his physique he was recruited into the army of the latest conquerors of the island, given a showy uniform, regular meals, and the prospects of travel. This army, like all those of the Northwest fringes, was much stratified and officered by the class-proud and arrogant, and he was at the bottom of it, with no hope of ever being treated any better than the ruling caste's domestic animals. For twenty years he was sent from one area of Shikasta to another, all parts of a (very short-lived) empire which was soon to crumble but was then at its zenith. The function of this victim was to police a multitude of victims. From the extreme east of the central landmass to the north of Southern Continent I, the poor wretch was set to lord it over peoples belonging to civilisations and cultures older, more complex, more tolerant, and usually more humane, than his own. He was permanently half-drunk: he had drunk too much from childhood, to forget the brutalities of his existence. He had a reddened, usually perspiring face, and a wooden look that expressed his determination never to think for himself: vestigial attempts in this direction had been at once punished, all his life. Sometimes an officer would write to his family on his dictation, and these letters would always include the words: "Here you have only to stick your foot out and the blacks clean your boots for you."

In every country he found himself—and he never knew more about them than their names before he got there—he took every occasion to seat himself in a chair in a public place, with first one foot thrust out, then another, a fatuous, proud, and condescending smile on his face, while some man made shadowy by poverty crouched before him, cleaning his black boots.

He would swagger around the policed areas of cities with a comrade, two gigantic men sometimes almost twice the size of the local people, in scarlet uniforms, braid and medals everywhere, and in one country after another this red face and fatuous smile, the shouted orders and abuse, the contempt and dislike written on the face of the barbarian, became a symbol of everything that was brutal, ignorant, tyrannical. To them he symbolised empire. And when the empire crumbled, partly because of the extreme dislike the conquered felt for their conquerors, this red-faced ox would remain an image in millions of minds—to be recalled with hatred, and with fear.

As for him, the climates of these territories where he had eaten and drunk too much for twenty years finally gave him a stroke when he was still in his middle years. He was sent home to an island where the poverty was worse than when he had left, and which was simmering with revolt and civil war. He decided to settle in the land of his own land's conquerors, and worked as a porter in a meat market. He married a countrywoman, who had been a children's nurse—eighteen hours a day, six and a half days a week, for her food, a roof, and a pittance. She had never had any prospect of escape but marriage and she was relieved to marry this strong soldier who stood nearly two feet taller than she, swaggering in scarlet, and soon to be pensioned off.

This tiny pension was to her security, a haven; and in fact it did ward off the extremes of poverty, which were exacerbated by his drinking.

There were four children alive from seven born.

The wife and the children would sit in their wretched rooms in the evenings, waiting for him to crash and stumble up the stairs, hoping for the best that could happen, which was that this man would not shout and rage and threaten to hit them, and then weep and sit sobbing himself off to a maudlin sleep; but would be in a good mood, and would sit at the head of the table, master of his household, great legs stretched out, his swollen and scarlet face complacent as he told them: "In them countries I had only to stretch out my foot and those blacks came fighting to clean my boots." And, "We 'ad only to show our faces and them black buggers ran for it."

He died in a paupers' hospital. He sat propped on pillows, his medals pinned to his pyjamas, his great face bursting with apoplexy, his little blue eyes popping from folds of red flesh, and his last words were: "We 'ad only to show our faces and them black beggars ran for their lives."

ILLUSTRATIONS: The Shikastan Situation

This particular incident took place in the southern part of Southern Continent I, but it was repeated in a thousand ways during the time the Northwest fringes used an advanced technology to conquer other parts of Shikasta so as to rob them of materials, labour, land. This particular geographical area was well favoured, being high, well watered and wooded, with a healthy dry climate. The soil was fertile. It supported a wide variety of animals. And it was lightly populated by a tribe with a particularly agreeable nature, being peace-loving, good-humoured, laughter-loving, natural storytellers, and skilled in the crafts. All the inhabitants of Southern Continent I were embedded in music: singing, dancing, the making and the use of innumerable musical instruments were the ground of their natures. They lived in balance with their surroundings, taking no more than they were able to put back. Their "religion" was an expression of this oneness with the land they lived in, medicine was an extension and an expression of their religion, and their wise men and women knew how to cure the sicknesses of the mind. This admirable state of affairs had not been long-lived: all Southern Continent I had been raided for slaves over centuries by other peoples, but the traffic had recently been stopped, and there had been a period without invaders from outside, or wars among themselves.

These people had heard tales from the south about the white people, who conquered and made slaves, who stole land: there had been explorers and travellers of various kinds, some of them "religious." The wise men and women, seers and warners, had said that this part too would be visited by white people, and that they would have to fight for their existence. But the temperament of these tribes did not make for anxiety and foreboding.

One day appeared a long column of white people, on horses or in carts. The watching black people were amazed, because of the bizarre appearance of these invaders. Also because of the horses. Someone laughed. Soon they could not stop themselves laughing. Everything struck them as comical. First, their colour, so pallid, and unhealthy. Then their clothes: they themselves wore very little, since the blessed climate made this possible. But the intruders were loaded with bunches and protuberances and excrescences of every sort, and they had extraordinary objects on their heads. Then, their stiff solemnity, their awkwardness. *They could not move.* Never before had the watchers had to think of their own accomplishments, but now they looked at each other and themselves and saw how well they stood, walked, sat, and how they danced. The changing pulses of the landscape they were part of fed their own flow of movement, but these newcomers they were examining with such incredulous laughter were unable to stretch out an arm or take a step, were as clumsy as if they had been cursed. And then, their impedimenta: What sort of people were these who could not travel without enough baggage to load down so many waggons, drawn by so many oxen? Why did they need it? What did they do with it all?

They wondered, they marvelled, and at evening they saw these sticks of people, so encumbered with their clothes, standing stiffly upright, their arms down by their sides, and emitting sounds . . . but what sounds could these be? There was no music in it, no rhythm, it was like the howling of hyenas.

But. There were the horses. These people did not know horses except by rumour. The variety of "deer" used to pull the waggons intrigued them, and the way they were ridden made them wish to do the same. And there were guns, which could kill at a distance. First they laughed, then admired; and only later were they afraid.

When emissaries from the invading column came to ask for the use of their land, permission was readily given. The concept of ownership of land was unknown to them: land belonged to itself, was the substance of the people and animals who lived on it, was saturated by the Great Spirit who was the source of all life.

And within a couple of years, they found their traditional lands and hunting grounds gone from them, and themselves being chased away, like animals. But above all, they were treated with a coldness and contempt which they did not understand, had no experience of, and which shrivelled the spirits of these amiable and warmhearted people. They had as little defence against this withering thing as "primitive" peoples in other parts of the world had against the diseases the white people brought with them.

Their wise men and women did not agree about what course was to be taken, or even about the probable outcome. That they had to fight for what had been stolen from them was clear. It was as if the invasion of these aliens had stunned the natural feelings of the natives, stopped their instincts and intuitions. How should they fight? When? Where? Above all, *why?*—when the country was so large and there was so much room in it. But the invaders seemed to be everywhere, already.

The subjected ones, seeing that they would shortly have nothing left, rose in rebellion. The intruders, using the technology of their foreign culture, suppressed the rebellion with extremes of cruelty and ruthlessness.

It is necessary to describe the cold distaste and dislike felt by the whites for the blacks, which remained their characteristic until the time came—shortly, but not until the culture they dominated was smashed, in ruins—for them to be thrown out again. Nothing is more astonishing than this characteristic, contemptuous dislike, described again and again by the conquered, and by many, too, of the conquerors, for not all the whites despised the blacks, some liked and admired them, though these were thought of as traitors by their own people.

We may perhaps find illumination in the work of one of Shikasta's own experts. (Marcel Proust, sociologist and anthropologist.) A servant of a rich family is ordered to prepare a fowl for the evening meal. She is chasing this fowl around a courtyard, muttering Filthy Beast, Disgusting Animal, and similar imprecations, while she catches the bird and kills it.

So, too, a torturer new to his job, who has to inflict pain and humiliation on some person he knows nothing of save that this is the enemy: there in front of him or her stands, or lies, or sits a puzzled frightened creature, just like himself, but there is a remedy: the torturer will work himself up to the task by calling the victim all the frightful things his tongue can come by. Soon this individual exactly like himself is a disgusting beast, a filthy animal, and the work can begin. One might describe this process as a tax exacted by fellow-feeling (SOWF) on natures not yet entirely brutalised.

And thus with the conquerors of a country, who will persuade themselves that these people whose land they are in the process of stealing from them are dirty, primitive, cruel, communists, fascists, capitalists, nigger lovers, white trash, or anything else that comes to mind.

Thus it is that seldom in Shikastan history has any race or people conquered a pleasant civilised and amiable race of people quite competent to manage their own lives.

The white people who overran Southern Continent I, using every kind of trickery, lie, brutality, barbarity, cruelty, and greed to grab everything in sight, could never speak to a black person without a cold cutting edge of contempt, due to him or her as a backward and unenlightened person.

Their religion reinforced their disabilities. Of all the major religions the most self-righteous, the most inflexible, the least capable of self-examination, this religion of the Northwest fringes, imposed often by force on peoples in perfect rapport with themselves and their beliefs as children of the Great Spirit, was officered by individuals incapable of doubt as to their own capacities and rights. To add to the confusion and damage they caused, some were often of great bravery and dedication, with the utmost probity, and capacity—not to say thirst—for self-sacrifice. That they, too, were *victims*, of a religion as bigoted as Shikasta has ever seen, does not aid the chronicler of these events.

But whatever the reasons, whatever the motives, whatever the excuses and the rationalisations, the dominating characteristic of these conquerors was their armour of righteousness, their conviction that they were in the right. Because of their empire. Because of their religion.

Thirty years after this particular geographical area was subjugated, this was the scene: land that had been the home of people whose living on it had left no mark, no signs of depredation, had been parcelled out among white farmers there on favourable terms for the specific purpose of keeping it out of the hands of the blacks, who had been moved, by gun and by whip, into special reservations of the poorest land, from which they were forbidden to move unless to seek work. Great farms of many thousands of acres were in the hands of single families, and were already largely denuded of trees often cut for mine furnaces, were scarred by mine workings and prospectings, threatened by erosion, swept continually by fires.

On each farm were "compounds" of black farm workers, forced out to work by the imposition of taxes. The black people could be only labourers and servants.

Their masters represented extremes from their own countries in the

Northwest fringes. They might be the most enterprising, who needed more scope for energy and talent than an increasingly overpopulated area allowed them. They might be criminals hoping to escape notice, or people with criminal tendencies knowing that there would be room for these here. They might be too stupid or disabled to compete among their own kind. All these people, good or bad, competent or not, lived at a level higher than they could possibly have done in their countries of origin, and many became extremely wealthy.

Let us eavesdrop on a moment of peculiar clarity among the subjected.

The place is a white farm, and the black compound on that farm. This is a haphazard collection of mud huts thatched with straw, leaking, tumbledown, squalid: a pathetic version of the villages used by these peoples in their natural state.

A big fire burns in the centre of this compound, as burns always in the villages, but there are subsidiary fires as well, and not only for the purposes of cooking: it is not one tribe here, but several, for workers have come from over a wide area containing many tribes. A dozen languages are being spoken, and this compound, based on the village whose nature it is to hold people together in a whole, is riven into factions, sometimes hostile. By one of the subsidiary fires a group of young men crouch, listening to an older man, who before the white man's coming was a chief. A young man on the edge of this group softly taps a drum. Other drums sound from other parts of the compound. From the bush all about come the sounds of insects and sometimes animals, but the process is already well advanced that will shortly clear the area of its stock of natural animals and birds: species are becoming extinct.

There was a fight this afternoon among two young men of different tribes. Its cause was frustration.

The white farmer had then lectured the two on their warlike spirit, their primitive ways. It was backward and primitive to fight, he had said. The white people were here to save the unfortunately backward blacks from this belligerence, by their civilised and civilising example.

The older man was sitting upright, the firelight moving on his face, which was showing relish and enjoyment. He was entertaining them: his family had been the traditional storytellers of his subtribe. The younger men, listening, were laughing.

The older man was surveying the white culture from below, the sharp slave's-eye view.

He was enumerating the white farms and the white men who owned them.

This was about five years after the end of World War I, which had been presented to these black people as one fought to preserve the decencies of civilisation. There were half a dozen farmers in the area who had fought on the other side in that war, who also presented their part in it as a defence of the fundamental decencies.

"On the farm across the ridge, the man with one arm . . ."

"Yes, yes, that is so, he has only one arm."

"And on the farm across the river, the man with one leg . . ."

"Yes, only one leg, one leg."

"And on the road into the station, the man who has a metal plate to hold his intestines in."

"Yes, what a thing, that a man must keep in his intestines with a piece of iron."

"And on the farm where they are mining for gold, the man who has a metal piece in his skull."

"Ah, yes, it is true, his brains would spill everywhere without it."

"And on the farm where the two rivers meet, the farmer has only one eye."

"True, true, only one eye."

"And on the farm here, this farm, which is not our land, but his land, the farmer also has only one leg."

"Ah, ah, a terrible thing, so many of them, and all wounded."

"And on the farm . . ."

Special benefits had been offered to ex-soldiers who would emigrate and take over this land. And so it was that to the eyes of the black people, the white people were an army of cripples. Like an army of locusts, who, after a few hours on the ground, show themselves legless, wingless, dozens of them, unable to take off again, when the main armies leave. Locusts, eating everything, covering everything, swarming everywhere . . .

"The locusts have eaten our food . . ."

"Aie, aie, they have eaten our food."

"The locusts blacken our fields."

"They blacken our fields with their eating mouths."

"The armies of the locusts come, they come, they come from the north, and our lives are eaten to the ground . . ."

As a chant popular in the compounds had it.

And again and again during that evening, these people dissolved into fits of laughter, putting together the white cripples of the area, the solemn lecture by the crippled farmer, and the picture of their two healthy young men, fighting briefly in the dust. They laughed and they laughed, staggering with laughter, rolling with laughter, howling with laughter . . .

Meanwhile, on that same evening, up on the hill where the farmer's house was, the man with only one leg was preparing to go to bed. His leg had been cut off halfway up the thigh. He was alive at all only because of this wound: his entire company had been wiped out in a great battle two weeks after he had suffered the good fortune of having his leg crushed because a shell burst near him. Of course he had often wondered if he might not have done better to die with his company. He had been extremely ill, and had nearly lost his reason. Previously he had been a man who lived in his body, danced, played football and cricket, gone shooting with the local farmers, walked, and ridden. This active man had had to face life with one leg. He managed well. When he got up in the morning, he tightened his mouth to an expression familiar to his family, one of patient determination. He manoeuvred himself to the edge of the bed, lifted the stump into the air, and fitted over it one, two, up to ten stump socks, according to the amount of weight he was carrying. He fitted the heavy wood and metal bucket over his stump, and pulled himself up by the edge of a table. Standing, he buckled the straps around his waist and over his shoulder.

His day could begin. He walked. He rode. He went down mine shafts. He sat up through nights to watch the temperature in tobacco barns. He stumped around fields, along drains, contour ridges, balanced and staggered his way across fields tumbling with great newly ploughed clods. He gave out rations, standing for hours by the sacks and bins of grains.

He was a man fighting poverty. The way he saw it.

At night, he dragged the metal and wood limb off him and collapsed back into bed, shutting his eyes, breathing deeply. "My God," he would mutter. "My God, well, that's done, for today."

And he would drift off to sleep, listening to the drums from the compound.

"They are dancing down there, I expect," he was thinking. "Dancing. They dance at the drop of a hat. Got a gift. Music. A gift. Threshing beans today, they make a dance of it, they dance their work, and they make up a song to go with it."

Re: Colonised Planet 5, Shikasta

ILLUSTRATIONS: The Shikastan Situation

[This Report by Johor seems to us a useful addition to the Illustrations. *Archivists*.]

Some areas of the Northwest fringes are still comparatively un-affected by technology, and there people live (as I transmit this) not very differently from the way they have done for centuries. A village in an area of extreme poverty has been set apart from others because every year there is held the Festival of the Child. This has always attracted local visitors, and during this era of tourism, tourists. The village has never had an inn for visitors, who put up in the homes of relatives, but now there is a government-maintained camping place, and mobile shops arrive for the period of the festival. A town not far away expects to benefit at this time, and makes provision of all kinds.

The Church is the centre of the occasion, but all the village is decorated: shops, the bar, the central square. And also the homes of the villagers, who have never relinquished their own rights in the matter.

Since the last report by Agent 9, there is a new development. On the night before the main event there are fireworks and dancing in the square and the streets leading away from the square. The tourists are always in time for this—to them—most interesting part of the festival, contrasting sharply, in their good clothes and the avidity that is their mark, with the local people, who observe their rich guests with good humour not unmixed with irony.

This night of dancing and drinking is conducted by the secular authorities but the priests keep it within their grasp by appearing at sundown on the steps of the church, with emitters of sweet smoke, and songs of a solemn kind. Nearly everyone is up all night, dancing and singing, but at the first sign of daylight, they are supposed to be in their places in the church, in abasement and in fawning postures, to be threatened and admonished by the priests.

The church "services" continue all morning, the people taking each other's place in batches, for the building is too small to hold them all at once.

Exactly at midday a troupe of priests, all decked out in every variety of finery and ornament, unlocks a door at the back of the church and brings out the Child. This is a gaudy statue without pretensions to realism, with staring eyes, highly coloured hair and skin, and smothered in laces and stuffs of all kinds. This figure is placed in a small litter covered with flowers and greenery and carried out of the building by a team of children chosen by the priests. It is carried three times around the square (which is no more than a small dusty space that has a few trees around it) by the children who are dressed no less fancifully than the image, while they, the villagers and the priests, chant and sing. The statue is put on an elevated place in the porch of the church, guarded by priests, and the singing continues all afternoon until sunset.

Meanwhile, all the children of the village, including the bearers of the litter, are lined up by their parents under the orders of the priests, and are hustled forward two by two past the statue while the priests "bless" them. When this is over they are rewarded by a feast of cakes and sweet drinks as fine as the poor village can provide.

While even a few years ago this festival was entirely for the children, the economic pressure of the tourists has operated so that there are entertainments and food and drink for the adults as well. This year, for the first time, there were television cameras, and because of this, everything was more elaborate than usual. When the statue has been taken in and put away into its cupboard, dancing begins again, and continues until midnight.

This is a pleasant enough festival, and offers much needed relief to people whose lives are hard indeed.

It has not become much more elaborate since the report of Emissary 76, four hundred years ago. But we must expect that while tourism lasts, every year will show new feats of imagination.

There is no use left in this festival from our point of view.

I could not prevent myself wondering as I observed these lively (but well-policed) scenes, what would happen if I were able to stand forward and relate the real origins of the festival.

"Over a thousand years ago, a visitor came to this village. The Northwest fringes were backward, regarded as savage by other, more developed areas—such as those on the far side of the great inland sea you call the Mediterranean. These advanced cultures often sent people northwards, in various disguises, to wander from place to place in order to impart techniques and ideas that could lighten the appalling conditions. This particular visitor came with three young pupils, who were learning from him the art of bringing more advanced ideas to backward areas. Arriving at this bitterly poor place, they discovered that there were no softer influences here at all, nothing for miles around, except for some monks who lived sequestered from the lowly concerns of the villagers.

"The atmosphere of the village was appropriate, and the villagers ready to listen to tales about civilisation whose whereabouts they could not really understand, since they knew as little of geography as they did of their own origins—and future.

"The visitors stayed unobtrusively in the village for many weeks. They imparted information of a practical kind, about cleanliness, the usefulness of bathing in avoiding illness, the necessity of clean water supplies, the care of the sick, elements of medicine, all things these poor people knew very little of. When a few of the more intelligent had taken in enough to be able to pass it on, there came information on crafts like distilling, dyeing, the preservation of foodstuffs for famines and hard times, and certain techniques of husbandry and agriculture that were new to them.

"And then these visitors began to tell the villagers, in simple terms, sometimes in the form of tales, stories, songs, a little of their history, and what this meant for them—what they really were and could become.

"These people whose struggle to feed themselves, to keep themselves clothed and housed, was as much as they could sustain, heard the news without resistance, and this was already a great deal, for people whose lives are so close to an edge may very often simply refuse to listen: even good news, a message of hope, may be too much for them to bear.

"In the evenings as the light went and the villagers came back from their work in the fields to eat and rest, our visitors would sit in this place, the square—which was very like what it is now—and they talked, and told stories and sang.

"There would be smoke rising from the huts and houses. Children played in the dust. Ribby and ravening dogs scratched or scuffled. Skinny donkeys stood about.

"The villagers sat quietly in the half-dark. Women held their infants in their arms.

"A woman was sitting on a stone, rocking a child and humming to it.

"The older man asked if they might take the baby from her for a short while, and she assented. He sat with the baby on his knee. It was drowsy and blinking, and he hushed his voice so that it might not be roused, and all the villagers had to lean forward to listen. He asked them to regard this child, which was one they all knew, was not set apart in any way from others, a child like any other, whose life would be like everyone's here, no different in any way, just as his children's would be, and his children's children. . . .

"At which the woman leaned forward to say apologetically that this child was a girl.

"But this child, went on the visitor, was not what she seemed—no, it did not matter in the least if she was a girl, for a girl was as good as her brother. . . . Ignoring the slight restlessness that occurred at this point, he went on. This child, girl or boy, was not what she seemed. No, what mattered was that she—or he—was the equal of anybody in the village, or in the villages around about, or even in the big town (which few of them had visited, though they had heard about it) or in the towns across the seas (which they had heard about, for a boy from the village had become a sailor and returned to tell them amazing and improbable tales which on the whole they thought it safer to disbelieve) or anybody, anywhere at all. They did not know it, but this village, which seemed to them so large, containing their lives and everything they knew, was only a tiny part of a great world. They must multiply this village by as many times as there were wheat grains in that field there, and the great towns by as many times as there were stones on that hillside—the light had almost gone, the moon was rising, and the hillside glimmered with white stones. The villagers were sitting silent, listening, listening . . . by now they trusted these people who had arrived 'like angels' among them, had taught them so many useful things which had already proved themselves. They all felt that amazing and wonderful things were being told to them, but it was all so difficult, so hard to understand. When the next town was the limit of their imaginations, how to believe in many such, and in cities a thousand times larger. . . .

"There were cities in the world . . . cities of people as many as stars in the sky. People like angels, for it must not be thought that these visitors of theirs were in any way remarkable or out of the ordinary.

"The villagers listened, trying hard.

"There were cities in the world where people had all they wanted to eat and more. They had clothes, enough to warm them and keep them dry. Their houses were many times the size of these houses here, in the village. Yes, all this was true. But what mattered was that there was space and time in the lives of these wonderful people to learn all kinds of things, not just cheese-making and how to keep a cow from falling ill of the stagger-disease. No, people had room in their lives to study, to think, to dream. They knew all kinds of extraordinary and true things— yes, true, true, what was being said tonight was true.

"These people were able, for instance, to study the movements of the stars, which were not so far away as might be thought here, in this village, or in other poor villages. No, each star up there was a world, each one, made of substances everyone here knew as well as he, she, knew their hands, or feet, or the hair on their heads. Those stars up there, they were made of earth—like this; and of rock—like this. And of water. And of fire, yes, of fire swirling and turning.

"Next evening, and the next, and the next, our visitors sat, and borrowed a child from the crowd, any child, insisting that it did not matter whose child, or whether a boy or a girl, or what age, and, holding this child before the people, they insisted that this child, if it were to be taken away—no, no, that was not the intention (because the crowd suddenly stirred and muttered), the child was sitting here on this knee, in these arms, just to remind them of something—if this child or any other was taken away and brought up in one of these fabulous cities where people did not have to spend every minute in labour, but had time to learn, to study, then this child would be just the same as those. And if he, or she, were taken off on a visit to—let us say that little star up there? Yes! That one! Or that one!—then . . .

"The people were laughing as they looked up, their mouths falling open as they gazed at the heavens, which on this evening were floury and thick with stars.

"Yes, that one. If this baby sleeping here was taken off to that star there, then he would be a star baby, would become a giant perhaps, who knew? Or grow wings, and feathers—who could tell?

"They laughed. Great shouts of laughter went up. But it was a marvelling and trustful laughter.

"Or become a child who could live in water, or in fire, perhaps!

"And this is the point, you see, this is always the point which they must remember: that every child has the capacity to be everything. A child was a miracle, a wonder! A child held all the history of the human race, that stretched back, back, further than they could imagine. Yes, this one here, little Otilie, she had in the substance of her body and her thoughts everything that had ever happened to every person of mankind. Just as a loaf of bread holds in it all the substance of all the wheat grains that have gone into it, mingled with all the grain of that harvest, and the substance of the field that has grown it, so this child was kneaded together by, and contained, all the harvest of mankind.

"These words and ideas, that were like nothing these people had ever heard or imagined, came into them, evening after evening, and always a child was held up in front of them.

"Remember, remember, that after a long time, not in your time, or your children's, or even your grandchildren's—but it will come, this time—your labours, and your hardships, and the burden of your lives, all will be redeemed, will bear fruit, and the children of this village and of the world will become what they have it in them to be . . . remember this, remember it . . . it will be just as if men came down from that little star there, twinkling away above those dark trees, yes, that one! and suddenly filled this poor village which is so full of hardship and of trouble, with good things and with hope. Remember this child here is not what he seems, is more, is everything, and holds within her, or within him, all the past and all the future— remember it.

"One morning very early a girl came running to the hut, where the four men slept, and knocked hard on the door saying breathlessly that she worked in the monastery as a servant in the kitchen, and the monks had heard of these visitors, and they had sent a messenger to 'the king himself,' and soldiers were coming. Yes, they were on their way. . . .

"When the soldiers came, there were no strangers in the village, they had gone away into the dangerous forests leaving behind them a pattern of stones on the hillside, a necklace around a child's neck, some designs drawn with coloured clays and earth on the walls of the only stone building in the village, which happened to be a storehouse. The villagers said that it was a false rumour, the talk of a foolish girl who wanted to make herself important, for of course it was the girl herself who had talked in the monks' kitchen, and then had become afraid of the results.

"When the soldiers had gone, a band of monks arrived.

"They visited the village perhaps once a year. They despised the villagers, though they were not much better themselves, being almost as poor, and not much less ignorant. This was when men, and women, might crowd together in shelters of various kinds calling themselves monks and nuns, as protection against the brutalities of the time.

"The monks had been instructed by the soldiers in the king's name to make sure undesirable vagrants did not shelter in the villages.

"This the monks impressed on the villagers, and returned to their stone rabbit warrens over the mountain.

"The villagers agreed with everything that was said to them.

"But they were as if stars had come closer and lived in their homes, their lives, and then suddenly disappeared. They kept what had happened close and secret, treasuring the crafts they had been taught, which soon spread among the villages around about—and even more, what had been told them.

"They would take a child up, and hold it, and repeat to each other what they could remember.

"None of the people who had been in the village in those days ever forgot. The children who had been held in the arms of the strangers were pointed out for all their lives. Something truly amazing had happened, and every one of them knew it, and soon the villages nearby knew it, too.

"The children of the children who had been held up before the little crowd in the village square kept a little of that quality in them or about them.

"But now it was not remembered exactly what had been said, or done, and who it was who had come—angels, was it?

"One evening, after a hot, dusty summer's day, when people sat around in their doorways, while the children ran about, the dogs scratched, and some ribby donkeys tried to find fresh grass where they would find none for weeks yet, they were saying: Do you remember?—No, it was not like that—Yes, my mother said—But that was not what—when a man who was the son of one of the baby girls held up before everyone picked up his own son and held him prominently on his knee and said, 'Let us try and remember exactly what was said, and then we will repeat it, and we will do it regularly, so that we will always remember.'

"Every year, this man held up his child before everybody, and they repeated to each other what they remembered, and looked up at the skies, laughing and shaking their heads. 'That star there!' 'No, that star there!' 'People made of fire!' 'Or of feathers!'

"This was kept secret, as many things were kept apart from the monks and the soldiers, but of course the ceremony came to be known. At first the monks forbade it and punished, but this made no difference. Every year, on a certain evening, in one of the homes of the village, a child was chosen, and held up, while they repeated the phrases they had decided must be remembered.

"By now much of this sounded like the envious talk of the poor about the rich anywhere on Shikasta—or anywhere else, for that matter.

" 'I am as good as he, my child is as good as that rich man's, dress me up in her clothes and I'd be a fine lady, too.'

"Then monks and soldiers came and several people were taken away, and were put to death for rebellion, talk against the king, disobedience to the monks.

"The monks then instituted, on orders from above, the Ceremony of the Child, which took place every year, and which they conducted. A small church was built in the village, which previously had had none, and this was afterwards built and rebuilt many times. The Child was the Christ-child, the monks said, but the ceremony never lost its roots in that visit so long ago, for there was still force enough to make the people hold stubbornly to the knowledge that *they*, not the monks, had been blessed, that *they*, not the monks, had been shown the Child. By whom, though? By what? People who came from the stars? No, no, that could not be. People from the moon? What nonsense! But there had been someone, or several, and these had come, and had promised, and been chased away. . . .

"And one day they would come again, and then there would be an end to these burdens and this labour and this terrible hardship which holds us all down in the dust and prevents us from rising. . . .

"And this, good people, and visitors, and priests and tourists, and campers, and people from the neighbouring villages, this was the origin of the festival which you hold every year. This is how it was. And now I shall run for my life. . . ."

[During the course of Johor's transmissions in this phase of his embassy he supplied information of a factual kind not requested by us believing (and he was not without reason) that our Colonial Service does not always appreciate certain local difficulties. The long view of planetary maintenance and development does not need, nor can depend upon, the sympathies, the empathies of the near, the partial, views. Yet to find oneself on Shikasta (two of the Archivists responsible for this note have themselves undergone the Shikastan experience) is to become affiliated with powerful emotions which have to be shed on leaving. We submit this piece, and another, believing that students may find them of use in more ways than one. Archivists.]

ADDITIONAL EXPLANATORY INFORMATION. I.

The Generation Gap: to employ a Shikastan phrase in constant use at this time, and in every context and by every type of "expert."

A phenomenon known in every animal is exaggerated and distorted during these last days of Shikasta. There is always a moment when a female pushes away an overgrown youngster coming to suckle, or a bird tips a fledgling out of the nest. The moment when a child is considered adult has been made into public and private ceremonial in every culture: in that sense "the generation gap" is to be considered an innate sociological fact, and if it is not expressed in ritual, a psychological one.

There have been civilisations on Shikasta that were stable for hundreds, even thousands, of years: stable of course within the limits of the wars, epidemics, natural disasters that are the Shikastan lot. Most of these civilisations were within the time when Shikastans lived much longer than they do now, sometimes ten, twenty times as long, though the life-span has always dwindled, faster or slower. A youngster coming to adult consciousness looked forward to a very long span of life compared with later times. Every youngster knew the moment when he or she had to fight for personal psychological independence, and this might lead to a short period of insecurity, and perhaps some readjustments on the part of the parents. But the norm was for off-spring to live very long adult lives alongside their parents. Childhood was a short preparation for a life. Parents giving birth to their allotted number of one, two, three children were adding to the population of people with whom they expected to enjoy perhaps several hundred years of a special affection.

As the life-span so dramatically and tragically shortened, there remained in what Shikastans call the "race memory" the same expectation as was appropriate for when people lived a thousand years—or even, sometimes, the two thousand or three thousand years of the earlier originating species: the hybrid. Every young person looks forward to an immensely long life. Its end is so far off that very few indeed are capable of *really* believing he or she will die. An individual who will live, if very lucky indeed, eighty years, has in his bones and blood the knowledge that he will live eight hundred. Or perhaps three thousand.

It is this fact, not suspected by Shikastans, who have relegated their former long lives to the region of myth, which is the cause of so many of their psychological maladjustments. But here I am considering only one of these, the effect on the relation between the generations.

It is known among Shikastans that "time" has a different movement for the young and for the old. Subjective appreciation of the passing of "time" is, for the child, very slow, never-ending, almost eternal. A child can scarcely see the end of a day from its beginning, and this is when the gene-memory of previous expectation of life is strongest.

A unit of "time" for a child is, then, different from that of a young adult, and different again from that of a middle-aged person, and an old one. As a generalisation one may say that a Shikastan life at the present has a curve peaking in middle age, in about the fifth decade. Before that an individual will be in the "I will live for a thousand years" dispensation, but after it is as if veils have been torn away, and very quickly indeed each one of them understands that when young they lived in an illusion.

An individual of middle age looks back over half of his life, of his "allotted span," which after such expectations of endlessness seems like a very short, vivid, but slippery dream. And he or she knows by then that all that can be expected is another short, illusive dream. That when he, or she, comes to die—and it will be soon—they will look back on experiences no more substantial than what they wake up from each morning: events and atmospheres exciting or pleasant or horrifying that have slid away and are already half-forgotten.

They look hopefully towards their children, their offspring, their continuance—but these heirs are regarding them with disappointment or worse.

One reason is that the parent is identified with the horrible condition of Shikasta: the previous generation represents the chaos and terror everywhere visible. This is an emotional fact, not an intellectual one, for most young people, asked something like, Surely you don't believe your parents are personally responsible for the Century of Destruction? would reply, Of course not! But this is what is often *felt*: a sullen rebellious dislike of the parents for what *they* have allowed to happen.

Another reason is that the people of Shikasta, being as they are now, at this time, the children of technology, of materialism, have been taught they are entitled to everything, can have everything, *must* have everything. Each young person—I am talking of the generality, not of the rare individual—confronts parents in antagonism because, having been promised everything, he soon understands that this will not happen: and the balk, the disappointment, is felt as a promise that has been broken—and is added to the reproof directed towards the parents.

They do not know what their own history is, as a species, nor what are the real reasons for their condition: they know nothing, understand nothing, but are convinced because of the arrogance of their education that they are the intellectual heirs to all understanding and knowledge. Yet the culture has broken down, and is loathed by the young. They reject it while they grab it, demand it, wring everything they can from it. And because of this loathing, even what is good and wholesome and useful left in traditional values is rejected. So each young person suddenly finds himself facing life as if alone, without rules, or laws, or even information he can trust. How can they possibly believe that anything good can come from the brutal anarchy they see around them? Yet they are equipped to make judgements, and use their minds in certain ways—so they have been taught. They are equipped for self-sufficiency and individual judgement, and they proceed to carve out their emotional territories with the total ruthlessness and self-interest that characterised the Northwest fringes when these animals overran the world grabbing and destroying—but now it is no longer only people from the Northwest fringes, but everyone and everywhere. For in front of them stretches this long life, without an end, without bounds—there will be time to put right mistakes, take different turnings, change wrongs into rights. . . .

And they are watched by the adults who are in despair.

Nothing that the adults can say will be *heard* by these infants wandering in their highly tinted deceiving mists.

Most of the adults, and particularly those of the northern hemisphere, or the affluent classes anywhere, have lived their lives on the principle that there will be *nothing to pay*, and are washed up, stranded on various bitter shores, surrounded by the results of their piratage when young. Most would undo what they have done, would "do things differently if I had my time over again." They long to communicate this to their young. "For God's sake, don't do that, be careful, you have so little time left, if you do that then this and this and this is bound to happen."

But the young "have to learn for themselves." This is their right, their way of self-definition, an essential for them. (Just as it was for their parents who know how futile it is to suggest they may be wrong.) To relinquish this *right*, their self-development, self-expression, self-discovery, means succumbing to pressures felt as intolerable, corrupted, bogus.

The old watch the young with anguish, pain, fear. Above all what each has learned is *what things cost, what has to be paid*, the consequences and results of actions. But their own lives have been useless, because nothing they have learned can be passed on. What is the point of learning so much, so painfully, at such a cost to themselves and to others (often the offspring in question) if the next generation cannot take anything at all from them, can accept nothing as "given," as learned, as already understood?

And these old ones who have lived through everything know very well that every horror is possible and indeed inevitable, but the young are feeling that well, perhaps, it will be all right after all.

The old live waiting, longing, for the young to come to their senses and understand they personally have so little time left, and the planet has so little time left: "For God's sake! There is no time left, no time left for you, and not for us either, while you peacock about and play little games. . . ."

But there the young are, in their hordes, their gangs, their groups, their cults, their political parties, their sects, shouting slogans, infinitely divided, antagonistic to each other, always in the right, jostling for command. There they are—the future, and it is self-condemned.

The old have no future, because particularly for creatures who must die almost before they come to their senses, the young have to be a future. The old, looking back on their little space of tinted mist, say, "I haven't lived." And it is true. But they look at their young—and know that these will not live either.

This is one of the powerful forces at work here, now, on Shikasta. Among the innumerable divisions and subdivisions, peoples, races, subraces, ideas, creeds, religions, one operates everywhere, in every geographical area, the gulf that separates the young from the old.

JOHOR *reports:*

Here is a list of the individuals I was asked to check. Where their situations are satisfactory and their growth according to plan, I have not included them. I have however added some our agents suggested might be in difficulties, whose situation was not yet known in Canopus, and therefore their names were not on the original list.

These are listed separately from the individuals I had to locate and help because of Taufiq's dereliction: they did not fall within his scope.

[Shikastans spend a good part of their time being surprised at each other's behaviour and commenting on it. This is partly because their knowledge in the area they categorise as "psychological" is faulty, and partly because they do not apply what they do know.

Most of the surprise, pleasurable or otherwise, felt by them because of some development, is when an inner drive is working its way out by means of encounters or clashes of personalities. Folk wisdom encapsulates the knowledge that people often are drawn towards those who are bound to cause them pain. And it is true that the hidden power, or force, that drives Shikasta along its difficult and painful roads, and which is felt by some of them as a "guide" or "inner monitor" is not one that may consider "happiness" or "comfort" when it is operating to bring some individual nearer to self-knowledge, understanding.

It is not necessary, most of the time, to direct an individual into this or that relationship or situation—components of his or her personality, aspects of themselves they may not be aware of at all, will push them, by the laws of attraction or repulsion, into the places, or near to the people, who will benefit them. Very often two people, or a group of people, may meet in forceful and beneficial situations, and onlookers may even cry out that this must be the result of a "miracle" or "divine intervention." The couple, or group, have been drawn to each other sometimes across oceans, or overcoming "impossible" hazards, because they need each other—need to learn from each other. But often this process, to the uninstructed onlooker, seems like a meaningless or wasted conflict, or a stalemate, or even damaging.

And of course sometimes such encounters are indeed mistaken, wasteful, damaging. How could it be otherwise on poor Shikasta, in its extremity, at the end of the long processes that have brought it to such a shameful state?

But again, very often not: and the people involved may later say to themselves, to each other, of that time they experienced as difficult, or painful almost beyond bearing, or mistaken: What a lot I learned then! I wouldn't have missed it for worlds! *Archivists.*]

33.   Her undertaking was to manage a vast family fortune, she being the sole heiress. She was not seduced by wealth, to which she remained basically indifferent, but by the men attracted to her fortune. She married several times, never usefully to herself, though one of the men did profit by the experience to the extent that an aspect of himself was fully completed and he was able to move on to work on another. But she was not able to pull herself out of the cycle of "falling in love" and then becoming disillusioned. Discussions with Agent 15 suggested that her fortune should be drastically, even grotesquely, increased in ways never expected by her and which underlined her responsibilities. It is probable that the shock of this will return her to responsibility. Agent 15, who has undertaken this assignment, will arrange, too, for her to meet No. 44 who remains in the doldrums, and whose influence on her will be, we believe, constructive.

44.   If he does not benefit, Agent 15 will move him on to something else. But he cannot be in a worse situation than he is now, and the risk of a setback from an involvement, even a business one, with a woman so infantile must be taken.

14.   Her undertaking was to devote herself to caring for a crippled and difficult widowed mother. She did this from the age of thirty. The relentless, unremitting task was within her capacity until she herself became elderly and suffered an illness which enfeebled her. She was unable to pull herself out of the resulting depression, and was considering suicide, or even abandoning her mother, now senile, into an institution. I added to her burden, causing her to become responsible for an aunt in as bad a condition as her mother, but with a vigorous, abrasive, and humorous nature. 14 did not go under, but rallied, and under the stimulus of the blow, "took on" the visiting and care of other old men and women in the neighbourhood. She is restored to her former capable and optimistic condition.

21.   This man, of the oppressed black race in Southern Continent I (southern area), had undertaken to withstand oppression for the sake of others. He fell early into political action, as was expected and planned, for there was no other means of expressing self-reliance, self-respect, in that area, at that time. He was imprisoned, tortured, and became crippled as a result. It was at this point that he lost his way, becoming embittered and discouraged. He had turned in on himself, and was solitary, known to his fellows as the Angry One. If he had continued in this state, he would soon have attracted to himself an

early death. He was earning his living as a vegetable seller in a "black" township, when he was again arrested in some civic disorder and unjustly imprisoned. This added to his rage. It was obvious to everyone in the prison that he could not last long, for he combatted authority and his fellows in every way possible. I caused him to be put together with a man as crippled as he, as unjustly treated, and who had accepted his state with the aid of one of the—very many—local religious cults. These two men served out their prison sentences as friends. Now, released, they continue friends, and work for the improvement of conditions for the many crippled and handicapped children in the "black" township.

42. The undertaking was to live as normal and wholesome and ordinary a life as was available in a time of such horror, reminding others forced into extraordinary situations by war, destitution, political hazard, of the possibilities of a simple, family life, and particularly of how parents may care for and guide their children. He was brought up by a mother who, unexpectedly widowed, consoled herself with food: indulgent, she taught him self-indulgence. He was obsessed with food. This is not an uncommon condition: food has assumed an importance that astonishes every one of us visiting Shikasta. There are many factors that have gone to create this situation. First, innumerable people never get enough to eat, and so they are obsessed with the need for food: and if they are in fact released from indigence, food becomes more than a necessity. Second, wars have imposed on vast areas of Shikasta periods when food becomes something to be dreamed of, longed for: when food returns, these habits remain. Third, as has been commented on, the economies of large parts of Shikasta are geared to consumption, so each individual, every minute, is being pressured into thinking about food and drink, and very few are able to withstand it. And then of course there is Shammat the greedy, whose poison is at work in the bodies and minds of every Shikastan. So extreme is this situation that it is not thought shocking, in a world where most of the inhabitants starve and half starve, for individuals to travel from one city to another, or one country to another, or even one continent to another, for the sake of good eating, attracted by places whose cuisine is notable. In describing the attractions of a city, first of all will be listed the food that is available and even the details of the cooking.

When 42 married, he chose a woman, who like nearly everyone he met, thought about food more than almost anything else. Their household was dominated by the buying, cooking, and eating of food. Their children were brought up to consider food of supreme importance. Agent 9 in the report before this one explained that it was arranged for 42 suddenly to lose his livelihood, and positioned where he could choose to run a restaurant. The intention was he might come to regard the processes of eating and cooking in a more objective light. But he, his wife, his children, and some of their friends became obsessed with a restaurant that was famous not only in his own country but in several others. Food was never out of their minds, and it was clear that things were worse than before. I have arranged for him to be invited by a certain international agency because of his knowledge of every aspect of nutrition to become adviser to a nutritional programme in certain extremely poor areas in Southern Continent I. I believe that he and his wife may accept this invitation, and they, plunged into daily, hourly contact with the extremes of hunger, may be shocked out of their preoccupation. This leaves the problem of the children, additional to my assignment, and I have asked Agent 20 to intervene here.

17.   She undertook to risk her sanity—in a time when more and more people become mad, or live on the edges of madness, or who can expect to "break down" several times in a life—in order to explore these areas calmly and chart them, for the benefit of others. This was more than she was able to sustain. She had to undergo more and worse pressures than we expected, due to the early death of her mother. Some individuals near her have learned from her as to the possibilities and risks and lessons of mental imbalance, but she herself has not kept balance. A great part of her life has been spent in mental hospitals, or in sheltered situations, at the others' expense, both financial and emotional. A previous report described her condition, with suggestions for positive intervention, but these did not lead to improvement. I contacted her in a mental hospital where she was by choice, and found her stubborn and recalcitrant: to keep herself going with even the intermittent and tenuous hold on sanity she does possess, means that she has to be stubborn and suspicious: she has been treated with stupidity and brutality too often. I have arranged that a certain doctor with unusual insight into these conditions, working silently and with discretion inside his profession, shall contact her and work with her, suggesting ways in which she may describe what she experiences so as to help others. This will be of benefit to both, but I do not hold out much hope.

Re: *Colonised Planet 5, Shikasta*

NOTE: I was wrong. See added material, Lynda Coldridge, attached.

4. At a time when the convention has been that information about scientific discovery should be freely available, but when in fact great areas of research mostly, but not all, to do with military possibilities, have remained concealed, so that the public knows only part of the horrors being brewed for them, this man undertook to work inside a military scientific research establishment. He has been remarkably good at his work, and early became eminent in his field, though his name was not known outside a small circle of similar searchers. But he has been and is in a key position. Slowly he became obsessed with the horrific nature of his work, which resulted in neurosis—conflicting duties to "country," "science," "family," etc., and so on, which he was unable to solve, made him ill. He was ill, privately, and secretly, for years, for there was no one with whom to discuss his situation. While maintaining an ability to work, and even furthering discovery in a field which he increasingly considered criminal, inwardly he has been in a nightmare of guilt. I arranged for him to meet, at an international conference on another topic, a man working in the same field as himself in an "enemy" country—I put this in quotes because these are times when enemy countries may become allies overnight, or may be secretly allied in some ways while at war in others. These two men, both with difficulty carrying the weight of their burden of knowledge, encountered each other at once, drawn together because of their real inner preoccupations. They have arranged for leakages of some of their more deadly information, in ways that will make it less lethal, and postpone its use. This man is therefore back on the road he chose. His time will be spent more and more in the dissemination of this secret information, until he is arrested and imprisoned.

Now follow the individuals whose situation was brought to my attention as needing assistance. I number them according to System 3.

1 (5). This individual's chief characteristic was a critical sense: accurate, and keen. Various influences during upbringing reinforcing this equipment, any situation he found himself in was "seen through" by him at once. He left his own milieu early, rebelling against a parental situation in which he could see nothing but hypocrisy, and married young. He had three children, found himself entombed in "mediocrity and hypocrisy" and left for various unconventional arrangements with women, three illegitimate children resulting. He married again, had two children, but the marriage did not hold. Again he

married, and divorced, with one child. At the age of fifty-five he was alone, much impaired and made nonproductive by guilt. He has earned his living always on the fringes of the arts, often as critic and satirist. But a sense of derision that has never allowed him to succumb to any situation has always been complicated by a warm and generous heart—which attribute is strengthened by guilt, and causes him continually to fluctuate from "no" to "yes."

After discussion with Agent 20, we arranged matters so that one of his progeny was inspired to turn to him for help. He has taken her in and become responsible for her. Others of his offspring, hearing of it, appealed to him for refuge. At this time when children often flee their parents as if to remain in contact with them is to perpetuate in themselves all the vices of Shikasta, it is common for adolescents to leave home and seek surrogate parents: in this case, he is the surrogate parent, for he had not seen any of them for years. This man found that his home was crammed full of children and adolescents and young adults in various difficulties, and moved to a large house in the country. His attitude towards "ties," "duties," "conventions," "false allegiances," "hypocrisies" being well known, he has become quite an exemplar. Much more than an ordinary conventional man, whose children will have left home by the time he is in his fifth decade, he is burdened with postdated responsibilities. A former mistress, becoming ill, has been taken in. Another, in breakdown, followed. A husband of a former wife, falling into financial difficulties, is being assisted by him. This man is now responsible in one way or another for some twenty people, and has been cured of his stagnant and unwholesome condition. For one thing, his critical sense is now usefully at work in the diagnosis of his charges' ills and needs. As he carries such a heavy burden, I have arranged that Agent 20 keep a check on him, with powers to intervene if necessary.

1 (13). This man, after a hard struggle in childhood and youth against poverty and lack of education, became a journalist. For many years he was a dubious figure in the eyes of the authorities, for he was one of those—sharing a critical and analytical capacity not dissimilar from that of 1 (5)—who were continually attempting to present a factual picture of events and processes to the public very different from that of the majority view. This from a nonpolitical viewpoint, though he was branded as a socialist at a time when it was unfashionable and ill regarded. As happens often on Shikasta, the viewpoints he had

represented for three decades, side by side with a minority of similar men and women who had a hard time of it, suddenly became a majority view, and almost overnight he was something of a hero, particularly among the young. There are areas of Shikasta where critics of society may be hunted and persecuted all their lives. In others, they are absorbed. Over and over again, people who have been kept on the move mentally, always having to defend and sharpen and refine their perceptions of events, will suddenly find themselves in a spotlight focussed on them by the many publicity machines, will be made national figures, will be frozen, in fact, in public attitudes. Again and again, valuable people become neutralised, made into—often—figures of fun, at the least lose their impetus, their force. The man listed here fell into this trap, and had not understood that he was repeating and repeating old attitudes. I have arranged for him to meet a woman from Southern Continent I, who has had to fight so hard all her life even to survive that she has energy for two: he will marry her, and become revivified, and forced out of his pattern. Their children may be expected to be remarkable, and I have arranged for them to be watched by Agent 20.

1 (9). This woman has always been oversensitive to influences of any kind, and lacking in robustness and self-definition. She was sheltered by a strong family and then by a strong husband. He died and she was quickly a victim of depressions and states of sorrow that became addictive. This condition attracted vampires in Zone Six of a particularly virulent and persistent sort. It was clear that she could not live long and that in Zone Six she would be awaited by no helpful entities. I wondered whether to attempt another marriage for her, but it happened that a woman with strength of character and decisiveness capable of repelling any amount of debilitating and miasmic influences was in a condition of indecision about her life. They are now living together and the resulting energies are successfully rebuffing the malignant entities from Zone Six.

DOCUMENT, LYNDA COLDRIDGE.

(No. 17, this Report.)

I am writing this for Doctor Hebert. I keep telling him I can't write, I never write, I never have. He says I must. So I am. He says if other people read it they will be helped. But the reason he wants me to write things is that *I* will be helped. That is what he thinks. Well he will read this first so he will find out what *I* think. Although I do keep telling him. Doctor Hebert is a nice man. (You are a nice man!) But you don't listen. Doctors are always like this. (Not only doctors.) I often talk to Doctor Hebert for hours at a time. But he wants me to write my thoughts down. That seems to me funny. *Crazy.* But it is *me* who is crazy, not Doctor Hebert. Doctor Hebert knows everything that ever happened to me. He knows more about me than any other doctor. More than Mark does. Well that goes without saying. Or Martha. Or even Sandra or Dorothy did. Doctor Hebert says it is important that he knows about me. He says I have had every form of treatment ever used in mental hospitals. He says I have survived them. This is wrong. I have *not* survived them. I tell him how I was when I was a girl. I was mad *then*. According to their ideas. Then I tell him how I was mad when I was mad in the way I was mad when they started giving me treatments and putting me into hospitals. Because the two kinds of madness are different, not the same. Do you understand this Doctor Hebert? (You say I should call you John but I don't see why. Calling you John doesn't make you mad or me sane.) When I was a girl all kinds of things went on in my head, and now I know that was mad. Because so many people have said so. But it was lovely. I often think about that. I have not known that niceness since. (But sometimes I do get little flashes but I'll write that later. If I ever get to it.) And when *they* began the machines and the injections and the *dreadfulness* what was in my head was different from before. But they wouldn't see that. Do you, Doctor Hebert? Do you? I am *telling* you. In words. Words, but on paper. I shall begin again here. I get muddled. I meant to say something else first of all.

Doctor Hebert has ideas of all kinds. Some of them are good. I applaud them. I applaud you Doctor Hebert. Clap Clap. This is one of my childish days. Doctor Hebert says that I feel myself to be useless. (But I am. Anyone would see that at once.) He says that I can be of use to people who have just gone mad and who don't understand what is happening to them. He says I should go to such a person and say This is what is happening to you. He says that then they will feel better. And make me feel better because they feel better. But what he doesn't understand is, what will make them feel better is that they feel better. I.e., it all stops, it goes away, they aren't crazy any longer. He says I must say to some poor loon, all shaking and crying and hearing voices, sometimes coming out of walls, or seeing horrible things that aren't there (but perhaps they are!) I must say . . . new sentence. Look, I must say. Do not be afraid. You see, it is like this. (I am talking to this poor loon now.) We have senses adjusted to a very small range of sight or hearing. All the time sounds are coming in from everywhere, like a waterfall. But we are machines set to accept only let us say 5 percent. If the machine goes wrong then we hear more than we need. We see more than we need. Your machine has gone wrong. Instead of seeing just daylight and night and your cousin Fanny and the cat and your ever-loving husband, which is all you need to get along, you are seeing a lot more i.e. all these horrors and peculiar colours and visions and things. The reason they are horrors and not nice is that your machine is distorting what is there, which is really nice. (So says Doctor Hebert, but he is a nice man. You are a nice man Doctor Hebert, and how do you know?) And instead of hearing your husband saying he loves you or your wife or a bus going past you are hearing what your husband is really thinking. Like, you are an ugly old bag. Or what your children think. Or the dog. (I can hear what the dog belonging to the caretaker thinks. I like him better than most people. Does he like me better than most dogs? I shall ask him. If people knew what dogs are thinking they would be surprised. Just as well, really.) Well, if I say all this to the poor loons, they will cheer up and feel better. Says Doctor Hebert. To understand all is to forgive all. But I say to Doctor Hebert, that is not so. If you have voices sometimes it seems a hundred of them hammering away in your head, then you don't care why. You can do without original thoughts about percentages believe me. You want them to stop. And if you keep seeing monsters and terrible things you want them to go away. Is it going to cheer them up? I mean, knowing that we (people and for all I know dogs too) are geared to see only Aunt Fanny and the cat and the street because outside this everything is horrors? (Doctor Hebert *why* are you so positive the horrors aren't there? I mean, *why?* I really want to know. I mean, what world are you living in, Doctor Hebert, because I don't think it is the same as mine. Well I suppose that goes without saying, because you aren't mad and I am.) I shall start again. What you are wrong about is this, that people will feel better if I or you say things like this. Because nearly everyone has been brought to believe that the 5 percent is all there is. Five percent is the whole universe. And if they think anything else, they are peculiar. And if the machine then goes wrong and in comes let us say 10 percent then as well as being frightened about voices coming out of someone's elbow or the door handle, and what these voices say which is nearly always silly, then they will know they are *bad*. *Wicked*. Because you can't change people's ideas. Not just like that. Not suddenly. As it is, the poor loons are coping with *silly* voices that they *know* are silly, which is bad enough, but the voices are saying they are wicked and disgusting. Nearly always. And then on top of that, they have to cope with knowing that they are open to more than 5 percent, *which is bad by definition*. When they were children it is more than likely they saw and heard all kinds of things more than the 5 percent, like having friends they could see others couldn't, and their parents when they told them said they were lying and wicked. I am getting upset. I shall stop now.

Last night a poor loon was brought in. She was frightened. Doctor Hebert asked me to sit with her. So I did. She is schizophrenic. Well that goes without saying I suppose. She loved a friend and they were going to marry this week. He broke it off. She was upset. She didn't eat. She didn't sleep. She cried a lot. Yesterday she was walking across Waterloo Bridge and then suddenly she was about twenty feet up looking down at herself walking across the bridge. It happens to me quite often. What it means is this. We are several people fitted inside each other. Chinese boxes. Our bodies are the outside box. Or the inside one if you like. If you get a shock, like your best friend saying no I won't marry you I am going to marry your friend Arabella instead then anything can happen. I like watching myself from outside. It makes this living on and on and on and on seem not important. I look at me, poor old bag, which is what I am (Doctor Hebert says I must put on my nice dresses and make my face up.) But little does he realise, little do you realise Doctor Hebert that the Chinese box that stands outside and looks at poor bag Lynda doesn't care. What I really am is not poor bag Lynda all bones and the shakes and the shivers. I stand outside her and look at her and think, Well cry if you like, why not? *I don't care*. But this poor loon yesterday night. Her name is Anne. I suppose Doctor Hebert you think she would feel better if I said to her, You are a set of Chinese boxes, and when you walked across Waterloo Bridge all miserable and ill, they got separated for a bit, and so one of them looked down at the others, or other. Because Doctor Hebert it takes a lot of getting used to. You can't just say it, announcing good news. If she is religious yes perhaps. The soul. But this Anne is not religious, I asked her. She might be frightened if religious but it would be an idea she had heard of. I'd say soul and not Chinese box. But most religious people anyway think about the most unimportant Chinese box and about burying it or laying it out and how it will be in the grave or cremating it or something. So if they are like this then even soul would not be much good, let alone Chinese box. Words. Chinese box *bad*. Soul *good*. If Christian. Sometimes some poor loon comes in and I can talk to him. Her. A child is best. I mean, they are often not frightened when they see themselves walking away in front or something like that. It's second nature to some. It is a game. But they must keep quiet. I did it when I was a child. My parents quarrelled. When they started I used to take myself off outside the room. Of course they thought I was there with them but I wasn't. I sat there with a silly grin on my face but I was away outside, thinking other thoughts. I shall stop now.

Anne is very bad. I have been sitting with her. She is frightened more than anything. She hears the usual voices saying she is bad and wicked and all that. Also she keeps seeing her friend who is marrying Arabella. She sees them talking. Also making love. She told me this. She is frightened to tell Doctor Hebert. I told her not to tell Doctor Hebert. I am telling Doctor Hebert now. Doctor Hebert is one thing but there are other doctors here. This way Doctor Hebert will know but the other doctors won't. I told her that all she was doing was using "second sight" and she must have heard of that. I said a lot of people have it. I asked her if she saw things when she was a child. She said she did. I said it is like playing the piano or riding a bicycle. Practice makes perfect. I said all that kind of thing. Sensible. Second sight that's all it is! Looking down at yourself from twenty feet up, think nothing of it! Well it didn't make her feel better at all. Because when these things happen strongly enough to make people ill it is because the 6 percent of whatever is a *wavelength*. It is a voltage. It is a thousand volts instead of one. It is not just that you are the same as normal and then suddenly looking at yourself from outside or hearing voices, which can happen like a sort of glide sideways or up from where you were, and *not* an increase in voltage, but then at other times or with other people the voltage goes up suddenly and you feel you will shake to pieces. The 5 percent of sight hearing etc is *energies*. That is the whole point. So much voltage of sight, hearing. And if it is a bit more the machine shakes to pieces. That is the point. This is the point Doctor Hebert. Anne wants it to stop. She can't bear it.

Last night Doctor Hebert and I had one of our sessions. After lights out. In his office. He was on night. He had read all this. He had a sensible thought. It is this. When some person, let us say a Scottish lady in the Highlands like an old nurse I had once has second sight, and she says: A tall dark stranger will cross your path, and he does, or Someone will die this week and he does, then this person isn't shaking to pieces because the voltage is too high. Or children looking down from the branch of a tree at themselves sitting on the ground playing in the dust. They aren't shaking to pieces. They aren't shaking and crying and screaming and wishing it would stop on the contrary it all seems the most normal thing in the world.

The answer is some people are *born* to receive not 5 percent but perhaps 6 percent. Or 7 percent. Or even more. But if you are a 5 percent person and suddenly a shock opens you to 6 then you are "mad." I am sure I was born a 6 percent person, not mad at all. But they made me mad because I told what I knew. If I had kept my mouth shut I would have lived a peaceful life. With Mark. Poor Mark. Oh poor Mark. He is in North Africa with Rita. He writes to me. He loves me. He loves Rita. He loves Martha. Love love love love love. If I had liked it when he slobbered all over me and stuck his hands and things into me then that would have meant I loved him I suppose. That is how he looked at it.

The talks I have with Doctor Hebert are like the talks I used to have with Martha. Not as long, not all night or days at a time because Doctor Hebert works hard. He has to look after things. But we talk about the same things. Doctor Hebert says I have learned so much and I don't use it. He says what is the point of Martha and me finding out so much, and then not doing anything. Doing *what?* Writing a letter to The Times. (That is Mark talking.) Standing on platforms? (Arthur. Phoebe.) I told him that when Martha writes to me again I'll ask her to come and see me and then he and Martha can talk too. Martha is in the commune place. I've been there to visit Francis. I suppose it is all right. But why do people have to get into one place and live together?

Like dogs curled up in a basket licking each other. Lick. lick. People who are like each other are together anyway. That is what I think. They don't have to go lick lick.

Doctor Hebert wants to come with me and visit Martha and Francis and talk the whole night through. I don't mind.

Doctor Hebert wants me to work every day on my "faculties." I say to him (I am saying to you now) that sometimes my "faculties" are strong and sometimes not and it is no good talking about "every day" like office work. But he is very keen on 9 to 5, or maybe 2 to 4. Mondays to Fridays? Do I get Saturdays and Sundays off? He says people who come in here and who are not too frightened should join. Join what? He is very curious about "what I know." Suppose what I know isn't very nice? Suppose I know things about what is going to happen, but I would much rather not know. Doctor Hebert talks very easily about knowing this or that. I ask him (I am asking you again Doctor Hebert) why do you suppose we are all set or most of us for 5 percent, with a few people set to 6 percent and even fewer to 7 or 8? (But we wouldn't know about those, would we? They would be like Gods, I think. Taking it from our point of view.) Do you think the reason might be that whoever sets us poor little machines knows very well how much we can stand? Because Doctor Hebert *I* can't stand it, and I try hard not to think about what I know.

When I wrote that I forgot to put in something important. If a person is a set of Chinese boxes, one inside another, then is that what the world is? I am writing this down because it is important. When I take a look at myself from outside I want to laugh. I see Lynda the old bag all bones with bleeding fingers. But that isn't what the person is who looks. It is not important about the old bag in a not very nice dress. (I couldn't get into the ironing room again today, the key was lost, Doctor Hebert if you really mean about looking nice because of self-respect.) So perhaps there is another world that looks at our world, this dreadful place. *Hell.* Did you know this was hell Doctor Hebert? Do you? I said it and you smiled. It is her illness you thought. But this is hell, Doctor Hebert. But supposing what I thought is true, another world, a sort of lighter replica of this heavy lump of misery in the chains of *gravity*, gravity, it is so *heavy* and so thick—suppose this other world slips off like a glove and looks back at *hell* and shrugs its shoulders. And another world, and another. Round Chinese boxes. Does that amuse you? I feel a smile on my face so I suppose it is amusing.

Sometimes Martha and I sat and laughed and laughed. Sometimes Dorothy laughed. Not often though. Sandra didn't laugh, not ever. But Dorothy killed herself and Sandra got better. No one liked Sandra. It was because they said she was common. Well she was. Being in all these hospitals I haven't cared about that. Not for years and years. What matters is, you say something and then it is understood. Mark was my husband. He isn't now because I told him he must divorce me so that Rita could have children properly. Mark loved me. He loved me. He drove me mad loving me. I used to listen to how he loved. He wanted to wrap my filthy dirty smelly hair around his hands. Love. Darling Lynda I love you. But he never understood anything I said to him. Meanwhile he was loving Martha. Well good luck to them. I thought so then and I think so now. Then Rita came. Kiss kiss lick lick gobble gobble. Rita never understood a word Mark said. But never mind that, when it was Rita and Mark the house had a good feel, it was different from before. So from that I conclude there is no point my trying to understand about sex. Love so called. It is a waste of time. I'm not equipped, that's obvious.

Doctor Hebert has taken in what I said about 9 to 5, office hours. He wants me to come to him when I am in the mood, so that I don't waste anything, and he can make experiments on me. He didn't say experiments because he believes I am frightened of that sort of thing. Doctor Hebert you don't listen when I say things. I can never be frightened again, because if bad things happen, I just step outside my body and go off somewhere else. I don't mind if you want to make experiments. But it won't make any difference. Are you going to convince your confreres? Is that what you have in mind? I'm not going to be a guinea pig at conferences or meetings of doctors. No, no. What you don't understand is, people never believe these things. Not until they experience them. Then when they experience them they become people other people don't believe. Hard lines. Martha and Francis say the military do research into this kind of thing and use it. Why don't you ask the army? They don't tell the truth to ordinary people. Death is more important.

Doctor Hebert is being transferred to another hospital. He says I can go with him. I shall go with him. I want to stay in hospital. They say I could leave and manage, but I am too badly deteriorated and I shall stick to that. I could live in that commune place but I'd have to behave all the time. Lick lick lick. I shall leave here next week to go with Doctor Hebert. One hospital is like another. Doctor Hebert says he wants to go on working with me.

Since Doctor Hebert, I have been sometimes just for short moments like I was when I was a girl. Before they grabbed me and forced me into the hospitals. The voices when I was a child were friendly. It was a friend talking to me. They would say: Yes Lynda, it is all right, do that. Or this. Or, Have you thought about doing that, because you can if you try. Lynda, Lynda, don't be sad. Don't be unhappy. And once when I was crying and crying because my parents quarrelled all the time, the voice said right through all that fuss I was making, *What is the matter, Lynda?* Meaning, what a fuss about nothing. All these years I have remembered the friendliness, and wondered where it had gone to. Since the doctors all I heard was voices saying I was wicked, horrible, cruel. But now it is coming back. That is because Doctor Hebert is a kind man. I mean kind in himself, not just his words. Words are nothing. The thing that is there, the friendly thing in a person or place is *sweet*. It is a sort of sweetness and closeness. I keep telling Doctor Hebert, the voices that torment poor loons, saying you are horrible and all that, I will punish you, could just as well be saying, I am your friend, trust me.

ILLUSTRATIONS: *The Shikastan Situation*

This took place in a part of Shikasta controlled by an obscurantist religion that spread its bigotry and ignorance over all aspects of life, and that held, as an absolute truth, that "God" had created humanity on a certain date about four thousand years before. To believe anything else was to court reprisals that included social ostracism, the loss of opportunities to earn a living, the reputation of "ungodliness" and general wickedness. The reaction against the narrowness and dogmatism seldom equalled even on Shikasta manifested itself in certain intellectuals who worked in the fields of human history, biology, evolution, offering as an alternative belief that the peoples of the planet had evolved, slowly, through many millennia, from the animal kingdom: certain types of ape being designated as the ancestors of all Shikastans.

Religion reacted with violence, and civic authority, at that time almost indistinguishable in fact if not in theory from religion, was touchy, incensed, punishing, arbitrary.

These few individuals fought back with courage and spirit, opposing "superstition" with "rationalism" and "free thought" and "science." In one way or another, each had to suffer for his stand.

I offer here the history of one, "a small soldier in the cause of free enquiry"—his description of himself. He was not from a wealthy family, but was poor, and a teacher of the best sort, whose passion had always been—and remained—to inspire the young into useful lives free from the tyrannies of ignorance, and ready always to follow any *fact* whithersoever it might lead.

He was in a small town, where public opinion was in total subjection to religion. He began to teach the children under his care the new "knowledge"—that all of humanity had descended from animals—and after reprimands, lost his job. The girl he had hoped to marry said she would stand by him, but succumbed to pressures from her family. He was sustained by his conscience, and taught himself carpentry, and with great difficulty—for most of the people of the town shunned him— earned a precarious living. After a time the priests made even this impossible. He had to leave his home town, and went to a big city, where his history was not known. He was able to get work as a carpenter. He accumulated a library offering the "new knowledge," works of free thought of all kinds, works of science, some to do with genetics, which was a field in which rapid advances were in fact being made. The library he offered to fellow spirits, particularly young people, of which there were far more in this city than there could be in a small place where "everybody knew everybody else." More than once, his library, his opinions, his fearless conversations with anyone who would listen, caused visitations from local religious representatives. Once his library was burned by local bigots. He had to move his home twice. He did not marry. He lived for sixty years in poverty and alone, sustained always by the belief that he was in the right, and that "the future will absolve me" and "I have stood for the truth."

This stand by him and a few other brave spirits who were open to the mental currents and discoveries of the time, some of them true and valuable, but generally sloganised by a derisive populace as "If you want to be a monkey no one is stopping you!" was in fact the beginning of a successful and widespread movement to destroy the stranglehold of this particularly destructive religion over large parts of Shikasta—in some places it had maintained an absolute tyranny for hundreds of years.

This man, in his old age, going to the shops, or sitting on a bench in the sun, would be harassed by children, and sometimes adults, shouting, "Monkey! Monkey! Monkey!" And he would smile at them, his back held very straight, his head up, fearless, sustained by Truth.

JOHOR: *Agent 20, asked for a report, contributed this.*

I am in a large city in the Isolated Northern Continent, with extremes of rich and poor. This is a living area, where tall buildings house innumerable people. All the men, and many of the women, leave during the day, to work. The poverty here is not of the extreme kind, a fight to eat and keep warm, but of the variety common in the affluent areas of Shikasta: a great deal of effort goes into maintaining a certain standard of living, which standard is arbitrarily dictated by the needs of the economy. Family life has broken down. Couples seldom stay together for long. The children, left to fend for themselves from an early age, and given little affection, form gangs, and soon become criminal. Much expert thought is given to this problem, and its solution is frequently announced to be a greater parental attention to the young. Exhortations to this effect are made by authority figures, but with little result.

An interesting aspect is that stories of idealised family life are continually shown on the various propaganda media, but these are from past epochs, and are hard to relate to the present day, yet they are very popular. The contrast between the warmth and responsibility shown by adults in these tales, and what can be observed every day, adds to the cynicism and alienation of the young.

It is of little use to approach these gangs of children—who of course very soon become young adults—as an individual. As an individual, my scope is limited.

To approach the adults, particularly the mothers, has better results, but it is often too late.

Sometimes I have wondered if among the many thousands of families crammed into these towering buildings, there is one with the moral energy or even the conviction to bring up their young as well as an animal would.

And I am not talking of the cruelty that is hidden here, physical and mental, inflicted even on infants, but of an indifference, a lack of interest.

I live in a room in an old house in a street adjacent to the acres of bare asphalt where the tall buildings are crowded. Rare indeed to find a garden, or trees, but my room, on the ground floor, overlooks a little patch of earth where some flowers grow. There are two trees, one smallish and one well grown.

The woman who has the room across the hall tends the flowers and keeps cats. Like many women she makes a great deal of pleasure and interest for herself out of very little.

A she-cat she took in one cold night gave birth to four kittens. She gave three away. The she-cat, already old, died. There was one cat left, a black-and-white female, pretty and engaging but stupid. I think she was even feebleminded. She slept nearly all the time, was timid, and kept herself indoors. When she came on heat, she mated with a large black cat who had made it clear to the other cats that this garden was his territory. The woman believed him to have a home, but fed him when he seemed hungry. She did not want him in her room, but when the female had her first litter of two kittens, a tabby male and a black female, the father asked to come in so persistently that she allowed him, and he would sit by the box where the family was, and call to the little mother cat, and sometimes lick the kittens.

The woman was intrigued by this paternal behaviour, and called me in to see it. We called the female cat his "wife"—with a smile, but sometimes the woman showed embarrassment, with a laugh that was shame for the human race.

The little black-and-white cat was a good mother as far as the feeding went. And she kept the kittens clean. But she seemed unable to instruct them in the use of a dirt box. It was the male cat who did that. He took them to the box, made them sit in it, and rewarded them with a male version of the "trill" that a female cat uses to encourage offspring. He would give a gruff purr that sounded humorous to us, and then lick the kittens.

He was not at all handsome. We believed him to be very old, since he was bony, with torn ears and a poor coat, in spite of the feeding he was getting in this new home, for that was what it had become. He was not importunate, or greedy. He would wait for our return from somewhere, and then, his yellow eyes on our face, like an equal, he asked with his demeanour to be let in.

As for food, he waited, sitting quietly to one side while his "wife" ate, never much, but thoughtless of her kittens, as if she hardly noticed them crowded at the dish with her. When she was filled, she went at once to her box. The male cat waited until the kittens had finished, and then he came in and ate. Often there was not much left, but he did not ask for more. He licked the dish clean, sat with the kittens, or watched them curl up around each other, and crouched near them, on guard.

When the time had come for the kittens to be introduced into the garden, the mother cat did not seem to know it. She made no effort to take them out. There were steps into the garden. The male cat sat at the foot of the steps and gave his strange gruff purring call to the kittens, and they went to him. He took them around the garden, slowly, while they played and teased him and each other, but he introduced them to everything, every corner, and then showed them how to cover their excrement cleanly.

This scene was watched by the woman, from her window, and by me, from mine.

There was another young cat from a house nearby who was a natural climber. He was always at the top of a tree or putting one paw in front of another carefully as he balanced the ridge of a house.

The kittens, seeing this dashing hero at the top of the big tree, shot up after him and couldn't get down. He, ignoring them, jumped from the top of that tree down into the branches of the smaller tree, and from there to the ground—and vanished.

The kittens were in a panic, crying and complaining.

The black cat, who had watched all this from where he sat on the steps, now went thoughtfully to the bottom of the big tree, sat down, and looked up, considering the situation. There, above him, were the kittens, clinging tight, fur disordered, letting out their plaintive panicky wails.

He issued instructions for a safe descent, but they were too distracted to listen.

He climbed the tree and carried down one, then climbed it again and carried down the other.

He spoke to them severely about their foolhardiness, with gruff purrs and cuffs to their ears.

Then he went to the smaller tree, called them to him, and went up it slowly, looking back, and waiting for them to follow. First up went the tough little tiger, and then the pretty little black kitten. When the tree began to sway under his weight, he grunted, making them look up at him, and began to descend slowly backwards. They, with many complaints and cries of fear, did the same. Near the ground they jumped off, and chased each other around the garden, with relief that the lesson was safely over. But he called to them, and now went half-way up the big tree. They would not follow him. He remained there, halfway up, his four legs locked around the tree, looking down and urging them to join him. But not today. The next day, the lesson was resumed, and soon the kittens were able to climb the big tree and get themselves safely down.

All day he was in the garden watching them, and when they went indoors to their mother he lay out on the wall, or sometimes followed them. He would sit by his "wife," where she lay unobtrusively tucked up in her box, and look at her. He seemed to be wondering about her. This young animal was like an old woman, with no energy left for more than the minimum demands of life, or like a young one who has been very ill and was left depressed. There was never anything in her of the fierce joyous possessive energy one may see in a young nursing cat. Sometimes he put his ugly old head close to hers and sniffed at her, and even licked her, but she did not respond at all.

The kittens grew up and went to new homes.

The autumn came on. Some brave hunter with an airgun took a shot at the black cat and there was a bad wound which was a long time healing, and left him with a limp. But he was stiff in walking anyway and we thought it age.

When the winter came he did something he had not done before. He would sit on the steps, looking up at the woman's window, or at mine, and soundlessly miaow. If the woman let him in he sat by the female cat for a while, but when she took no notice, lay down in a corner by himself. But the woman did not really want him there, so he would direct his soundless call to me instead. In my room he would wait until a blanket had been put down for him, near a stove, and there he slept, and in the morning he went to the door, purred his gruff thanks, wreathed my legs politely and went out. It was a bad winter. Sometimes he could hardly drag himself out, he was so stiff, and he stayed in my room on his blanket. He might crawl out for a few minutes to relieve himself. This seemed to be happening very often. I put a dirt box in the room, for there was deep snow outside. He used it often. There was a cold on his kidneys, I thought. Well, he was old. Discussing it with the woman, we decided that being so old he should not be harassed with doctors and attempts to keep him alive. Medicine was got for him, though.

He was extremely thin and did not eat.

Once or twice he visited his "wife" who seemed quite pleased to see him. But when he came back to my room she seemed hardly to notice.

It was evident that he was in pain. Settling down on his blanket he did it gently, first one muscle and then another, and he would suppress a groan.

Sometimes, moving himself, he held his breath, then let it out carefully, his yellow eyes looking at me as if to say, I can't help it.

I wondered if he was afraid, poor beast, that I would throw him out into the snow if he made a nuisance of himself, but no, I soon came to believe that this was the self-control of a noble creature, mastering pain.

His presence in my room was always a quiet friendly force, and if I put my hand down to him gently, knowing he was afraid of sudden or rough movement, he gave a short grunt of thanks and acknowledgement.

He did not get better. I wrapped him up carefully and took him to the cat doctor, who said he had a cancer.

He said, too, that this was not an old cat, but a young one, who was a stray, had fended for himself, and become rheumatic from sleeping out in the cold and the wet.

JOHOR:

ADDITIONAL EXPLANATORY INFORMATION. II.

[This is to be regarded as, in a sense, a continuation of Additional Explanatory Information. I. Archivists.]

It is a long time since Shikastans were able to bear their lives without drugs of some kind. I look back, back, and see that almost from when the flow of SOWF was cut down, they had to dull the pain of their condition. Of course there have always been individuals, a few, for whom this was not true.

Alcohol and the hallucinogens, the derivatives of opium, cocoa and tobacco, chemicals, caffeine—when have they not been used? By whom? I begin with the crude ones, the obvious comforters, and softeners of reality: but there is no need to infringe on areas of work done by colleagues and about which information is plentifully available in our archives.

Of the emotional props there have been no end. . . .

But now, in this time, few retain their substance, their solidity. I can define what I mean exactly by saying that on this visit of mine now to Shikasta, I could use exactly the same *words* to describe—let us say—a religion, as I did: but that a major fact would be left out: this is a feeling, or atmosphere.

The religions of Shikasta are no less, even though they have lost their power to tyrannise: new religious sects proliferate, and ecstatogenous sects most of all. But what has happened is that the skies of Shikasta have been lifted: they have sent men to their moon, and machines to their fellow planets, and most people believe that Shikasta is visited by spacecraft from other planets. The words, the languages, of religion—and all religions rely on emotional, image-breeding words —have become weightier and more portentous: yet at the same time transparent and slippery. A Shikastan saying Star, Galaxy, Universe, Sky, Heaven, uses the same words but does not mean the same things as did his fathers of only a century ago. A certainty has gone, a solidity. Religion, always the most powerful of the reality-blunters, has lost its certainties. Not long ago, a hundred years, it was possible for members of a religion to believe it was better than any other, and *they* were the only people in the whole world likely to be "saved." But now this frame of mind can stand only as long as they keep their minds closed to their own history.

The nationalisms of Shikasta, that pernicious new creed which uses much of the energies that once fed religions, are strong, and new nations are born every day. And with each, a generation of its young men and women steps forward ready to die for the chimera. And, whereas so recently, not more than a generation, or two generations, it was possible for a Shikastan to spend a life thinking not much further than a village, or a town, only just able to grasp the concept of "nation"—now, while "nation" is strong, devouring, so is the idea of the whole world, as an interacting whole. To die for a country cannot have the conviction it did. So recently, a hundred years ago, or fifty, it was possible for the members of a nation to believe that this little patch of Shikasta was better than all others, more noble, free, and good. But recently even the most self-regarding and self-worshipping nation has had to see that it is the same as the rest, and that each lies, tortures, deludes its people, and bleeds them in the interests of a dominant class . . . and falls apart, as must happen in these terrible end days.

Politics, political parties, which attract exactly the same emotions as religions did and do, as nations did and do, spawn new creeds every day. Not long ago it was possible for members of a political sect to believe that it was pristine and noble and best—but there have been so many betrayals and disappointments, lies, turnings-about, so much murdering and torturing and insanity, that even the most fanatic supporters know times of disbelief.

Science, the most recent of the religions, as bigoted and as inflexible as any, has created a way of life, a technology, attitudes of mind, increasingly loathed and distrusted. Not long ago, a "scientist" knew he was the great culminator and crown of all human thinking, knowledge, progress—and behaved with according arrogance. But now they begin to know their own smallness, and the fouled and spoiled earth itself rises up against them in witness.

Everywhere ideas, sets of mind, beliefs that have supported people for centuries are fraying away, dissolving, going.

What is there left?

It is true that the capacity of Shikastans to restore the breaches in the walls of their certainties is immense. The exposed and painful nature of their existence, subject to myriad chances beyond their control or influence, their helplessness as they toss in the cosmic storms, the violences and discordances of their damaged minds—all this being intolerable, they still hide their eyes and pray, or add to the formulas in their laboratories.

Each one of these alliances of an individual with some greater whole, the identification of an individual with a mental structure larger than himself, was a drug, a prop, a pacifier for children. These were greater even than alcohol and opium and the rest, but they are going, thinning, dissolving, and the insensate and furious, fanatical and desperate struggles that go on in the name of this or that creed or belief, the very fury, is a means of stilling self-doubt, numbing the terrors of isolation.

What other ways have Shikastans used to ward off from themselves the knowledge about their situation which is always, always threatening to well up from their depths and overwhelm? What else can they clutch to them, like a blanket on a cold night?

There are the varieties of pleasure, implanted in them for the sake of their survival, the needs for food and sex which, as the whole species is threatened, rage in an instinctive effort to save and preserve.

There is something else, and stronger than anything: the well-being, the always renewing, regenerative, healing force of nature; feeling one with the other creatures of Shikasta and its soil, and its plants.

The lowest, the most downtrodden, the most miserable of Shikastans, will watch the wind moving a plant, and smile; will plant a seed and watch it grow; will stand to watch the life of the clouds. Or lie pleasurably awake in the dark, hearing wind howl that cannot—not *this* time—harm him where he lies safe. This is where strength has always welled, irrepressibly, into every creature of Shikasta.

Forced back and back upon herself, himself, bereft of comfort, security, knowing perhaps only hunger and cold; denuded of belief in "country," "religion," "progress"—stripped of certainties, there is no Shikastan who will not let his eyes rest on a patch of earth, perhaps no more than a patch of littered and soured soil between buildings in a slum, and think: Yes, but that will come to life, there is enough power there to tear down this dreadfulness and heal all our ugliness— a couple of seasons, and it would all be alive again . . . and in war, a soldier watching a tank rear up over a ridge to bear down on him, will see as he dies grass, tree, a bird swerving past, and know immortality.

It is here, precisely here, that I place my emphasis.

Now it is only for a few of the creatures of Shikasta, those with steadier sight, or nerves, but every day there are more—soon there will be multitudes . . . once where the deepest, most constant, steadiest support was, there is nothing: it is the nursery of life itself that is poisoned, the seeds of life, the springs that feed the well.

All the old supports going, gone, this man reaches out a hand to steady himself on a ledge of rough brick that is warm in the sun: his hand feeds him messages of solidity, but his mind messages of destruction, for this breathing substance, made of earth, will be a dance of atoms, he knows it, his intelligence tells him so: there will soon be war, he is in the middle of war, where he stands will be a waste, mounds of rubble, and this solid earthy substance will be a film of dust on ruins.

She reaches for the child that plays on the floor but as she holds its fresh warmth to her face she knows that it is for the holocaust, and if by a miracle it escapes, then the substance of its inheritance is being attacked as the two of them stand there, close, the warmth of their mortality beating between them as the child laughs.

He looks at the child, thinking of nature, the creative fire spawning new forms as we breathe. He has to, for he knows that the species dwindle everywhere on Shikasta, the stock of gene patterns is being destroyed, destroyed, cannot come back. . . . He cannot rest in thoughts of the great creator, nature, and he looks out of the window at a landscape seen a thousand times, in a thousand different guises, but now it seems to thin and disappear. He thinks: Well, the ice stretched down as far as here, not so long ago, ten thousand years, and look, it has all remade itself! But an ice age is nothing, it is a few thousand years—the ice comes, and then it goes. It destroys and kills, but it does not pervert and spoil the substance of life itself.

She thinks, but there are the animals, the noble and patient animals, with their languages we don't understand, their kindness to each other, their friendship for us—and she puts down her hand to feel the living warmth of her little cat but knows that as she stands there they are being slaughtered, wiped out, made extinct, by senselessless, stupidity, by greed, greed, greed. She cannot rest in her familiar thoughts of the great reservoir of nature, and when her cat gives birth, she crouches over the nest and peers in, looking for the mutations which she knows are working there, will soon show themselves.

He thinks, as the loneliness of his situation dizzies him, standing there and whirling among the stars, a species among myriads—as he has only recently come to know—that these thoughts are too grand for him, he needs to put his arms around his woman and to feel her arms around him, but as they turn to each other, there is tension, and fear, for this embrace may breed monsters.

She stands as she has done for millennia, cutting bread, setting out sliced vegetables on a plate, with a bottle of wine, and thinks that nothing in this meal is safe, that the poisons of their civilisation are in every mouthful, and that they are about to fill their mouths with deaths of all kinds. In an instinctive gesture of safety, renewal, she hands a piece of bread to her child, but the gesture has lost its faith as she makes it, because of what she may be handing the child.

When he is at his work—if he has any, for he may be one who is being merely kept alive, not being used, or stretched, or developed through his labour—he, at his work, again and again, because the need is so old, renews himself in the thought that this work of his benefits others, that it links him with others, he is in a creative mesh and pulse with all the labourers of the earth . . . but he is checked, is stopped, the thought cannot live on in him, there is bitterness and anger, and then a weariness, disbelief: he does not know why, she does not know why, but it is as if they are pouring away the best of themselves into nothingness.

She and he, making order in their living place, tidying and cleaning their home, stand together among piles of glass, synthetics, paper, cans, containers—the rubbish of their civilisation which, they know, is farm-land and food and the labour of men and women, rubbish, rubbish, to be carried away and dumped in great mountains that cover more earth, foul more water. As they clear and smooth their little rooms, it is with a rising, hardly controllable irritability and disgust. A container that has held food is thrown away, but over vast areas of Shikasta it would be treasured and used by millions of desperate people. Yet there is nothing to be done, it seems. Yet it all happens, it goes on, nothing seems to stop it. Rage, frustration, disgust at themselves, at their society, anger—breaking out against each other, against neighbours, against the child. Nothing they can touch, or see, or handle sustains them, nowhere can they take refuge in the simple good sense of nature. He has seen once a pumpkin vine sprawling its great leaves and yellow flowers and sumptuous golden globes over a vast rubbish heap, where flies sizzle and simmer—at the time he hardly noticed it, and now it is an image for his imagination to find rest in, and comfort. She watches a neighbour trying to burn bits of plastic on a bonfire, while the chemical reek poisons everything, and she shuts her eyes and thinks of a broken earthenware bowl swept out of a back door in a village, to crumble slowly back into the soil.

In all of man's history he has been able to restore himself with the sight of leaves in autumn that will sink back into the earth, or with the look of a crumbling wall with sun on it, or some white bones at the edge of a stream.

These two stand together, high above their city, looking out where the machines that are destroying them rush and grind, in the air, on the earth, under the earth . . . they stand breathing, but the rhythm of their breath shortens and changes, as they think that the air is full of corrosion and destruction.

They turn taps and handles and water runs out willingly from the walls, but as they bend to drink or to wash they find their instincts reluctant and have to force themselves. The water tastes flat, and faintly corrupt, and has been already ten times through their gut and bladders, and they know that the time will come when they will not be able to drink it, and, setting out containers for rainwater, will find that, too, undrinkable from chemicals washed from the air.

They watch a flight of birds, as they stand together at their windows, and it is as if they are sorrowfully saying goodbye, with a silent corrosive, tearing apology on behalf of the species they belong to: destruction is what they have brought to these creatures, destruction and poisoning is their gift, and the swerve and balancing of a bird does not delight and rest, but becomes another place from which they learn to avert their eyes, in pain.

This woman, this man, restless, irritable, grief-stricken, sleeping too much to forget their situation or unable to sleep, looking everywhere for some good or sustenance that will not at once give way as they reach out for it and slide off into reproach or nothingness—one of them takes up a leaf from the pavement, carries it home, stares at it. There it lies in a palm, a brilliant gold, a curled, curved, sculptored thing, balanced like a feather, ready to float and to glide, there it rests, lightly, for a breath may move it, in that loosely open, slightly damp, human palm, and the mind meditating there sees its supporting ribs, the myriads of its veins branching, and rebranching, its capillaries, the minuscule areas of its flesh which are not—as it seems to this brooding human eye—fragments of undifferentiated substance between the minute feeding arteries and veins, but, if one could see them, highly structured worlds, the resources of chemical and microscopic cell life, viruses, bacteria—a universe in each pin-point of leaf. It is already being dragged into the soil as it lies there captive, a shape as perfect as a ship's sail in full wind or the shell of a snail. But what is being looked at is not this curved exquisite exactness, for the slightest shift of vision shows the shape of matter thinning, fraying, attacked by a thousand forces of growth and death. And this is what an eye tuned slightly, only slightly, differently would see looking out of the window at that tree which shed the leaf on to the pavement—since it is autumn and the tree's need to conserve energy against the winter is on it—no, not a tree, but a fighting seething mass of matter in the extremes of tension, growth, destruction, a myriad of species of smaller and smaller creatures feeding on each other, each feeding on the other, always—that is what this tree is in reality, and this man, this woman, crouched tense over the leaf, feels nature as a roaring creative fire in whose crucible species are born and die and are reborn in every breath . . . every life . . . every culture . . . every world . . . the mind, wrenched away from its resting place in the close visible cycles of growth and renewal and decay, the simplicities of birth and death, is forced back, and back and into itself, coming to rest—tentatively and without expectation—where there can be no rest, in the thought that always, at every time, there have been species, creatures, new shapes of being, making harmonious wholes of interacting parts, but these over and over again crash! are swept away!—crash go the empires and the civilisations, and the explosions that are to come will lay to waste seas and oceans and islands and cities, and make poisoned deserts where the teeming detailed inventive life was, and where the mind and heart used to rest, but may no longer, but must go forth like the dove sent by Noah, and at last after long circling and cycling see a distant mountaintop emerging from wastes of soiled water, and must settle there, looking around at nothing, nothing, but the wastes of death and destruction, but cannot rest there either, knowing that tomorrow or next week or in a thousand years, this mountaintop too will topple under the force of a comet's passing, or the arrival of a meteorite.

The man, the woman, sitting humbly in the corner of their room, stare at that indescribably perfect thing, a golden chestnut leaf in autumn, when it has just floated down from the tree, and then may perform any one of a number of acts that rise from inside themselves, and that they could not justify nor argue with or against—they may simply close a hand over it, crushing it to powder, and fling the stuff out of the window, watching the dust sink through the air to the pavement, for there is a relief in thinking that the rains of next week will seep the leaf-stuff back through the soil to the roots, so that next year, at least, it will shine in the air again. Or the woman may put the leaf gently on a blue plate and set it on a table, and may even bow before it, ironically, and with a sort of apology that is so near to the thoughts and actions of Shikastans now, and think that the laws that made this shape must be, must be, must be stronger in the end than the slow distorters and perverters of the substance of life. Or the man, glancing out of the window, forcing himself to see the tree in its other truth, that of the fierce and furious war of eating and being eaten, may see suddenly, for an instant, so that it has gone even as he turns to call his wife: Look, look, quick!—behind the seethe and scramble and eating that is one truth, and behind the ordinary tree-in-autumn that is the other—a third, a tree of a fine, high, shimmering light, like shaped sunlight. A world, a world, another world, another truth. . . .

And when the dark comes, he will look up and out and see a little smudge of light that is a galaxy that exploded millions of years ago, and the oppression that had gripped his heart lifts, and he laughs, and he calls his wife and says: Look, we are seeing something that ceased to exist millions of years ago—and she sees, exactly, and laughs with him.

This, then, is the condition of Shikastans now, still only a few, but more and more, and soon—multitudes.

Nothing they handle or see has substance, and so they repose in their imaginations on chaos, making strength from the possibilities of a creative destruction. They are weaned from everything but the knowledge that the universe is a roaring engine of creativity, and they are only temporary manifestations of it.

Creatures infinitely damaged, reduced and dwindled from their origins, degenerate, almost lost—animals far removed from what was first envisaged for them by their designers, they are being driven back and away from everything they had and held and now can take a stand nowhere but in the most outrageous extremities of—patience. It is an ironic, and humble, patience, which learns to look at a leaf, perfect for a day, and see it as an explosion of galaxies, and the battleground of species. Shikastans are, in their awful and ignoble end, while they scuffle and scrabble and scurry among their crumbling and squalid artefacts, reaching out with their minds to heights of courage and . . . I am putting the word *faith* here. After thought. With caution. With an exact and hopeful respect.

JOHOR *continues*:

Warnings that it will be dangerous to delay any longer have been received. Before I enter Shikasta on the necessary level, I must make a final check on two possible sets of parents suggested by Agent 19. It is even more difficult than was envisaged to choose circumstances that will allow me to develop quickly, and with time to become independent, and without incapacitating damage.

JOHOR *reports:*

There is not much to choose between the two couples.

First Couple. He is a farmer, a farming technologist, and will not find himself unemployed. She is similarly employed. There are already two children. This is a healthy, intelligent, practical pair, not likely to split up, and with a responsible attitude towards their offspring. There is one disadvantage: both are natives of a certain island of the North-west fringes, and suffer from a characteristic disinclination or inability to adapt to other races and peoples. As I have, of course, in view of one of the major tasks in front of me, no alternative to choosing parents who are white or partly so, this problem must be circumscribed. By, I think:

Second Couple. They combine between them many useful capacities. His parents came from the central landmass during World War II and he was brought up speaking several languages. They had the energy that often is to be observed in immigrants and refugees, and he has this, too. He is a doctor, an administrator, and a musician. Her mother is a native of the extreme western islands of the Northwest fringes: being "working class" and much handicapped by her origins in a class-obsessed society, though she was able to overcome these to a certain extent by energy and ability, she has made sure her daughter was equipped with as good an education as is available. Her father is of mixed race, which will almost certainly be an advantage. This woman has therefore as much energy and effort in her background as her husband. She is trained in medicine and sociology and writes books of an informative sort. This couple is not likely to divorce. They, because of their cosmopolitan background, are particularly able to view the world scene with competence and comparative lack of regional bias. They are healthy, well balanced, likely to be responsible parents. They have no children as yet. They are, because of their dispositions and their work, likely to travel.

This couple seems suitable.

JOHOR *reports:*

I had taken so much power from the Giants that I did not expect to see anything left of that sad habitation, its pitiful occupants. I travelled as fast as I could across blowing sands, and saw that these were deeper and wider, the rocks starker and blacker, no green anywhere, no life— just as on Shikasta the deserts spread while the forests were levelled or died of disease. The halls of the Giants were like a mirage, shimmering towers, battlements, courts, broken walls—ghosts and illusions, all, all, and I walked through them as through a soap bubble. In the great hall the thrones, the dais, the banners, the crowns, and the sceptres glimmered into sight and vanished, so that one moment I stood in a deceiving dream of halls and princes looking for Jarsum or for anybody at all who might survive there, and the next on empty sands that lifted and settled around my feet with a small hissing sigh. When the scene appeared, I saw the transparent wraiths of my old friends, Jarsum among them, but they dissolved, and I waited for a reappearance, and tried in that moment to grasp at least his hand— but when I stood where he had been a moment before, waiting for him to be there again, and he came, his great eyes yearning awfully towards me, he was like a reflection on water. Jarsum, Jarsum, I said, or called to him, through the shaking and dissolving reflections, Jarsum, you may not know it, but you and your companions have been of use in your end, you have helped us, you have steadied and speeded me in what I had to do . . . and then it *was* the end. It was as if a fountain had faltered and gone, the last emanations of that power that had sustained them from those millennia long ago faded and went and there was nothing. And never would be again.

I left there and walked towards the borders of Shikasta. I passed many possibilities of slipping over into the other Zones, Zones Four and Five in particular, and, remembering the lively scenes I had observed or taken part in on past visits, it was a real effort to make myself move on.

Besides, there was an unpleasant region of Zone Six to pass through, and I was not looking forward to it.

All around the boundaries with Shikasta, on a certain level, crowd the avid ghosts, and not one of us enjoys contact with them.

They are souls who were unable to break the links with Shikasta when they left it. Very often they are unaware they *have* left it, are like goldfish who find themselves inexplicably outside their bowl yearning in, not knowing how they got out or how to get back. Like hungry people at a feast: but while the food and festivities are real, they are not, dreams in a real world. These poor wraiths crowd around every part of Shikasta, as thick as bees. Some scenes, places, occasions, attract them irresistibly. Around the proud and the power-loving, there they cluster, trying to partake of what they yearn for, because in their lives they were powerful and proud and cannot stop themselves wanting that sweet food, or because they were beaten down and humiliated and wish now for revenge. Oh, the revengeful and bitter ghouls that surge all about the pomps and the powers of Shikasta! Scenes of sadism, cruelty, murder—there crowd those who allowed themselves to be sunk in the aromas of pain and the inflictions of it, and who never got their fill of it, and who want to feel it, or to deal it. . . . Sex: there they crush and crowd, for of sex one can never have enough, that is its nature, and most of those who stand hungry there are those who in life fed most on sex. Food: around the kitchens and the dining places throng the greedy, whose lives were spent in eating or thinking about it. Those who spent their lives on their own beauty, or on thoughts of the superiority of their family, or race, or country, those who . . . but every spendthrift passion has its attendant courtiers, swarming close, invisible, seeing everything, hungry, wanting, never fed, and never to be fed. . . .

And there are those who long for the subtler fulfilments, for not all by any means of these hungry ones long for the sensational and violent, the crude or the ugly.

Around those beds where lovers lie obsessed, what accomplished beings hover, savouring each caress, each long drunken look, each kiss— of all the intoxicants, this is the most powerful, and these are not savage or brutal ghosts, no hungerers for pain or to inflict it, not owners of comfortable bellies and soft beds—no, these may be among the most refined and responsive souls, most closely tuned to Canopus, but who allowed themselves to be tangled in these Shikastan nets and could not free themselves before they died. Among the fascinated crowds are uglier beings, the succubi and the incubi, the many varieties of vampire, those who have learned how to feed off the energies of Shikasta.

Around the accomplished and the talented, those who have easily, or through some lucky combination of circumstances, become artists of all kinds, the tellers of stories, musicians, makers of images or of pictures—the souls who linger here are to be pitied more than any. These knew what it was to feed the needs of poor mankind with the nourishments of art (part food though it is, only shadows of what they might have had) but who could not, for some reason to do with the oppressions and hazards that are the very nature of Shikasta, which chokes off and destroys so much vital creativity. These are not souls to be feared or shrunk from. As I passed by a scene, perhaps, of a scientist calculating the nature of stars and star-forces, or a woman at work on a tale that may help others to see a situation or a passion more clearly, I recognised friends crowding hungrily there. Poor ghosts. "Move on, move on," I urged, "leave here, don't allow yourselves to be fastened here around these glass walls, go—free yourselves. Find useful work in the other Zones, or return the hard way to Shikasta—those are your ways out. You may yearn and lean and pine here for long ages and never know anything but frustration and emptiness and longing. . . ." But they cannot hear, these bewitched ones, hanging there, eyes fixed on scenes which to them have a wonderful attraction, a glamour which makes them forget anything they ever really knew of the truth.

I passed through crowding souls who, knowing of the imminent and awful trials of Shikasta, tormented with anxiety for their children, their friends, their lovers, sigh and pine around the council rooms and discussion chambers where the powerful talk and make decisions as to the future of Shikasta—or think they do—and found there many old friends. They recognised me, some of them. "Johor," they cried, "Johor, look, let me back, let me tell them, let me, let me, me, me, me, me . . ." and great wails and groans go up, as they stand listening to the infantile wranglings of the conference tables, the matchings of strength with strength, power with power—and ahead lies destruction, where nothing will remain alive across continents but an occasional diseased animal, a demented child. "Johor, Johor," they cried, grasping me, pulling me back, "let me in, let me through, let me slip through now, and stand there among them and tell them, warn them . . ."

"Leave it," I said, "go, leave these frontiers. You've played your part, and it wasn't chosen by you—and if you did not do as well as you should, then turn your back on what you may not change now. Or if you want to be one who *can* change, then don't crowd there like little children who cannot do anything but *imagine* competence in a future they are unable to direct, children who are nothing at all except in their imaginations. You may not help your families, your friends. Not this way. Come back into Shikasta, but the hard way . . ."

But they cannot hear me, hear only what they want to hear. They return to their lamentings around the conference tables and the committee rooms.

Oh, the borders and frontiers of Shikasta are very terrible, not for the easily swayed to pity, not for the easily horrified. Many have faltered there, eyes so filled with what they see they are blinded to what they have to do. And I, too, pushing my way through, felt faint, and lost my strength to these bitter and famished ghosts. As I had done before, of course, and that helped me, being able to recognise what I felt—though this visit was so much worse than the last, things are so much worse, oh, poor Shikasta, its dramas being played out on such a stage, and with such crowded tiers of observers.

I left this region and approached the entry posts where the lines waited. I looked for Ranee, who had again worked her way halfway up her line, having lost her position to go and deal with the emergency. She was alone there. I could not see Rilla and Ben. I asked her where they were, and she said that she had brought them to the region of the lines, put them together, and returned to her own place. I stood by her, looking everywhere, then went up and down asking for them. At last I was told that a couple similar to those I described had been seen. They were in their places at the end of a long line, but had strayed off, attracted by something, and had not been observed to come back.

And now what should I do! Already late, and weakened—yet I had to go and search for them.

I did not have to go far into the scrubland. I saw before I came close, some coloured blobs or balls floating and playing in the air, and found that I had come to a standstill, watching, enchanted. It was as if these flying tinted balls had life and intention, and could direct themselves. As if they were playing a game, teasing each other, evading, then chasing and gently bumping, before swerving off again. I realised I had been there for some time, quite absorbed. I made myself go on. Soon I came on Ben and Rilla, sitting side by side on the warm white sand between shrubs, staring up, smiling, delighted, altogether lost. "Rilla! Ben!" I called, and called again. It was some time before I could attract their attention away from those delightful fleeing and pursuing balls or bubbles that now I was close under them seemed like animated soap bubbles, globules of differently tinted light, transparent, or seeming to be, for as one hung immediately above me—perhaps to observe me, I wondered?—I saw that inside transparent surfaces were moving sparks and flashes, always changing. At any moment Ben and Rilla would have forgotten me again, and I called to them to stand up and follow me. They did not, at least not at once. They looked up, they looked down, they looked anywhere and at anything but me. I saw Rilla was concealing something, and heard, or felt, a small pulse of complaint and fear. I went to her, and pulled up her fist, and made her open it, and she had captured one of these lights or bubbles which, through being confined in her hand, had lost most of its colour and vitality and was a dull sick thing pulsing feverishly, as if breathing for its life. I held my hand under hers, and lifted both, till our palms lay one above another in front of us, with the damaged creature recovering there, slowly regaining its life, and then suddenly it sped up and off and resumed its games among the others. And again I found I was standing staring, just as Ben and Rilla did, for I had never seen any- thing so pretty and engaging as the game of the lights, or the crystals. I put one arm around Ben, and one around Rilla, and walked them away from that place, while they hung back and dawdled and looked over their shoulders—just as they had with the scenes of the churning sands. And then, as we got away from the enchantments of the place, Rilla began scolding me. "Why did you take so long! I thought you'd be back to fetch me before this!" I could not help laughing, it was so absurd, and Ben laughed, too, but Rilla certainly did not, and kept up her scolding as we approached the long lines of waiting people.

I found Ranee, and left Rilla in her care, with precise instructions. For I reckoned that by the time Ranee reached the entry post, it would be time for Rilla to enter.

Then, taking Ben by the hand, while of course Rilla complained that I was abandoning her and favouring Ben, I went forward with him, past the lines, keeping a firm hold of him. He had understood suddenly that the time had come and was afraid, and I could feel him indecisive.

I said to him, "Ben, you have got to. Now. Trust me."

He sighed, and shut his eyes, and held on with both hands to my forearm.

Behind us the lines of waiting people stretched, winding away into a distance. I could not see their ends. Once they would have held a dozen or twenty souls. But as the wars of Shikasta, the hungers of Shikasta, the diseases of Shikasta, ate up people, now there were oppor- tunities, and opportunities again . . . some in those lines had been there when I entered Zone Six on this same visit, and had in the meantime gone in to Shikasta, had succumbed to some hazard—illness, accident, war—and were here again. How many brave faces did I see then, as I held fast to Ben, and he to me, as we went forward into the whirling, tinted mists. The throngs of waiting souls fell behind, disappeared into cloudy dark. We stood, the two of us together, in an opalescent mist. There was a singing hush, a stillness that throbbed. And throbbed . . .

At that moment it was necessary to collect oneself as at no other time. We had nothing to sustain us but the imprint of the Signature, which would emerge, like a brand on flesh that could show itself only in heat or under pressure. It was as if we had chosen deliberately to obliterate ourselves, trusting to an intangible we had no alternative but to trust.

We were like those brave souls on Shikasta who, believing that they stand for what is right and just, choose to defy wicked and criminal rulers, in the full knowledge that the penalty will be a deliberate destruction by corrupted doctors of their minds, their familiar under-standing of themselves, through drugs, psychological torture, brain damage, physical deprivation. But they trust, within their deepest selves, that they have resources which will sustain them through everything. We were like people jumping from a height into a pit of poisonous shadows, trusting that we would be caught . . .

In a thundering dark we saw lying side by side two clots of ferment-ing substance, and I slid into one half, giving up my identity for the time, and Ben slid into the other, and lay, two souls throbbing quietly inside rapidly burgeoning flesh. Our minds, our beings, were alert and knowing, but our memories had already slid away, dissolved.

I have to acknowledge—I can do no other—that this is a moment of fearful dismay. Even of panic. The terrible miasmas of Shikasta close around me and I send this report with my last conscious impulse.

DOCUMENTS RELATING to GEORGE SHERBAN (JOHOR)

RACHEL SHERBAN'S JOURNAL

I see I must plunge in. The more I think about it, the harder it gets. Facts are best. I told George I was actually starting this, and he said, Get your facts straight first.

I have two brothers, George and Benjamin, two years older than me. They are twins. Not true twins. I am Rachel. I am fourteen.

Our father is Simon. Our mother is Olga. Our name is Sherban, but it was Scherbansky. Our grandfather changed it when they came to England from Poland in the last war. (Second World.) Our grand-parents laugh when they say no one could pronounce Scherbansky. I used to get angry when they said this. I do not think the English are funny. They are stupid. My grandfather is Jewish. My grandmother not.

I see that our education has been far from ordinary. I am seeing a lot of things for the first time, as I think how to write this. Well of course that's the point I suppose.

First. Our family was in England where we were all born. Both our parents worked at a big London hospital. He did organising. She was a doctor. But they decided to leave England and got work in America. It was because England was so bureaucratic and stick-in-the-mud. They did not say this was why they left England never to return. Not to work. After America we went to Nigeria and then Kenya and then Morocco. Which is here. Usually our parents work together in a hospital or project. We always know about their work. They tell us what they are doing and why. They take a lot of trouble telling us. As I think about this so as to write it I see that this doesn't happen much to other children. Sometimes my mother Olga has to work somewhere by herself. I go with her. Even when I was a small child. It is funny I took it for granted. I must ask her why I was with her so much. I have asked her. She said, "In countries that have not become bureaucratic there is a lot of latitude." Then she said, "Anyway, they like children, this isn't England."

Our parents criticise many things about England. Yet they have sent us there quite a bit.

I have learned all sorts of things, but have not been regularly at school. I know French, Russian, Arabic, Spanish. And English, of course. My father has taught me mathematics. My mother tells me books to read. I know a lot about music because they are always playing music.

My brothers were sometimes with my mother, but these days mostly with Simon. When he went to seminars to give lectures or conferences he took them too. Sometimes our parents had us in school properly for a year or two years.

In Kenya this happened. I have just seen it. The headmaster was a friend of ours. He kept shifting us from class to class, pretending we didn't fit in, or had gone beyond a class or something. But what he was doing was making sure we learned a lot of different things. He did this with other children from outside Kenya and some of the black children too. He is a Kikuyu. We learned a lot of geohistory there, and geo-economics. We have had tutors all the time too. There is one thing to be said for being educated in this mad way, you don't get bored. But if I am supposed to tell the truth, then it is true that often I longed to be in one place and stay there and have friends for a long time. We seem to have a lot of friends, but they are often in another country. In fact more often than not.

We children have been sent for holidays to England three times. We stay in London, and then go to a family in Wales. They are farmers. We learn how to look after animals and about crops. My brother George was there for a whole year, December to December, to learn about the cycle of the seasons. Benjamin was critical about George going there, and didn't go himself, but he could have done. He was in a bad phase then. More than usual, I mean!

I was sorry when George went, I did not see him for a whole year.

I must tell the truth again. I have been jealous too much. When I was small I was jealous of the twins. They were together such a lot. When they were they often did not take any notice of me. George did more than Benjamin.

Benjamin always wanted to be with George when he was younger. People used to think Benjamin was younger than George. They are so different. Benjamin is not cheerful and confident like George. George was always telling Benjamin, Yes, you can do this, Yes, you can do that. Benjamin used to sulk and went away by himself. But when he came back he used to make George take notice of him.

And George always did. That is why I was jealous.

That is why I am still jealous.

When George was away for a year, I thought Benjamin would take notice of me, but he didn't. I didn't care all that much because really it is George I want to take notice of me.

Now I shall write down the <u>facts</u> I remember about when we were children.

I shall write what I think <u>now</u> about things that happened then. Not what I thought then.

When we were in New York we had a small apartment and we three children were in one room. One night I woke up and saw George standing by the window looking out. We were high up, twelve stories. It looked as if he was talking to someone. I thought he was playing, and wanted to join in. He made me be quiet.

In the morning I said at breakfast that George was at the window in the night. Mother was worried about it.

Later George said to me, Rachel, don't tell them, don't tell them.

When Mother or Father asked about it I said I was teasing.

But there were a lot of times I woke and George was awake. He was usually at the window. I did not pretend to be asleep. I knew he wouldn't be angry. I once asked him, Who are you talking to? He said he didn't know. A friend, he said. He seemed troubled. Not unhappy.

He was sometimes unhappy though. Not in the way Benjamin was. When Benjamin was in a bad mood all of us had to take notice and be upset too.

George used to get silent and go off into a corner. He pretended to be looking at a book. I could see he had been crying. Or wanted to. He knew I knew, just as he knew I knew about his being awake so much in the night. He just shook his head at me. That's all. Not like Benjamin. Benjamin used to quarrel and he hit me sometimes.

Once in Nigeria something happened. The boys had a room to themselves and I was alone. I hated this. I missed George so much. Sharing a room I was close to him and now I wasn't. He came into my room one night. I was asleep and woke up. He was sitting on the floor on some straw matting, leaning against my mosquito net. I put my head out of the net. There was moonlight outside and on the floor and I could see his face all shining because he had been crying. Not making a noise. He said to me, Rachel, this is a terrible place, it is a terrible place, it is a terrible . . . His voice was stuffed up and I could not understand at first. I tried to comfort him, saying Well, the family would move again, our parents had said we were going to Kenya. He did not say anything. Later I saw he was not talking about Nigeria. I can see that he came into my room because he was lonely, but I wasn't any help to him at all.

I see that he was very lonely then. I know Benjamin did not understand a lot of the things he said. And it is only now I understand some of them.

I have suddenly understood that Benjamin was so blustery and raucous often because he knew George was wanting him to understand but he couldn't.

I was eight when we went to Kenya.

George slept outside on the verandah of the house. The climate was different from Nigeria, healthy. He liked to be under the stars. I knew that he was awake often, and he did not want our parents to know how much. I sometimes crept out of the window of my room on to the verandah and sure enough he would be sitting on the verandah wall, staring out. This was outside Nairobi in some hills. Our house looked over a lot of country. It was beautiful. Sometimes we sat for a long time on the wall, and it was often moonlight or half-moonlight. Once an African came past very silent and he saw us and stopped to look. Then he said: Ho, ho, little ones, what are you doing there, you should be asleep. Then he went off laughing. George liked that. When I got sleepy George lifted me down from the wall. He pretended to stagger because I was heavy, but he didn't really think I was heavy. He staggered all over the verandah with me and we nearly killed ourselves not being able to laugh out loud. Then he helped me back through the window into my room. I loved those times with George, even though we never said much. Sometimes we sat there a long time and never said one word.

Once he did say something I remember. That afternoon our parents had had visitors. They were all people with important jobs in Kenya. There were black people, white people, brown people. I did not think of that sort of thing then because I was a child and I was used to everyone being different. Sometimes we have been the only white family in some places but I don't remember thinking much about it.

It was a party, a celebration of something. We children had helped serve drinks and food and stuff. Our parents always made us do jobs like that. Benjamin often did not like to do it. He used to say we had servants and why didn't they do it.

During the party George caught what I was thinking, and he smiled his special smile at me. This meant: Yes I know, and I agree. I had been thinking how silly they were, the grownups, not our parents, but the others, they were showing off the way grownups do.

Sitting in the moonlight that night on the wall, George said, There were thirty people there.

I already knew from his tone what he meant.

I was thinking, as I did so often then, that I knew exactly what he meant, but Benjamin usually didn't. But then he said something I hadn't expected. I remember that night because I cried a lot. For two reasons. One was that I did <u>not</u> always know what he was thinking, any more than Benjamin did. The other was that George was so lonely thinking that kind of thought.

George said, Passing teacups and glasses of booze and saying please and thank you . . .

Well, I was laughing at that, seeing what he saw.

But then he said, Thirty bladders full of piss, and thirty backsides full of shit, and thirty noses full of snot, and thousands of sweat glands pouring out grease . . .

I was upset, because he was speaking in a rough angry voice. And when I heard this voice, I was always ready to believe it was me he was angry with.

He went on and on, A room full of shit and pee and snot and sweat. And cancers and heart attacks and bronchitis and pneumonias. And three hundred pints of blood. And please and thank you and yes Mrs. Amaldi, and No Mr. Volback, and Please Mrs. Sherban, and Oh dear me Minister Mobote, and I am more important than you are, Chief Senior Register Doctor.

I could see he was angry. He was restless too, as he sometimes was, knotting himself together, and tying his legs around each other.

He was furious. He started crying.

He said: This is a terrible place, a terrible place.

I did not like it, and I went to bed, and I cried in bed.

Next day he was nice to me and he played with me a lot and I was not sure at all about liking that, because he was treating me like a baby.

I have not yet written down the facts of how we look. We are all different. It is because of the mix of the genes, our parents say.

George first. He is thin and tall. He has black eyes. His hair is black and straight. His skin is white but not like the white of white people from Europe. It is an ivory colour. In Egypt and here in Morocco there are plenty of people who look like him. It is our Indian grandparent coming out in his skin.

Now Benjamin. He takes after Simon. He is rather heavy. He gets fat easily. He has brown hair and blue-grey eyes. His hair curls. He is always sunburned, a reddish-brown.

Now me. I am more like George. I am not thin unfortunately. I have black hair. I have brown eyes, like Mother. My skin is olive even when I am not sunburned. In England no one notices me because I am not unusual. They think I am Spanish or Portuguese. Here no one notices me because I am not unusual. Everyone notices Benjamin.

What happened to us children that changed everything was when George spent the year on the farm in Wales. Olga and Simon said I was wrong to "pine" after George. And they made me do a lot of things in that year, two languages, French and Spanish, and taking guitar lessons. I wasn't pining. I was lonely. And when he came back I was still lonely. He was thirteen when he went to Wales, and fourteen when he came back. He was grown up. I did not understand that, but I do now.

During the whole of that year, Benjamin was difficult. He did not work well at school. He moped a lot. When George came back though, he tried to win Benjamin over and after a time he did. But I can see now that George had grown up, but Benjamin hadn't. Benjamin has always done everything to get George's attention. I don't think our parents know how much. That isn't because they are too busy to notice. Well, sometimes they are too busy. They spend a lot of time thinking about us and how to bring us up well. But a sister sees things that parents don't see. I suppose they have forgotten. I think they remember the overall thing, but not the smallness of things happening every day.

I see now that one of the reasons they wanted George away was to free Benjamin from George. Apart from George learning the cycle of the seasons. But that made things worse, the way I see it. Benjamin felt George had been given something he hadn't been. Yet he didn't want to go to Wales, and scorned George for being a farmer's boy. Benjamin is a bit of a snob.

I see there are a lot of facts I have taken no notice of at all. I wonder if you have to spend your whole life suddenly understanding facts that were perfectly obvious all the time.

When George came back he asked me several times, What has happened? Tell me what has happened? So I told him about Spanish and French and played him my guitar.

He was impatient, but he tried not to show it. He said, No, I don't mean just you. So I told him about Benjamin, though he knew about Benjamin, he spent so much time with him, and then when he was quiet, and I knew that that wasn't it, I said about our mother organising the big new hospital, and our father helping her. That was better, but it wasn't right. For he said, Rachel, our family isn't everything, we aren't all that important. So I got panicky. I do, when I know he is disappointed in me. I gabbled on about Mother and Father and what they had said, but he lost interest. He went on being kind to me, when he had time. But he was very restless just then. He could not keep still ever. He was with a group of boys at the college a lot and they were wild and noisy and I could not believe this was George. But I did understand that they talked about things I wasn't interested in then.

I started to listen when my parents discussed the state of the world and I enrolled in the Current Events classes at the school, and I listened a lot to the News and Information programmes.

I see that our family is different from most others in this way. Everywhere we go, everyone is passionately for some Party or other. Or pre-

tends to be. It is easy to see when they are pretending. Our parents
often say people who pretend must not be blamed. It is surviving, and
that is more important than waving flags. Sometimes when they say
that people are shocked. But I know they think politics is a mistake.
They think that political people are on the wrong track. All they are
interested in is doing things, like reorganising hospitals and making
things work. They don't often say this, except with us or close friends.
They don't say it so much actually, it's what they <u>don't</u> say that makes
it obvious. But everywhere politics is so important, and I can see that
this must have been a big problem for them, now I think about it. I
mean, it must be like saying you were an atheist in the Middle Ages.

Facts. <u>England</u>. The first two times we children visited it were before
the Dictatorship, and there was nothing much to notice but things
being inefficient. But the third time, food was short, even though it was
on a farm, and Mr. Jones and Mrs. Jones were worried. I have been
asking Simon and Olga and they say that a lot of people were in prison
and people got arrested suddenly and then vanished. Well, there's
nothing new in <u>that</u>. And the people who couldn't get work, particularly
the young ones, were rampaging about. That was before they were put
in armies and kept in camps. Wales and Scotland were the same, although they were Independent. The Dictatorship was trying to be all
English, and not to have so many foreigners. When George went for
his year farming, it was hard to arrange. Travel got difficult after the
Dictatorship and anyway, people couldn't afford it. Mother says that it
was only because of <u>special</u> <u>contacts</u> that George was allowed in. Although we are all English. I mean, visits are all right, but difficult, but
living there for a whole year was nearly impossible. I have underlined
the special contacts because I see more and more how important that is.

<u>America</u>. Olga and Simon say that it is so rich anyway, the crisis was
masked. But I remember seeing lines of people waiting for food. And
Olga says it was the same, like England, the unemployed milling about
and rioting and smashing things, and when we were there the beginning
of camps and uniforms and keeping them under military discipline.
Nigeria was different because people had been poor anyway. Perhaps
that is better than having been very rich and then getting poor. I have
just had that thought. In Nigeria we saw hungry people and sick people.
That was when I began to go with my mother everywhere. Into hospitals and relief camps. There was an epidemic. My first epidemic. I
went with her. Of course I was inoculated against <u>everything</u>. But they
weren't sure what the disease was. To this day she says they don't really

know what it was. Now I think how brave she was to take me every-where. She says when I asked her (just now) that I have to be ready for danger and emergency. And that is one of the reasons all three of us have been taken to so many places with our parents, even into camps full of illness and epidemics and famines. In Nigeria there weren't so many unemployed, because most of them got on to the land somehow. In Kenya it wasn't so very different—poor people, and different kinds of illness. Olga and Simon were working on a big team for six months with people who had escaped from a bad famine. They were doing hygiene in the camps. There were a lot of young people with no work and they were put into uniforms too. What big armies everyone has now. I hadn't thought of it like that before. Simply because of no work. In Egypt it was different in some ways. Very very poor. Illness, again. Olga and Simon at it as always, camps and relief. I remember watching the kids running along the streets breaking everything and screaming and setting fire. I was afraid that our building, the one we had a flat in, would be set on fire. Two buildings in that street were. All the city was full of burning buildings. More armies! More uniforms! And now Morocco. Well, it is different again, but n ɔt so very, if you come to think of it. Different words, but the same things. Poor people. Armies. Not enough to eat.

I see I have got away from politics. I meant to write about all the political parties. Governments. That kind of thing. But it seems to me that in each country our family has been in, the same things have happened. Are happening. But America is a Democracy. Britain is Socialist. Nigeria is a Benevolent Dictatorship. (I have just asked Olga and that is what she said.) Kenya is Free and Developing. (Mother says, Benevolent Oligarchy.) Morocco is Islamic and Free and Socialist and Developing. (Benevolent.) I don't know if this is the sort of fact I ought to be dwelling on? I can't believe it matters. Well, everyone else seems to think it matters. But it seems to me to show that our education has been very peculiar to say the least. Nearly everyone is passionate about whatever political party it is. When we have visitors, they have certain things to say, and they say them, one after the other. Often I and George have had to stop ourselves giggling. And even gone out of the room. And this happens in each country, it doesn't matter what the govern-ment is. Of course Mother and Father are never part of any political thing, but they are always Experts employed by the Government. That means, if you are in the habit of thinking like that, they must be supporters of that government. Or might be. And this means that visitors have to say certain things for the benefit of Mother and Father and for the other visitors. It is very boring. Well, that is all I am going to say about that.

Special contacts. I see that this is important. I see that it has been important always and I didn't understand that. Because of writing this I keep seeing things. I am trying to be careful to write down everything as I think now and not as then, but it is difficult, because I keep slipping back into that frame of mind.

The first thing I have to think about is Hasan. Soon after George came back from the year on the farm, Hasan came to the house and George began spending time with him. If you come to think of it, it is funny how it happened. Because nothing much seemed to happen. Hasan was an ordinary kind of visitor, one of the people in the Medical Association. But he was George's friend right from the start. And we didn't think anything of it. Correction, I didn't think anything of it, because it has always happened like this.

The first time, it was New York. George must have been only seven. There was a woman who came a lot, and she used to take George out to see things and do things. Once or twice Benjamin went too but he didn't like her. I asked George what they did and he said, We talk about things. I didn't think much about that then, but I am now. And then on holiday in Wales, the three of us. There was a man came from Scotland. We believed he was an expert in connection with farming. Perhaps he was. Now I wonder. He took George off to camp once, and fishing too. And other things. I've forgotten what. I wasn't taking much notice but now I wish I had. Benjamin went camping once. He didn't like it much. He was always finding things boring. That was his style. I see it was not so much what he really thought but a style. To protect himself. I have been sitting here wondering if I was asked to go on these trips. Why didn't I go too? But what I do remember is I loved the farm so much I never wanted to go a step from it, they could have invited me to do anything and I wouldn't have left Mrs. Jones. But I do remember going for a walk with George and this man. I remember something about him. Which I could recognise now. He was called Martin. George liked him. And then there was Nigeria. When the epidemic was on and our parents so busy, we weren't always with them. We started to have tutors then. One tutor came from Kano and he taught us mathematics and history and Arabic. Also how to notice everything. He made a great point of that. He was a tutor for all of us, but now I see that George went off with him a lot. And in Kenya we had tutors as well as the school. It was the same there. I mean, it was always George, I see that now.

I have asked Mother about it. (Have just finished asking.) <u>She</u> <u>knew</u> <u>exactly</u> <u>what</u> I <u>was</u> <u>asking</u> <u>from</u> <u>the</u> <u>first</u> <u>word</u> I <u>said</u>. She had been expecting me to ask her one day and had wondered how to answer. I could see all that as soon as I asked her. She set herself carefully to answer all my questions. She has always been patient about questions. I have understood this because of watching other mothers with questions from their children. When Mother gets asked a question she makes it clear that she thinks it is important and she is taking it seriously.

I said I was writing this. Well she knew that. I said I had to get my facts right. And then I told her that as I wrote I was understanding things. She was not at all surprised by that. She told me a lot about Martin. Who he was and that kind of thing. And about the tutors and the woman in New York. But when she had ended with saying that they were like this and like that and did this kind of work or whatever, she said to me, as if I had asked some exact question, I <u>don't</u> <u>know</u>, <u>Rachel</u>. The way she answered that, framed the question I hadn't asked.

I will put down where this is happening. We are in a little house with a flat roof. We like it better than the big block of flats where we were first. This is in a part of the town where it is nearly all local people, i.e., <u>Natives</u>. So called. They are most of them lovely and we have friends among them. I mean, real friends. At night we often sleep on the roof. It is lovely. We lie out, on mattresses and look at the stars and talk. This is the best time ever for us all. I get so happy I don't know what to do with myself. When the family is together at last. Because that isn't often. Father for instance is away this minute, organising hospitals with a team of doctors. Doctors "All-Sorts," Benjamin calls teams like this, meaning, all races. Father is working very hard. Well, I suppose that goes without saying.

There are some small rooms around a court. The rooms have earth floors. This is not a house "people like us" live in often. Some of the white people say we are "eccentric." I'd rather be eccentric and sleep on the roof and look at the stars and the moon.

Mother is at this minute in the court, writing a report for the WHO. The court is not just for us but for several families. There is a lot of noise. She works with everything going on, kids playing etc. There are some lilies in a big terra-cotta pot, and a rather dingy little pool, dusty, but it is better than nothing.

Mother is sitting on a cushion on the edge of the pool writing. I sat on the edge of the pool too.

I didn't have to prod her after she said, I don't know, Rachel—I just sat and waited. I thought perhaps she would not say anything at all. I understand her when she doesn't. We are together so much, we know what we are thinking. I knew that Mother knew I was in one of those times when we understand things suddenly, all at once.

She said to me, What do you think about it?

That surprised me, I must confess. She said it in a low voice, not frightened, not like that, but as if truly not knowing what to say, and as if she truly thought I might be able to say something she hadn't thought of.

I said, Well, Olga, it seems to me as if there is something very funny about it.

She said, Yes. Yes.

We sat there quite a long time. It wasn't as if this was a good time to have an important talk. I mean, because of the children. The baby from the room across the court would have fallen into the pool if I hadn't got hold of it, for instance.

I said, It is only now I have had a sudden feeling that there was something all the time.

Yes, it started very early. George was seven.

Yes, with the woman in New York.

Miriam.

She was a Jewish woman?

Yes.

It hasn't ever mattered what they were.

No.

Then I said to her, in the same tone of voice she had used to me, low, and in my case it was because I was a bit afraid, really, George is special in some way?

Yes, that must be it.

What does Simon think?

He saw it first. I was quite frightened about it all at one point, Rachel. But he told me not to be. He told me to think about it. So I did. I have never thought about anything so hard in my life. I believe that since then that is what I have been thinking about. Yes, I can say that, Rachel.

That was all for then. I took the baby back to its mother. There is one thing about living like this. No one could say we aren't integrated with Moroccan life at its roots.

I have been sitting here thinking. This room is my bedroom. It is more like a cubbyhole. But I like it. It is very cool. It is all mud. It has an earthy smell. A damp smell, because I sprinkle water in the morning before the sun gets hot. And I throw down water outside the door morning and evening, to keep the dust down, and the smell is gorgeous.

When I look out of the door, there is blue sky. That's all. Blue sky. Hot.

There are two things on my mind at this moment.

One is this. Benjamin. One of the reasons Benjamin is so difficult and <u>awful</u> and sulks so much, and tries to quarrel with George is, he is jealous because George goes with Hasan so much. But Hasan has more than once asked him to go out to a café or something but Benjamin never will. That is because he thinks he is being put off with a café or a walk in the evening. I know this because unfortunately I have only to watch myself to know. I think of George having all kinds of really deep experiences with Hasan, I don't know what, and cafés aren't much. But I've asked George at nights when we lie out on the roof and he says: We talk, that's all.

Now when I look back at all the places and people, and I've asked him, he has always said, We talk, that's all. Or, He tells me things.

Benjamin has refused the <u>special</u> <u>contacts</u> from the very first. From when he was seven in New York and he didn't like Miriam. That is the truth. He has always had the opportunity, just as George had, and Benjamin has always refused it. You can think about it and think about it. I am thinking about it, and there is something so <u>awful</u> there I don't know what to do with myself, because of course I am thinking, What have I refused? I have always been offered everything too, but I always had some good reason not to. Like loving Mrs. Jones and wanting to be in the kitchen cooking with her and feeding the chickens.

Benjamin. It has always been the same. What he has wanted, right from the beginning, has been something <u>more</u> than what he was offered. He wanted to be asked by himself with Miriam or Hasan or whoever. I bet he wouldn't have said Miriam was boring if Miriam had asked him out by himself. And when we had tutors and George went off with one of them, Benjamin never went. He said, once, Stupid black man. The funny thing is, this isn't what he <u>really</u> thinks. I mean, he doesn't think that blacks are stupid or anything like that. He says this kind of thing as part of his <u>style</u>. And that is frightening when you think of it. I mean, anybody can put on an act, but then you are stuck with it. Like that mime with the mask on his face he couldn't get off. There is something frightening about all this. Benjamin truly doesn't like living here. He makes jokes about "the native quarter." Yet he adores sleeping on the roof and he makes friends with all the local kids, and he is sweet with the little kids. But he means it too. He would like a nice boring modern flat in a nice boring modern building with nice boring people. What I think is, now I am thinking, is that Benjamin says this sort of thing simply because he isn't treated as special. But George hasn't been treated as special. George has always gone along with what was there. He has seen it, but Benjamin hasn't.

Yet it was never anything much. So you would think at the time.

You could even say that nothing at all has ever happened. Well, what did? George has made trips, and gone camping, been taken to tea or a museum or something by someone or another. Or a tutor has said, Let us go to the park. Or a mosque or something. Or just sitting and talking under a tree on the edge of a street. Once I saw George with Ibrahim sitting on the earth under a tree. He was about nine. Or ten. In Nigeria that was. They were talking. Just talking. I looked at them and I wished I was there too. But I believe I must have said no when I was invited. I can't remember it, but I believe so.

<u>What</u> these people are, that is the point. After they have been coming for a while to the house, then I say to myself, Here it is again.

What is it, then?

That is the point.

Well, that is the second thing on my mind, <u>what</u> these people are.

I liked Hasan from the start, but I thought he was old. I suppose he isn't. Mother says he is about forty-five. That is about Simon's age.

Hasan talks to George a great deal. Hasan spends more time with George than any of the other "special contacts" have done.

George is with Hasan nearly every day. He went away with Hasan to the Sacred City for a week too. Now I am <u>thinking</u> about it. That was only last month. When George came back, I noticed our parents didn't ask him what had happened there. They both treat George as if he is grown up. He is sixteen. Are they afraid of him? <u>That</u> <u>is</u> <u>the</u> <u>wrong</u> <u>word</u>. There is a right word, but I don't know what it is.

What I mean is this. The more you think about all this, the more amazing it is. But not in a dazzling way, as you say, How amazing. I mean, your mind keeps going deeper and deeper in.

Every day there is more to think about. (This is being written a bit at a time every day.) And I think a lot in between, and I go and ask Mother questions. When George comes in, I try to talk to him, but that doesn't happen very often. He isn't unkind. He doesn't tease, the way he used to, before he was grown up.

I wish we could go back to before George was grown up. I don't want to grow up. I want to stay a little girl. I am writing this because I am supposed to be telling the truth. So that is the truth. Sometimes (recently) I have watched Simon and Olga at their lives, and it is so hard for them always, I can see that, not only the working so hard, I have only just understood that they have <u>heavy</u> lives. That <u>is</u> the right word. For once. And I see George at this time, and I know he is finding it hard.

I would say that he is thinking furiously. This is what I think is the main thing going on. He sometimes has a look on him that I feel on myself when I sit here thinking and thinking. As if things are crowding in too fast and you are afraid you can't catch them all. You <u>know</u> you are not catching them all.

He sits by himself a lot. Sometimes he is in the courtyard and all the children of this house and a lot of the houses nearby are there too. He plays with them and tells them stories but he is thinking. He is so restless! He gets up and moves off as soon as he has sat down sometimes, as if a pin has been stuck into him. As soon as the sun goes, he is up on the roof. He forgets about eating. Sometimes I take him a plate of something. He often gives it to the kids. It goes without saying that they are all hungry most of the time. He sits with his back to a little bit of roof, with one leg out and his arms on his other knee, which is raised, and he is looking out over the roofs and into the sky. And he is thinking. Sometimes at night I wake up and I see him sitting up awake, looking at the sky. And our parents wake too, but just go to sleep again. And now I wonder if they knew all the time that he often didn't sleep at night when he was four or five, let alone seven when Miriam came first. Have they known all that? I have tried to get near the subject with Mother, but she doesn't like to talk about that, I can see. I think she did know all the time but only understood what she thought about it later, like me. But that in itself is difficult. <u>Heavy.</u> Because if what we think now is different from what we thought then, we can take it for granted that what we think in a year will be different again. Or even a <u>month</u> the way my thoughts are changing at the moment. Your thoughts are the last thing you can rely on.

Yet for all that, something else is there you can rely on. Behind the thoughts.

Although this very strange thing whatever it is is going on now, our family life is quite ordinary and normal: even Benjamin is normal, I suppose. There are other families with sultry children. Father says Benjamin is "very sultry" when he gets exasperated with him.

Benjamin is really awful actually. But I know that what is making him like this is that he doesn't understand where he has gone wrong. He must know he has said "no" to what George is doing now. He must think about it. Benjamin may be "sultry" but he isn't stupid. He is being driven quite crazy by George. He thinks of nothing else.

When George came back from the week in the Sacred City he would not ask one question, but he hung about George all the time like a thunderstorm. George is always kind with Benjamin. Well most of the time. As he is with me. But I know that often he is too preoccupied with thinking to know we are there. And he probably wishes we weren't. I hang about too. I am always on the lookout for a word or a look from George. Let alone a smile. When he was still a child he had a marvellous smile. It was a warm friendly smile. But he is less likely to smile these days. He moves about all hunched up. It looks as if he had an invisible weight on his shoulders, and he is trying to stop himself from throwing it off. Sometimes he looks quite tormented.

And then suddenly, usually when the family is together at table or on the roof, he gets very funny and lively and plays all kinds of games and is very affectionate with us. I watch Mother and Father and they are relieved. They love it when he is like this. And Benjamin gets like a little boy, and shouts and laughs too much, but that is from relief. I am afraid I am just the same.

I hope I am not such a weight on Simon and Olga as Benjamin is.

I have just shut my eyes and looked at the expression on their faces when they look at Benjamin. It is patient and humorous. When they look at George their faces are sweet, and joyful. That is the exact word. I love looking at their faces when George is being funny and sweet. It is exactly as if they had been given a wonderful present. Well I don't think they feel that Benjamin and I are wonderful presents. Not to judge by their faces.

I see that this piece about Facts is all about George. I didn't know that was going to happen when I started.

It was Hasan who said I should write this journal.

I hadn't actually forgotten it was Hasan, but that fact was at the back of my mind. I wouldn't be surprised if I wasn't capable of forgetting it altogether.

It is extremely funny what we remember and what we choose not to. What happened was this.

It was just after sunset. The moon was coming up. There were hardly any stars yet. It was lovely. It is wonderful after the hot day is over. The dust is so strong and sweet, because the water has been sprinkled on it. And the cries and the talk from the town around us are mysterious. And the Call to Prayer, too, I love it. I shall hate leaving here. I hope we won't have to, not for a long time. But I suppose it won't last. And the smells of the spices in the cooking. I get quite drunk on it all every evening at sunset time.

George had gone up on the roof by himself. I couldn't help myself, I went up there too. He smiled when I got up on the roof, but then went on sitting as if I weren't there at all. I was miserable because he didn't take any notice of me. Shortly after that Hasan came up. George didn't seem surprised to see him. Hasan sat in another angle of the roof. He did not say anything for a time. The heat was coming out of the mud of the roof into my back and into my feet. I can't remember how the conversation started. Now that I am looking back, and linking this with other times I was with George and Hasan I realise that I often did not take any notice of the beginnings of conversations. George and Hasan were talking, mostly Hasan, with George listening very intently. George sometimes nodded or gave a quiet smile as he does when something pleases him. I understood that evening. I understood that I was understanding. I could have understood before, that when George is with Hasan and Hasan is talking, George is hearing things in what Hasan is saying that are quite beyond me. That I can't hear at all. I could see from George's face that in quite ordinary things that were said was much much more. I just couldn't grasp it. It was going too fast for me. It was above my head. The conversation was apparently about not very much. I was thinking in an agonised sort of way, that they weren't talking about anything important or special. Yet George's face kept lighting up as he understood the things that were there.

I was so miserable and frustrated that I was nearly crying.

Hasan noticed, and kept an eye on me, and went on talking to George for a while. Then he turned straight to me, so that he faced me, and he began talking to me, not in the same way, but simpler. He asked me if I kept a diary or anything like that. I said that I had a little diary, and I wrote in it things like, Had an Arabic lesson or guitar lesson or went to college. He said he would like me to write an account of my childhood.

Now I must confess something. The truth. When he said that, quite casually, I felt a terrific surge of resentment. He wasn't my tutor or anything! Why did he say, as if he had every right to it, that <u>he</u> wanted me to do this or that! But even while I was being resentful I was thinking that if he had asked me if I wanted to spend every afternoon with him, while he talked to me, and George wasn't there, I wouldn't have felt angry or resentful at all. On the contrary!

I knew that he understood exactly what I was feeling.

Then he gave me a little nod, as if to say, It will wait, don't worry.

Then he went on talking to George, in that way which was above my head.

I wanted him to talk to me again, ask me questions. I was longing for him to say again that he wanted me to write something for him. I had all sorts of ideas in my head. I would write him essays about when I went with Olga to the virus epidemic and I helped nurse there for a whole month. I wanted him to see me as someone sensible and responsible. Olga said to me that I had been invaluable in the epidemic and she could rely on me to do exactly as I said I would. I was proud enough to die when she said that, but I wanted Hasan to see me like that. And then when they took no notice of me I started thinking rude and silly things like, Oh, if you think I'm just a young miss, all insipid and ordinary, well then, I shall be. And I was sitting there, all derisive inside (just like Benjamin) thinking I would write an essay like the silly ones I have had to do in some schools, What I Did in the Holidays.

While I was thinking this, I wasn't listening at all to George and Hasan, and yet now I would give <u>anything</u> to have that chance again— just to sit there, trying to <u>hear.</u> I had not been offered such a chance before. Not being with George and Hasan for a couple of hours, quite alone, while they talked. And why should I be offered it again? I spoiled that one when it was given to me. I see now that this happened <u>on purpose.</u> I had been wanting and agitating all the time to be with George and Hasan, doing all the exciting things that I imagined they did—I don't know <u>what!</u> But it turns out that all that happens is that Hasan talks in that very ordinary but special sort of way, and George takes it in. He is riveted by it. He is so absorbed that you could throw water over him and I believe he wouldn't notice it.

But when I <u>was</u> offered the same, then I did not know how to listen, my emotions got in the way, I was sitting there all raging and wanting them to look at me, talk to me, like a little child.

I see now that this was made to happen so that I could see—I was being made to see—what stood between me and being able to learn from Hasan.

Anyway, since I am telling the truth, here goes. I rushed down off the roof, and got an essay I had written for English Comprehension. I was proud of this essay. I got good marks. But now I wonder. I shall put in the essay here. It wasn't long. This was because I was trying to give the impression in the essay that my noble emotions silenced me, or something of the kind.

THE OLD MAN AND THE DYING COW

On the television last night I saw something that affected me and changed me forever.

The television set was in the public square and a lot of people saw it. They were all poor people, who never have had enough to eat.

It was a programme about the famine in the Sahel. Several famines in fact, because they had taken shots from different programmes to make a general report.

One of the shots stays in my mind.

An old man is sitting by a cow.

The old man is extremely thin. His ribs are showing. His collarbone and his upper arms are like a skeleton.

But he has a patient wise air, and his eyes are thoughtful. And very dignified.

The cow is so thin, she is just skin stretched tight over her ribs, and the pelvis bones are sticking right out. You can already see how she will be when she dies in a few days.

But her eyes look into the camera, and they are patient and wise.

There is nothing but dust everywhere for miles around. Nearby is a patch of withered sticks which is the millet that was planted for the food for that year. But the drought has killed it all.

The cow has walked until she staggered and subsided to the earth. She will never get up again. She will die here.

The sun is burning down.

The old man has built a little roof to shade her. It is some reeds stretched across four sticks. This gives a little thin shade.

This cow is his friend.

The old man is sitting by the cow. She is in the stripy shade from the reeds, but he is in the full sun. The dust is blowing over them.

There is not enough water for everyone.

The old man has a little water in a tin cup. The cow sometimes pants and her tongue starts lolling out and then he puts some drops of water on the tongue and he swallows a few drops himself.

There they sit. He will sit with the cow until it dies.

The cow knows it is going to die.

The cow thinks that she has belonged to this man and his family all her life. But the wife and the children have died. The cow is wondering why she has to lie here not able to get up, by the old man, and why the dust is everywhere, and there is no rain and no food and no water.

The cow doesn't understand.

The old man doesn't understand. But he says it is The Will of Allah.

I don't think it is The Will of Allah.

I think it is wicked, wicked, and Allah will punish us all for letting the old man die there and his poor cow die in the hot dust.

Why? Oh God!

Why? Oh Allah!

Well, I got back up to the roof with this in my hand, ready to give it to Hasan. He was talking to George and not about to take notice of me. I sat down again.

By then all the sky was full of bright stars, and it was the time when everyone in the little houses was eating. I knew that soon our supper would be ready for us.

Then Olga did call up, Supper.

Hasan finished what he was saying, and got up. He was wearing the usual white robe, and he seemed very tall and a bit shadowy. My heart was aching. It was aching badly. I did not know what to do. I was frantic.

George got to his feet and stood by Hasan. I saw to my surprise that George is very nearly as tall as Hasan.

Both were looking at me while they stood there, tall and shadowy, with the stars all around them.

Hasan smiled. I held out my essay but he did not take it. Of course he didn't. He hadn't asked for it!

So then I said to him, tumbling it all out, I want to do it, I'll do the diary, I want to, really.

Good, was all he said.

And believe it or not, I <u>again</u> was full of resentment, because he hadn't taken my precious essay. And as if he should have congratulated me or made a fuss of me or something for saying I would do this journal.

First I went down the outside of the house on the stairway. Then George behind me. Then Hasan. I was longing for Hasan to come in to supper. He had come several times.

But at the foot of the steps he said goodnight, and George said good-night and that was that.

Benjamin was not at supper, thank goodness.

That is how I came to write all this.

And now I know why he wanted me to write it.

This bit is being written several weeks later. Nine to be exact.

Two <u>facts.</u> One is, several times I have <u>found</u> <u>myself</u>—I put it like this because it is always by accident apparently, with Hasan and George when they are talking. Or rather Hasan is talking and George listening. At least now I don't emote and grovel inside. I can listen. Sometimes I have just caught the drift of what is being said. But the truth is that I know that after being in on a conversation like this, George has under-stood one thing and I have understood another. That is the nature of this kind of talk.

The second fact is that George has done something I'd never never have expected not in a thousand years. He has become the leader of a whole <u>gang</u> of boys at the college. They are just as <u>silly</u> and <u>noisy</u> and <u>awful</u> as any of these gangs anywhere. They are always rushing about and making speeches, full of self-importance.

And George is with them.

I think it is awful.

I know that Mother doesn't like it, nor does Father.

As for Benjamin, of course he is having the time of his life, being full of scorn.

But George sees Hasan all the time as well. I don't know what to think.

This is being written later. Months.

George has been to India, to visit Grandfather's family.

He is even more grown up, if possible, but he is still boss of that ghastly gang and he is with Hasan more than he is ever with us.

History of Shikasta, VOL. 3014, *Period Between World Wars II and III.* Armies: Various Types of: The Armies of the Young.

"Coming events cast their shadows before." This Shikastan observation was of particular appropriateness during an epoch when the tempo of events was so speeded up. Small harbingers of major social phenomena could be noted, not one or two centuries, but a few years before, sometimes even months. Never was there a time on Shikasta when it was easier to see what was coming; never a time when it *could* have been so easy for them to understand the simple truth that they were not in control of what was happening to them.

Already in the eighth decade every government on Shikasta was preoccupied, often fearfully and secretively, with the consequences of mass unemployment, and particularly among the young. By then it was evident that the new (and often unforeseen) technologies would make mass unemployment inevitable everywhere, even without the world economic crisis which was due mostly to the spending of the wealth and resources of the planet primarily on wars and the preparations for wars: inevitable even if the population was not increasing at such a rate. (The checks on this increase by deaths due to famines, epidemics, and natural disasters—these last enormously increased due to the cosmic pressures—did not impose a significant effect until later.)

By that time knowledge of mass psychology, crowd control, the psychology of armies, was sophisticated within the limits Shikasta had imposed on itself. [SEE SUBSECTION 3, "The Shifting Criteria and Standards in the Scientifically 'Respectable' and Permitted. Scientific Bigotry Analysed and Compared with Political, and Religious Bigotry in Several Cultures." VOL. 3010, CHAPTER 9, "Results of Secret Research in Military Scientific Establishments and Their Impacts on Civilian and Revealed Science."]

All governments had a pretty clear idea of the dilemmas they faced; and most engaged, to one degree or another, in intensive and permanent discussions with experts on the control of populations.

By the end of the decade no one could be in ignorance as to what must be expected from large numbers of permanently unemployed youth. Already the cities were helpless before the aimless, random, unorganised violence characteristic of small groups of the young, male and female, who "for no reason" destroyed anything they could. The amenities on which the cities of Shikasta were dependent for even an approximation to comfortable living—telephones, transport, parks, public buildings, anything in fact that came into the public domain— might at any moment be destroyed, defaced, or made temporarily inoperative. The cities were no longer safe at night, for these groups of young robbed, assaulted, murdered, always on impulse—and without ill-feeling, almost as a game.

The remedy, an increase in policing—a general increase in militarisation, in fact—was already highlighting the nature of the problem. What is begun has a momentum: the consequences of greater police surveillance, sharper penalties, and the further cramming of prisons already overfull, must be even greater police surveillance and powers, sharper penalties, and a criminal population becoming steadily more brutalised. But these were the beginnings of the problem: its infancy. Rampaging crowds of—at that stage—mostly male youth, on special occasions, such as public games and spectacles; the occasional, sporadic, apparently motiveless violence of small groups—these symptoms were the faint shadow of things to come, a harbinger, even though the public life of cities was already transformed, and the older people mourned lost civil standards and amenities, for it must be remembered that while we may look back at, and can study, a century of deepening barbarism, of increasing horror, a family wanting no more than to live without challenge or drama could easily find a quiet street, and "peace," provided they were fortunate enough to live in a comparatively sheltered and favoured geographical area, and provided they were able to make the mental adjustment to relegate war—and its consequences—into something that happened elsewhere and did not affect them; or something that had happened to them, but between such and such dates, and then taken itself off.

In innumerable cities during this epoch of almost permanent war, when the wealth of Shikasta was poured into war, when every information channel poured out news of war and war preparations, it was possible, for short periods, to live, by means of making constant mental adjustments, in a state of quite comfortable illusion.

But this was not possible for the governments, which had to face the problem of multitudes of people, nearly all young, who had no prospect of any kind of work, who had never worked, and whose education fitted them only for idleness.

At some point their numbers had to increase to the point where much more than occasional and haphazard violence, casual vandalisation, could be expected. Crowds, masses, would, as if at a signal, but seeming to themselves "by chance," pour through cities, smashing everything they could find, killing—casually and without reason— those they found in the streets, and when the orgy of destruction was over, return sullen and bewildered to their homes. Hordes, or small armies, or bands, or even smallish groups, would rage through country- sides, killing animals, overturning machinery, burning crops, working havoc.

It was clear what had to be done. And it was done. Numbers of these potential arsonists and destroyers were taken into various military organisations that had civilian designations; what was done, in fact, was what always was done in times of such disturbances on Shikasta: the thief was set to catch the thief, the despoilers were controlled by the despoilers, put into uniform and made into public servants.

But there would be more, and more, and more . . . there *were* more and more: millions. And millions.

Armies have their own momentum, logic, life.

Any government putting men, or women, into uniform, and keeping them in one place under discipline knows it has to exercise this mass constantly and vigorously, to make sure its *energies are safely har- nessed*: though few Shikastans understood that phrase in its di- mensions as they could, and should. Masses of individuals in military conditions are no longer individuals, but obey very different laws, and cannot be allowed idleness, for they will begin to burn, loot, destroy, rape, from the sheer logic of the mass of their diverse powers.

The remedies were not many, and not effective, or at least not for long. One was to create not one army, owing allegiance to one slogan, commander, idea, but as many as possible, and in many uniforms. In each geographical area were dozens of different subarmies, encouraged to think of themselves as different from each other. And encouraged to compete in as many ways as could be devised. Sports, public games, mock battles, treks, hikes, climbs, marathons—the whole of Shikasta was overrun by energetic young people in a thousand different uni- forms, competing energetically and vociferously in what were being kept, by dint of much official vigilance, harmless ways.

And still the millions increased.

Even more the wealth of the planet was being spent on war, the nonproductive.

These armies were fed, were kept warm, were cared for, but outside the armies the populations were fed increasingly badly, and there were fewer and fewer goods to go round. Terrorised by their "protectors," dependent entirely on the good will of the uniformed masses, the civilians, the unorganised, the unmilitarised, the uninstitutionalised, sank always more into insignificance and helplessness.

The gap between the young—in uniform or hoping to be—and the old, or even the middle-aged, was almost total. The older people became increasingly invisible to the young.

At the top of this structure was the privileged class of technicians and organisers and manipulators, in uniform or out of uniform. An international class of the highly educated in technology, the planners and organisers, were fed, were housed, and interminably travelled, interminably conferred, and formed from country to country a web of experts and administrators whose knowledge of the desperateness of the Shikastan situation caused ideological and national barriers to mean less than nothing between themselves, while in the strata below them these barriers were always intensifying, strengthening. For the crammed and crowding populations were fed slogans and ideologies with the air they breathed, and nowhere was it possible to be free of them.

These myriads of armies of the young, with their variegated uniforms, or, at least, banners and badges, were only one type of the armies of Shikasta.

In every country were small specialised armies, trained quite differently from the young. These were armies whose function was actually to fight. The high technology had made mass armies of the old sort redundant. The specialised armies were mostly mercenaries: that is, people recruited from volunteers who had an aptitude for killing, or experience of it in previous wars, or a desire to find an excuse for barbarism.

Although most of those in the armies of the young had been given very little education, and that of no relevance to the problems that faced them, this did not mean that they had been left without what was in fact an extremely thorough indoctrination, mostly into the virtues of conformity, through the propaganda media. The various forms of indoctrination did not always coincide with what was imposed on them in the armies. And it must be remembered that even the simplest and most basic facts taught to a young Shikastan in the latter part of the Century of Destruction were bound to be more accurate—nearer reality—than anything his father and grandfather could have approached. To take one example, the ordinary, mass-produced geographical maps in use in classrooms: the information in these, for accuracy and sophistication, was beyond the wildest dreams of geographers of even two or three decades before. And geography is the key to an understanding of the basics—much more than most Shikastans had any idea of at all. Even the most sketchily educated and ill-informed youngster had at his or her fingertips *facts* that had to contradict, in all kinds of ways, obvious and implicit, the propagandas which afflicted them.

What Shikastans had early on in the Century of Destruction called "doublespeak" quickly became the rule. On one hand every Shikastan used the languages and dialects of indoctrination, and used them skillfully, for the purposes of self-preservation; but on the other they at the same time used the ideas and languages of *fact*, useful method, practical information.

Always, in epochs when the languages and dialects of a culture have become outstripped by development of a practical sort, these languages become repetitive, formalised—and ridiculous. Phrases, words, associations of sentences spin themselves out automatically, but have no effect: they have lost their power, their energy.

What happened very soon was what every government had foreseen, been terrified of, had tried to prevent: the armies of the young began to throw up leaders, not those designated by authority. These young men and women were able to understand, because of the amount of information still available (though governments always tried to suppress it) the mechanisms of the organisations they were in, the methods used to control them: their subjection, in fact. And these they explained to the masses under them.

Very quickly, the masses of youth were conducting what amounted to self-education in their own situation. That they had been set to compete with each other, make formal enemies of each other, were not allowed or at least, not encouraged, to mix and mingle, had been taught to see uniforms and badges not their own as the mark of the alien, the feared; that their very existence made governments tremble; that the arrangement, organisation, every moment of their lives was a function of their redundance, their uselessness in the processes of production of real wealth—their lack of worth to society—all this was taught to them by themselves.

But understanding it did not make their situation any better.

They had the misfortune to be young in a world where ever-increasing multitudes competed for what little food there was, where there was no prospect of betterment save through the deaths of many, and where war could be expected with absolute certainty.

From country to country, everywhere on Shikasta, moved the representatives of the youth armies, their own representatives, conferring, explaining, setting up organisations and understandings that completely undermined or went counter to the ukases and ordinances of the ruling stratum, the experts and administrators—and it was as if everywhere on Shikasta arose a great howl of despair.

For what could be done to change this world that had been inherited by the young?

They were locked more and more into a sullen and despairing loathing of their elders, whom they could see only as totally culpable—and, realising, at last, their power, began issuing instructions to their superiors, to governments, the overlords of Shikasta. As had happened so many times on Shikasta before, the soldiers had become too strong for a corrupt and feeble state. Only this time it was happening on a world scale. The governments, and their dependent classes of military and technical experts, tried to pretend that this was not the case, hoping that some miracle—even perhaps some new technical discovery—would rescue them.

The armies covered Shikasta. Meanwhile, the epidemics spread, among people, and among what was left of the animal populations, among plant life. Meanwhile, the millions began to dwindle under the assaults of famine. Meanwhile, the waters and the air filled with poisons and miasmas, and there was no place anywhere that was safe. Meanwhile, all kinds of imbalances created by their own manic hubris, caused every sort of natural disaster.

Among the multitudes worked our agents and servants, quietly, usually invisibly; sometimes, but seldom, publicly: Canopus, as we always had done, was working out its plans of rescue and reform.

And there, too, moved the agents of Shammat. And of Sirius. And of the Three Planets—all pursuing their private interests, unknown to, for the most part invisible to, the inhabitants of Shikasta, who did not know how to recognise these aliens, whether friend or enemy.

RACHEL SHERBAN'S JOURNAL

Our family has the four little rooms on the corner of this mud house, if that is the word for a building that is made of little rooms with doors out into the streets, inner doors opening in on to the central court. I can't imagine that one family could live here, not unless there were dozens of people in it, like those Russian families in novels. So it means the building was made to house a lot of poor families. Above our rooms is our patch of roof. There are six other families, each with its little patch of roof, separated from the other patches by low walls, which are high enough to hide you sitting or lying down but not standing. Mother and Father have one tiny room. Benjamin and George have another. There is a cubbyhole for me. Then the room we use for eating and sitting in if we aren't on the roof. The cooking place is outside. It is a sort of stove made of mud.

We are on good terms with all the families, but Shireen and Naseem are our particular friends. Shireen adores Olga. And Shireen's sister Fatima loves me.

Naseem went to school and did well. He is clever. He wanted to be a physicist. His parents did without everything so he could go on studying at college, but they did not stop him marrying, and so he had a wife and a baby before he was twenty. That is a western way of looking at things. He had to support them, so he works as a clerk. He says he is lucky to get this work. At least it is regular. I often wonder what he thinks about having to be a clerk, working seven a.m. to seven p.m., and with this wife and five children and he is twenty-four.

I spend quite a lot of time with Shireen and Fatima. When Naseem goes to work, and all the men leave the building, except for the old ones, the women are in and out of each other's homes, and the babies and children seem to belong to everyone. The women gossip and giggle and quarrel and make up. It is all very intimate. Sometimes I think it is awful. Like a girls' school. Women together always giggle and become childish and make little treats for each other. East or West. When Shireen has nothing in her rooms but two or three tomatoes and onions and a handful of lentils and has no idea what she is going to feed her family that day, she will still make a little rissole of lentils for a special friend across the court. And this woman puts some sugar on a bit of yoghurt and gives it to Shireen. It is always a feast, even with a spoon of yoghurt and seven grains of sugar. They spoil each other, caress each other, give each other little presents. And they have nothing. It is charming. Is that the word? No, probably it isn't.

Shireen is always tired. She has an ulcer on one breast that heals and breaks out again. She has a dropped womb. She looks about forty on a bad day. Naseem comes home tired and they quarrel and shout. She screams. He hits her. Then he cries. She cries and comforts him. The children cry. They are hungry. Fatima rushes in and out exclaiming and invoking Allah. She says Naseem is a devil. Then that Shireen is. Then she kisses them and they all weep some more. This is <u>poverty</u>. Not one of these people has ever had enough to eat. They have never had proper medical care. They don't know what I mean when I say medical care. They think it means the big new hospital that is so badly organised it is a death trap and being treated like idiots. They don't go there. They can afford only old wives' tales when they are sick. A doctor that really cares about them is too expensive. Shireen is pregnant again. They are <u>pleased</u>. After they have quarrelled I hear them laugh. Then there is a sort of ribald angry good humour. This means they will make love. I've seen Shireen with bruises on her cheeks and neck from love-making, and then Fatima, the unmarried sister, has to blush and the married women tease Shireen. She is <u>proud</u>. Although she always has a backache and is tired she is good-humoured and wonderful with the children. Except sometimes. That is when she is so exhausted she sits rocking herself, crying and moaning. Then Fatima croons over her, and does more work than usual, though she always works very hard helping Shireen. Then Naseem caresses her and swears and is angry because she is so worn out. Then there is more laughing antagonism between them. This is mysterious, the ebbs and flows. I mean there is a mystery in it. I don't understand it at all. I watch them and I want to understand. They respect each other. They have a tenderness. Because their lives are so difficult and awful and he can't ever be a physicist, or anything but a little clerk. Often he goes mad thinking about it. And she will be an old woman at forty. And some of their children will be dead. Mother says that two are weak and won't live. Because not one of the children has had enough of the proper things to eat, they may have brain damage, Mother says.

Sometimes I see an old woman, and I think she must be seventy at least, then I find out she is forty, and has had ten kids, four of them dead, and she is a widow.

I can't stand any of this. I can't understand it.

I am of the West and I believe in the equality of women. This is what I <u>am</u>. So does Olga. But when Olga is with Shireen and Fatima she is exactly like them. She laughs and is gay and intimate. These women have a marvellous time. They make fun for themselves out of nothing. I envy them. Believe it or not. They are supposed to be miserable and downtrodden. And they are. The dregs of the dregs. And so are their husbands. When you compare these lives, pared down to nothing, with what I can remember only too clearly of America I want to vomit. The fat vulgarity of it. When these women get hold of an old American magazine, a women's magazine, they all crowd around it and laugh and get such pleasure from it. One tattered old magazine, the sort of thing you leaf through at the dentist and think what a load of old rubbish, they handle with such respect. Each rubbishy advertisement gives them entertainment for days. They will take an advertisement, and go off and stand in front of the only mirror in the building. It is an old cracked thing and the woman who owns it takes it for granted everyone must use it. They pull some cheap dress around one of them, and match it with the advertisement, and laugh.

I watch and think of how we throw everything away and nothing is good enough.

Sometimes they say they are going to learn languages like clever me and they sit around and I start off with French or Spanish. They sit, with the children all crowding around wanting attention, then one has to go off and another. I am sitting there, handing out my marvellous phrases, while they repeat them. But the next time there is a lesson, there are fewer of them, and then only one or two. Fatima is learning Spanish from me. She says she could get a better job than she has. She is a cleaning woman. If you can call a seventeen-year-old girl that. The language lessons haven't come to much, but they made an occasion for fun while they lasted.

Shireen is delighted she is having a baby, though she is too tired to drag herself about, and it means even less food. And she worries all the time because it is time Fatima is married.

Fatima is very slim, and not pretty, but striking. She knows how to make herself attractive. She uses kohl and henna and rouge. She has two dresses. She washes and cares for them. Benjamin says they are fit for a jumble sale. But he would. I hate it when Benjamin comes anywhere near these people. They are all so slight and elegant and quick-moving. Like air, because of never having eaten enough. And then there is Benjamin, a great brown hairy bear. George fits in with them. He is like them. Quick and thin.

Benjamin knows he is out of place and that they find him amazing so he keeps away.

Shireen wants Fatima to marry a friend of Naseem, who is a clerk in the same office. Naseem thinks he will marry her. They joke about it. Naseem says, Have a heart, or words to that effect, why do you want the

poor thing to be married and saddle himself with all this misery. In-
dicating Shireen and the five children. He laughs. She laughs. Fatima
laughs. If I am there and I don't laugh, they all turn on me and tease
me, saying I look so solemn and boring, until I do laugh.

And then there is a sudden wave of black bitterness. It is awful, an
irritability that gets into Naseem and Shireen and they hate each other.
The children whimper and wail. The two rooms seem full of children's
dirt and vomit and worse. Flies. Bits of food. It is horrible, squalid and
awful.

Naseem then jokes that perhaps his friend Yusuf would like me
instead of Fatima because at least I am educated and can keep him in
luxury. At which Fatima calls me into the cubbyhole she shares with
the three older children, and she takes down her best dress from a hook
in the mud wall. It is a dark blue dress, of a soft cloth, very worn. It
smells of Fatima and of her perfume, heavy and languishing. The dress
has beautiful embroidery on it in lovely colours. Fatima made the dress
and did the embroidery. This dress is a big thing in her life. She puts
on me gold earrings, long, to my shoulders, and then about a hundred
bangles. Gold, glass, brass, copper, plastic. Yellow, red, blue, pink, green.
The gold bangle and the earrings are precious to Fatima, they are her
dowry. But she puts them on me and is delighted.

This has happened several times. She loves doing it. It is because
she admires me for being so educated and able to do what I like. So
she thinks. She thinks I am marvellous. My life seems quite beyond
her and utterly amazing.

Yesterday afternoon she put all this on me and then made up my eyes.
She made my lips a dark sultry red like a tart's. She stood me in front
of the cracked glass in the neighbour's room, and the women came
crowding around to watch. They were all excited and delighted. Then
she took me back to her sister's rooms and sat me down to wait for
supper. Yusuf was coming. I said to her she was mad. But it was the
wrong note, I could see that. She had to do it. Meanwhile, Shireen was
all worldly-wise and smiling. Naseem came home, worn out. Thin as a
rake because he does not eat what little there is for him, he always
gives it to the children. He laughs when he sees me. Then in comes
Yusuf. He is handsome, with dark liquid eyes. A sheikh of Araby. He
laughs. He pretends I am his bride. It is funny and sweet. As if everyone
is forgiving everyone for something. I say to them, cross, that all this is
silly because I have no intention at all of getting married. But I am
quite wrong to say it, because it is a sort of game. They are making an

alternative event. A possibility. Their lives are so narrow. They have
so little. So here is this spoiled western girl Rachel. But they like her
really. But they have to <u>manage</u> her. And after all, she might marry
Yusuf, who knows! Strange things do happen! Yusuf might fall in love
with Rachel! Rachel might fall in love with Yusuf! A romance! But of
course they don't believe this for a moment. And so it is a sort of
acted-out possibility, no hard feelings. It was a feast. Vegetable stew
and meatballs. They hardly ever eat meat. And I had insisted on bringing in a pudding Mother had made for us. It was a pudding of yoghurt
and fruit. Shireen made sure the children stayed up to get some of it,
after their share of the stew. She couldn't waste the chance of their
getting some nourishment into them.

There I sat, all dolled up, a sacrificial calf. It was a lovely meal. I
adored it. All the time I was furious. Not at them. At the awfulness of
this poverty. At Allah. At everything. And it was all ridiculous because
Fatima and Yusuf might just as well be married already. There is that
strong physical thing, and the antagonism. They quarrel as if they are
married, and are sure of each other.

After the meal, the feast-feeling faded away. The children were excited and a nuisance. Everything was a mess. Naseem and Yusuf went
to a café. Shireen put the kids to bed. Fatima cleaned things up. Then
she sat with me and said, Do you like him Rachel? Quite seriously, but
laughing. I said, Yes I like him and I shall have him! Oh, you are going
to marry him then? Yes, I shall marry him, I said. She laughed, but
looked grave, in case there was a chance in a thousand I might mean it.
And I kissed her so she should understand of course I wouldn't marry
her Yusuf. All the time I was wanting to howl and weep. But I personally think on reflection that I am extremely childish and they
are not.

Then Fatima took me into the court.

It was a night with a moon, last night.

People were sitting around in the shadows of the court. We sat by
the pool. It is a tiny rectangular pool. The lilies in the earth pot at one
end were smelling very strong. Olga was there, sitting quietly in the
dusk. She had one of the babies on her lap. It was asleep. I don't know
where George was or Benjamin. Olga knew I was in with Shireen and
Naseem and Fatima because I had asked to take the pudding. She knew
about Yusuf. She was worried in case I hadn't behaved well. She didn't
want me to have hurt their feelings.

When I came out and sat by the pool with Fatima she was looking at my face to see if I had behaved well. So I gave her a look which meant <u>Yes</u> <u>I</u> <u>have</u>.

The moon was overhead. It should have reflected in the pool. But there was this dust on the water. Also little bits of twig. Also bits of paper. The water is never clean. A woman will take a child that has made a mess and wash it there. Or someone will bend and splash water over his face, in the heat. Olga began by trying to stop people using the water but she has given up. She says by now they must be immune to any germs. Fatima leaned forward, and began carefully with the side of her palm to scoop the dust and rubbish off the water. Then Shireen came out from her quarters and she sat by Fatima and she too creamed off the dust. She knew what Fatima was up to, but I didn't. And Olga didn't. They were obviously up to something. This went on for some time. People sat quietly around, tired after the hot day, watching the sisters using the sides of their palms to scoop off the dust and wondering what would happen next.

Then Naseem came back from the café. He had been gone only an hour. He was tired, and kept yawning. He stood for a while leaning against a wall watching the sisters. Then he sat down by his wife, close but not too close, because they behave with dignity in public. He was close because he wanted to be. His leg and thigh was at least six inches from Shireen's folded-up leg, but I could feel the warmth of their being close. I could feel the understanding between them, in their flesh. They were conscious of every little bit of each other, even though they scarcely looked at each other and Shireen went on clearing the water. I was amazed by that thing between them. I mean the strength of it. If I could only understand it. Those two sitting there together in the dusk on the edge of the little pool, with the moon shining down—all the rest of us might just as well not have been there. I don't know how to say it. I was staring at them and trying not to.

And all the time Shireen went on competently scooping and skimming, and Fatima scooped and skimmed. And I was sitting there, all dolled up. Then the pool was clear. It was a little dark rectangle of water with a slit of moon shining brightly in it.

Then Fatima, smiling and delighted, and Shireen, smiling and pleased, came to me, one on either side, and gently pushed me forward to look in the pool.

I didn't want to. I felt ridiculous. But I had to. Naseem was sitting there, cross-legged, alert, watching, smiling, very handsome.

I was made to look at myself. I was beautiful. **They** made me be. I looked much older, not fifteen. I was a real woman, their style. I hated the whole thing. I felt as if Shireen and Fatima were holding me and dragging me down into a terrible snare or trap. But I loved them. I loved that strong physical understanding between Naseem and Shireen and I wanted to be part of it or at least to know what it was. It wasn't just sex, oh no.

The girls kept exclaiming over my reflection and softly clapping their hands, and making Naseem bend forward to look into the pool and then he clapped his hands, partly sardonic, and partly genuine. And the other people around the pool were smiling.

I was afraid of George coming in and seeing this charade going on. Because he hadn't seen what had led up to it. I could feel the tears start running and I hoped no one would notice. But of course Shireen and Fatima noticed. They exclaimed and kissed me and scooped the tears off my cheeks with the side of their palms that were still damp from the pool, and they said I was beautiful and lovely.

Meanwhile, Olga sat there watching, holding the sleeping baby. She did not smile. Nor did she not smile.

Olga, I will put down here as a fact, is not beautiful. This is because she is always tired and doesn't have time. Olga is English to look at, in spite of her Indian parent. She has the stubby solid look. She has dyed blond hair that is not always properly dyed. She has dark eyes that are sensible and considering. She is in fact too fat. This is because she forgets to eat sometimes all day, and then goes ravenous into the food cupboard and absentmindedly crams in bread or anything that is there to fill herself. She doesn't care. Or she will eat pounds of fruit or sweet stuff instead of a meal while she is writing a report.

She has nice clothes which she buys all at once to get it over with, but then she forgets about looking after them.

She sat there looking at this daughter of hers, who was so beautiful and exotic.

She was most interested in it all. I knew perfectly well she was thinking that all this would be good for me. Educational. Just as living in this poor building in this poor part of the town is good for us.

I could not stop crying. This disturbed the girls very much. Suddenly they did not understand it at all. Soon Naseem made them go off with him to their rooms, but first Shireen and Fatima hugged and kissed me, very affectionate and concerned, and I wanted to howl more than ever.

I stayed there on the edge of the pool. So did Olga. Then the others went off to sleep. They all had to get up early and they are tired with their hard lives.

That left Olga and me. I leaned forward and took a good look at the glamorous beauty. I have got thin in the last year. Sometimes I look at myself naked. The Queen of Sheba has nothing on me. Breasts and lilies and goblets and navel and the lot. But I don't want it. How could I want to be grown-up and marry and have six kids and know they are going to die of hunger or never have enough to eat.

When there was no one but me and Olga, and no chance of anyone coming out into the court, I did something I had been wanting to, but I couldn't while Shireen and Fatima were there. I loved them too much.

I took some sand from the pot around the lilies, and gently strewed it over the still surface of the gleaming water. Gently. Not too much. Just enough so that when I looked in I could no longer see the beautiful exotic Miss Sherban, Rachel the nubile virgin.

Olga watched me do this. She did not say a word.

I leaned over the pool, to make sure I couldn't see myself, only the blurred outline of the beautiful moon, shining down from the stars.

By the morning, if Shireen and Fatima remembered, and chanced to look, all they would think was that the winds had blown dust across the sky and some had fallen into the pool.

Olga got up and took the baby off to the room it belonged in. Then she came and put her arm around me and said, Now come on, go to bed. And she led me into our quarter. She hugged me and kissed me. She said, Rachel, it really isn't as bad as you think.

She said it humorous but a bit desperate.

I said, Oh yes, it is.

And she went off to bed.

I went through to my little mud room. I sat on the door-sill, with my feet in the dust outside, and I watched the night. I was still in Fatima's best dress of course, with her precious bits of gold. Being in that dress that she had been in a thousand times was something I can't describe. If there is a word, I don't know it. The cloth of the dress was full of Fatima. But that wasn't it. It smelled of her and of her skin and her scent. It was as if I had put on her skin over mine. No dress I have ever had in my life could possibly feel like that. It could never be that important. If I had a fragment of that cloth, wherever I was in the world, if I came on it in a drawer or a box, I would have to say at once, Fatima.

Re: Colonised Planet 5, Shikasta

The feel of that warm soft cloth on my skin was burning me.

I understand that old thing, about a woman rending her bosom with her nails. If I had not been in Fatima's precious best dress that she would need to get married in, I would have raked my nails through the dress and into my bosom. And I would have raked my cheeks with my nails, too, but the blood would have hurt Fatima's dress.

I sat there all night until the light began to get grey. There were some dogs trotting about in the moonlight. The dogs were very thin. Three of them. Mongrels. So thin they had no stomachs, just ribs. I could feel their hunger. Living in this country I have a fire in my stomach which is the hunger I know nearly everyone I see feels all the time, all the time, even when they sleep.

Then I go into meals with the family and eat, because of course it is ridiculous not to. But each mouthful feels <u>heavy</u>, and too much, and I think of the people who are ravening. I am sure that even if I lived in a country where everyone had enough to eat all the time, and lived there for years, I would still have this burning in my stomach.

I did not go to bed last night. When the sun came up I took off Fatima's beautiful dress and folded it and put the earrings and the dozens of different bangles with it. Later I shall take these things over to her. One day soon I expect that I and Shireen will help Fatima into this dress so that she can marry Yusuf.

A *letter from* B E N J A M I N S H E R B A N *to a college friend*
Dear Siri,
Here is my promised account of the circus.
On the afternoon before leaving, George "received"—the only word for it I am afraid!—representatives of the three organisations he was to represent. The Jewish Guardians of the Poor. (Female, black.) The Islamic Youth Federation for the Care of the Cities. (Male, a very superior fellow, combining a brand of marxist socialism peculiar to himself and I gather perhaps four others, with an ancient lineage of which he has no intention anyone shall remain in ignorance.) The United Christian Federation of Young Functionaries for Civil Care. (Female, brown.)

These three entrusted inordinate quantities of messages, briefs, reminders, cautions, and good wishes to their delegate and departed to three different far-flung areas of Morocco, well pleased.

I travelled with George only because he seemed to insist, and on our arrival we were put up in the house of one Professor Ishak. The usual interminable confabulations went on from dusk until after midnight, and again George seemed to need my support, otherwise I would have gone to bed. The pre- and/or post-conference junkettings have never held any appeal for me.

Over a thousand delegates from all over the world assembled in the Blessings of Allah Hall, which is modern, air-conditioned, large, surrounded by snack bars, cafés, eating nooks attractive to east and west, north and south, and everything of the best. From the first moment the goodies were being eagerly sampled by one and all, but particularly by those delegates from Western Europe, and most particularly from the British Isles, who seem pleased enough to get even half a square meal inside themselves whenever the opportunity offers.

Opening speeches at nine a.m. George delivers one of them. All things to all men. Not to mention women. Half of the delegates are female and not a bad-looking bunch even to my connoisseur's eye. There were nearly as many different uniforms as delegates, of every shade imaginable, and the place was like a sample room of a dye factory. Medals blazed. Ribbons glowed. Is it really possible that so much valour, intelligence, accomplishment, devotion to every conceivable variety of duty, were all together at the same place, and at the same time?

Your poor friend was not among those in uniform. I wore my post-Mao tunic, and the badges of our college. George wore a cotton suit that could give offence to no one, and with it his three badges, the Jewish Guardians of the Poor, the Islamic Youth Federation for the Care of the Cities, and the United Christian Federation of Young Functionaries for Civil Care, thus outtrumping, and outmanoeuvring any number of local interests without even trying. He was of course as handsome as the evening star (as I overheard some delicious morsel whisper) and there wasn't a soul, male or female, left unmoved at that winsome modest manly form.

The subject of the Conference being the general togetherness and co-operation and sharing of information and love and good will (etcetera and so on) among the Youth Organisations of the World, of course it was necessary first of all, before descending to these perilous shores of unanimity, to establish boundaries, banish misconceptions, and stake claims. The familiar verbal aggressions (yawn yawn) began at once.

Battle was joined by the Communist Youth Federation (European Branch, Section 44) for Sport and Health, with a few routine references to running dogs of capitalism, fascist hyenas, and so-called democrats.

A conventional, indeed modest, opening move.

It was countered by the Scandinavian Youth Section of the League for the Care of the Coasts with references to tyrannical enslavers, jailors of free thought, and perverted diverters of the true currents of soaring human development into the muddied channels of repetitive rhetoric.

In came the Soviet Youth in the Service of the World (Subsection 15) with opportunistic revisionists and scavengers of the riches of the marxist theoretical treasuries.

Were the delegates from the Socialist Democratic Islamic Federation of North Africa content to remain silent? Deteriorated inheritors of the corrupted revolutionary ethics, and contaminators of the true ideals of the socialistic heritage by self-appointed custodians of dogma—was the least of it.

And now, what said the Chinese Youth Representatives of Peace, Freedom and True Liberty? You ask, do you? With earnest dedication to exact definition, they offered: the use of superstitious and archaic religious dogmas to enslave the masses, and the empty rhodomontade of bankrupt pawns of the antediluvian economic system.

Insulters of the absolute and eternal truths enshrined in the Koran!

Unleashed oppressors!

Rancid invective!

Polluters of the true heritage of the ever-welling mental wealth of mankind's toiling masses!

This dazzling exchange was halted by the Norwegian Youth Against Air Pollution, her blond plaits swinging, and her breasts all agog, while she shouted that this was feeble hogwash masquerading under the guise of free and flexible thinking and was no more than she expected from so many male prisoners of their own decaying doctrines.

But here in came the plenipotentiary from the British Young Women's Armies for the Preservation of Children, disagreeing with Norway on the grounds that in her opinion, Delegates 1 and 5 had been correct, but Delegates 3 and 7 certainly not, and as for her, she could see only racism among the humanistic hogwash, and prejudice blatantly evident in the fat guzzlers in the styes of post-imperalistic self-indulgence.

This took us to the first break, and we thronged out, brothers and sisters all, laughing and jesting and exchanging addresses and the names of hotels, and the numbers of hotel rooms, and those who had insulted each other five minutes before were observed to be already cemented in the closest friendship.

Half an hour later we were at it again.

I will not weary you with the names and styles of the purveyors of antique insult, but merely transcribe some of my observations, the first one which comes to mind being the absolute necessity of the animal kingdom (what our elders have left us of it) to occasions of higher mentation.

Running dogs, and hyenas, we have had already, but soon entered fat cats, pigs—to the indignation of the Semites, Arabs and Jews—cooing pigeons of hypocrisy, snakes (slippery and otherwise), poisoned shellfish from the shores of mental pollution, crocodiles, and rhinoceroses charging blindly through the subtleties of the marxist revelation.

And what of natural phenomena, could we do without them?

After lunch, which was most ample and amicable, once again bringing much-needed sustenance to certain hungry ones, we returned to the hall, united in beaming fondness for each other, and I noted: dawn dews bringing the refreshing life of Islam to the empty sands of irreligious impiety. Flowers of Our Master's Thought. (Whose Master? I forget.) Tsunamis of ignorant obscurantism. Sandbanks of obstinate misinterpretation. Tainted winds from poisoned minds. Stagnant pools of dogma. (Again, I forget which pools. Marxist? Islamic? Christian? And who cares? They certainly did not!) Waterspouts of confusion. Depleted reservoirs of bankrupt theory. Badlands where nothing grows but the parched thistles of dying creeds. Deserts of internecine strife. Clouds of superficial brotherhood. King Canutes trying to hold back the ever-springing seaswells of marxist inspiration. Clay feet. Dusty but unbowed heads. Eroded brain cells. Quicksands of . . . overflowing rivers of . . . mildewed boughs of . . .

And thus we arrived at our evening meal, and it could be observed that some of us were putting back everything we could, our first square meal ever from the look of some of us. And then, the dance! There we all were, male and female, a perfect flowerbed of colourful uniforms, and some girls with a tentative blossom or two in their hair, and even one or two in proper dresses! These had suitors around them in what a disapproving maiden called "a sexual assault," but it was only one carping voice in a perfect feast of love and harmony. Making my usual enquiries, performing my usual one-man survey, I discovered that for many of these poor deprived souls, this was their first "real" festival, meaning the first time they had encountered others than their own kind, having never met any but socialist revisers, Islamic New

Thoughtists, or whatever. These were particularly having the time of their lives, absolutely stunned by the richness of thought possible in this teeming world, "oh brave new world that has such people in it!" and had to be protected from their inexperience by certain watchful souls, myself among them (deputed to this end by George), for while there was nothing against people waking up in beds they had <u>chosen</u>, we were trying to prevent sad awakenings in the dawn in the arms of <u>perfect</u> <u>strangers</u>. And so to bed. (Alone.) But George was up talking away all night as usual.

Next day a feeling of urgency was making itself felt, for the real meat of the agenda had still to be set before us, but no, the preliminaries were not yet over.

A military mode prevailed. Target identification obscured by empty rhetoric . . . automated invective . . . calibrated marksmanship on the sociological front . . . keeping enemy positions in the sights of social revolutionary acumen . . . target identification obscured by faulty weapons of analysis . . . vigilance on the ever-shifting frontiers of social change . . . booby traps in the social sector . . . invincible battalions of dialectic . . . depth-bombing of our intellectual bastions . . . fatally low-altitude penetration of theoretical bases . . . pointless camouflage of an already collapsed ideological position . . . demolition of . . . destruction of . . . spin-off from . . . checksights . . . height-finding . . . range-finding . . .

You think that this <u>must</u> be the end? Well, nearly, we had reached the mid-morning break, with only the rest of the day left for our real purposes.

But there were still a few mutterings from the dying storm . . . bourgeois communists . . . bourgeois socialists . . . bourgeois democrats . . . bourgeois technocrats . . . bourgeois pseudophilosophs . . . bourgeois pessimists . . . bourgeois opto-polymaths . . . bourgeois bureaucrats . . . and bourgeois racists and bourgeois sexists.

With an hour left to lunch and the hounds of time snapping at our ever-moving heels, we got down to it, and since by then we were all cemented into one soul, we passed without debate resolutions about unity, brotherhood, co-operation and so on. These being the principles which we all serve. And it was after lunch easily and quickly agreed that it was urgently necessary to establish subsidiary armies and camps and organisations for the innumerable young children without homes and parents everywhere. A subcommittee was elected to deal with this, on which I was abashed to find myself, since I had no such expectation. I know that George put Ali up to it, but I have no proof and I don't mind, at least it is useful. In fact urgently necessary.

A lot of subcommittees were set up in not very much more time than it is taking me to write this, on a large variety of on the whole useful tasks, such as crash courses into <u>real</u> national and regional differences (note that the tetchy obligations of the hostile rhetoricians were by-passed neatly in this one nonabrasive word—understood with small pleased smiles by everyone present) and on survival, and on the ex-changing of sample groups from country to country. And so on.

The conference ended in a rush with the bands playing very fast, because we had run overtime, a vast number of national anthems, organisational songs, and martial music of every kind, type and style, but thank heavens, the delegates were already streaming out to catch their coaches, many in floods of tears at interrupted friendships and loves, making improbable plans to meet again, kissing, hugging, waving. Never has there been such a scene of—surely?—<u>treason</u>, for these enemies were entwined together like barley-sugar sticks on a rainy day, and they could hardly be dragged apart.

And so ended the Conference.

George was pleased. He was in very good spirits on the drive back, singing and playing games. The life and soul of the party one could say, and I do. I suppose he is not so bad, my sainted brother. But what was he doing there at all?

RACHEL SHERBAN'S JOURNAL

It is a long time since I wrote down anything. Eighteen months to be exact. We are in Tunis now. A modern block. Unfortunately. <u>I</u> say unfortunately. I felt perfectly at home in that mud rabbit warren. I loved living there. Benjamin was relieved to get out of it. As soon as he walked into this boring flat he was at home. You can see him positively expanding in every breath. Smiling and <u>relieved</u>. I have not heard from Shireen and Naseem. Fatima married Yusuf just after I left. They are in a room next to Shireen's and Naseem's rooms. Soon I sup-pose Fatima will have five children. Who will help Shireen with her babies then? I would help if I were there. I felt they were my family just as much as this family is. I <u>love</u> them. Here today and gone tomorrow. In this block of flats no sleeping on the roof. That was the best thing I ever knew.

Well, at least here we aren't called eccentric.

The reason I am making myself write this is that I don't know what to think about anything. Particularly about George. I hate all this youth movement thing. I think it is childish. I simply can't see how any of them takes it seriously. It is obvious to the meanest intelligence why the kids join it. It is because they wouldn't have any privileges otherwise. I think that is despicable. And George is in it up to his ears. Of course a lot of them have to join something. It is the law.

The last time I wrote things down I understood what was going on. So I am trying again.

It was Hasan who said I should last time.

Where is Hasan? He has completely vanished from our lives. And George left Morocco apparently without a pang. Apparently, but who knows what he feels? I don't think he has seen Hasan though and he saw him every day in Marrakesh. I asked if he missed Hasan, and he looked bothered, and then he sighed. Because of me, of course. I asked him again and he said, Rachel, you are making things much harder than they need be.

Since we have been here, George has made another visit to India. He has not talked about it. Olga and Simon haven't asked. So I didn't. Benjamin did. But in a sarcastic sort of way. When he is like that George doesn't answer. Anyway he was invited to go and he wouldn't. But George is spending time with Benjamin. Often in the evenings they go to cafés. I hardly ever go. I am working for my exams. I am taking geopolitics, geoeconomics, and geohistory.

I have seen something. I work for exams. Benjamin works for exams. George doesn't work for exams. What he does is this. Wherever we go he attends college or university or something. Or tutors come. Or he goes off on trips with Father and Mother to places, though hardly ever now, that was when he was younger. Now it is trips with someone like Hasan. But he doesn't take exams. He knows as much as we do, though. More, by far. What happens is, he is with a class or a tutor for a month or something like that, and then he knows that subject. Mother and Father have never made him sit for exams. Yet we always have to. But they take a lot of trouble to make sure he learns all kinds of things. Mother is off in the South at the epidemic, so I shall ask Father.

I did. Obviously he had been expecting this question. What he said was, It was felt that George would not need exams. It was felt. I did not notice at once that he had said that. Then I said, Felt by whom? I was being cross and a bit sarcastic. (The way Benjamin is.) Father was quite patient, affectionate but definitely on his guard. Not cagey, though.

He said, You must have understood the situation, Rachel.

That checked me. Because of course I believe I do.

I said, Yes, I think I do. But what I want to know is, who said to you and Mother in the first place that George should be educated like this?

He said, The first time it was suggested, was in New York.

Miriam?

He said, Yes, that's it. And then there were the others.

I suddenly knew exactly how it was. It had been exactly like those moments when Hasan talked and I suddenly understood something, though apparently nothing very much had been said. I saw that it had been the same with Father and Mother. Obviously Miriam and then afterwards one of the tutors or someone had said quite casual simple things that rang in their minds, and then slowly they understood.

Writing that down has made me feel I have to know more about Simon and Olga. How is it they are like this? Why did they understand so easily? Or perhaps it wasn't easily. But they did understand. I don't know any other parents, of my friends, I mean, who would understand. Now I am looking back on our education, all of it, all the odd things, the tutors and the special courses and being with Olga and Simon in all kinds of peculiar and sometimes dangerous places, and how they have allowed George to be taught in that way, and I see how different they are. For one thing, and before anything else, they take so much trouble with us. Most parents aren't bothered.

I have just been to ask Father. He is working with his papers on the desk in the bedroom. I knocked and went in and he said, Wait a minute Rachel. He finished doing some calculations. Then he said, What is it?

I sat on the bed where I could see his face with the light on it. I felt quite fierce, but I didn't know what to ask.

He pushed his chair right round and faced me. Father is getting old now. His hair is grey and he is always too thin. He is very tired at the moment. I could see that he wished I had not come in just then. The light from the window was on his glasses and I wanted to see his eyes.

As I thought that, he took off his glasses. I thought that this was just like him. I suddenly felt very affectionate and I blundered straight in. I said, I want to ask something difficult. Ask away, then. I want to know how it is that you and Mother are the sort of parents you are. <u>Why?</u>

He did not seem surprised. He saw at once. But he was thinking about what to say. He sat with his legs stretched out, almost to the bed where I was sitting. He swung his glasses back and forth. This always drives Mother <u>wild</u>. It is hard to get glasses at all, let alone repaired.

He said, Strange as it may seem—This is how he begins saying things he finds difficult. Humorous. Strange as it may seem, this thought is not a new one to either your mother or myself.

Strange as it may seem, I am not surprised to hear it. I suppose <u>as usual</u> you have been waiting for this moment of truth and you have your words ready.

Something like that, he said, swinging his glasses.

Mother will kill you if you break those glasses.

Sorry. And he put them down. Look, Rachel, I think you understand all this just as well as we do.

Oh <u>no</u>, I said to him, really furious. I thought he was going to slide out of it. I mean, I said to him, It is impossible. Listen! There you are, you and Mother and three children, Mum and Dad and three dear little kiddies, in New York, and you of course all set to do the very best for them. And then along comes a perfectly ordinary woman called Miriam Rabkin and buys ice cream for all the kiddies and says, Oh no, don't bother to send George to an ordinary school, just let him pick things up as he can, that is by far the best way, and meanwhile I'll just trot him off to the Museum of Modern Man. And <u>you</u> said, But of <u>course</u>, Mrs. Rabkin, what a good idea, we'll do just that.

Silence. There we sat. He was smiling and friendly. I was smiling and <u>desperate</u>. I am feeling quite desperate these days. <u>That</u> <u>is</u> <u>the</u> <u>truth</u>.

Something like that, he said.

Very well then. In Marrakesh George spent exactly half a term in Mahmoud Banaki's class. When he came out he was fully versed in the History of the Religions of the Middle East, back to Adam at least if not further. Right?

Right.

But who told you to send George to that class at that time?

Hasan.

You mean he breezed in one afternoon and said Mr. Sherban! Mrs. Sherban! I am Hasan and I am interested in George, a very promising lad you have got there, and I want you to see that etc. etc. And you said, But of course! And it was done.

He was being definitely on the defensive but patient.

You forget Rachel, that Hasan came along after quite a lot of people of that kind.

Saying of that kind, in that way meant I had to accept those words and all the thoughts I had had on that subject.

All right, I said.

He was sitting there, rocking about on the back legs of his chair, looking at me. And I was looking at him.

And then he said what I had all this time been waiting for him to say.

You must see, Rachel, that being George's parents meant we had to see things differently.

Yes.

We have been taught to see things differently. Do you see?

Yes.

At the beginning, when it started, often enough your mother and I thought we were mad. Or something like that.

Yes.

But we went along with it. We did go along with it. And it worked.

Yes, I said.

Then he said, Rachel, you must run along, I've got to finish this, I have to, do you want any help with your homework? If so, I can after supper.

No, I said, I can manage.

I have seen something. During the term when George was doing the History of the Religions of the Middle East at the Madrasa, he also took classes from a Christian and from a Jew. In other words, while he was learning the curriculum, he was simultaneously learning the partisan points of view that wouldn't be in the curriculum. Not to mention God knows what from Hasan. That means he couldn't take exams, because what he had learned would never be contained in the exam questions. Though of course he could narrow everything down, after all Benjamin and I have to do that all the time. But that isn't the point. He is being educated for something different.

By whom?

What for?

Meanwhile he is a star figure in the local youth movements. And it makes me sick. Benjamin says George needs to show off. Well, that is of course what I cannot help thinking. But in my experience what Benjamin thinks is nearly always wrong. It comes out of his being jealous. Like me. At least I know that I am jealous and Benjamin doesn't seem to. Anyway I come more and <u>more</u> to the conclusion that what I think isn't worth anything. I seem to myself more and more a sort of sack full of emotions. Swilling around. I am angry. I don't know what about. I am so angry I could <u>die</u>. Sometimes I watch these emotions go surging past. Hi there anger! Hi there jealousy! Hi everyone! This is Rachel saying hello!

I have to put down what I feel about Suzannah. I think Suzannah is awful. Mother is very patient when Suzannah comes, and Father is extremely humorous. She is a loud, vulgar, stupid, flashy girl. She is crazy about George. Well girls crazy about George are like the sands of the seashore. So why Suzannah?

I asked Mother. (She is back from the epidemic. But she is leaving for the famine next week.) She said: George is seventeen and a half. She said that George was seventeen at least ten times in half a hour. That was about all she could say about it. Meanwhile I could see she was wishing I would stop yapping at her. Yap yap yap, like a little dog. I could see myself. I asked Father. He said, Suzannah is extremely physically attractive. I can't bear this. Furthermore I don't believe George sleeps with Suzannah. I said to Benjamin who was making a lot of coarse remarks, George certainly does not sleep with Suzannah. He said, Darling little sister, what do you think they do during these starlit nights? I said he was stupid and didn't understand George.

I said to George, Do you sleep with Suzannah, and he said Yes.

When he said that what I felt was that he had hit me. So I cried a lot. If George could sleep with Suzannah, then nothing mattered. How can he? It is an insult. I mean, to girls who are serious. I just feel that everything is spoiled. And Benjamin is quite right I am afraid. He says George is a power-lover and he is. So that's that.

I wrote that last bit several weeks ago. It has been a very bad epoch in my life. Benjamin suddenly started being very nice to me and I and Benjamin went out a lot. Several times, quite by chance—though I know our parents don't believe this, Benjamin and I were in cafés where George was with Suzannah. When George is with Suzannah, so it would seem, he is quite different from what he is at home with us. He is very <u>funny</u>. He laughs a lot. Not a care in the world. <u>Showing off.</u> I just wanted to be sick. But then Benjamin started to show off too, and more than once called across to George and Suzannah with all sorts of Jokes. I wanted to die. So then I said I wouldn't go out with Benjamin. I stayed at home. I did badly with my school work. And then Mother talked to me. She was disappointed in me. I know she and Father had talked. <u>I'm</u> not stupid. She came into my bedroom one night. I was crying. I said to her at once, All right, you and Father think I am jealous of George. She said to me, That's not the point at all. I said to her, All right then, what?—for already I could see a new perspective. She said to me, George isn't a saint, he isn't some sort of a paragon. But the point is, he is not yet eighteen years old.

I said, I think it is all disgusting.

She said, as humorous as you can get, Rachel, <u>what</u> is disgusting?

I said, Olga, George is a person who sits in a room and think that if there are thirty people in it, then there are thirty intestines full of shit, thirty bladders full of pee, thirty noses full of snot, and three hundred pints of blood. So I suppose if he is in a café with Suzannah, with those fat boobs of hers hanging out, he is thinking, two intestines full of shit, two bladders full of pee, two noses of snot, two bodies full of sweat, and twenty pints of blood. Not to mention 700 million sperm and an egg. And an erection and a vagina.

Olga sits down. She lights a cigarette. She leans back. She folds her arms. She sighs. She says, <u>When</u> did he say things like that? Getting at once to the point.

He was . . . it was a long time ago.

I daresay he might have added a dimension or two since then.

Well, I can't stand it, I said to her. I can't stand life. That's the truth of it.

I had half a thought that she would put her arms around me and comfort me. But although that is what I was wanting before she came in, when she was actually there I would have been ashamed if she had.

She said: You do not have any alternative, Rachel. Because you can either stand it, or commit suicide. Or live in such a way that it is as good as committing suicide. And there is evidence to suggest—here she was being humorous the way Father is, she has caught it off him—there is evidence to suggest that there is hell to pay. Literally. But in any case, <u>we</u> <u>do</u> <u>not</u> <u>commit</u> <u>suicide</u>. And the way she said this was different from anything I had ever heard from her, full of pride. Really grim. It was as if she had slapped me or flung me into freezing water. I suddenly saw her quite differently. I saw that she was a person. Not my mother. She had thought it all out. She had wanted to commit suicide. She would never commit suicide. On that night I grew up. Or so I would like to believe.

I have been thinking about Olga's life. I have been trying to put myself in her place, always in camps full of refugees, dying people, starving people, people dying of diseases, babies dying. When I was with her in the epidemic that time I saw her crying over a room full of dying babies. No one else was there. She was very tired, that was why she was crying. Ever since I can remember, my mother has been working with people dying in one way or another. She is always in places where it is truly hell. Always. And that is true for my father too. I see that I am extremely childish.

What I am writing now happened three nights ago. I could not write it down before, it was too difficult. Now I have thought about it. Very late I heard George come in. It was four in the morning. It was very hot. It was that time when night is still absolutely here but morning <u>is</u> here but you can't see it only feel it. Outside in the streets it was silent in that particular way. I would know any city I have been in by the silence at four in the morning. George had come in. I could hear him in his room. I went to his door and knocked. He did not answer. I went in. He was just slipping down his trousers and I saw him. Our family has never made a thing about nakedness, but what I was thinking was, <u>That</u> has been inside that awful cow. He turned his back, so I saw his buttocks and his back and he put on his pyjamas. Then he got into bed and lay down with his arms behind his head. George is very beautiful. But if he were ugly it would be the same. He was very tired. He wished I wasn't there. Exactly like my parents, affectionate and patient. He said to me, Rachel you aren't being kind. I was expecting him to say, <u>Fair</u>. When we use words like Fair, Olga and Simon always laugh and say we haven't stopped being British and childish. But he said Kind. So I said to him, I don't care, George. I <u>don't</u> understand. So he said, Well Rachel there isn't anything at all I can do.

There I was standing at the door, and he was in bed and his eyes kept closing.

He said, Rachel, what is it you want?

At this I was slapped in the face again. Because of course I wanted him to say I hate Suzannah, she is a clumsy vulgar idiot. But he wouldn't in a hundred years.

Sit down, he said.

I sat on the bottom of the bed.

I was expecting some illuminating remarks, I see that now, but of course his eyes kept closing.

He did look so handsome. But he was so tired. And I started to think about his life. He never has slept more than three or four hours a night.

I thought he was asleep. So I began to talk. I was talking to George. I said, It is absolutely intolerable, all of it, it is awful, it is ugly, it is disgusting, and life is absolutely unbearable.

His chest rose and fell, rose and fell. I wanted to put my head down on it and go to sleep.

He suddenly said, with his eyes closed, Well Rachel . . . I am listening. And he was asleep again. Absolutely gone. I stayed there a little, thinking he might wake up. But the light came in at the window. There were the dusty palm trees along the streets. The smell of dust. Hot. George slept and slept. I felt ashamed and angry and I went to bed.

I have been thinking about Suzannah. Suzannah has been in George's life for nearly a year. That is a long time. I look back over a year and it seems forever. And I have grown up so much in that time. Suzannah comes to supper here a lot. She is very eager to please. She never takes her eyes off George. I am sorry for her. I did not realise that I am, until now. It is because she knows quite well she is not good enough for George. She wants to marry him. I once would have thought she was insane. But if George can sleep with Suzannah then he can marry her. I said to George, Are you going to marry Suzannah? He said to me, My dear little sister! I hate that, it is what Benjamin calls me, and anyway, I am over sixteen now. But what about Suzannah, I said. She is twenty-three years old, he said. I was shocked to the spine when he said that. In the first place because she is so much older. And then because he thought it could make any difference to her. He said, She knows very well that marriage is not on my agenda. At this, I was shocked again.

I can't remember George ever being stupid before. I said to him, George, Suzannah wants to marry you. She thinks of nothing else, day and night. He said to me, my little sister, you were born to be my tormentor, my hair shirt. At which he picked me up and whirled me around the room.

This was in the living room. Benjamin came in at this point. He wanted to be part of it. The moment he came in, things were different, I mean, George whirling me about became a different sort of act, hostile and against me, and not friendly. Which it had been. I could feel George slowing down because he knew this too. Benjamin tried to join in the whirling about, as if I were a prize to be grabbed away. George set me down against the wall and stood in front of me. Benjamin kept dodging about in front of George because he wanted to throw me up and down and whirl me about. By then I was crying with rage. At the same time I was grateful to George.

After a minute, Benjamin felt ridiculous and he went to sit down. Then George sat down.

Rachel believes that I ought not to be sleeping with Suzannah, said George to Benjamin. I may say that this was quite serious. He had taken me seriously.

Of course you should sleep with her. Fuck them all, I say, said Benjamin. The minute he had said it, we could both see he was sorry. He looked embarrassed.

There sat Benjamin in one chair. Large, hairy, brown. Like a peasant. And George, thin and lithe and elegant. Both embarrassed. I stayed where I was, because I was afraid Benjamin would come after me.

Well, little sister, said Benjamin, so you think George shouldn't be sleeping with Suzannah? But why not?

I said, Oh sleep with anyone, who cares, I don't care, I used to think it matters, but I can see that it doesn't matter at all.

I was crying so that tears were literally splashing on to the floor.

George was looking at me. He kept looking at me. He was obviously unhappy. I was full of triumph because he was.

George said, Well little sister, tell me, who should I sleep with?

At which Benjamin said, Obviously, Rachel.

Then nothing happened for a few moments. George looked shocked and amused. Both. Benjamin was ashamed again.

It was one of those times that I recognise more and more: you can see alternative scenes parallel to what is really happening. Because of

Benjamin, what <u>he</u> was, I could see very clearly that I could fling myself across the room, and try to scratch his eyes out. Then George would get up, pick me up off Benjamin, and sit me down.

That was <u>Benjamin's</u> <u>scene</u>. What <u>he</u> imposed.

But George being there prevented this happening.

Because George was there and looking as he did, I walked out and away from the wall and sat down by myself.

This is a serious conversation, said George to Benjamin, and Benjamin shut up.

So who should I sleep with? he asked me. I am a normal male. I shall not be marrying for five years.

At this, both Benjamin and I were stopped in a different way. There was a long silence.

I really want to know, said George. There are brothels by the hundred in this and any city. And of course there is chastity. There are a lot of girls who want to sleep with me. Suzannah is one.

All this seemed to be so off the point, I could hardly believe it.

And when you are finished with her? I said. What will she do when <u>you</u> marry?

Good God, said Benjamin, listen to that!—He was acting the part of resigned astonishment. The eternal feminine—The absolute absoluteness, the ultimate ultimatum.

Well go on little sister, said George, I want to know.

She loves you, I said.

She loves you, said Benjamin to George, as before.

Yes she does, I said. It's funny you can't see it. Why can't you? Why are you like this? Why are you suddenly stupid? You are the most important thing that ever will happen to her.

Well that's true enough, said Benjamin. False modesty will get you nowhere.

For George was in fact looking quizzical.

I said, You can marry fifty other women and she can marry some fat stupid speech-making politician, and she can be a big lady and make speeches and run around in a uniform, and you will still be the most important thing that ever happened or ever could happen.

George was extremely embarrassed. He was red. I have never seen that before, with George.

Benjamin for once was looking quite sensible, and even grown up.

Benjamin said to George, She's right.

Re: Colonised Planet 5, Shikasta

George said, Well, so what am I supposed to do?

Benjamin said, very dramatic, Trapped!

I have been thinking.

What I have concluded is this. You don't understand something until you see the results.

What made me think about this is the Conference of Youth. When he said he was going I was sick. Later I heard he was the delegate for some Muslims, some Jews and some Christians. Well, there isn't anybody else who could do this. I don't know how he does. And he could have represented socialist groups and marxists and business groups. They asked him.

I couldn't go to the Conference. I wasn't asked. How could I be when I never go near youth groups?

Benjamin went. First he said he wouldn't go if it killed him, but he went, of course.

I heard everything that happened. From Benjamin. But after he had finished I thought out what had happened from my own point of view.

Benjamin says that George was ever such a success and the belle of the ball, and hinted that George spent the night with some woman. Suzannah wasn't there. I could ask him and he would tell me but I won't, never again.

But since he came back, there have been messages all day, from everywhere. I am not going to list the countries because I can see there won't be an end to them. Because George went to that Conference in that way he can travel to anywhere now and be welcome. And various people have turned up at this flat and talked about George and what he said at the Conference. He was talking, they say. They mention particularly about his talking. And Benjamin said he "spouted" all night. If he spouted, then how could he have been with some woman? I said this to Benjamin and he said he never suggested George had done anything but talk.

They keep turning up here, white, black, brown, pink, and green, day and night, day in and day out, and it is perfectly clear that they want to hear George talk. I have seen something. George talks as Hasan talks. George has caught it from Hasan. That is what I have seen. And I sit and listen and so does anyone else who is around. So do Olga and Simon. And so does Benjamin. He doesn't say a word. He can jeer as much as he likes afterwards, and sometimes he has no idea at <u>all</u> about what <u>is</u> going on but he listens like the rest of us. So <u>as</u> <u>usual</u> I have to say this: my feelings are one thing. But what I am thinking is quite another. As for what I <u>understand</u> when George is talking, then . . . but obviously there is no point in saying anything about that.

From TAFTA, SUPREME LORD of SHIKASTA,
to SUPREME SUPERVISORY LORD
ZARLEM on SHAMMAT, *Greetings.*

Submission, O Great One!

Your instructions have been carried out!

The Four National Areas have been tested.

Head of Government One: Receiving our directive to tell the truth exactly, accurately, without concealment, to his subjects, he informed his council of ministers that this was his intention, because "it had come into his mind." He was at once incarcerated in a prison for the mentally deranged, and it has been given out to the subjects that he has resigned on grounds of ill health.

Head of Government Two: This man, having just been "elected into power," took the first opportunity (a television appearance) of informing his subjects that conditions were much worse than he had imagined before actually taking office and becoming possessed of certain information that is available only to heads of government. He considered it his duty to inform them of this material, which ought not to be secret. In order to survive at all it would be necessary for them to face certain facts: these were the facts. . . . When the television appearance was over, he was informed by the faction that had "put him into power" that he had lost their support. He has had to resign.

Head of Government Three: This man, determined to tell the inhabitants of his geographical area (because of our promptings) certain facts that had been withheld from them, was assassinated by the military before he could do so: because of their total espionage cover, they knew of his determination at once.

Head of Government Four: In the midst of a worse than usual crisis, he made hitherto inaccessible facts public and found no one believed him: there was such a gap between what they had been told and what he was telling them now. Becoming emotionally unstable with the effect of impressing the truth on them and finding over and over again this had no effect, he had a heart attack and died.

These tests have proved that the planet is immune to truth.

There is therefore nothing left to bar our progress.

Re: *Colonised Planet 5, Shikasta*

Excelsior! Glory to us! We have overcome!

Submission, O Great One!

––––––––

The PAN-EUROPE FEDERATION of SOCIALIST DEMOCRATIC-COMMUNIST PEOPLE'S DICTATORSHIPS for the PRESERVATION of PEACE.

Integrated ALL-EUROPEAN SERVICES for the VIGILANT SUPERVISION of ENEMIES of the PEOPLE and the PREVENTION of CRIMES AGAINST the PEOPLE'S WILL.
DEPARTMENT 15. (BRITAIN) TOP LEVEL. SECRET.

To our Great Leader, All Hail! Our grateful thanks to Him whose Life guards us all with its fearless farsightedness in the Service of an unremitting advance into the future. Our homage to Him who stands like a bulwark between us and the forces of degeneracy. Words fail us when we think of His sacrifices in our Sacred Cause!

[This was a report on seventy-four leaders who emerged from the youth movements or who retained influence from the past, who were not, that is, appointed by the ruling bureaucracy. The report was based on material supplied by spies and agents. It was begun just before the taking over of Europe by the Chinese and completed and in some cases rewritten by a Chinese official. We choose this particular document to exemplify the superior abilities of the new overlords. The choice of these three representatives is of course ours: neither the British official nor the Chinese official thought he was of particular interest and both laid greater emphasis on others. *Archivists.*]

Benjamin Sherban. No. 24. What can we say about this decadent philistine whose filth pollutes the glorious struggle transforming the ownership of the means of production for the benefit of all the toilers of mankind. The lesson of such degenerates is that we have far to go to achieve total victory on the political and ideological fronts. We have to gird ourselves to wage a protracted and ever-hawk-eyed struggle against the reactionaries enslaved to the undertow of capitalist influences from the filthy past in order to mount the heights of true socialist achievement. This enemy of the people has impudently assumed so-called leadership of the Junior Youth of the Youth Movements of North Africa (Section III) and is openly challenging the will of the true fuglemen of the People. Under the false and patently transparent guise of speaking for the children (eight to twelve years) of those territories he imposed his vomit of subjective twaddle on their defenceless minds in contradiction to the true conclusions arrived at by the methods of comradely inner-Party discipline and the recommendation is that he should be arrested in the name of the People's Will when he attends the Pan-Youth Congress in the autumn. If this should prove impossible due to the contradictions of the existential situation then he should be ruthlessly exposed for what he is.

George Sherban. No. 19. This hyena is brother to the last entry. Due to unscrupulous and pitifully debased opportunistic methods never before surpassed in the history of the glorious class struggle he has imposed himself as a representative of several Factions in the name of so-called Fairness, little reckoning that his feeble wrigglings in the dust of historical subjectivism are seen through by the clear-eyed masses in their glorious climb up the mountains of Truth. He has visited various countries in our glorious Federation in the last two years and imposed his slime wherever his low ambitions have led him. What can we say about such unscrupulous and debased criminals who trail with them the germ-laden and polluted dust from the dead past? We must resolve to be ever-watchful! Ever-ready to expose errors! Ever-open to opportunities to speak out of a whole-hearted and disciplined empiricism so that never again will such jackals sully the spirit of the glorious masses. This man must be arrested on his next impertinent appearance on our glorious European soil and put on trial if he refuses on his own accord to step down from history. If this should prove impossible for any reason then our propaganda is always ready to expose the contradictions and to impose the correct line, and must unmask him.

John Brent-Oxford. No. 65. This pitiful relic of the past has at times served the People's interest but those who can follow only the old routines in a revolutionary period are utterly incapable of grasping the new and the ever-growing. Under the banner of allsidedness and objectivity he has defended those misguided comrades who have erroneously set their faces against the Truth and has ever taken his stand with members of the old Labour Party whose crimes and criminal errors have long been exposed. In spite of every care and attention from the Re-educators, he obstinately refuses to allow his mind to open to the Truth, and as we need every place in our glorious prisons for the reception of the criminal element of our population it is recommended he be sent to No. 5 Penal Settlement. Our new Europe has no room for such refuse from the past!

[Notes on the above Report by Comrade Chen Liu, in charge of the People's Secret Services, Europe. *Archivists.*]

24. Benjamin Sherban. Emotionally unstable. In my view he will respond to re-education. He should be *invited* to attend re-education. With the usual rewards. He should then be *asked* to return to his present position at the head of the children's movement, as our representative and with an important title.

19. George Sherban. He is intelligent, well educated, with an appealing personality. He is skillful at handling people and groups. He is in my view dangerous. There is no question of re-education. There is no question of arresting him on his next visit or using him in a Trial: the repercussions would be undesirable. He should be disposed of by any "accident" that seems appropriate. I have given the necessary instructions.

65. John Brent-Oxford. This man is a nuisance. He has influence among the older generation who remember him as Member of Parliament and representative of

Britain in the early Pan-Europe councils. He is of a good moral type. He cannot be convicted of corruption or delinquency of any sort. He has deteriorated badly in prison. He suffers from diabetes. The prison diet makes no allowance for this. In or out of prison he will not live long. I suggest he should be given a position of moderate authority in the administration attached to any one of the youth organisations. Their contempt and disregard for any old person will hasten his death. He should be treated with respect by us in order not to alienate those who remain of the old socialists who may yet be won over to work with us.

Private letter sent through the Diplomatic Bag,

AMBIEN II *of* SIRIUS, *to* KLORATHY, CANOPUS

In haste. Have just been looking through our reports from Shikasta. In case—which is unlikely I know—you have not got this information, Shammat called a meeting of all its agents in one place. This in itself seems to us symptomatic of something long suspected by us—and I know, by you, too. Conditions on Shikasta are affecting Shammatans even more than Shikastans, or affecting them *faster*. Their general mentation seems to be deteriorating rapidly. They suffer from hectivity, acceleration, arrhythmictivity. Their diagnosis of situations—as far as they are capable and within the limits of their species—is adequate. Adequate for certain specific situations and conditions. The conclusions they are drawing from analyses are increasingly wild. That Shammat should order this meeting, exposing its agents to such danger, shows that the mother-planet is affected; as much as that the local Shammat agents should obey an obviously reckless order.

This condition of Shammat and its agents, then, seems to us likely to add to the spontaneous and random destructivity to be expected of Shikasta at this time.

As if we needed anything worse!

Our Intelligence indicates that you are weathering the Shikastan crisis pretty well—not that anything else was ever expected of you. If all continues to go well, when may we expect a visit? As always we look forward to seeing you.

RACHEL SHERBAN'S JOURNAL

I see that I am going to write again about what is going on. This time it is because everything is too much. So much is happening all the time and I can't grasp it. George says I have to try, and not switch myself off. He says I switch myself off.

This flat is always full of people now. They come to see George. It is a big flat, that isn't the point. Particularly now Benjamin is hardly ever here because of his Children's Camps. And Olga and Simon are nearly always away on a crisis. But Benjamin and I, both of us, had been thinking that George would probably get an office of his own or something of that kind because of so many people. But he didn't. Benjamin got quite sarcastic about this flat becoming a public seminar. Olga and Simon said nothing but waited. I watched <u>them</u> wait and watch. They wait in the same way I wait. The way to understand something is to watch what is happening. The results are the explanation. This means you have to be patient. What is happening is that when people come to the flat all agog to see George, he doesn't even take them into his own room. Which is quite large enough. No, he sits talking in the living room with the doors open and everyone coming through. That means he wants us to be there too. And so I am whenever possible. And Olga and Simon too. And Benjamin when he is here.

They are from every country there is. Mostly our age. But sometimes old, as well. George met these people on his trip through the Youth Armies of Pan-Europe. Nearly all actually met him or heard something that struck home. They were <u>struck</u> and couldn't believe it and came to find out. I know this because of myself. Over and over again I experience the same. No, it is not possible, I think, but then it is. Sometimes their getting here is impossible. But somehow they do it. If they don't wangle some official thing, and God knows that is hard enough these days, they come illegally or even in disguise. Several times I've been in the living room when someone comes. Then this person, he or she, takes off a uniform and some hair or beard or glasses, or becomes the opposite sex and suddenly you see it was a disguise. Well, everyone seems to be in disguise anyway. They don't go back to their organisations or places if George says they mustn't. Nearly always they are sent off to some other place. Always a very definite place, with an exact time they have to stay there before they leave again.

George has been on at me. He says I've got to start thinking more. He says what is the use of all my education, the kind of education I've had. You've got to be useful, he said. You surely are not saying I should be an administrator and run things, I said. Really appalled. George said, Why not? Look at Olga and Simon, they do it and do it well. I said, Running things, what's the point? He said, If you can't beat them join them! Oh, very funny. George says, Rachel, you are too soft, and you have to toughen yourself up. Toughen myself up for <u>what</u>?

At which he manifested the humorous patience I know very well from Olga and Simon.

I see that I have been having this conversation, one way or another, with myself, or with Olga and/or Simon, or with George, all my life.

Very well then. The new items for today are: (1) Ban on eating any fish anywhere around coastlines. Extinction fishermen. The great nations challenging each other in the middle of oceans over deep-sea fish. The Antarctic seas showing signs of poisoning in the fish. (2) Food in the British Isles now down below World Minimum Standard. Third World Countries say they have no compunction in starving Europeans who have always treated them like dirt. They are getting their own back. Charming. (3) There are four million people in prisons and penal camps in Europe. They are there to die. Mostly old people. (4) There is a new bad famine in Central Africa. (5) Cattle diseases. Sheep diseases. Pig diseases. Trees dying. The Governments are saying this is not pollution as such. (6) Youth Armies are on the march.

Good for them.

That is enough for one day.

Olga came back from the famine yesterday. She looked awful. I ran her a hot bath and put her into it. I felt as if I was her mother. I made her eat some sandwiches. I put her into bed. She was quite dazed and gone. I sat with her while she lay in bed. I turned the lights off when she asked so she could see the stars through the window. I understood sitting there that Olga will not live long. She is worn out. More than that. She is far away from me. From us all. When she is with us, you would say she is being absentminded if you didn't know her. Olga is never absentminded, because she is always interested in everything going on. What is happening is that she is going away inside.

Today in the living room there was George and some people, mostly Chinese, not official Chinese. Mother was sitting with us. George was telling them where to go, what to do, what not to do. Then Benjamin came in. He has become quite different now he is so successful. That is malicious. Now that <u>he</u> is <u>so</u> useful. That is the exact truth. But he is bluff King Benjamin. He wears a uniform invented by himself of jeans and bush shirt and a keffiyeh. Usually he sits and listens but today he must have had something very good happen because he was full of himself and kept breaking in and talking. The Chinese were waiting for him to shut up. But he didn't. George just waited. But Benjamin seemed too large for the room, he is so big and everyone else in it was small in comparison and well behaved and courteous. Suddenly Olga began crying. It was out of exhaustion. I could see quite clearly that years of Benjamin had suddenly become too much. She kept sobbing, Oh do stop it, stop it, Benjamin. He was absolutely <u>devastated</u>. He collapsed. George signed to me, and I took Olga out and put her to bed again. In a minute Benjamin came to the room, and asked to be let in. He sat by Olga and held her hand. She was still crying. He was crying. I was crying.

Simon came back today with his Peripatetic Hospital. He has been working twenty hours a day for weeks. He and Olga sit in the living room like two ghosts. They hardly talk. I see they don't need to. I see that our family often sit in the living room for hours and say practically nothing, George too. George has been spending hours sitting with Olga and Simon saying not a word. Being <u>with</u> them. Benjamin came marching in and asked about Simon's trip. By then Simon had recovered a bit. He said this and that, and then Thank God they were Chinese. Meaning the Overlords. (People's Representatives.) Where he had been travelling. I have seen that Simon and Olga often say Thank heavens he or she or they were Chinese. But what I am suddenly asking myself is, <u>Wh</u>y the Chinese? I mean, why is it that absolutely everywhere you go there are Chinese. Ever so efficient and useful of course. Never put a foot wrong. Tact personified. Simon and Olga say, common sense personified. Last month when Olga went to the famine, she actually grabbed a Chinese from some office or other and took her too because they are worth their weight in gold. In common sense. There are six Chinese doctors in Simon's Peripatetic Hospital.

This afternoon has been peculiar. George came back from college at three. He lectures there on Systems of the Law. Because he says it is a good thing that people are reminded that such a thing as Law is possible. There were people waiting for him. I had given them mint tea and cake. Then I saw they were all hungry so I gave them what we had ready for supper. They were two Germans, three Russians, one Frenchwoman, a Chinese, and one Britisher. When George came in and greeted them and sat down, at once there was something different. An atmosphere. Usually what happens is that there is some small talk, and news about what is going on, and then George begins to talk in his way. Sometimes you can catch when he begins, and sometimes it is all happening before you have seen it. People who know him watch for it. But those who don't, blunder about spoiling it all. Until they catch on. This afternoon I could see at once these were people who had been with him before, somewhere on his trips. There was the attentive atmosphere. But there was something wrong too. It was someone there who was wrong. I wondered who? Someone there was dangerous. I saw it was the Britisher, Raymond Watts. Once I had seen it I couldn't understand why it had taken me so long. It was obvious that he was a spy. I saw that the others who had arrived with him had not seen this but they knew something was wrong. Slowly one after another they got it. It was very nasty. Soon everyone was sitting looking at Raymond Watts. Who was uneasy and false. He was scared. He had good reason to be. I was waiting for George to say something. Or do something. But he sat smiling as usual. Then the others, the Russians first, got up and said they were going. I could see it was all dreadful. The others went out after the Russians. Not Raymond Watts. George looked at me. I stayed. He went out into the lobby with the others, and he was there some time. I tried to talk with Raymond Watts but he was shaking and sweating. The voices from the lobby were loud and angry. I knew they were wanting to kill Raymond Watts and George was saying no. Then they went off and George came back and nodded at me and I went. Later I said to George, Are they going to kill him? George said, No. I told them that Raymond would change. I thought a bit, seeing quite a few things. I said, Oh, it has happened before. George began to grin. I saw that it had. Often? George said, There are as many spies as not, these days. He was looking at me. I knew perfectly well what was coming, more about me toughening up. George said, First of all, people have to eat. And then, for many people, being a spy or something of the kind is the obvious thing. They have not been given an alternative. Don't you see? No, I said, I don't see. At which point, he said, Rachel, you really must try to be stronger. You have had a sheltered life in many ways. That made me angry. I said to him, What has been sheltered about it? He said, First of all, you have never been tempted to do something you shouldn't because someone you loved was hungry or because you were hungry. And secondly, you have been all your life with advantaged people.

I said to him, Like Naseem and Shireen, for instance. Advantaged?

Yes. They were brought up to be decent. They were good people. But most people now are not brought up to be decent, but the opposite and it is <u>not</u> their fault.

It took me some time to hear what he had said. I said to George, Are they dead then? George said, Naseem died a month ago, of an infection. He got chilled. I said, You mean, he died of not having enough to eat. That's right, he said. And Shireen died in the hospital in childbirth.

So what has happened to the children?

He said that two of them have died of dysentery, and the baby Shireen died of is being looked after by Fatima. The other three have been taken into a Children's Camp.

By then I was crying, though I had decided not to cry.

George said, Rachel, if you can't face all this, then you'll have to come back and do it all over again. <u>Think</u> <u>about</u> <u>it</u>.

I have been trying to think about it.

I wish I was dead with Naseem and Shireen.

I have to write down that George is not beautiful the way he was only two years ago. He is actually ugly sometimes with being tired.

I have seen that Simon will not live long. He is like Olga, a long way from us. George sits with them, every minute he can. I go in too, then I leave because I want to cry, and they are certainly not crying, but very serene.

George has said that he wants me to help Benjamin with his work in the Children's Camps. I couldn't believe it. He said, Yes, Rachel, that is what you have to do. I said, Oh no, no, no. He said, Oh yes, yes.

Benjamin came in, great sunburned <u>oaf</u>, and I couldn't. George wasn't there. I knew quite well George had made sure I was alone with Benjamin. Benjamin kept saying, Where is George, where is Mother, where is Father. Simon had gone off to work at the hospital, and Olga was lying down. I saw that Benjamin was feeling left out. At last I made myself ask him if I could come and help him at the Children's Camps. His face, well! I was glad I had asked. I see that when Benjamin comes in here he needs very much to be liked. Now I am going to actually have to face doing it, I don't think I can. George isn't here, he has gone on a trip to a Youth Army in Egypt.

I went with Benjamin to his Camps. He uses a light army truck. He stopped at the Peace Café to offer lifts. We took seventeen people, all for the Camps. Benjamin's Camps are fifteen miles out. Benjamin says this is far enough out to prevent them coming in to tear the place to pieces in the evenings. He said that about the little kids, and it was exactly the same as old people and ordinary people saying about the Youth "tearing everything to pieces." The place of the Camps isn't very pretty. It is flat and dusty with some low hills around. Suddenly we came to a barbed-wire fence. It is electrified. Benjamin said there has to be a fence. To stop people getting in as much as to stop the kids getting out. Quote unquote. There are five thousand boys in the one Benjamin lives in. There are breeze-block sheds, fifty boys to a shed, five sheds to a group, twenty of these groups. There is a standpipe for each group of five sheds, and a block of showers and lavatories. There are central offices and buildings. The Camp is built like a wheel, with the sheds as spokes, two groups of sheds on each spoke.

There are half a dozen palm trees. A few hibiscus and plumbago bushes. The place swarms with children, but always in squads and files. Not at random. They are called by loudspeaker at 5:30 each morning. The sheds are hot and stuffy so they are pleased to get out. They do physical exercises, with a proper physical instructor. There is a palm-thatch roof over a cement floor that has mats spread on it, where they sit for meals in sessions of five hundred each. Each sitting has twenty minutes to eat. They have porridge and yoghurt for breakfast. This eating place is almost continuously in use. After breakfast they do lessons and games. The lessons are done in classes of a hundred, most of the time. There isn't a proper place for lessons, so they go on everywhere, and in the eating shed too when it is not being used to eat in. The teaching is shouted at the children, sometimes through loudspeakers, and the children chant after the teachers. When anything up to fifty different classes are going on at the same time all over the camp it is weird, the capitals of the world being chanted here, then heroes of history chanted a hundred yards away, principles of hygiene on the other side, duty and respect to the elders next door, then addition or the multiplication table with the aid of a blackboard the size of a house, all this going on at once, and then from right across the Camp the sounds of a class chanting the Koran, or doing some dance. Well, the one thing these kids won't suffer from is compartmentalisation of their minds. They have an early lunch. Vegetables and beans. They lie down. Then they are crowded into the eating shed practically sitting on top of each other and they have history and current affairs. Indoctrination. Then they have lessons on the Koran and Mahomed and Islam. The Christians and Jews being fewer are done in the sleeping sheds. Then it starts to get a bit cooler thank heavens, and there are more games and supper. Then Prayers, and a sort of sermon, which is very emotional and uplifting. Then off they march to bed. They are never alone. Never, never. Not for one second, ever at any time. They do nothing by themselves. They are like people in big cities, always careful of their limbs and where they put themselves in case they bump or tread on each other. They are very polite and disciplined. They have bright staring watchful eyes. Then suddenly, you'll see a group of them that have broken out of a line or a squad, go wild, crazy, tearing about, flailing their arms and screaming and pummelling each other. The young men who look after them rush in and break it up. These young men are volunteers from the Youth Camp five miles off.

I said to Benjamin that the psychology of these children must be completely different in every way from those in ordinary families, and when they grow up they will be completely different. Benjamin said, Yes, very true, would I prefer them to be dead?

I wonder what Naseem's and Shireen's three children are like now in the Camp. These children are all orphans from one of the crises.

Benjamin slops about the Camp, smiling and full of good will, and available to everyone. The kids like him. The supervisors like him. He likes them. I can see that I underrated Benjamin. If people did not always contrast him with George, he would be admired. He is very efficient. He keeps everything working properly. Nothing would work if someone didn't co-ordinate things, not with so many children and not enough facilities. Benjamin is trying to get several more sheds like the eating shed, for teaching in. He doesn't seem hopeful. He says his main concern day and night is that there shouldn't be an epidemic.

Benjamin gave one of the uplift talks. The sermon, in fact. He did not tell me he was going to do it, because I know he was embarrassed. The moment I saw him there standing up ready to start, what I was thinking was, Don't you dare try to be like George! But he was absolutely different, rather like the pep-talks at assembly in school. All for one and one for all, we are brothers, we must help each other, and God will help us. God and Allah, I would say 70 percent Allah, 30 percent God, being fair to everyone. But he did it well. What else can he do? What else could be done?

He drove me back after the children had gone to bed. We brought in some of the helpers from the Camp. We kept picking up Youth on the road. The truck was so overweighted it had to crawl. Benjamin said two things during this drive back. One. That I should have a boyfriend. I knew that meant I am unhealthy about George. I said to him, Don't bother, I know you mean George. But you are quite wrong about what I feel. So he said, I understand perfectly well. I am not an idiot. But if you are waiting for someone to turn up as good as George you are going to be a virgin all your life. At this we were silent a good bit. I was angry, needless to say, but I was feeling that I was unjust, because I could see he meant it well and he had spoken not at all in his usual style. He said, After all, we are both of us going to have special problems because of George, aren't we? I digested all this. Then I said, I am not going to add to the population of the Children's Camps. At which he said, I've known only one girl who has so resolutely chosen to live in another century. May I present you with an elementary manual on birth control? At which I said, I don't know why you think I am some sort of an idiot. I have thought about it. I am not interested in the sort of partnership couples set up now, no children, no home, they might just as well not be married. Why do they bother? Well, said Benjamin, being humorous, there is this thing called sex. Well, I said, I'll apply to you for a healthy and congenial partner when I can't stand it any more and I think I can't find one for myself. At this we began laughing. I cannot remember ever having this kind of nice easy time with Benjamin before. Not ever. For the first time I really like Benjamin.

But then he said he wanted me to "undertake" the Camp for the girls which is the partner to his Camp. I said of course I couldn't, how could I, I couldn't possibly run a thing like that. He said, Why not? I didn't know how until I did it. And anyway I don't "run" the Camp. The helpers do it.

At this we got into an argument, but not a painful one. The helpers come from the Youth Camp, all about our age, eighteen and nineteen years old. It is always the younger people in every Youth Camp who do the looking after the children. There are no women in the boys' Camp, and this is what we argued about. He said, It was a Moslem country. I said, I didn't care if it was Moslem or Mars, it was cruel to have all those boys without a woman in sight. He said, What did I suggest, a mother-figure for each shed of fifty boys? I said, No, but half the helpers should be girls. He said, Good God, he has the mullahs breathing down his neck as it is, but if there were girls working with the boys day and night, the Authorities would go crazy. I said, They were a filthy-minded lot. He said, I was being a westerner and showing no insight. I said I didn't care about all that, it was very simple, it was common sense to have some women.

I went out with Benjamin to the girls' Camp. There is no contact between the two, in spite of there being only five miles between them, and quite a lot of brothers and sisters being separated. But every week the brothers and sisters are taken separately to a neutral place in the Youth Camp, and spend some hours together. I suppose it is something. I had not said one word of criticism about this, because I had made up my mind not to, but Benjamin said, Well what do you suggest?—just as if I had criticised.

The Camp is identical with the boys' Camp. The girls and the boys wear the same clothes, a sort of suit of light white or blue cotton, trousers and short-sleeved tunics. The boys wear keffiyehs. The girls wear tight little caps over light muslin veils. Today a wind was blowing dust and sand everywhere and all you could see were dark eyes over the veils that were wound around mouths and nostrils. I wished I had a veil myself.

The helpers are mostly Tunisians and of course some Chinese. They all enjoy looking after the children. There are long waiting lists in the Youth Camps to work in the Children's Camps.

The day was the same as the day in the boys' Camp.

In the afternoon I was in the thatched shelter where they had lunch, and some bands of little girls crept out from where they were supposed to be resting in their sheds and stood around watching me. I was a new face. I wasn't in uniform. I wore a short red dress over some pale blue trousers. The dress had short sleeves. I was quite proper. But I was very strange to them. Exotic. Not because of my looks. In fact I look like them. I said hello and was friendly, but they were serious and silent. They kept staring and crowding in, and in. I had such a sense of them crowding in on me, not smiling, thousands and thousands and thousands of them. What will they be when they grow up? But they seem grown-up already with their hard little faces and hard careful eyes. I sat down on the mat and hoped they would come and sit by me. They pressed in around me, looking down at me. I said to them, Please sit down, come and talk to me. First one slowly sat, and then they all did, all at once. And they sat very close and stared and said nothing. Then Benjamin came striding along, and they all ran away at once, without even a glance back.

Re: Colonised Planet 5, Shikasta

Benjamin said, Come into the administration hut. That was because we were creating a disturbing sensation being together in the all-girls Camp. So I did. It was just an administration hut, like one anywhere.

He said, Well will you do it? I said, But what am I to do?

Be here, he said, quite fierce and urgent, and I saw how he saw what he was doing. You must be here, and always be available for everyone at any time and see that things are co-ordinated.

I said I would think about it.

After supper he gave another sermon, practically word for word the same as last night's. Everyone adored it. Love and good will all around. I suppose I could learn to give a sermon, there's obviously nothing in it since everyone does it all the time, political speech or sermon, what's the difference.

It was nearly night when we left. The girls were all in lots of fifty, with two girls my age one in front and one behind for each batch, marching around and around the Camp for exercise, keeping in step, singing away. The moon was coming up.

I said I'd think about it and I am.

Today I had decided I would not take on the girls' Camp. No sooner had I decided than George came back. He brought two children, a boy and a girl. One for one Camp and one for the other, I suppose? Kassim and Leila. Parents died of cholera. They are here in this flat. Very quiet. Behaving well. They go off into George's room when he is out and shut the door. I suppose they cry.

I was in the living room by myself. George came in and sat down. All the doors open. Anyone can come in any time and that is the point. But we were alone for a change. I said, All right, I've seen the Camps.

He waited.

I did not say anything, so he said, Have you told Benjamin? I said Yes, and he said at once, very concerned, but putting up with it, Then he must be upset.

Yes, he was, I said. He sat there waiting, and so I said, I have been thinking about how we were brought up. He said, Good!—And I've had a thought you will approve of. . . . He was already smiling, very affectionate. I said, How many people in the world have been brought up as we have been?

He nodded.

All the time, more and more Camps, enormous schools, everyone herded about, slogans, loudspeakers, institutions.

He nodded.

I went on talking like this. Then I said, But all the time, a few brands plucked from the burning. Well I don't think I am up to it.

He sat back, he sighed, he recrossed his legs—he made a lot of quick light movements, as he does when he is impatient, and wishes that he had the right to be.

Then he said, Rachel, if you start crying, I am going to get up and go out. He had never spoken like that before.

But I wasn't going to give in. I felt as if I were definitely in the right.

Then he said, These two children, I want you to look after them.

Oh, I said, you mean, not Benjamin, not the Camps?

No. They come from a family like ours. Kassim is ten, and Leila is nine. It would be better if they did not go into the Camps. If it can be managed.

I was sitting there thinking of what it would involve. Of our parents, and how they had brought us up. How can I do anything like that? But I said, All right I'll try.

Good, he said, and got up to go.

I said, If I had agreed to work in the Camp, then I couldn't have looked after Kassim and Leila. Who would you have asked?

He hesitated, and said: Suzannah.

This really, but <u>literally</u> took my breath away. I just sat there.

Suzannah is kind, he said. This was not a criticism of me, but a statement about Suzannah. He nodded, smiled and went away.

Today George came into my room, and he said he is going off on a trip again. Everywhere, through all the armies in Europe and then down to India, and to China. It is going to take him a year or more.

I could not take this in. It seemed to me he had only just got back, and we hadn't even talked properly yet.

George said, Rachel, this will be my last trip.

A first I thought he was telling me he would be killed, then I saw that wasn't it. What he was saying was, it would not be possible after that to make his sort of journey.

He told me that a lot of people will be coming here, and he would leave me with instructions of what to say.

Re: Colonised Planet 5, Shikasta

Not Simon and Olga? I asked and he said, No.

Of course I knew what he meant.

Then, just as I was thinking that now Benjamin is sensible and nice he can help with everything, George said, Benjamin will be coming with me. This was more than I could stand, all at once. George sat, quite relaxed and easy, watching me, concerned, but waiting for me to be strong. I didn't feel able.

George said: Rachel, you've got to.

I didn't have any breath in me to say anything. George said, I won't be leaving for a month, and went out.

Then I went off to lie down.

Today it was announced that the All-Glorious Pan-European Socialist Democratic Communist Dictatorships for the Preservation of Peace welcome the Benevolent Tutelage of the Glorious Chinese Brothers. Well, why bother? What a joke!

But when George heard it on the radio he was very serious. I said to him, But you knew it was going to happen, obviously? He said Yes, but not so soon. He sent a message to Benjamin by someone leaving from the Peace Café (because the telephone wasn't working again) to come as soon as possible. He spends a lot of time with Benjamin now. Every afternoon. He goes out to the Camps, and he is with the children, and then he goes with Benjamin to have supper in the café. Benjamin has had an invitation from the Chinese to go to Europe. He is flattered. He is ashamed of being flattered.

Every morning early before breakfast, I bring Kassim and Leila to my room and I teach them geography and Spanish. And the history of recent politics and religions. This is what George says they should learn. When I get back from teaching at college in the afternoon I teach Kassim and Leila Portuguese and geohistory. Otherwise they are with George all the time. Olga and Simon have hardly noticed the children. It is too much for them. Olga has gone back to work at the hospital. She is fighting a battle with bureaucracy. Well, what's new! Simon is taking a week's holiday because he had a minor heart attack. George told him he must. They talk a lot, or sit quietly together. The other day Olga said, I feel as if I have finished what I had to do.

I said to her, Olga, do you mean, it doesn't matter now because we three are grown up? Olga said, Something like that. I said, But I don't think I <u>am</u> grown up. She was <u>affectionate</u>, and said, Well, hard lines! And so we laughed. This is how things are with us at the moment.

This evening George and Benjamin were in the living room and about ten people who had come to see George. One of them was from India, and she talked about a girl called Sharma, and from Benjamin's reaction I realised she was a girl George was interested in. There was a packet of letters from the girl to George. When the visitors left, and George went off with Kassim and Leila somewhere, Benjamin was with me. I said, Who is the girl?

I could see that if I wasn't careful we would slip back into the awful quarrelling way we used to be in.

She seems to have taken George's fancy, said Benjamin. It was <u>he</u> who was keeping us nice and sensible and not quarrelling and I was grateful.

I said, Is it serious?

I thought you were going to say, What about Suzannah!

I was in fact thinking about Suzannah.

At this point I saw that I would start shouting at Benjamin, if I didn't leave the room, and that would have been unfair, because he hadn't done anything. So I got up and left.

I slept hardly at all thinking of this girl and George. I dreamed. It was awful, everything taken away from me. I know I am not being strong. This afternoon George came into my room when I was teaching the children Portuguese and I knew it was because he knew I wanted to talk about this girl. He nodded and the children went out. Then he sat in a chair opposite to me, and leaned forward and looked straight at me.

He said, Rachel, what is it you want me to say?

I want you to say I love this girl, she is the most marvellous girl in the world, she is beautiful and sensitive and intelligent and remarkable.

All right, he said, I've said it. And now, Rachel?

It goes without saying that as usual I felt <u>lacking</u>, and sat there with all my emotions rioting around, of no use to anyone.

I couldn't speak, and then he said, It is not difficult to feel love for someone, in the sense that something is called out of you by possibilities. Potentialities.

Her qualities are not the ones you need? I asked. It sounded feebly sarcastic, but I hadn't meant this at all. So he didn't take it like that.

You surely must see, Rachel, that none of us is going to have the things we want.

I know that.

Very well, then.

You haven't mentioned Suzannah, I said.

I didn't think it was Suzannah on your mind.

I didn't say anything.

Then he said, Rachel, I want you to listen very carefully.

But I do, always.

Good. Listen now. When I and Benjamin leave, I want you to stay here, in this flat, and look after Kassim and Leila. I don't want you to leave here. I want you to remember that I said this.

When I heard what he said, I was engulfed in a sickness. A blackness. It was horrible. I knew that what was happening was terrible. I wanted to grasp what was happening. I felt that I should be absorbing something and I wasn't.

I was faint and not seeing well, but I heard him say Rachel, please remember, please.

When I had stopped being faint, he had gone out. He sent the children back in and I went on teaching them.

I have been waiting for George to talk some more with me alone, but while I often sit with him and his visitors, he doesn't talk with me alone.

We heard today that Simon died in the Sudan. Of one of the new viruses. George telephoned from the college on a special permission but Simon was already buried. George and Benjamin and I sat in the living room together, by ourselves. No visitors. It is very hot tonight. We were waiting for Olga, and she came in late, but she had been told already. Then the four of us sat. Olga is so worn out, I don't think she felt anything at all. I could see from her face that it was not that she couldn't take it in but that she had a long time ago. The four of us went on sitting there, quietly, until Olga said, It is going to be morning soon. She has gone to bed. George and Benjamin are still sitting in the living room.

George and Benjamin left today for Europe. With a contingent of twenty-four, all delegates from different parts of Africa. Olga and I are here, and the two children. Olga is almost invisible, she floats around.

She does go to the hospital, but she comes in early at night and lies down. She has some life in her in the mornings, and she sits in the kitchen with Kassim and Leila and tells them stories about George as a child, and then as he grew up. When she forgets something she looks at me, and I fill in. I see she wants to be sure they know about George. I sit and listen to her, and what she says is quite different from what I remember. I mean, because she is so tired and <u>gone</u>, the things she says are halting and flavourless. I sometimes can't believe this is George she is talking about. Then I have to wonder if the things I wrote down about George are lifeless in the same way. Sometimes what she says sounds as if it comes out of a very old dusty book. She repeats anecdotes. She tells them things about George that she knew, and I didn't. She talks and talks and talks about George.

Leila and Kassim sit watching her. They are very attractive children. They are thin, from too little food, wiry, with alive brown faces, straight black hair, soft dark eyes. I contrast them with the children in the Camps and I feel they are precious. Of course that isn't fair to the children in the Camps. Every one of them needs someone to love them. Each one of them.

Suzannah comes in every evening just about suppertime. She is very quiet and <u>humble</u>. She is exactly like a dog that hopes it will not be sent away. Yet whenever she comes everyone is kind. Olga is particularly. She sits beside the children at the supper table. She is nice with them, simple and sensible. They like her. I look at her in her loud smart blouse and her commonplace face and her waved hair and I simply cannot believe it.

Olga woke me in the night and said I had to take her to hospital. I rang Suzannah who came with her army car. We took Olga to hospital, and I asked Suzannah to go back and be with the children. Olga was taken to a little room off one of her own wards. There were a lot of bright lights, and doctors and nurses. She said to the chief doctor, Please don't . . . meaning, don't give me drugs. He works under her usually. He took her hand and smiled and nodded, and nodded at the other doctors and nurses and they all went out and left me with Olga. She was very tired. Her face was grey. Her lips were white. She made a movement with her hand and I held it. She was looking at me from a very long way off. I could see that it was all she could do to breathe. She said, in a loud sudden voice, Rachel. I waited, and waited, and waited. The bright lights battering down. Then she smiled, a real smile, so I knew she was going to die at once, and she said, Well Rachel . . . in a friendly sort of way. Then she stopped breathing. I closed her eyes after a bit. Before that she had been looking at me. So it seemed. I stayed with her until she was cold. I did not feel any grief because it did not seem to be indicated. Anyway, I don't believe in death. And anyway, I wished I was with her. Then I called a nurse in, and said that if there were any documents to sign, I would have to, because now I was the only member of the family left here. They gave me a cup of coffee and brought me a form to sign. Then I walked home. It was light by then. Suzannah was asleep on the sofa in the living room. That made me like her, because there were six empty beds she could have put herself in. She did not fuss or say anything silly, but made me more coffee and then got the children up and gave them breakfast. We sat together in the kitchen, and I told them that Olga had died, and that I would look after them. And Suzannah too, they asked? And of course I said, Yes. It seemed completely the right thing to say this.

I have seen that of course George will marry Suzannah. How was it I didn't see that before? She is a member of the family already. She has been for a long time.

Now George and Benjamin have gone away and Mother and Father are dead, this flat is full of space. I have put Kassim in George's room, and Leila in Benjamin's room. This is something very important for them. Before they have felt like refugees taken in. But now you can see they feel part of the family. I have given them jobs to do, like keeping the flat tidy, and shopping, and both Leila and Kassim can cook some things. I still haven't sent them to school. I don't know where or how. I have even thought of trying to find Hasan to ask him. Perhaps these children are important the way George was? For all I know Hasan is dead. Over and over again, you think of someone you haven't seen for a time, and then you hear: dead. George didn't leave instructions for the children except that I had to look after them. I cannot possibly teach them all they should know.

Last night Suzannah came for supper, in the way she does, her eyes saying she must be asked, but of course ready to leave in a moment if she isn't. As we were talking at supper, the subject of school came up. Suzannah is good at math, so she will give them lessons. Then she said she would take them sometimes with her to her job. She teaches physical culture and hygiene and diet and that sort of thing at one of the

Youth Camps. I said No, I didn't want Leila and Kassim influenced by all that. I saw that both the children were looking amused in their polite way. Suzannah said, You must not overprotect these two. I always get furious, inwardly, when she says things. It is her manner. Everything she says has the same quality. Pushy. But it is a result of something I didn't undertand, because of not liking her. It is strength that makes her insist on what she thinks. She insists and is too loud because of her experiences. The usual bad ones. She has had to fight for everything. And so she does fight. She was a refugee. She has never even known her real name. The Camp administrator called her Suzannah. She has not had any name but that. She was for six years in a girls' Camp. She taught herself all kinds of things in the Camp. She got the helpers who knew math and hygiene and diet etc. to teach her. She fought her way out.

Suzannah was going to her job as it happens this morning and it would have been sensible to ask her to stay the night. I didn't. I wanted to but I couldn't make myself. I felt taken over by her. So she went home, leaving just in time for the curfew. I felt guilty. When I was helping the children to go to bed, Kassim said, Rachel, are you trying to protect me and Leila from things we have already experienced? I don't know very much about them. I don't ask them, because it must be painful, and if George did tell me I wasn't listening. Perhaps they want to talk about it and I don't let them. I will but give me time.

People are always coming here asking for George but not nearly so much. Like a stream's steady current suddenly reducing its flow. And that makes me wonder. For everything has always seemed so haphazard, the people coming, and how they came, it always being so difficult, but now he is not here, only a few come. I am being careful. Benjamin said I must be on the lookout for informers and spies. How do I know when a person is a spy? I have been left to manage much more than I can. I must be making bad mistakes I suppose.

Yesterday Raymond Watts came. Of course I am careful of him. But why is he still here? George was always telling people to go here and go there, but he didn't tell anyone to stay here. Late in the evening some boys from Holland came in. They got here in the usual crazy way, hit and miss. Suzannah was here. She made a sign at me and beckoned me outside. Of course they saw this. I suppose she imagined that they didn't. She "whispered" to me that I should be careful of them. They heard, because they left at once. I asked Suzannah how she knew. She said, When one has had certain experiences, one senses these things. So I asked her about Raymond Watts, and she said, Oh he is all right now.

Raymond Watts came again. I have seen that he is in love with me. Well, if he wants to waste his time. He was talking about things, and I heard he was a schoolteacher in England. I asked him how long he would be here, and he said, Six months, unless fate was kind, meaning me I suppose, and so I asked him to give Leila and Kassim lessons.

Last night Suzannah was here because she had taken the children to her Camp with her, and made them help her with her work, and then she taught them math, and then she had supper. Then I made myself ask her to stay the night. I put her in Father's and Mother's room. She was nearly collapsing with emotion. Well, so was I. She has a little box of a room on the edge of the town where the sand is in drifts right up to the door and mangy dogs roam about. The room is too hot for her to be in at all in the afternoons. It is quite like the little mud room I loved so much, but the house doesn't have a court with a pool, and she doesn't have a roof to sleep out on. This morning I said to her it would be sensible if she moved in here. I didn't do it nicely, I am afraid, but I did it, so I suppose that is something. I know she is going to start throwing her weight around, but she won't even see anything wrong in it, and there is nothing I can do, and I know it isn't important.

When I put Kassim in George's room, I told him I would clear out the cupboards for him and today I did. I brought George's things into my room. He never has had much in the way of clothes, so what there was left here went in with mine. Of course I could not help crying. I miss him so much I ache all day and all night. I miss Benjamin too, strange as it might seem. I don't miss Olga and Simon much. That is because they had gone so far away before they died. What I do miss is what I can remember of them when I was little. But that is stupid. And when I think of how tired they were, that makes me want to cry. But they wouldn't value that. Well, I don't value it either. I have given up worrying about me being childish. I have put George's papers in cartons. I found letters in his papers. I don't know if I should have read them or not, but I did. One was from his great love in India. All I can say is, she doesn't understand much about George. Also a letter from George to her, which he didn't send. She hasn't read it, but I have.

So it seems to me, judging by <u>results</u>, *that this letter was more for me than for her. I take it for granted that I am being dishonest.*

Letter from SHARMA PATEL
to GEORGE SHERBAN

Dear Comrade,

I only heard last night that the bearer is going your way, so this last letter (I have been writing to you every spare minute I get, which isn't saying much!)—it has to be short, this letter.

When are you coming? You promised. Luis says you are to come on another all-round trip, India just one of your ports of call. I am waiting —you know how impatiently.

But I have something concrete to put forward. At the next Pan-Europe Conference of the Youth Armies, it is on the cards India will be elected into Convenor's position. This is what everyone is expecting. That will make your Sharma boss of Europe for that year. (Of course I am only joking, as you know!) But I am looking forward to it, apart from the travelling to each of the countries. I talked to Luis about my idea. I asked him to think it over carefully. I told him that if you <u>were prepared to put yourself forward for it</u>, you would very likely represent North Africa. Are you prepared to put yourself forward? You didn't seem wholehearted when we discussed this. You are wrong! It isn't correct to vacillate and hang back when you know you are right for a position! Selfish ambition is one thing. I am not advocating that. I don't think even my worst enemies could accuse me of that. But it is not modesty to refuse to undertake responsibilities you are right for! And you are the right man for the job. And you deserve it. Your style of work and your achievements are well known. And there is your Indian background, which is not unknown! I hear on all sides how highly you are thought of. So, I hope that I will hear from you that you have put yourself forward for the path that now lies open to you. Which brings me to my plan. What I asked Luis was this. It would be a step forward on the right path to link Europe and Africa. At the present these links are intermittent and tenuous. We should correct this. I propose that you, as representative of North Africa (you <u>will</u>, you <u>must</u> agree!), should be elected with me Joint Heads of the Armies for the year. And of course this year might very well become two or even more, it tends to happen! I can see your dear smile! I can hear you pointing out that this plan of mine depends on three unknowns. But I have a hunch. I have a feel for how things are likely to work out.

Re: *Colonised Planet 5, Shikasta*

I have been right often enough, admit it! So I am working this end for the success of this plan. We can travel together through Europe and North Africa. I don't have to say what that would mean to me. And to you, I know. Our lives together, our love, will fuse into the great upward march of mankind, which is led by the uncorrupted youth of the world.

Oh I can't wait to see you again! But I have been so busy, all day and half the night as usual, I haven't had time to be sad. I know this is what you would want to hear from me when we meet.

But I do allow myself one little indulgence . . . I remember . . . do you remember?—that jewel of a night after the Conference at Simla . . . one day nights like that will be the heritage of all mankind, and so I don't feel selfish when I think of this jewel of a night. Oh George, when will I see you again? The bearer will be returning here before going on to Peking and will bring me your letter. Which will agree, I hope and trust, to my proposals.

Your Sharma

GEORGE SHERBAN *to* SHARMA PATEL

I have read your letter very carefully. I will see you during my visit to India and I will tell you then why I will not allow myself to be put forward, as you suggest. But Sharma, I did tell you, I explained everything to you.

I have been dreaming. Would you like to hear my dream?

There was a civilisation once—where?—it doesn't matter. The Middle East perhaps, China, India. . . . It lasted a long long time. Thousands of years. We can't think like that now: continuity, cultures not changing very much, generation after generation. It was a civilisation where there were rich and poor, but not great extremes. It was well balanced, too, trade and agriculture, and the use of minerals, all in harmony with each other. People lived a long time, perhaps a thousand years. Perhaps five hundred. But it doesn't matter, a long time. Of course now we despise the past and think that children were mostly born to die because of ignorance. But these people were not ignorant. They knew how not to have too many children and to live at peace with their land, and their neighbours.

Imagine what a marriage might have been then, Sharma. Nothing frantic and desperate, no fear of death as we all have it, making us rush to mate and marry and the having and holding because we know that everything may so suddenly be taken away.

And lifetimes stretching in front of you . . . a young man may have parents two hundred years old, think of that Sharma, how sensible and experienced they must be . . . he sees this marriage, and its strength and its sense, and he knows he wants the same. And there is a girl like him. They may have known each other all their lives. Or have heard of each other, for there is plenty of time to hear of this one and that one —to listen to someone growing up nearby, and to wonder, would we be right with each other? But there is no hurry, no rush, no desperation. Behind them stretches their civilisation, and the wise men and the historians and the storytellers tell them of it, and in front of them stretches their world, and will go on and on. . . .

But marriages are made young, of course, for that is the time for marriage. The families make slow and thoughtful approaches to each other. What they are thinking of is how they can carry the best they know into the future of the race, their culture. They see themselves, feel themselves, as the bearers of culture. Yes, they discuss family characteristics—this is a good family, the mother is good and balanced and beautiful enough, and the father is also these things, and his line too. When these young people know these things are being discussed, it is not with a sense of personal affront, which is how we would, now, in these days, experience a discussion about—not our wonderful and precious selves—but our importance as representatives. When they meet, it is without panic and grasping. They talk and they visit and they wait and they get to know each other's families, and all this may take a long time, years even, for there is no hurry. And they know that if they decide not to marry, then in any case they will be friends for so long they cannot see the end of it. Meanwhile they love, of course, and choose how they may live, in this place or that, he will work at this or that, and she too, and all the time their children are implicit in what they say and think and do, for the knowledge of how to keep a strong, continuous healthy civilisation is the deepest thing in them.

Can we even begin to imagine, in our feverishness, our consumption of possibilities, the slow, full texture of their days, their years?

They marry, when the time has come for it. What is he? A merchant perhaps and she will travel with him and work with him, or a farmer? A maker of artefacts, these two, tiles, household vessels, everything satisfying and good in their hands, and to look at. Or they will choose to live in a house near their bakery, or is it a leather goods shop, or is he a carpenter, or does he work with metals. What they do with their hands brings them satisfaction, pleasure, every gesture they make must have use, and necessity. There is no hurry. No fear. Of course people die, but after long lives. Of course there are accidents and even, sometimes wars, but these are skirmishes along the edges of their civilisation, bordering another just as fine and old as their own. There is respect between these two cultures, and often marriage and much trading.

This couple have their children and educate them and they are absorbed into the stream of inheritance which carries them like a river. I can see these two young things—like us, Sharma—in love, and loving, but not in the service of some "cause," and not grabbing love as a shield against horrors. <u>Which</u> <u>is</u> <u>what</u> <u>we</u> <u>are</u> <u>doing</u>, <u>Sharma</u>. They are kind, and playful . . . I can see them doing simple pleasant things like walking along a riverbank, and swimming naked in fresh good water with their friends. And visiting each other's houses, visiting friends. Can you imagine what friendship must have been like in those days? Now our friends are usually in another continent, or are going to move away next week. I like to think of what friendship must have been then.

And I can see these two with their young children, enjoying them, enjoying every minute, because there is not the sort of pressure we know. And watching how they grow and show this trait or that, show the past which they are carrying into the future.

And I can see them, still young people, very young, a hundred, two hundred years old, vigorous and lively, and their family is grown and self-supporting but not flown as we take for granted must happen. Imagine the relations between children and parents who may know each other for hundreds of years? I wonder what kind of bond that might be. Imagine, it might take three hundred years or more for a person to reach maturity. You can think about it, and think about it all and not really grasp it, it is too hard for us. The high marriage. A real marriage. It happened once, I am sure of that.

Do you like this dream, Sharma? I wonder . . .

Or, if you don't, how about this . . . we are back in time, back, back . . . people are physically very different from these I have just written about, and of course different from us, with our diseases and our degenerating organs and our pitiful little lives.

That was a time when this earth had close links with the stars and their forces . . . does this annoy you, Sharma? You probably think it <u>not</u> <u>useful</u>. You are a very practical girl, and I admire you for it. Any situation offered to you—in no time you have grasped it, summed it up, seen how it may develop into the future. It is a capacity rooted in the deepest part of your nature—you value the capacity but not what it is rooted in! There isn't anything I value in you I could tell you about, and you would be pleased! Do you know that? Isn't that amazing? You think I value what you value in yourself—your cleverness, your ability to manage situations, your brilliant sensible speeches, the way you are so concise and quick in committees. Even your humanity. . . . Do you know, you would be angry, if I told you what I love to see in you . . . it is a marvellous grasping of the <u>actual</u>, a sense, a gift, an instinct. I watch you pick up a bowl of rice and your hands have in them a language of understanding. You put up your hand to adjust your sari. I could watch that gesture forever. It has such certainty in it, such knowledge. One of the children come running, and it is not what you say, but how you touch and hold. It is a miracle, this thing in you. I can never have enough of it, I watch you, how you put your feet on the earth, so absolutely right, every step, and the movement of your head as you turn it to listen. I tell you, Sharma, there is something there that I—I simply give up! I salute it, and that's all.

In those days of this other older dream of mine, there were few people on the earth. These people who did live here knew what their lives were for. Because we don't, we have no idea at all. They existed to keep life flowing into this planet. It was they who regulated the cosmic forces, powers, currents, so many, and so different, and all with their patterns and flows and rhythms. The lives of these people were regulated, every minute, by their knowledge. But this did not mean a clockwork regularity, which is how we have to think and feel, but a moving with, and through, these always changing flows of the currents.

When a man and a woman married, it was not "to have children" or "to make a family," not necessarily, though of course children had to be born and when they were, it was exact and chosen. No, these two would be chosen, or choose each other, for they were born with the knowledge of <u>how</u> to do this—because they were complementary, and this was judged always by how they stood in relations to stars, planets, the dance of the heavens, the forces of the earth, the moon, our sun. It was not even that they chose each other, rather that they were chosen by what they were, where they were. When they "married"—and we cannot even begin to guess how that seemed to them—their being together was a sacrament, in the sense that everything contributed to the harmony. And when they mated, this was a sacrament, in the true and real sense, used consciously and exactly to adjust, fuel, add to, lessen, powers and currents. And what they ate was the same. And what they wore. There could not be disharmony, because they <u>were</u> harmony. Everything, their thoughts and movements . . . they were suspended, on this earth, between earth and heaven, and through them flowed the lives of stars, and through them flowed the substance of the earth to the stars. . . .

That was how marriage was then, Sharma. I can see your face as you read this.

I must end now. My personal life has been sad recently. My father and mother died. They were wonderful people. There are family problems.

I will see you soon.

RACHEL SHERBAN'S JOURNAL

A lot of refugees have arrived from the new war, and we have had twenty of them in this flat. Fitting in somehow. Now they have gone on to a camp. Survivors. Surviving. I can't understand why they try so hard. Each one, a story of amazing escapes.

A million people died last week. Why then should it matter if Rachel Sherban stays alive? That is my question. I don't know who to ask it of. There must be a reply to it. If George was here, what he did would be the answer. He is always at it, rescuing people. One way or another. Mind you, I wonder if some of the people he rescues would be pleased if they knew they have genetic value. Genetically useful, said George once when I asked about someone.

A million people. I try to take it in. The people that were milling around in this flat are alive. But the unlucky ones are dead. Why one alive and one dead? It makes no sense to me at all. Out in the streets at night, all the rioting and shooting and then someone dead on the pavement. It might just as well be me. I went out last night. Curfew or no curfew, I walked about the city. All night. Soldiers. Trucks. Shooting. I did not even cover my face. No one saw me. I walked back into this flat this morning quite alive thank you. Well, answer that, whoever you are. Suzannah was out of her mind. Do you want to kill yourself, she shrieks.

I have seen something. I wonder how it was I didn't before. Who is it needs this killing, this agony, this suffering, the death, death, death, death. The blood and the blood. The reek of blood going up from this planet must be in somebody's nostrils. Somebody needs it. Something. There isn't anything that doesn't have a function. What happens always fits in with everything. What happens is <u>needed</u> by something. It happens because it is drawn out of a situation by need. There isn't anything that happens that is extraneous. There is somebody or something that needs this savagery and the blood.

The Devil, I expect.

I feel as if I have suddenly found a key in my hand.

I read that the cleverest trick of the Devil is that nobody believes in him. It. Her. Well, we have been very stupid.

I feel very odd. As if I am not here at all. Don't exist. A wind is blowing through me. I can feel it, blowing through my cracks and crannies. I am always cold.

I walk about this flat and I keep feeling myself float off into <u>unreality</u>. That is a word. I look at that word and it isn't anything. Once again there isn't a word for it. Yesterday I felt so gone, that I looked back into my room to see if I could see me sitting at the window. Because I couldn't feel myself where I stood at the door.

When this place was full of the refugees it was all right because I spent every minute getting things for them and doing things. But even then I felt very light. Porous.

Suzannah is worried. She keeps exclaiming and looking at me.

Suzannah is so strong. When I sit near her I can feel heat beating out of her. No, not heat, strength. I feel actually burnt by it. It envelops me. But when I go and sit near her on purpose to feel this, because I think it may warm me, then it is as if I was being crushed, or fanned away like dead grass. She put her arms around me last night and hugged me. She rocked me. This was exactly the way a mother cat gives a kitten that has got cold or upset about something are really rough licking, so hard the kitten can only just stand up or even gets knocked over. It is to make the blood flow. To shock the kitten into its senses. Those words, into its senses, are exact. Alive. They tingle. I can feel them. As I write this some words are alive and I can feel them pulse, but others are quite dead. Like Reality. Suzannah held me roughly and shook me, from the same instinct as a mother cat's.

But I was just nothing. A little bit of stick or cold shadow inside those great arms of hers.

I did put my head on her shoulder. Partly because it would please her. I even went to sleep. I am not here at all.

The night before last I woke up and saw Olga sitting on my bed. She was smiling. At once I could see it wasn't Olga, it was the moonlight, and the curtains moving. But what I felt for that second I thought it was Olga, was a sweetness and a longing. That made me afraid, because I never felt anything like that for Olga when she was alive.

I feel as if something very strong is pulling at me, a sort of sucking and dragging, and I want to let go into it. There is a strong sweetness somewhere close to me, tugging at me.

Suzannah follows me around and looks at me. She loves me. Because I am George's sister.

I look at her, so strong. And so ugly. She was washing her hair. I thought, she is going to shape it into those awful ridges and curls again, making herself so thick and ugly. When her hair was wet I went to her, and took the comb and parted her hair and made it straight and flat. She knew what I was doing. She had a little smile. Patient. She is so <u>nice</u>, Suzannah. I looked at her when I was finished, and there was a plain middle-aged woman. More like a servant. She knew what I was seeing. She had tears in her eyes. She was thinking, Rachel is beautiful. Suzannah does not envy me. She is not jealous or malicious or nasty in her feelings, like me.

I gave her back the comb, and she turned to the mirror and carefully did her hair as usual, fluffing it out and crimping it. Then the kohl and the lipstick. So she was back to normal. She did not look at me when she had finished. She had a stubborn air. Holding on to what she has. We had supper, Suzannah and me and the children. I was looking at her and wondering where she gets her strength. I put my hand into hers and she rubbed it and rubbed it. She knew why I had wanted her to fold my hand inside hers. She knows this kind of thing. She says to me, Poor little one, poor Rachel.

I really don't know what I can do, or say. I don't think I exist at all. There is a transparency around me, like a film I can't brush aside. A sort of faint rainbow.

Raymond Watts was here and said that someone had just arrived from over there and had information for me. This person had hoped to find George here. But that is strange in itself. Why should he. I told Raymond to bring this "someone" here.

I have to go, must leave at once. The "someone" said he "had access to" information that George was going to be killed by the Overlords. He didn't know George had already left here. He is part of the Administration. That means the Youth people wouldn't trust him. Raymond

Watts trusts him because he said he had "gone bad" from the Administration's view.

I have to tell George. Warn him. He might not know.

Suzannah has been at me all night. I said she would take me over and she has. How is it possible? A year ago Olga and Simon were alive and were my parents, and George was here and Benjamin, and now I am here in this flat alone with Suzannah and two children I hadn't seen this time last year and they are my family.

What right has Suzannah to say what I should do. I could not stop myself loathing her, sitting there, leaning forward, all earnest eyes and great boobs, telling me, Do this, do that. She says I have to stay here.

This is your home, Rachel, this is where you belong. And of course you must be with Kassim and Leila, they need you. Over and over again.

Why do they need me? They need her! Why should the world need Rachel Sherban if it has Suzannah!

Of course she would be only too delighted to be left here in this flat in complete charge and <u>owning</u> the children. She is <u>here</u>. She is in my parents' room. She is positioned just right for George when he gets back. If he gets back.

I don't mean the things about Suzannah I wrote there.

She says and says and says that George doesn't want me to rush off after him. How does she know? Yes of course George did say I should stay here, but did he know then that this man was going to turn up? I have to go quickly, I know how I can do it, I have been thinking how. Suzannah said, You can't go Rachel, if for no other reason than "I am such a princess" and "they"—meaning the Youth Army people—wouldn't like my attitudes. "Surely you can see that Rachel," she said. Not bitchy at all, oh no, it is what she thinks, so she says it.

When I said that I was going, Suzannah said, Then at least let me tell someone who I know can help you. Meaning, with the transport and disguise. That "at least" made me furious. It is funny, how Suzannah makes me furious. <u>Rubs</u> <u>me</u> <u>up</u> <u>the</u> <u>wrong</u> <u>way</u>. That is one of the phrases that are <u>alive</u>. Every word right. I said, I would meet anyone and do anything, all I wanted was to get across to Europe at once and tell George. I will not let them kill him.

I shall disguise myself to look like him. We are very alike, everyone says so. And they will kill me instead of him. It is easy. All these thousands of different uniforms and ways of dressing make it easy.

Re: Colonised Planet 5, Shikasta

I am ready to leave. Suzannah follows me around saying, Don't go, Rachel, don't go. She is in tears half the time. She keeps saying, You are mistaken Rachel. She says my name in that heavy earnest way. The Jewish Ra-chel. I like my name like that. I have always been pleased when people said Ra-chel. But when she says it, it is as if she was taking me over. Through my name. I am thinking all the time, suppose George did know they were going to try and kill him and that "someone" would come here and I would want to rush off and warn him. He knows all sorts of things before they happen. But suppose he didn't? This is the most important point. Sometimes I think one way, then another. I cry all the time, though I try not to. Suzannah cries. She wrings her hands. I did not know wringing one's hands was something actually done. But she does. She would! Everything in her is very <u>pure</u>. She accuses me, Ra-chel, you are wrong, you are very wrong!—her eyes flash, they brim with tears. <u>Accusation</u>. How can you Ra-chel! It is wrong, oh I would not have believed it of you! <u>Reproach</u>. She makes some ridiculous mistake, perhaps in cooking, wasting some little thing. Oh, how could I do a thing like that, oh how could I! <u>Remorse</u>, her eyes widen and stare as if at an avenging accuser, her hair actually stands on end.

And so now we are two women, weeping and wringing our hands. I watch us doing it.

Here we are, in this flat, the two of us with two children, a family, and she leans all over me and makes me cups of soup and gives me her rations, and says, You must eat, Ra-chel, you must sleep, Ra-chel. She has altered all the furniture in Mother's and Father's room. There is no reason why she shouldn't. I've watched her stand in the door smiling in at the room, as if she had been given something wrapped in pretty paper and she doesn't want to unwrap it for fear of spoiling the paper.

When I saw this I kissed her. I loved her for it. I wished I could give her everything wrapped in pretty paper to make up for the awful things that have happened to her, and that she came through. I can't imagine anything that could defeat Suzannah. If they put her down in a desert with Kassim and Leila, all by herself, a thousand miles from anywhere, she would say, Now Kassim, now Leila, this is what we must do, listen carefully. We must be sensible and . . .

I am leaving tomorrow.

COMRADE CHEN LIU, *to* PEKING:
re the GEORGE SHERBAN *situation*

Attempts to dispose of this dangerous man have failed: What went wrong is not clear. A woman impersonating him, who we later discovered was his sister, appeared in various places, but not where he was scheduled to be: he has never made any attempt to disguise his movements. This woman was wearing the uniform of Section 3, North African Youth Movements, while leaving Tunis and arriving in Spain—aided by the Youth networks, and getting lifts with various types of military vehicle. In the south of France she changed to clothes commonly worn by the said George Sherban, and succeeded in passing for him, but only for a few days. Appearing in towns and encampments where he was not expected, and behaving in a bizarre manner, "he" was reported to have suffered a mental breakdown. Meanwhile the real George Sherban was in Brussels. This period of less than a week sufficed to start rumours that this "holy man"—as in some quarters he is taken to be—has the capacity to be in two places at once. The rumours spread widely and the real George Sherban was reportedly embarrassed. At any rate, in Amsterdam he addressed a meeting of hysterics, denying he had any such capacity, but such was the fervour of the crowd, he had to make a getaway. He went to Stockholm where he disappeared from our agents' view for some days. In the meantime, while our agents were still taking Rachel Sherban for him, she was involved in two serious accidents outside Paris, but escaped from both with minor injuries. We tend to believe that he was attempting to reach her, or to send messengers of some kind to her. But she was arrested by the Paris People's Police on our instructions, and before she could be questioned, killed herself.

These theatrical events are not all that obscure this situation. For instance, we expected George Sherban to seek election as representative for all North Africa, and we are informed that he would certainly have succeeded. But he did not, and made no attempt to do so. He is travelling through the Youth networks representing an assortment of miscellaneous organisations, some with status, some without influence to the point of being ridiculous. I can only believe that his ambitions are pitched much higher. I can make no guess at what this man is aiming for. This is by no means the first opportunity for fulfilling *apparent* ambitions that he has despised. There have been others that were his for the picking and he ignored them.

Re: Colonised Planet 5, Shikasta

Looking for factors that distinguish his career as representative of so many various and different Youth organisations, our agents can offer only a few consistent facts. One is that wherever he has been a handful of individuals abandon the positions they hold and make their way to other destinations. We can find no common denominator in these individuals, who are of every race and nation, and of both sexes. Nor in the places they go to. Or in the places they come from. Or in the work they do when they arrive. They may stay in the Youth networks or may not. Their work may be visibly responsible and respect-inspiring, or without civic value.

Taking these factors into account, I suggest that George Sherban be left alive for the time being, until we ascertain what it is he is aiming for.

The nine attempts to dispose of him have lost us five of our employees.

His brother Benjamin Sherban is in Camp 16, Czechoslovakia. He is undergoing Top Treatment on Elite Level. It is too early to assess results. George Sherban, reported to be on his way to India, spent a day with Benjamin Sherban. This was done in a way typical of his style of working. There was nothing illegal in his arrival or stay in Camp 16. Yet no one else has attempted such a thing, nor had we believed anyone would attempt it: it seems pointless. But it is outside our jurisdiction unless we decide to make our Benevolent Rule specific and obtrusive.

BENJAMIN SHERBAN, CAMP 16, CZECHOSLOVAKIA, *to* GEORGE SHERBAN *in* SIMLA

I have things to tell you, my little brother! But *how* is another matter. One thing after another, I hear you say? Right. Here goes. You were here the day before the "Friendship Tutorial" was destined to begin. We did not know what to expect. *I* thought luxury and opulence, carrying on the grand traditions of Karlovy Vary, that baroque consolation of the Bourgeoisie, for their hard lives, ditto of the Party Bosses and their hard lives. But not at all. In a splendid shell, all gilt and cupids and rubbishy splendour of all sorts, behold, functional cells for us students, and common rooms conducive only to spartan thought. Two hundred of us. Cream of the cream. All under twenty-five, including the Chinese, our mentors. Equal numbers of men and women.

And adequate austerity and no privileges for anybody, including the Chinese.

The other three of *us* arrived, in the end, but late: they had had difficulties. I made myself known to them and the instructions were passed.

The various artefacts were placed as advised.

We ate our meals in the former hotel dining room, lush to the point of lubricity, but the food was mostly potatoes-and-lucky-to-get-them.

The Chinese, ten of them, mingled from the start, very correct but friendly. They let it be understood that for the first few days nothing would be organised. The agenda: we were to get to know each other. The agenda when further pressed: informal discussions on the problems which face us.

Which are?

The relations between the Youth Armies and the European subject masses, correct attitudes towards said subject masses.

This was not at all what was generally expected. Which was of course tourist trips hither and yon, interviews with the Bosses, being photographed on cultural monuments, and probably a year in a Chinese city as honoured guests and all that crap.

Faced with this "agenda" you can bet there were informal discussions. At which the Chinese did not appear at all. They let us get on with it. We then concluded that the expected rewards for good behaviour and "co-operation" would be nothing so crude as above, but jobs and offices of various kinds in the new structure controlling the said populations. In other words, we decided—and still think—that the top layers of the structure of the Youth Armies will be incorporated into the Overlords Administration. Time-honoured stuff of course. But then, if it had not always been so effective, would it be honoured? In other words, we were being faced with the complete loss of autonomy of the Youth Armies—such as it has been—but we are not expected to mind: on the contrary, we must allow ourselves to be swallowed whole without a protest.

But do not think I carp! Since this is bound to happen, at some point and we all knew it, I, they, everyone, am, are, is, overwhelmed with admiration *as usual* at the smooth tact of our Chinese Benevolences, such a nice change compared to you-know-who, and what a pity they feel themselves too good to learn useful lessons from our Beneficial Rulers.

Right. So much for the framework, which is *not* the burden of my information, only the background.

The above-mentioned "informal discussions" went on day and night aided by (moderate) alcohol, (well-tempered) sex, eternal friendships being sworn between Alaskans and Brazilians, South Sea Islanders and Irishmen, lassies from Cape Wrath and denizens of the Cape of Good Hope, everything as usual.

Everything *exactly* as usual, and as to be expected, all the attitudes being struck that the Benevolences were obviously wanting us to get out of the way before serious discussions could begin: "Never will I bow my head . . ." "I would die sooner than . . ." "Do they think they can buy . . ." etc. and so on ad pukeam. *But after a few hours the atmosphere changed, and this is where I rely on your interpretation.* Bearing in mind that during this phase our mentors were always discreetly elsewhere, appearing only for meals, charm and friendly likeability personified.

The aforementioned atmosphere. It took me some time to understand what was happening, and then, to believe what was happening. On that very first morning I was with twenty other people, collected together at random, in a former billiard room, transmogrified into a setting for We Shall Not Be Moved! all sitting about casually, at ease, talking on the theme, if-they-imagine-they-can-buy-us, when it came into my mind that everything we were saying could be interpreted differently. On a different level. This seemed so wild that I put it all down to being up until four with Her Amiability from Abyssinia. (No, talking.) After lunch, turnips-and-lucky-to-get-them, I was with another group of about twenty, in another room. We were discussing the possibilities of co-operation with Their Benevolences, when I realised it was happening again, and this time stayed with it, and did not push it away with "but it's impossible!" The atmosphere was remarkable, *clear* and *cool*, those are the words I think. Everyone very alert, quick, getting every point, eye contact saying volumes where words did not. Not only I, but everyone realised something peculiar was happening. After all, I had had the advantage of being in on similar occasions with you, when operational. But everyone knew. Each one of us. And yet if the Beneficials had been present, they could have sat through from start to finish and not heard one subversive word.

And so the next three days.

You will not need me to spell it out.

I was always with different associations of people, according to how they formed themselves at the moment when an "informal discussion" was due to begin. Often in different rooms. But it was the same in all the groups. Our three particular friends confirm this: we did discuss it a little, but *there was no need to*. More and more it happened that after that kind of *transparent* talk, we would find ourselves sitting silent, for ten, fifteen, twenty minutes at a time. More. An hour once. Nothing said. No need to say a word.

And when we were actually talking, the two levels were unmistakable —clear, so easy to read that it was as if we all suddenly had been taught another language.

Well, while these informal and casual discussions were going on, we of course all came together in the big dining room for meals. At which we *all* sat in that high calm atmosphere that made us one. And the Chinese could make nothing of it. They kept starting discussions and themes, but after a minute these simply died out. We could see they believed we had got hold of drugs or something like that. We could see that they were beginning to be affected too. They didn't like it. We knew they were meeting to discuss it. Meanwhile, we enjoyed another two days of being by ourselves. There was one session when we—the usual random lot—went into a room, sat down, and not one word was said for the whole morning. There was no need for it. And then the Benevolences changed tactics and at each "informal discussion" each group had a mentor. They did not change what was happening. When we were actually talking, there was nothing to be heard by them that wasn't on one level "sensible." But once or twice there started the long silence, which *they* broke, out of nervousness.

Right.

End of good tidings.

Beginning of bad tidings.

There we all were, on the sixth day, *all* so far from our usual silly selves that it made us positively sick to remember them. And then, there appeared at breakfast a man who did not introduce himself, but he just sat there. The Chinese did not know who he was either. That was clear. Though they pretended after first surprise that he was *not* a surprise. Or at least some of them did. As usual, we were saved by the fact that it is quite impossible to brainwash everyone to the same degree all the time. Some of our mentors were able instantly to put on a good face, offer a united front, but others not. And this was how we knew this particular Benevolence was unknown to them.

But what a creep. Type international technocrat, enough said.

The Bland Man at once introduced himself into one of our discussions, the one I was at, as it happened. He came in smiling. He sat smiling. I tell you, I have long since reached the point that when I see a Certain Smile I wish only to reach for my gun.

The atmosphere was . . . not the same.

It *thickened*. We all of us kept starting topics, and in the spirit of the last few days, but anything said *fell flat*. Literally. That is exactly what happened. Words sent up like kites into the air of expectation guided by the string of concord went *clunk*. As if shot by an airgun.

Right?

We all sat there struggling to rise again like kites foundering on the hill of disappointment and inability.

Before lunch, I made the rounds and found, as I expected, that all the artefacts you had given me had gone.

At lunch there was a peevish and irritable spirit in the dining room. The Bland One sat there, as at breakfast, by himself.

Again the Chinese were obviously disturbed by his presence, though pretending not. Unmistakable however that emanation: this-is-incorrect-and-I'm-going-to-catch-it-if-I-don't-watch-out, if only because one has been so often conscious of emanating it oneself.

After lunch I did not stay in one room, but went from one group to another. The Smiling One was with a different group from the one he had honoured in the morning.

The atmosphere had gone completely. *Drained away*. Accurate, no? Sucked away?

We did not see His Blandness again. That is, he graced our deliberations for exactly one day. The Chinese, when asked, keep repeating, Oh, everything is in order, this was a Visiting Comrade.

Next day, our "informal discussions" were back to normal, the usual brawling jargon-filled idiocies.

Our particular three friends have simply disappeared. They are not here. Did His Malevolence spirit them away? I cannot find out. The Chinese say they will "make enquiries." They are all thoroughly upset by the whole thing.

Meanwhile, it is clear that people cannot remember what happened during those five days. I mean this absolutely and precisely. When I try to remind them, I see that look I know so well, the glazed empty look. It is funny that it has taken me so long to recognise that look.

And I myself have more than once found my mind going dim as I try to recall exactly that atmosphere, or even that it all did happen.

It did happen.

It happened.

What happened?

At least one knows *what is possible.*

I have recollected what you said to me as you left that morning: Well, you can't win them all!

Ah, what nonchalance! What insouciance!

Of course there is a question which you can't expect us at the very least not to adumbrate. Which is, Why take so much trouble if you know in advance it is a write-off? At the most a 1,000–1 chance?

No, don't bother to answer.

Just as you said when I told you about Rachel, Well, better luck next time.

O.K., O.K., I am joking.

But only just.

I babble. Of necessity. Forgive me.

I have not been able to find anyone to bring this before. We are coming to the end of the Friendship and Learning Month, which is tedious beyond belief. The usual interminable meaningless bickering discussions about things that will never happen. The Leadership of the Youth Armies has passed a resolution agreeing to "attempt to adjust their activities with the administration of Pan-Europe."

I have several times mentioned His Nastiness to our Benefactors, if for no other reason than that it is amusing to see their hasty, embarrassed and overcorrect manner as they assure us that his visit was entirely in order and approved of.

Ah, but by whom, that is the question.

So, what do you want me to do next.

COMRADE CHEN LIU, *to* PEKING,
COMMITTEE *of* PUBLIC DIRECTION
and COMPREHENSIVE CO-ORDINATION

I have yet again to report hardship due to insufficient food supplies allocated to European sector. The levies on farm produce have caused the predicted passive resistance by farmers throughout the area. Over-ardour on the part of the Local Administration in fulfilling the laudable and legitimate demands of the Centre is counterproductive. From

Ireland to the Urals, from Scandinavia to the Mediterranean (the area for which I have the honour to be responsible) the people are suffering famine. I took the liberty of saying in my last Report that in my view the inelastic attitude towards the Pan-European area is due to an un-verbalised desire for revenge for centuries of colonial oppression. I humbly begged that the Council should consider ways of making representations to the Aligned Committees for the Emergent Nations to consider well the results of their policy. If it is desired to exterminate the peoples of Pan-Europe, then this should be formulated and steps taken to put plans into action. I have been informed by my envoy to you that my words on this subject were considered offensive. I hope that my record of Service to the People will speak for me. It has never been part of our policy to inflict wholesale suffering on the countries we have taken under our Benevolent Tutelage. It has always been our aim to re-educate where possible even those recalcitrant sections of the population who show little signs of understanding. Therefore I took the liberty—and do again in this Report—to ask if it is the considered policy of our Council to support the Aligned Committees for the Emergent Nations?—if it is, in fact, the intention to empty Europe for colonisation from the South? If this is the aim, then I find myself im-pelled to protest, and purely on the grounds of expediency. Whatever happens in Europe will be ascribed to our Beneficent Guidance. All eyes are upon us. The fact that local representatives have ceased re-sistance due to our re-education, of various degrees of stringency, and have mostly been replaced by our guidance, adds weight to the argu-ment in favour of making sure that the policies followed by the Aligned Committees for the Emergent Nations will add to our reputation as the true Elder Brother of the Deprived peoples of the world.

Letter enclosed with this Report to CHEN LIU'S *friend, Chairman of the Council,* KU YUANG

I have not heard from you. Does that mean you did not get my last letter? Or that you did—I do not know which thought is worse.

If you did, you will not need to read this.

I beg of you to do what you can. Even in the camps and townships of the Youth Armies, which are at least regularly if insufficiently supplied, there is hardship. The suffering generally is offensive and severe. Is it that our Council now bows before the Emergent Nations? The Centre is dominated by the limbs? Is it that this is not weakness but policy? Do we no longer feel able even to express an opinion? Or we protest, but privately? Out here in the colonies of course it is hard to keep adequately informed. But I do what I can: for instance, an analysis of the innumerable meetings, conferences, councils, of the last twelve months through the southern hemisphere, reveals that there were over a hundred speeches on the theme of *revenge,* and not one (or one recorded) expression of moderation, or even of an intelligent intention to use and exploit human and other resources, rather than destroying them.

My old friend, I find myself in a mental and emotional conflict that keeps me awake at night, and destroys my pleasure in my work for our great People. When you told me you would send me to oversee Pan-Europe, I told you I was not necessarily the best man for the job. Your reply was that a man conscious of reservations and emotional difficulties would be better than one who was not. I wonder! I work daily, hourly, with our officials, men and women of the highest calibre, and who seem to suffer no indecision in their work. And yet, to repeat, for the last few months this work has not been—I hope?—the results of decisions from us, the Centre.

I loathe the white-skinned peoples. Physically they repel me. Their smell offends me. Their avidity and greed have never struck me as anything but disgusting. They are clumsy in movement, awkward in thought, unsubtle, overbearing. Their assumption of superiority is that of the country bumpkin, the big man of the little village, who comes to the city and does not know that the sophisticates find him ludicrous as he swaggers and boasts.

Their savagery has never done less than appal me. The cold-bloodedness of the intentions behind their imposition of opium, the wanton destruction of our cultural heritage, or its theft, their inferiority . . . but I need not go on, for we have discussed it often enough. I live among a race I dislike to the roots of my being. Even in their decline and their subjection, some of them, indeed, many of them, manage to behave as if they have been unjustly deprived of a sinecure, and a few even manage the airs of dispossessed royalty bravely suffering the rabble.

Imagine my situation, then, forced to stand by while a policy is being implemented that my emotions applaud, my lowest instincts enjoy, that returns *me* to savagery. My old friend, I am writing under pressures you will surely understand, and you will make allowances. I believe that our cadres here are in fact as cheerful and enthusiastic in their work as they seem to be. They can be so cheerful only because

(a) they applaud the policies of the Emergent Nations and approve what they see and have to do, or (b) they do not understand what it is they are seeing—do not understand what it means for *us* that these policies are being implemented, for surely they cannot be *our* policies, our Will? I watch them and wonder if it is possible that our Great People can so willingly agree to deliberate mass murder, or if perhaps they are able to persuade themselves that what is going on is something else.

Do we really have no objection to being compared with Genghis Khan?

I know that we all have forgone leave that is due to us in the interests of the general good, but I would like to talk to you. Is it true that you will be touring the southern hemisphere this autumn? If so, I could perhaps apply for leave and meet you somewhere.

CHEN LIU *reports to the* COUNCIL *in* PEKING

Further to my Report of a year ago. The decimation, if not destruction, of the peoples of Pan-Europe now being official policy on the part of the Emergent Nations, following the Conference in Kampala, I have no more to say on that topic, but merely report a consequent development.

Until now the Youth Armies have been relatively free of division on lines of race. This has been official policy with them, racialism having been identified with the old generation, with the past. While immigrants have been coming into Europe from India, the drought areas of Africa, the West Indies, the Middle East, and settling anywhere there was land or housing available (usually because the inhabitants have died from famine or disease), the Youth Armies have on the whole been scrupulous in respecting local land rights, local land policies, the integrity of areas. If Youth Sectors have commandeered empty villages or untenanted land, it has always been done within the style they have perfected, that of working within these limits, or at least nominally. Sometimes, of course, with the effect, calculated or not, of impertinence. But the real strength of these Armies is being eroded, quite simply, by hardship. For instance, a Pan-European Conference scheduled to take place this month in Switzerland is scaled down to less than half its projected strength because of lack of transport, shortage of fuel, shortage of food. And it will take place next summer, because their clothes are inadequate for the cold, and in Greece for easier access.

Generally, the work of the Youth is being diverted to their own maintenance. I am aware that it has been the policy to deplore the very existence of the Youth Armies, and I am not at this time arguing this point. But it seems to me that a great deal of our denigration of them has been—a perhaps necessary—rhetoric. For in many areas the Armies have been a useful, and indeed often the only, police force and control against every kind of anarchy.

For the first time a note is being sounded among the Youth to the effect that European delegates should take second place to those from the old colonies, on the ground of their inferiority of race shown by past barbarities.

I refer to previous Reports.

CHEN LIU *to his friend* KU YUANG

I have heard no word from you. Yet I can only believe that you have received my various private letters.

Do we wish to see these millions of young people, some of whom are of course totally misguided in their political thought, but who have proved themselves re-educable, millions who have created throughout the world their own organisations, styles of work, protective agencies, methods of self-discipline—do we wish to see them turn on each other? I cannot believe that this is something *you* would wish, any more than you can approve the present policies in Europe.

CHEN LIU *reports to the* COUNCIL *in* PEKING

As a development to matters referred to in the last Report: there is to be a Mock Trial staged on the highest levels of the Combined Youth Armies of the World. The Defendant is to be the White Races. The Prosecutors, the Dark-skinned Races. This will take place in summer in Greece. This Mock Trial is a matter of the greatest importance to the Youth Armies everywhere. I cannot emphasise this too strongly.

An individual, George Sherban, a man we have been observing closely since the start of our Beneficent Tutelage, and who before that was under the observation of the Pan-Europe Federation of SDCPD for P of P, is to take the part of Prosecutor. The man who will defend is John Brent-Oxford, an old member of the left wing of the Labour Party in Britain, with a record of work in various fields, mostly representing Britain in Europe for various Labour governments. He was imprisoned under the Pan-Europe Federation, and released on my recommendation to a low-level post in the Youth Supervisory Echelon, in Bristol, England. He is in bad health. He was a member of a well-known legal firm in Britain but his political activities took him away from the law. He is, however, well-enough equipped for a task which will need oratory more than any knowledge of current or previous legal requirements. The choice of both these men is astonishing. George Sherban is of British parentage, and his Indian allegiance amounts to a single grandparent. He is accepted however as an honorary Indian in the Youth Armies. John Brent-Oxford is over sixty. It is too easy to say that the choice of a member of the despised older generation is only to add to the emotional bias against the defendant: I am informed he is very well liked among the Youth who have worked with him. So this choice may be described as cynical, or careless.

George Sherban's brother, one Benjamin, an altogether less charismatic character, is to be one of John Brent-Oxford's "advisers." That is, he will be on the opposite side to his brother. He has recently undergone Top-Level Re-education, with no noticeable results.

This "Trial" must not be underestimated. Already requests pour in from every country, demanding facilities for travel. It is essential in my view that adequate food is allocated, and that accommodation in the way of tents is permitted. The mood of the Youth Armies, as I have more than hinted, is very different from what it has been. It is explosive, volatile, cynical—dangerous. I have already made arrangements for troops to be easily available, and on a large scale.

CHEN LIU *to his friend* KU YUANG

I beg of you to intervene. My orders that two regiments of troops should be available for the "Trial"—countermanded. My orders for special allocations of food—countermanded. My orders that plenty of space should be allotted for tents, that standpipes should be erected, that the area be cordoned off from the locals—countermanded, countermanded. All this without explanation. *I have not asked for one.*

In two months' time several thousand representatives of the Youth Armies of the World will congregate in Greece. Has it been seriously considered by the Council what effect it may have worldwide if this affair gets out of hand?

I write this in a state of mind that in the days of our old friendship I would not have to explain to you.

CHEN LIU *to his friend* KU YUANG

I got your message. I understand your situation. The agent who brings this is, as far as I can see, trustworthy. He will explain my situation. I was relieved more than I can say, to hear from you *personally*, even if the news is not very hopeful. I shall now describe the events of the "Trial," as you request, separately from the Report which will be sent via the usual channels to the Council.

First of all, George Sherban, the Chief Accuser, travelled to Zimbabwe, the slow way, by car, coach, lorry, train, and even in some places on foot, representing various Youth Armies, and being briefed by them. This journey was clearly critical on more than one occasion. The wars that decimate the area have dragged it down to the point where nothing happens as expected. The Youth Armies are anarchistic, badly organised, sometimes no more than organisations for looting and arson. The travelling party had to find their way through several war zones. George Sherban went with the full authorisation of the Co-ordinating Council of the World Youth Armies. He needed it. He was nearly captured on two occasions, *was* arrested once, but he talked his way out of it. His brother Benjamin went with him. This man has now been subjected to several separate stints of Top-Level education. I must report failure. But of an interesting variety. At no point was there confrontation, loss of politeness, failure to attend the allocated courses. On the contrary we have seldom had a more co-operative and intelligent subject. On the face of it, his acceptance of our Benevolent Tutelage has been complete. But he went with his brother on this prolonged journey against our expressed wishes. Of course if he had been where we enjoy a full and *overt* command, he would have been punished, but his position in the Youth Armies is too high to provoke possible dissatisfaction. Even on reporting his intention to make this journey it was with a perfect willingness to concur with anything we might suggest— short of not going at all!

In Zimbabwe a mass Conference was held in Bulawayo, on the site where Lobengula held court. The modern Lobengula was present, and released several thousand prisoners to indicate his joy at the occasion. It was there, in the heart of the erstwhile Dark Continent, that George Sherban allowed himself to be briefed to represent the Dark Races in the forthcoming Trial—which event was being spoken of by everyone as if it were to be a real Trial. They do not seem to be able to take in the concept, or perhaps the usefulness, of a Trial merely for propaganda effectiveness. Of course they may very well have found themselves confused at the situation, as were the—very many—representatives of the brown and other races (our own included) who had somehow made their way there. It was unprecedented, for its daring, its imagination, its success. This almost entirely white man was enthusiastically accepted by blacks as a representative, and moreover, as an Indian, the history of dislike of all things Indian up and down Africa apparently mattering not at all. My informants tell me that this was an occasion unprecedented also for its vigour, emotionalism, high spirits. I would have given a good deal to be there. Benjamin Sherban kept in the background, in a way which I would not have expected, if believing the many reports of an earlier ebullience and big-headedness. He was merely one of many assistants to George Sherban, the only one with a white skin. He has the advantage of representing the Junior Youth— eight- to fourteen-year-olds, and this is a powerful emotional stimulus everywhere.

This party stayed several weeks in Zimbabwe. They made an illicit trip over into the Transvaal, which I am informed combined daring and ingenuity quite remarkably. They then flew back to Greece, after being *blessed* (the word is used by Benjamin Sherban in a private letter reporting on the occasion) by the modern Lobengula.

They had already been informed that there will be no military protection, no extra rations, no co-operation from the authorities.

I am informed that their preparations are everything that we could wish.

I was not able to be present myself in this amphitheatre for the Trial, for had I been there it would have underlined a concern on our part that I did not wish to be evident. But I had plentiful observers, both open—in our own delegation, who are of course keeping me informed—and concealed, who are distributed among the various delegations. It is from these many, and very varied reports, that I am compiling this account.

The five thousand delegates were a sorry lot compared with what until now has been the norm. We have become accustomed to seeing such occasions as demonstrating the comparative well-being of the Youth Armies. These were ill-fed, shabby, some in obviously bad health. The mood of confidence in themselves as a viable future is gone. They are sombre, cynical.

Getting there had been difficult for all of them, although I had given instructions—which I had no confidence would be observed—that they should not be obstructed. Many had walked long distances: this was true mostly of the Europeans.

Pilfering and looting began from the moment the delegates arrived, but was checked at once, by an appeal to their sense of responsibility. But the damage had been done, and the local inhabitants, informed that they were being "honoured" by the occasion, must be imagined as a silent, sullen, closely observing crowd, always present around the camp, sometimes numbering hundreds.

The organisers had arranged guards, sentinels, everything needed for security, but this was precarious from the first and throughout, more from internal tensions than from external. It was arranged that the races should be distributed evenly through the camp, but almost at once the subject of the "Trial" showed its strength in separating the white race into a minority, a camp within a camp, separately sentinelled and guarded. From the start there were jokes, on the whole friendly, that the Chief Prosecutor was in fact white. From the very first day a song was popular among all sections, black, brown, gold, jade, and white: "I have an Indian grandmother," which of course was plentifully adapted, "I have a white grandmother" being the favourite. There were occasions when the entire encampment was singing "I have a —— grandmother"—white, black, brown, Irish, African, Eskimo, at the same time, at the top of their voices, and in the mood which was the style or stamp of the occasion: a mocking, sardonic nihilism, but which was not, in fact, devoid of good humour.

Who writes these songs? Where do they come from? The strength of the People is indeed great!

It was extremely hot. This was the key fact of the month, overriding everything. The large and commodious mess tents were partly in the shade of some ancient olive trees, but most of the tents were in the sun. The camp simmered and baked, day after day. Water was scarce. The sanitary arrangements were just adequate. By the end, this camp was an unsavoury place. If it had not been for some showers of rain the place would have been intolerable before the end of the first week.

I have spent several hours rereading the agents' reports, and this resulted in my reconsidering the event. There is something here that is puzzling. That these youngsters are brilliant organisers is no news to any of us: indeed, we can benefit from learning from them. But this went beyond ordinary common sense and even good timing.

I remind you that this "Trial" seemed to begin with almost a joke—
there was that quality in the first news of it. "The kids are deriding us
again"—that sort of thing. It seemed in bad taste, not to mention
pointless, considering the real and deep violence of the passion shown
everywhere on racial issues. And then, from our reports, it became
evident how seriously they were all taking it. Then there was the
amount of preparation that went into it—the visit to Southern Africa,
for instance, which was prepared for, and followed with interest, by
the Youth of the world. And finally, the participation of the highest
echelons of the Armies, and the presence, in the thick of everything, of
George Sherban, who always seems to be around at key moments.
Incidentally, he was recommended for removal but the orders were
countermanded, in order to give him time to show his hand—and I
believe he has done so.

To continue. Why Greece? Rumours were at first plentiful that the
"Trial" was to be held in one of the bullrings in Spain, but it was given
out, with more than adequate propaganda, that "this would prejudice
the issue, bullrings are places of blood." Without comment. The
amphitheatres in Greece? For Europeans these elicit associations of
civilisation and culture. The old Greeks, not noticeably a peace-loving
or particularly stable or democratic people—they were a slave-state,
despised women, admired homosexuality—were revered by "the western
tradition." Without comment.

The amphitheatres are circular empty spaces, surrounded by tiers of
circular stone seating, like benches. Uncovered. The climate is bitterly
hot or cold. Has the climate then changed, or were the ancient Greeks
impervious to cold and heat?

The "Trial" organisation solved the problem this way. They turned
day into night.

A session was scheduled every day at five in the afternoon, after the
worst heat, until midnight. Then there was a meal of salad, grains,
bread. The "Trial" began again at four in the morning, and went on
until eight. Bread and fruit were served. Between twelve and four,
there was, every night, energetic discussion and debate—informal. To
start with, the entire encampment was requested to sleep or rest from
nine in the morning until four. But this proved impossible. The heat
inside the tents was excessive, and there wasn't shade enough. Some
tried to sleep in improvised shelters, or in the mess tents, but in fact
very little sleep was had by anyone during the month.

It was *requested* that no alcohol be brought into the camp at all, because of the Moslems, and because of the difficulties of maintaining order. This was respected, at least at the beginning.

Permission had been refused by us for floodlighting, indeed, any supply of electricity. This led to some very interesting results. In fact, the extreme heat apart, it was clear that the lighting was the most important factor of the "Trial."

The arena itself was lit by torches set at intervals around the periphery. These were of the usual impregnated compressed reeds. When the moon was strong, the arena was clearly visible anyway. Without the moon, the effect was patchy.

We must imagine the tiers of seats rising from the arena, moonlit or starlit, but without other illumination, and the groups of contenders below, lit by the moon, or inadequately by the torches. The scene made a strong impression on all my informants, and it is clear the night sessions of the "Trial" were the more emotional and hard to control because of the lighting.

All around the upper rim of the great amphitheatre were guards, changed at every sitting, and arranged so that no race would claim preferment. There was a double line of guards, one line facing in to watch the crowds on the seats, and one facing out, because of the villagers who came as close as they were allowed. As the month went by, these uninvited visitors became very many, causing increased problems of organisation and of hygiene. They were nearly all elderly or very old, or small children. All were in a poor condition from hardship. That the youth were in not much better a state seemed to mollify them, and permitted some fraternisation.

I have never heard of, or experienced, any occasion which seemed to promise more opportunities for violence, riot, ill-feeling, and which in the event caused so little.

I now come to what the "spectators"—the wrong word for such impassioned participants—saw below them on that stage.

From the very beginning it was startling. The "Trial" was never anything less than *visually* challenging . . . surely not by chance?

The arena was not decorated in any way, no slogans, banners, pennants, on the ground of danger from fire. There were only the torches, thirty of them, each one with two attendants. These were from Benjamin Sherban's Junior Youth contingent, children of ten or so, equally boys and girls, and mostly, but not all, brown or black. The central stage, then, was ringed by children, all in responsible positions, for the torches had to be watched, and changed as they burned down, which happened every hour. Incidentally, torches which burn for three or four hours were readily available, but it was not these which were chosen. The children were in fact in control of an important aspect of the proceedings, and this set a certain tone from the moment the "spectators" took their places. The "youngsters," the "kids," the "in-heritors" were being forced to reflect, every moment they sat there, that they were shortly to be set aside by the newest set of "inheritors."

On either side of the arena was a small table and a dozen chairs. That was all. Tone, arrangements, atmosphere, were casual throughout.

On the prosecuting side was George Sherban, for the Dark Races. He has the ivory skin of a certain type of racial cross, but he is black-haired and black-eyed and could easily be an Indian or an Arab. But *visually*, white-skinned. With him, a changing group of every possible skin colour.

On the defending side, it was visually as provocative. The whites *always* included a few brown and black people.

The attending groups on either side changed with each session, and during the sessions there was a continual movement from the arena to the tiers and back again. There is no doubt that this was a policy de-signed to emphasise the informality. The Defender John Brent-Oxford was the only old person present. As I suggested before, this could be interpreted as a deliberate attempt to weaken the white side. He was white-haired, frail, obviously unwell, and needed to sit down, whereas all the others stood or walked about. He was therefore unable to use tricks of self-presentation—the sudden gesture; or stopping, arrested by new thought, in the middle of a movement; or flinging back the arms with a chest presented to the hazards of fate—all the little calcula-tions which, my dear friend, we know the effectiveness of so well.

He had nothing but his feeble presence, and his voice, which was not strong, but was at least steady and deliberate.

Throughout, and the point was of course lost on no one, he was attended by two of Benjamin Sherban's Children's Contingent, one white and one jet black, a Britisher from Liverpool in England. These, it was soon known, had a personal attachment to him, having been befriended by him when their parents died. He was, in short, in the position of foster-father.

Benjamin Sherban was nearly always stationed behind the old white's chair, in a posture of responsibility for the children. His posi-tion with the Children's Camps, which was well known to everyone, had its effect.

My informants were all, without exception, struck by this disposition of the arena, that there was no clear-cut, unambiguous target for their indignation. I feel I must remark that my reports throughout this "Trial" were far from boring: I wish I could say this more often.

I come to what was *heard*. Now comes an interesting point. Whereas every other one of my recommendations was contermanded—troops, extra rations, standpipes for water, proper lighting—one was permitted. This was provision for loudspeakers. Yet loudspeakers were not used at all.

Why were loudspeakers permitted? Perhaps an oversight! It is not too much to say that a large part of the time of every administrator must be spent in wondering about the possible inner significance of events that are in fact due to nothing more than incompetence.

Why did the organizers not avail themselves of them?

The effects were negative, increasing tension and irritation. To sit on crowded stone seats from five in the afternoon till midnight, straining to hear; to sit crammed on hard gritty surfaces from four in the morning through the rising heat of dawn until eight, straining to hear—this was hardly calculated to alleviate the general hardship.

One of my agents, Tsi Kwang (granddaughter of one of the heroes of the Long March), sat high up on the rim of the amphitheatre in order to be able to observe everything. She reports that to begin with, when she realised she would have to strain to catch every syllable, she was angry. Murmurings and complaints filled the tiers of people. Shouts of: Where are the microphones? But these shouts were ignored, and it was left to these five thousand delegates to infer that "The Authorities" (us, by implication, and on this occasion in fact) had not only refused extra rations and so forth, but also "even" microphones.

Tsi Kwang reports that at that height, "it was as if we were looking down at little puppets." "It had a disturbing effect." She felt "as if the importance of the occasion was being insulted." (All of our agents were of course emotionally identified with the antiwhite side, and were hoping that the Trial would show the whites up as total villains. Which of course it did up to a certain point. How could it not?)

With no microphones, only the unaided human voice, everything said on that small space far below (I am seeing it as I write through Tsi Kwang's eyes) had to be simple, because it had to be shouted. And this added to the challenge of the spectacle, for everything else was kept informal. Casual. (Except of course for the necessary guards.) But what was *said* had to be reduced almost to slogans, or at least to simple statements or questions, for from halfway up the tiers no one could have heard complex argument, legal niceties.

Everyone present—and all had come with their minds full of historical examples, memories of their own, or their parents' or their ancestors' experience of being oppressed, ill-treated—every person present had come burning with the need to hear *at last!* (as Agent Tsi Kwang put it) *the Truth.*

The "Trial" began straight away, on the first evening. The delegates were still arriving, were exhausted and some famished. Makeshift trestles stood about among sparse trees on the parched grasses, with jars of water and baskets of the local bread. These supplies vanished instantly, and everyone understood the signs of parsimony to come. The tents were going up over several acres. The first lootings had taken place and been stopped. Thousands of young people milled about. Some, from the extreme north, the Icelanders, the Scandinavians, were devastated by the heat. The deep burning skies were particularly noted by Agent Tsi Kwang. (She is from Northern Province.) The cicadas were loud. The usual dogs had arrived from nowhere and were nosing about for what they could find. At precisely four o'clock the word went around that the "Trial" would begin at once. And even as those travel-tired, hungry delegates crowded on to the hot stone seats under that scorching sky, with no preliminaries at all, the two groups of contenders filed down into the arena and took their places. The torches had not yet been lit, of course, but the children were in their places, two to a torch.

On the small wood tables were no books, papers, notes—nothing.

George Sherban stood by the table on one side, with his group, where the shade was soon to engulf them. On the other, in full sun, sat the frail old man, the white villain, whose history of course they all knew, since word of mouth is the fastest, if not most accurate, means of conveying information. Each young person on these tiers knew of George Sherban and that the villain had been of the old British left, had been imprisoned for crimes against the people, and rehabilitated, and brought here by the Youth Armies to defend an impossible case.

It was a restless crowd. They shifted about on the hard stone, grumbled because of the heat, the lack of microphones, that the "Trial" had begun even before many delegates had come. There were the greetings of people who might not have met for years or months, at some Conference perhaps halfway across the world. And there was an under-mood of desperation and of anxiety, which did not relate to the present scene at all, but to our general preoccupation that war is obviously imminent. And perhaps, even then, before so much as a word had been exchanged between accuser and accused, it was evident to everyone that the "Trial" was hardly central to humanity's real problems, that it is not enough to ascribe every crime in the book to any particular class or nation or race—I say this relying on your understanding, for I do not want it to be thought that my long (or so it seems to me) exile in these backward provinces has caused any softening of my ability to see things from a correct class viewpoint. But our human predicament is grave indeed, and it was not possible for those five thousand, the elected "cream" of the world's youth, to sit there in those surroundings face to face, in all their gaunt threadbare hungry desperation, and *not* to see certain facts writ clear.

They were allowed no more than half an hour for settling themselves, for the absorption of what they could *see*—of what they were being *forced to see*—when George Sherban opened the "Trial" by strolling forward two steps from the table and saying:

"I have been elected to represent the nonwhite races in this Trial by—" and he recited a list of something like forty groups, organisations, armies. Agent Tsi Kwang said the silence was profound, for almost at once the moving and the whispering and the coughing ceased as they all understood they had to remain completely still to hear anything at all. And this was the first opportunity they all had to absorb the assault on their expectations of the man's appearance.

He had no list in his hand, but recited the names, long ones some of them, and some often sounding absurdly bureaucratic (I make this comment relying on our old understanding of the necessary absurdity of some forms of organisation) without any aid to memory. He stood there, so said Agent Tsi Kwang, quite calm, relaxed, and smiling.

He stood back two steps, and waited.

The old white man in his chair then spoke up. His voice was weaker than George Sherban's, though clear, and the silence was absolute. It seems to me that this was a silence of more than hatred or contempt, for even Agent Tsi Kwang commented that he made "a figure you had to think about." For one thing, I believe that most of the youth do not see an old or elderly person from one year's end—or decade's end even—to the next, except as ancient creatures hurrying away from them in fear, or as clothed skeletons lying on the streets waiting for the Death Squads, or perhaps in glimpses of them forgotten in institutions waiting to die of neglect and famine. The youth do not *see* the old. They are not programmed to see the old, who are cancelled, negated, wiped out, "removed from the honourable record of history," as Tsi Kwang so happily puts it. She was unable, she said, to take her eyes off the "old criminal element." The sight of him filled her with "a correct and concrete loathing." She felt he should be wiped off the face of the earth "like a beetle." And similar remarks quite reasonable in the circumstances. You will have observed that I quote this agent as often as I do—and intend to throughout this account—because of what might perhaps be described as the classic correctness of her viewpoint. She can be relied upon always to supply the apt comment. The other agents, none of them up to her level, have been useful to me in my attempt to present a picture of appropriate light and shade.

What the old ghost said was that he represented the white races— and at that point there was no reaction of boos or jeers, only silence —and he had been appointed to do this by . . . and here there was no long list of organisations from every part of the globe, but only "The Combined Co-ordinating Committee of the Youth Armies."

He remained silent in his chair, while George Sherban stood forward again and called up loudly and clearly the following words, pausing between phrases, and looking around the tiers.

"I open this Trial with an indictment. This is the indictment. That it is the white races of this world that have destroyed it, corrupted it, made possible the wars that have ruined it, have laid the basis for the war that we all fear, have poisoned the seas, and the waters, and the air, have stolen everything for themselves, have laid waste the goodness of the earth from the North to the South, and from East to West, have behaved always with arrogance, and contempt, and barbarity towards others, and have been above all guilty of the supreme crime of stupidity—and must now accept the burden of culpability, as murderers, thieves and destroyers, for the dreadful situation we now all find ourselves in."

Throughout this there was not a sound, but as he ended and stood back, the great crowd let out a hissing groan, and "it was more frightening than if we had cursed the villains or hurled insults at them." This is the comment of another of our agents, not Tsi Kwang, who confined herself to: "No stone was left unturned to shame the criminals standing at the bar of history." Another comment was from a letter written by Benjamin Sherban, intercepted by us. "Farce has ever been my meat and drink, but I tell you that if I hadn't eaten too long and too full of sheer bloody lunacy so that I can't react any longer, I would have dropped dead from fright at that hissing." I quote this as contrast to our ever admirable and to-be-relied-on Tsi Kwang. (You will remember that Benjamin Sherban was standing immediately behind the Defendant.)

It is clear that the white contingent stood their ground with difficulty, looking straight in front of them, and not at the furious brown, black, and golden faces confronting them, and holding their positions only with an effort of will. There was a long and intense silence. The old white did not move. The two children on either side of his chair deliberately raised their heads and stared up and around the tiers of faces. It seems that Benjamin Sherban maintained a characteristic lounging and almost casual posture.

The sun was already going, the shadow had engulfed George Sherban's contingent, and the evening had arrived: a warm, gritty, uncomfortable evening.

"I am now going to call my first witness," shouted George Sherban —and these were the last words he was to say for many days. He was never absent from the "Trial" while it was in progress, but he kept himself inconspicuous among the group on the Prosecution side.

The first witness was brilliantly chosen. (From a certain point of view.) She was a delegate from Shansi Province. A girl of about twenty. She was, of course, well fed and neatly dressed and looked healthy and at once the atmosphere lost tension. We are not popular. This is the penalty we have to pay for our superiority! (I rely on our old understanding of the subtle, and necessary, and often ironic shifts and changes of events.) It is not that our Chinese Youth behave incorrectly. On the contrary, they are at all times enjoined to correct behaviour, wherever they may find themselves. But the fact is that they do enjoy certain advantages from the very nature of our Beneficent Rule, and—in short—it was not easy for the underprivileged Europeans, and the representatives of the Emergent Nations, to identify with her. Our Agent Tsi Kwang commented that she was pleased that the first witness was Chinese, and then "disturbed," for she felt it was "impertinent in a way she couldn't grasp without further analysis." The comment by the unfortunate Benjamin Sherban was:

"What a thing a crowd is! A conglomeration of *unstable elements*, would you say? If the Devil may quote scripture . . ."

This witness recited, for no more than fifteen minutes, slowly and clearly—as was the style imposed on everyone—the crimes committed by the white races on China, and ended (this was to prove the conclusion or summing up of nearly every witness) ". . . and were always guilty of insulting and inhuman contempt, and of stupidity, and of ignorance of the Chinese people and our glorious history."

It was by now nearly seven, and the arena was a well of dusk. The tiers were in semi-darkness. Our delegate, having finished, returned to stand with the others in the shadows, as the tiers called applause and clapped. But it was not the tumultuous applause that might have been expected for the first of the "witnesses," and that would have been forthcoming (I say this in a spirit of dispassionate comment) if the first witness had been an American Indian—for instance. No, the emotional temperature had dropped, and this is a conclusion quite inescapable after study of the various agents' reports. And besides, I am writing as the—I hope not altogether unskilled—organiser of a thousand public events.

The torches were then lit. It was done like this: from four different aisles through the tiers were seen descending great flaring lit torches, and under them shadowy figures that turned out to be of different colours, gold, brown, black, and white. They ran with these torches across the arena, inevitably evoking associations of the Olympic games, and similar emotional international occasions from the past, and handed the torches to the children who stood waiting to take them. The children were dressed in the various uniforms of their organisations. They reached up on tiptoe—this detail was mentioned by all the agents, so it clearly made an impression—to put fire to the bundles of reeds that stood out from the arena walls. One after another torches flared up, and illuminated the arena. This little ceremony was watched with great attentiveness. There was a murmur of appreciation. What this murmur meant was interpreted differently by the agents.

The lighting ceremony took some time. Being the first, there were snags. One torch fell from its place, the two children retreated, an older girl leaped down from the tier just above and took charge, inserting the torch again in its sconce, and helping the children to light it, skillfully—and dangerously—using the remains of a torch that had been carried down through the tiers: all this was obviously unpremediated and unorganised, and in tune with the informal atmosphere. Another torch had burned up too bright, and was sending up tongues and wings of flame too close to the people in the rank above, and it had to be brought down, put out, and another put in its place. By the time all this was done, the atmosphere was loose and relaxed, the delegates were chatting to each other, and it was quite dark. It was a hot and dusty dark, and the stars were not strong enough to relieve it. Below, the two opposing groups faced each other. And strong in the wavering and flaring light, was the old white man, sitting quite still, with his two children, white and black, on either side.

The moon came up from a bank of low cloud. I swear this was stage management! It was a half-moon, but brilliant, and Venus was near it. The setting was quite perfect for a Torch Pageant, or Banner Event, or a Dragon Dance.

Nothing happened for a few minutes. It is evident that everyone was silenced by the beauty of the scene, the drama of the arena. Then it was observed that the group on the prosecution side was conferring. Informally. That everything was to be kept informal had been indicated from the start, and then confirmed, and confirmed again. People from both groups had already left them and gone to sit in the tiers, and others had replaced them—a continual coming and going. The first "witness" had made her way back to the Chinese Delegation. Which, incidentally, had been put prominently and distinctively in a bloc in the very best position, low down and halfway between the two groups. This was the only national group which was allotted a special position and marked with a banner—the only one, in other words, to which attention was directed throughout the "Trial."

After a few more minutes of starlight, the rising moon, the ambiguous arena, and, of course, the charming children who were bravely and earnestly attending to the flaring torches—one of the group, but not George Sherban, strolled forward to confer with the accused, and then this person, a girl, shouted up that it was felt by the contenders that the proceedings had been opened, everyone knew how things stood, and people must be tired and hungry, and perhaps it would be a good thing if the Trial should be ended early, just for this one night. Did everybody agree?

No one disagreed.

And in that case, she shouted, the meal would be served at nine, for this one evening, and not at twelve, as it would on future nights. She then outlined the plan for the sessions, asked for tolerance, since food had not been obtained easily and would be limited, asked for everyone to be vigilant against looters, and to treat the local people with respect, and emphasised that they would have to "call on reserves of good will and comradely understanding during the coming month which would tax their endurance and patience to the limit."

That this girl was an ordinary delegate, not one of the "stars," and that most people did not know who she was, made a good impression.

The tiers emptied fast, as the delegates found their way in a half-dark. The camp was minimally lit, with hurricane lamps in the mess tents and at their entrances, and outside the latrines, which were tents over pits.

Somehow these people got themselves fed in the crammed mess tents.

That was the first day of the "Trial." I consider it a marvel of crowd handling.

After that first evening meal, most people slept, exhausted. Many slept where they were in the mess tents, while the servers stepped over them with their trays. Some slept anyhow outside their tents— inside was too hot. It was a scene of apparent disorder. But even so, the whites removed themselves to their self-created ghetto, and posted guards.

Next morning, at four, when the two contending groups stood in the arena under the newly lit torches with their yawning attendant children, the tiers were half-filled, and during that session remained half-full, for many of the delegates were too tired to rouse themselves.

So that dramatic early morning session was at half pressure, and when at eight o'clock the laggards staggered up to meet those who had been for four hours on the stone seats, with the dawn coming up red, dusty, and very warm, again to repair to the mess tents for their bread and fruit, it was to hear at secondhand a report of the proceedings. There had been two "witnesses," both much looked forward to, and of prime emotional importance. First, the representative of the Indian tribes of North America, and then the witness from India.

A young man from the Hopi tribe of the Southwest of the United States stood alone in the centre of the arena calling up into the half-empty tiers, turning around slowly so that all could hear and see, holding out his palms in front of him as if "he was offering himself and his case to us in his outstretched hands, poor fellow." (Benjamin Sherban.) When he started it was full night with thick stars. They dimmed as he went on.

Europe had been crammed with miserable starving people because of the greed of its ruling classes. When these downtrodden ones protested, they were persecuted, hanged for stealing even an egg or a piece of bread, flogged, thrown into prison . . . they were encouraged to leave and go to North America, where they systematically stole everything from the Indian tribes who lived there in harmony with the earth and with nature. There was no trick, or cruelty or brutality these white thieves did not practise. When they had filled the land from coast to coast, and killed off the animals and destroyed trees and the soil, they confined the Indians in prison areas and mistreated them. These people, whose very existence in this great land of the Indians was because of the greed and cruelty of their own kind, now forgot their recent history and became the same themselves. Very soon, the white thieves had divided themselves into rich and poor, and the rich were as cruel and oppressive and uncaring of their fellow humans as any in history. Due to the exploitation of the labour of the poor, the new rulers became very powerful, and exploited not only North America but other parts of the world. They imported slaves from Africa, again in the most cruel and brutal way, to do their work and be their servants. This great country, which once was inhabited by peoples who did not know the words for rich, poor, owning, possessing, who lived their lives through in communion with, and obedience to, the Great Spirit who rules the world (I am of course quoting from the agents' reports), this rich and beautiful country was despoiled, poisoned, made an arsenal of weapons. And from coast to coast, from North to South, every person in it was made to worship not the Great Spirit who was the soul of every person of mankind, but the accumulation of wealth. Money. Goods. Objects. Eating. Power. The poorest of the whites was rich compared with the subject Indians. The most deprived and exploited of the poor were privileged in law compared with the people whose real home this was. This United States—a term which he used with contempt, spitting it out —was a place of shame, wickedness, corruption, evil. And all these crimes had been committed in the name of "progress"—spitting it out. All, in a spirit of self-congratulation and self-approval.

And then, the summing-up, the indictment:

"At the root of this criminal behaviour was contempt, the despising of others not like yourself, an arrogance that prevented you from ever even enquiring into the real nature of the peoples you dispossessed and treated as inferiors, a lack of humility and the curiosity that is based on humility. The indictment against you is arrogance, ignorance, stupidity. And God will punish you. The Great Spirit is punishing you, and soon you will be no more than a memory, and a shameful ugly memory."

These words were called up, or half shouted, phrase by phrase, very slowly, and the young man had his face to the sky, and his hands always held open and out—by the time he had ended, the sky was paling. The old white man sat there unmoving, and silent.

Complete silence. No one moved.

The torches were smoking and the children, aided by George Sherban, put them out. The cicadas had begun.

Throughout this contribution, a few laggards were making their way down to seat themselves. The great amphitheatre remained half-empty as a young woman from North India, the leader of the Youth Armies, Sharma Patel, George Sherban's reputed mistress, walked forward to the centre.

She is beautiful, and made an impression at once. Agent Tsi Kwang described her as "striking, and with many personal advantages."

"Europe, mostly Britain, but other countries too, had seen India, as Europe always did, as a place to be conquered, exploited, used. For two and a half centuries India had been drained of its wealth." Here followed twenty minutes of statistics. This was not altogether successful: material and delivery appropriate to a seminar were used in this vast setting where it was necessary to strain the ears to hear anything. Before this part of her contribution was done, her audience was restless, if sympathetic. "India had been occupied 'for her own good,' of course, in the usual hypocritical mode of Europe, by armies and by police, and the continent's inhabitants, with their intricate ancient history, their many complementary religions, their diverse cultures, were treated by the white invaders as inferior. The rule of Britain over India had been accomplished and maintained by arms, and by the whip. The people who did this were the barbarians. They were . . ." and here came the familiar indictment: "They were arrogant. Their exploitation of India was done in the name of progress and of their own superiority. Superior! Those ugly clumsy people with their thick minds and bodies! Yet these superior people were incapable of learning even the languages of the people they subjugated. They were ignorant of our customs, our history, our ways of thought. They were never anything but stupid people, stupid, ignorant, and self-satisfied."

These two contributions took until eight.

The late sleepers had to hear about the first two "indictments" from those returning to look for their breakfast. "Well, yes, but we know all that" was the frequent comment. As if they were expecting more, or something different. But what? For this was a consistent emotion from the beginning of the "Trial" to its end. It is something I have pondered on, and still find an enigma.

Throughout that day, until five and the evening session, it was hot, uncomfortable, and difficult in the camp. Everyone understood that this indeed was going to be no easy time. There were too many of them. There was not enough water. Already sorties were being made in search of new supplies of food and water. The dust was on everything. This was the time they should be sleeping, but where? And the local people had already arrived, were arriving more and more, and stood about, watching the thousands of young people who milled around looking for more food, a little shade, places to sleep. What they did, in a resigned enough spirit, was to settle down in groups, perhaps playing instruments and singing, or talking, or discussing conditions in their respective countries. Such meeting times of the youth have always been—I have consistently maintained—not far-off legislative sessions! In effect, at least. And George Sherban and his brother and the other "stars" were everywhere, taking part in discussions and music making. The old white was there, too, received well enough by everyone, and indeed often finding himself the centre of interested groups.

The generality of the white delegates—about seven hundred of them, stayed in their enclave of tents that day, and when they emerged for a meal or other purposes, behaved quietly, avoiding eye confrontation, and if challenged, smiled, and were bland and polite. They behaved, in fact, as so many of their subject peoples have always had to do: they were trying to be invisible.

This day, and after that night's session, and next day, the whites were in real danger, but after that, the emotions lost force.

Our agents were assiduous. It is clear that all were misled to some extent by their very proper enthusiasm for justice. They talked of "a total victory" over the white races. But what could they mean? They seemed to imagine not only a "verdict in their favour," but even summary justice of some kind. But to be carried out how, and on whom? The person of John Brent-Oxford? On their fellow delegates? I can only conclude from these fevered (but of course entirely understandable) reports, that the atmosphere and feelings in the camp must have been running very high, and beyond any reason.

I was struck then, and am struck again, by the difference in tone between the early reports of our agents and the later ones. Because of what can only be judged by us as their wrong assessment of situations, must we now assume that their assessment of other matters is sometimes faulty?

For the second evening session, guards escorted the whites, in a body, to the amphitheatre. The guards were appointed by the organisers, and included both Sherbans, Sharma Patel, and other "stars." The white delegates sat together, during that session, and were positioned opposite to the place reserved for our people, the Chinese. This gave the impression of a confrontation, for as I said, no other delegates sat according to national or racial origin.

It is clear that the confrontation, whites vs. Chinese (which is how it *looked*) was disapproved of by our delegates, who had felt that an honour (a proper, justified, and appreciated honour offered to our Beneficial Rule) was being denigrated and even mocked, because the hated and despised whites were now being similarly set apart, and immediately opposite themselves. Even if for very different reasons.

Once again there was the opposition between the "accusers" led by the—silent—George Sherban, and his group, and the "accused," the old white, and his group.

Once again, the late afternoon fading into dusk, the lighting of the torches, the attractive children, the constant coming and going between floor of arena and tiers and between camp and amphitheatre, which was crammed, packed, jammed with people.

All of the second night's session was taken up by representatives from South America, young men and women from the Indian tribes. Thirty of them. Several were wasted with disease. It is hard to imagine how some made the journey at all.

I will not go into detail.

This indictment was even more powerful than that of the Indian from the United States, because the events described were more recent. Some of the victims stood before us . . .

The incursion of Europe into South America. The conquest of brilliant civilisations through rapacity, greed, guile, trickery. The savagery of Christianity. The subjection of the Indians. The introduction of black people from Africa, the slave trade.

The devastation of the continent, its resources, its beauty, its wealth.

The casual, or deliberate, murder of the Indian tribes for their land, by introduced diseases, by starvation, by depredation—crimes that have not even now been completed, since there are still pockets of exploitable forest left—and everyone knows that where there is something that is capable of giving profit, then exploited it will be. The destruction of the animals, the forests, the waters, the soil.

One after another, the Indians stood forward and spoke—or, rather, shouted, or called up their accusing phrases, so that all the intent and listening thousands could hear. The white people, particularly the Spaniards, in their place on the tiers, surrounded by their guards, sat directly accused, culpable, guilty—reaping the hatred of those massed young people, representatives in more than one sense, for now they *were*, for that time, the murdering destroyers whom—as themselves and as individuals—they certainly had never done anything but condemn. But now they might very easily be lynched . . . and the old white man was forgotten, for all eyes were elsewhere.

As the Indians ended their plea, or accusation, two of the Spaniards broke from their guards, and ran down into the arena, and stood just in front of the old white man in his chair, stretching their arms up and out, in a gesture reminiscent of the crucified Christ, submitting themselves to their peers.

And again there sounded the deep, hissing, blood-chilling groan.

Immediately opposite the Spaniards stood the small crowd of Indians, some of them being held up, because of their weakness and disease—these groups stood there with the lights of the flaring torches on them, while the thousands kept up their hissing groan. And then, at a signal from the prosecuting side, the children began to extinguish their torches. Soon the great amphitheatre was dark, shined on by the stars and the strengthening moon. And the crowd began heaving itself up and clattering away.

Our agents all said they expected that it would be found that the two Spaniards had been killed in the darkness, but it was not so.

That was the first normal night. At midnight, they all crowded around the mess tents, finding what food they could. The contingent of whites asked the guards to leave them—and this made a good impression. The two Spaniards had joined them, and it seems that shortly some sort of informal seminar was in progress, on affairs in the South American continent, with the Spaniards and the two Sherbans prominent. The old white was also popular. In fact, for every night of that month, from midnight until four and the start of the morning session, they all, particularly George Sherban, were to be seen everywhere, each the focus of attentive groups. Seminars. Study groups. Classes. These words were used by all our agents. The old white was sought after because I gather the youth were curious to hear about the last days of "British democracy" and the Labour Party—ancient history to them. Also they saw him as a figure redeemed by his willingness to confess his crimes to the People's Tribunal, and to offer the last days of his life to the Service of the Workers.

At four a.m., when the amphitheatre filled, the whites were again escorted to their place opposite the Chinese delegation, but when there, they consulted briefly, asked the guards to leave them, and then dispersed themselves to sit at random among the others. This gesture caused some people, Agent Tsi Kwang, for instance, indignation, as it appeared to her an insult to the Correct Judgement of the Masses. But on the whole, it was well received. The high point of ill-feeling, and the possibility of assault and worse, was in fact passing. Soon the whites mingled freely, but still withdrew to their own tents to rest. And it was not long before even this was dropped.

That day there was a switch in emphasis, much to the annoyance or disappointment of all our agents, who were hoping that "something concrete" would result from the previous night's crisis of feeling. They expected, it is clear, an acceleration or culmination of bad feeling.

But racially the temperature was lowered, because there followed a series of "witnesses" testifying to the effects of military preparations, the arms build-up, submarine warfare potential and actual, the fleets patrolling the oceans, and above all, the instruments policing the skies whose very existence threatens whole continents with sudden death at any time.

The evening session was taken up by a series of recitals, or accounts, which sounded like laments, because of the necessarily slow, emphasised, simplified words, of the progress of war—the First World War, a European war, and the way its savagery impacted on non-European races made to fight in it, or forced to give up raw materials; colonies "lost," or exchanged, or freshly conquered; colonies used as battlegrounds for conflicts not their own. The Second World War, engulfing nearly all the world, its appalling devastations, again fought mainly between the white races, but using the other races where they could, or needed to, and the savage culmination when the Europeans dropped the atom bombs on Hiroshima and Nagasaki. And then the

Korean War, and its total barbarity, its illogic, its destructiveness, its strengthening of the United States—and its corruption of the States. The French in Vietnam. The United States in Vietnam. Africa and its attempts to free itself from Europe. If this is to be an attempt at actuality, then I must report that at this point there were certain veiled references which could be taken as a criticism of us, as well as of the Soviet Union, in Africa.

This litany, or requiem, or lament, on the subject of war took three days. Meanwhile, the moonlight strengthened. The evening sessions were monitored by a brilliant, almost full, moon that dimmed the torches, and dwarfed the arena and its antagonists.

By the fifth day a routine had been established. And a self-imposed discipline: all could see its necessity.

This mostly concerned alcohol. There had been some unfortunate incidents. Again the suggestion was made that it should not be brought into the camp. Meanwhile, the locals were in throngs around the camp day and night, only too ready to sell or barter alcohol, and even a little food. Already the young people had begun to leave the camp immediately after "breakfast" (as the agents complained, the meals were becoming "invisible") and made their way to the sea, some miles away. There they drank wine, ate what food they could cadge or grab, and began to catch fish and cook it there on the shore —knowing of course full well that fish from that sea was not safe food. They swam, rested, made love—and were back by five o'clock. If this had not happened, the camp would have been even more intolerable. It was already extremely uncomfortable, mostly from shortage of water, smelly, dirty, and besieged more and more by the curious villagers, who never took their eyes off these visitors of theirs, nor stopped trying to squeeze onto the tiers for what they clearly saw as free entertainment.

George Sherban seemed not to sleep. He stayed in the camp, for the most part, always available to whoever wished to talk to him. He was often with the old white. His brother Benjamin was much occupied with looking after his contingent of children, who were becoming wild, undisciplined—and liable to turn at any moment into the children's gang of the type we are unfortunately only too familiar with. The energies of many of the delegates, male and female, were devoted to restraining these children.

On the fifth night, there was a brief but heavy shower of rain. The dust was laid, the air cooled, the seats in the amphitheatre washed, the tension eased. The opportunity was taken to fill in the latrine pits, and to dig others. This improved things a little.

After the sessions spent on war, there succeeded four days on Africa. The "witnesses" came from every part of Africa. The days of their testimony again sharply changed the atmosphere. How may I put it? Variegated in type and aspect as they were, nevertheless, all together, they presented a picture of such liveliness and exuberance, such strength, such uncompromising virility, such warlike self-sufficiency—of course it must be remembered that in some parts of that continent governments have been in power which strike some of us as less than suitable, and which have discouraged those parts of the population they disapprove of to the point where only the more martial seem to survive. However that may be—and of course, I am only putting together a picture as it appears to our agents—these nearly hundred delegates seemed to impress upon everyone their difference from the rest. One point, for instance: with rather more to complain about from the white man even than other continents, they were concerned to express opinions about the intervention of others, not all white.

I will return to particularities:

The first "witness" was a fine young woman comrade from Zimbabwe.

She was received with the closest attention, and in silence—not with the hissing groan that so often is mentioned by our informants. This was the first indication of the change in mood, and because of the current situation in Africa, one of wars, civil wars, economic chaos. What she said sounded like ancient history, which, since her starting point was the conquest of Matabeleland and Mashonaland by Rhodes and his lackeys that took place not much more than a hundred years ago—a fact that she lost no time in reminding them of—was amazing in itself. Our Agent Tsi Kwang, for instance, was moved to remark that it made her think.

Her indictment, obviously considered an exemplary one, perhaps because it could be contained within such a short time span, a century being but a moment compared to the stretches of centuries—not to mention the millennia—which some delegates found it no hardship to encompass, was given from four a.m. on the sixth day until eight a.m.—but she was supported during the last hour by a white witness, a lawyer, whose standing by her, calling at her indication up into the early morning sky all kinds of facts and figures, had a bizarre and even, to some impatient ones, risible effect.

The cutting edge of her indictment was not the expected one: that the white barbarians had conquered by arms a defenceless and hospitable people who did not expect treachery and guile, but on the contrary offered their country freely and willingly to these tricksters—only to find themselves butchered, massacred, and then enslaved. The point that concerned her was this one; and the fact that it would have been better made in more modest surroundings conducive to such moderate reflections, should not prevent us from actually considering it in more modest surroundings.

In this vast territory, the whites had been given "self-government" by the home country Britain in 1924, except, that is, for two aspects. One was Defence—which did not concern her. But the other was "Native Affairs," and this was reserved by the British government on the specific and expressed ground that they, the British nation, had the responsibility to protect the conquered native populations, to see that their rights were not infringed, that they were not to suffer hardship as a result of their "tutelage" by the whites. For it goes without saying that the whites saw their rule as educational and benevolent. (I inscribe this second word with reluctance, with the reliance on your understanding, and the reflection that one word may have to stand for a variety of shades of circumstance.) From the very moment the white conquerors were given "self-government" they took away the black people's lands, rights, freedoms and made slaves and servants of them in every way, using every device of force and intimidation, contempt, trickery. But never did Britain protest. Never, not once. She did not raise her voice, even though throughout this entire period of ill-treatment by the white minority, the black peoples were expecting to be rescued by their "protecting" government overseas, and believed that this rescue did not occur only because their white friends overseas could not really know of their situation. Not that they desisted from sending every kind of representation to the Queen and to Parliament as well, and through every sort of intermediary. But why did not one British governor ever notice what was happening and protest and report to his home government that the main clause in this famous agreement giving self-government to the whites was not being honoured? Why did not help ever arrive to the enslaved and betrayed people of the then Southern Rhodesia? It was because of a very simple fact. Because the government in Britain, the people of Britain, did not *remember*, had not thought it important enough to take in, the key fact that self-government had been given to the white minority on condition the blacks were not ill-treated, and that they had the obligation to step in. And they had been able to forget, simply not to take notice, because of their inherent and inbred contempt for peoples other than themselves. Worse was to come. When Africa began stirring in her chains (a phrase which gave particular pleasure to Agent Tsi Kwang), when a small section of "liberal" whites began to protest in Britain about the treatment of the betrayed blacks, even they did not seem to know that all this time the government of Britain had the legal right to step in at any time in pursuance of duty. They did not seem to have absorbed the fact that during a period of several decades when the blacks had everything taken from them, *Britain had had the legal and moral responsibility* to step in and forcibly stop the whites from doing as they liked. And more, when the blacks began fighting back under the rule of the infamous Smith and his cohorts, and the British government was at last forced into some attitudes of responsibility, even then no one seemed able to remember that the culpable one was not Smith, nor even his predecessors, but Britain herself, who had betrayed the blacks for whom she was supposed to act as guardian against the whites. For Britain it was who had connived at, allowed, and by passive indifference, encouraged the whites to do exactly as they wished. And when the last stages of that tragic struggle were going on, the British government, throughout, talked, acted, and seemed even to believe, that the whites of Rhodesia were responsible for the situation and not itself, as if something quite odd and unknown were happening, a great surprise, the grabbing of rights and land from the blacks—something that had had nothing to do with the British government. And all this led to one of the most absurd, contemptible sequences in late British colonial history—that Rhodesia could have been in the forefront of the news, day and night for years, the cause of the blacks so belatedly espoused by a thousand kind hearts, commented on ceaselessly by a thousand professionals, but not once during this time was the point made that Britain had been responsible for the situation in the first place.

"And how was this possible, this extraordinary state of affairs?"

"I will tell you," called up this young soldier into the morning sunshine above the amphitheatre. "It was because the British people and their government could not see us, they always had a blind spot for us, we blacks did not count. If we were dogs and cats they would have seen us but we were black people. In the War of Liberation these philanthropists cried out when a white person got killed, but if fifty black people got killed, and even if they were children, they did not notice it. We were always nonpeople to them. Why should they care about broken promises?"

I describe this in more detail than perhaps is necessary for you who have always taken such an interest in Africa and who indeed as a young man spent two years in Mozambique with the Resistance Forces. I describe it because it has caused me to reflect on the extraordinary persistence of certain phenomena in a given geographical area. (I rely on our old friendship, hoping you will excuse a slackness of thought or of phraseology or perhaps even an apparent irrelevance to the true and real issues of the Liberation of the People, but it is nearly four in the morning, and outside H.Q. I can hear the sounds of our patrolling soldiers, *our own*, as it happens—but who can rely on the permanence of anything in these stirring times.)

Of this persistence, or continuance, more in a moment. Meanwhile, I pause to comment that this young black woman's contribution was the most reasoned of all the indictments. I do not mean she was more *correct*. That is not my point here.

There is no end to the indictments against the white man. I say this and need say no more: one has only to mention any country and the stark facts and figures spring to mind. We did not need a "Trial"!

But this young woman was making a point others had not. "Stupidity," "ignorance," "arrogance," the crude self-satisfaction we have so often discussed—these are one thing, and these words or similar ones ended every one of the "indictments." But she was saying something more. *How was it possible* for a tract of country the size of Honan Province to be conquered by a handful of adventurers, and thereafter to be *forgotten* by the empire? Because that is what happened here. Brutality, yes. Ignorance, yes. Yes, yes, yes. But these have not been exactly unknown in history. But it was possible, in the British Empire, for a vast part of Africa to be physically conquered, put in the care of one hundred thousand whites—and the number of these never rose above half a million—and thereafter forgotten. Oh, governors were sent out—the type we know so well. I don't doubt that from time to time the British government was reminded by its financiers that there were interests there that needed guarding, but that was all. Serious undertakings, promises, obligations, were not reneged on so much as *over-*

looked. To the extent that the Rhodesian crisis when it finally matured could be discussed for years and years, and the key fact never mentioned.

And now to my point about a continuation of a trend, a strand, a factor in a place, or among a people.

This "Trial" took place—as far as the participants were concerned —for only one reason: to air grievances and complaints against the erstwhile colonial oppressors. The Imperialists. That was its function. This girl made her case for four hours, calling in the aid of her white lawyer, and she was listened to with great attention. And yet *her case got lost.* It was because of the general atmosphere—that there was so much to listen to, to work through, in conditions of such discomfort. Her point, that a great empire was able to conquer and then to forget, or overlook, a territory the size of Honan was not taken in. Is not that extraordinary? *In fact, what happened was what had always happened to that particular territory.* Yet a few hundred miles to the north, in Northern Rhodesia, shortly to be Zambia, uprisings, and successful ones, took place among the black peoples against the whites, and the key emotional factor was precisely that the British people, in the person of Queen Victoria, had made promises which had not been kept. *There,* effective. In Rhodesia, not.

Well, I at least find myself reflecting on this point. A geographical area keeps a certain *flavour,* which manifests in all its happenings, its events, its history. I cite for instance the lamented Soviet Union, or Russia, where events occur and continue to repeat themselves, over and over, regardless of whether that vast land is called Russia or the Soviet Union, or its dominant ways of thought are this or that or the other. And of course there are other examples we may easily think of.

I sometimes wonder if this thought may not be usefully taught to children at the start of their "geography lessons." Or would one call it *history?* If I seem to ramble, put it down to the long night of *anxious* wakefulness. The dawn is here and I shall not rest yet, for I wish to finish this long letter to you; the courier will leave this evening.

I return to the amphitheatre: Africa was the agenda for several days.

Meanwhile, in the camp itself, it is clear that the organisation was suffering.

Everyone was really hungry, lacking sleep, hot, dusty. By now nearly all of them flocked to the coast for the midday hours, and of course this made them even more tired.

There was by now a feeling of urgency. With the full moon blazing down, so that the thousands on the tiers were fully visible to each other, and the torches almost unnecessary, the contenders dealt fast with: the ruining of the Pacific, the imposition there of alien ways on ancient and peaceful societies, the forcible imposition of Christianity, the destruction of islands in the interests of western industry and agriculture, the use of the Pacific for nuclear weapons tests as if this ocean belonged to Europe. They dealt with: European rule over subjugated peoples in the Middle East, the irreconcilable promises made to Arabs and Jews, the arrogance displayed . . . "contempt, arrogance, stupidity, ignorance."

I interpose at this point that those so recent enemies the Arabs and Jews were inseparable, and took every opportunity of reminding us of their common origin, their similar religions, the compatibility of their cultures, and—so they intend—their common and harmonious future.

The "Trial" then dealt with: the white man in Australia, the white man in New Zealand, the white man in Canada, the white man in the Antarctic.

You will note that I have scarcely mentioned the Russians. One reason is that there were no Russian delegates, though there were from the Russian colonies Poland, Bulgaria, Hungary, Czechoslovakia, Roumania, Cuba, Afghanistan, parts of the Middle East.

By then, delegates were following each other every ten minutes, and they were in lines stretching up the aisles and waiting to recite, or to shout, their indictments, and to return to their places.

We have now reached halfway through the "Trial"—the fifteenth day. Rereading the agents' reports, what is striking is the note of frustration—annoyance. You will bear in mind that our agents are all active members of their representative organisations, not dissidents or oddballs. They act for us mostly without payment, and as a token of appreciation for our Beneficent Rule. They are emotionally part of the Youth Armies, and their value is that they share with, and cannot help but register, the prevailing common mood or moods.

I again have to ask, What was it that all these young people were expecting and that they were not given? For on the face of it, they were getting exactly what they had come for.

I quote Tsi Kwang: "There is an incorrect spirit. The cadres are not overcoming the difficulties of the situation. There is vacillation and also many mistakes. There is an insufficient readiness to boldly grasp the bourgeois distortions that cannot help but negate the true experience of the sincere Youth." And so on for several pages.

All our agents, during those days, turned in similar reports.

The egregious Benjamin Sherban: "The centre cannot hold, mere anarchy is loosed upon the world." I am told that these are lines from an ancient folk ballad. (I would like to hear the rest of it, for there may be guidance there in present difficulties.)

It is clear that the delegates were at breaking point and it was only because of the flexibility and tolerance of the organisers that the "Trial" could continue at all. For one thing, alcohol was now entering the camp and affecting discipline. For another, sex, previously discreet and within the limits of good sense, was now blatant, not only between delegates, but between them and the locals.

The prevailing mood was one of restlessness, dissatisfaction, a continual *movement* around the camp, from tent to improvised shelter to mess tents, where debates and "seminars" seemed continuously in progress, and from the camp to the shores—and by now some donkeys had been pressed into service, and derelict army trucks had been located and put into use (petrol being commandeered of course) and parties of delegates moved up and down the coasts entering towns and villages to try and organise food, and individuals wandered about as well, for as usual on these highly pressured occasions, there are always those who seem to spin off, as if from a centrifuge. These broke down, or threatened to, wept, complained of being underrated, discussed the possibilities of suicide, and fell hopelessly in love with delegates whom they certainly will never see again.

All this did not mean the sessions were not fully attended. The amphitheatre was crammed, attentive, centred on the events in the arena, from four until eight, and from five until midnight. But now they were less silent, intervened often in the "indictments," adding comments and facts and figures. There was total participation between audience and—I was going to say—actors.

There seemed no reason why the supply of witnesses should ever end, but already it was being asked when the old white, who was sitting there hour after hour, day after day, silent, on his chair, was "going to defend himself." But meanwhile, of course, he had been continuously in conversation with everyone interested—and this by now was everyone—whether hostile or not, during the hours of leisure, if that is a word that may be used for such a frenzy of restlessness. In short, he was not being thought of as enemy, and the epithets (correctly of course) used of him by our informants seemed to me to lack the fervour they had had at the beginning.

It was being openly said that the "Trial" could not run its course of a full month, for conditions were becoming impossible.

It was at this point that something new happened. Aircraft appeared, evidently keeping watch. The first was on the night of the full moon: a helicopter hovered over the amphitheatre for some minutes, and proceedings had to be stopped until it decided to go. This attentive, *unmarked* machine made its effect: our agents report fury, exasperation, a pent-up rage—if the machine had been within reach it would not have survived. There were "jokes" about surveillance from the Russians. Also by us. (I report, merely, without comment.) On the next night, a different craft appeared, also unmarked, and remained over the amphitheatre until its point had been made. Again the reaction was fury. An almost hysterical rage. Do you think it is possible that in some quarters it is not appreciated what horror and loathing are felt by many for the products of our human ingenuity and technological progress? Various and different craft kept appearing in the skies at all hours of the day and night from then on, some very low, some so high as to be almost invisible, most unknown to the—very expert—youngsters watching them. "Jokes" were made about spacemen, flying saucers, international police forces, flying squads of vigilantes, guided spy satellites.

And the imminent war became suddenly the chief topic. If this was what the surveillant craft wished to achieve, they succeeded.

Now the moon was past its full, appearing later each evening, the torches were again exerting their strong emotional effect on everyone.

Abruptly, on the ninth night, George Sherban, who had said practically nothing at all during the actual sessions, came forward to remark, and in a casual way—which annoyed some of our agents— "that it seemed to him time that the prosecution rested its case." This had not been expected, or at least, not then. But no sooner had he said it, than at once it was felt by everyone that he was right, for what could be added to the indictment they had already heard!

They had, however, been expecting a summing up, but all he said was: "I rest my case, and call upon John Brent-Oxford to speak."

At first there was a strong reaction. But it changed from disappointment to approval, and the young people were saying to each other that this was a correct, if daring approach.

The silence was absolute. The old white did not stand up. No one expected it: all knew his health was poor. Sitting in his chair, from which he had not moved for all those sessions, he said, clearly, but with no effort to be heard:

"I plead guilty to everything that has been said. How can I do anything else?"

Silence again.

He did not say anything more. Muttering began, angry laughter, then a stirring, and indignation.

This tension was broken by some young man calling out in the jeering but good-humoured way which was, it is clear, very much the note or style of the "Trial": "Well, what are we going to do? Lynch him?"

Laughter. Some of our agents report that they did not find the moment amusing. There was lacking, claimed Tsi Kwang, a proper respect for "the healthy verdicts of history."

There was also considerable confusion, and a good deal of anger.

After some minutes the old white held up his hand for silence and spoke again:

"I want to ask all of you present: Why is it that you, the accusers, have adopted with such energy and efficiency the ways you have been criticising? Of course some of you have been given no alternative: I refer to the North American and the South American Indians, for example. But others have had a choice. Why is it that so many of you who have not been forced into it, have chosen to copy the materialism, the greed, the rapacity of the white man's technological society?"

With which he stopped speaking.

There was indignation, and a loud murmur of talk, which became a clamour.

Then George Sherban called up, "Since it is nearly midnight, I suggest we call a halt and resume the discussion at four a.m. as usual."

The tiers emptied fast. That night very few people left the camp. It was seething, and pervaded by a spirit which, after very carefully perusing the reports, I am going to take the liberty of describing as jocular.

The four hours were spent in energetic discussion. Everywhere they were speculating about the defence they were about to hear. They were *joking* that it was obvious that the white man, always in the right, was about to accuse them, particularly those nonwhite nations which had taken efficiently to industry and technology—which I am happy to say includes us—of many of the crimes *he* had been accused of. In a spirit of part anger, part burlesque, in hundreds of conversations between couples, among groups, in "seminars," these probable accusations were being framed and elaborated, and even offered to the old white for use.

Our agents all expressed indignation at this turn of events, calling them frivolous and insulting.

Towards dawn it rained: another heavy shower. Just as there was a movement to the amphitheatre to light the torches, it rained again. It was a wet, and even chilly dawn. The word went around that the session was cancelled, to give the amphitheatre time to dry out. A great many went to sleep where they were, because of the easing of the tension due to the drop in temperature—and due also, to the general feeling of anticlimax.

As they woke again, through the morning and early afternoon, the conversations and debates began anew, but on a lower note, more seriously, with less laughter. But the mood was one of amiability.

It is clear now, reading the reports, that the "Trial" had in fact ended. At the time though, there was a certain eagerness to know what would happen next.

It was lucky that it rained, but if it had not, I feel that events would have petered out in much the same way.

By five the amphitheatre was dry, and the delegates crammed the seats.

Everyone was looking towards the old white, with many ironical speculations as to what line he would take, but it was George Sherban who went into the centre, held up his arms for silence and began:

"Yesterday the accused made a counteraccusation. It is one that I know has been thought about and discussed ever since. But today I want to put forward a self-criticism, which I feel we may agree is not outside the spirit of this gathering of ours."

This was unexpected. Not a sound from anybody. The woman Sharma Patel came forward to stand beside him.

"We have heard for many days now, accounts of the ill-treatment by the white-skinned races of the Dark Races—to which, as you know, for purposes of this Trial, I have the honour to belong . . ."

This was greeted with a great roar of sardonic laughter, and from various places around the vast gathering came singing. "I have an Indian grandfather," "I have a Jewish grandmother."

He held up his hand, the noise stopped, and he remarked, "As it happens, a Jewish grandfather, from Poland. And of course it now seems at least possible that this ancestor of mine originated with the Khazars and not in Israel or anywhere near it, so that gives me two non-European grandparents out of four. But otherwise, of course, I am that common mix, Irish-Scotch, both of them subject races."

Another roar of laughter. There was a danger the singing would start again, but he stilled it.

"I want to make a single observation. It is that for three thousand years India has persecuted and ill-treated a part of its own population. I refer of course to the Untouchables. The unspeakable treatment meted out to these unfortunate people, *barbaric, cruel, senseless—*" these words were thrown up, one after another, with pauses between, like challenges, up into the tiers as he turned slowly around to face every part of the audience—"this unspeakably cruel treatment is matched for baseness by nothing the white races have ever done. At this time millions upon millions of people in the subcontinent of India are treated worse than the white South Africans ever treated any black—as badly as any white oppressor ever treated a black man or woman. This is not a question of a year's oppression, a decade's persecution, a century's ill-treatment, not the results of a short-lived and unsuccessful regime like the British Empire, not a ten-year outburst of savagery like Hitler's regime in Europe, not fifty years of savagery like Russian communism, but something built into a religion and a way of life, a culture, so deeply embedded that the frightfulness and ugliness of it apparently cannot even be observed by the people who practise it."

At this he stepped aside and Sharma Patel took his place.

"I, an Indian born and bred, ally myself with what our comrade has said. I am not an Untouchable. If I were, I would not be standing here. Because I am not, I am able to stand forward now to say that I heard nothing during the days we have sat here listening to the indictments, that cannot be matched by what I know—what we all know—is true, of the treatment of Indians by Indians. Thousands and thousands of years it has been going on, and still it seems that we are unable to put an end to this monstrous wrong. Instead we come here to criticise others."

With which she went back to stand with her group, and George Sherban followed her.

A long silence. Nothing was said. Then began the restless stirring and muttering which always means a crowd is going to express itself in some way.

John Brent-Oxford now raised his voice, but not very much, so that everyone was forced to silence themselves so as to listen.

"We all know that at this time, now, there are nations, nonwhite nations, which dominate and subjugate by force other nations, some equally nonwhite, but other nations that are white."

Silence again.

Then: "Do you want me to remind you of the many instances in history when black, and brown, and light brown, and gold-coloured and cream-coloured nations treated themselves, or other nations badly?"

Silence.

"For instance, it is not news to any of us that the slave trade in Africa was conducted largely by Arabs and was made possible by the willing co-operation of black people."

At this point, a latecomer, running down one of the aisles between the seats, called out, "It seems we are in for a seminar on man's inhumanity to man." Various people near him enlightened him on what had been happening, he called down an apology, and during this little stir, it was noticed that people had begun to leave the stadium.

Then a girl stood up and shouted, "I've had enough of man's inhumanity to man. What is the point of all this anyway?"

She was German. A Polish girl stood up from the opposite side of the amphitheatre and shouted across, "I'm not surprised you have had enough. You can leave if first you stand up like others have done and do some self-criticism. I want you to tell us of the crimes committed by the Germans in the Second World War."

"Oh no!" "Oh for God's sake!" "Let's get out of here," was now heard from everywhere.

The old white was trying to make himself heard. Other people were calling out that anyone who wanted to make similar points should come down to the floor of the arena and make them properly, clearly, and correctly.

The German girl, pigtails flying, was running down into the arena to face her opponent, who was already there: the Polish girl, a large young woman who was wearing a costume our agents one and all found "disgusting"—dirty white shorts and a brassiere. But by then all the costumes had become a matter of individual whim, and often exiguous.

A lot of people were standing up to shout that they hadn't come to listen to "private quarrels."

This caused more interventions, verbal and otherwise: there were some scuffles. In a moment everything was quarrelling and disorder.

George Sherban brought the proceedings to an end. As he did this, a helicopter appeared, directly overhead, very low. It was large, noisy, with violently flashing lights of different colours.

Suddenly everyone was standing, shaking their fists and screaming. It was by then almost completely dark, the torches were flaring: a scene of confusion and impotent rage.

They all streamed back to the camp. By then everyone recognised the "Trial" was over. People were talking about returning to their respective countries. They were hot, dirty, tired, irritable, and very hungry. All night, there were aircraft coming and going. This made it impossible to sleep or to rest. When the light came, everyone streamed away down to the sea, walking, jogging, running.

Not everyone left the camp.

About seven in the morning, a single aircraft came over, flying rather high, and dropped a single well-aimed bomb into the amphitheatre. This was totally destroyed. Some debris fell among the tents. The old white, who was sitting by himself not far from the amphitheatre, was hit by a piece of stone and killed. No one else was hurt.

When the thousands of young people came streaming back, they found a scene of devastation. Some left at once, making their way on foot to towns and villages along the coast where they could begin their long and dangerous journeys home.

By that night very few were left. The camp had been dismantled, the disgusting latrines filled in, the local people had gone.

Our Chinese delegates were taken away by special coaches.

Resentment and anger were expressed, as it was seen that food had been brought, and our delegates were already eating and drinking as they were driven away.

By next morning there was nothing left but the usual half-starved dogs nosing about.

So much for the "Trial."

While it was still in progress, I was getting reports of rumours—very strong and persistent—particularly in India and Africa, that there were plans for "mass transfer of populations" to all parts of Europe. By implication, these included plans for pogroms and massacres and the compulsory attachment of land. The rationale for these invasions was always variations on the theme of the white man's culpability, that he had "proved himself unfit to play his part in the brotherhood of nations."

Our attitude was expected, was *assumed*, to be one of sympathetic noninterference.

Shortly after the delegates left Greece, scattering over the world, these rumours ceased.

Are we then to believe that the highly rhetorical and oversimplified (though of course in essence entirely correct) "indictments" had exhausted a certain allowance of anger and desire for revenge? Or that these young people returning home with an *account* of what had taken place, a description of the arguments and counterarguments used— this had the effect of damping certain fires?

I am without any rational explanation. But the *fact* is, coincidence or not, massacres, a determined and planned wiping out of the re- maining European populations was on the cards, and being actively endorsed—and now nothing is being heard of it.

This rather minor, and bizarre, and suspect event, the "Trial," to begin with almost a joke (not I hasten to add because of its subject), is in fact being commented on everywhere.

This although we allowed no news coverage. Of course accounts— inadequate and inevitably garbled—found their way into the news- papers of the world, including the official organs of the People's Will. But always in a minor and unemphasised way. There was no television, and it was mentioned hardly at all on the official radio wavelengths.

The question of George Sherban. This "Trial" succeeded in elevat- ing him to a position of undisputed leader and spokesman, even though he spoke, during the "Trial" itself, perhaps not more than a score of sentences. What did he expect to gain by this exposure of himself in this particular way? Which was accomplished, I remind you, without even the aid of certain positions he could have had for the asking?

I can only report that whatever one may have reasonably expected to happen, the fact is that he disappeared when the "Trial" was over. No one seems to know where he is, and yet the Youth organisations and Armies of fifty countries are clamouring for him to visit and "instruct."

Many of the delegates to the "Trial" have also disappeared, and people with whom they are known to have been in contact.

What were the subjects of conversation during those days and nights when he was always on view in the camps, talking, discussing, "holding seminars"?

Studying my informants' reports, I can come to no conclusion.

He is a fluent and witty conversationalist—yet on no particular subject. He makes a strong impression, yet does not seem to leave people with the memory of strong opinions. He does not take any particular political stand, he has never stood for a class or other position that could be defined. Yet he is trusted by young cadres for whom politics are everything.

Our Agent Tsi Kwang when reporting conversations she was— obviously—fascinated by, since she mentions over and over again that she has been in his company, says, "The delegate George Sherban fails to satisfy the soaring aspiration of the People's glorious militancy. He lacks revolutionary sweep. He lacks an ability to base his actions on the highest interests of the broad masses. He suffers from wishy-washy idealism and enthusiasm for humanistic ideas unrelated to concrete requirements. Weak-minded elements with insufficient bases in correct doctrine find his utterances attractive. He should be exposed and re-educated."

I have reissued instructions for his elimination.

I send you comradely greetings. My remembrances, memories of an old friendship are one of the few pleasures of my exile.

[This Overlord was recalled shortly after. His friend Ku Yuang had already been removed from his position by an opposing faction. Both were sequestered, and underwent "beneficent correction" until their deaths. *Archivists*.]

History of Shikasta, VOL. 3014, *Period Between World Wars II and III*. SUMMARY CHAPTER.

This was a period of furious activity.

The inhabitants of Shikasta, engaged in destroying themselves, soon to face the intensive, if short, final phase of their long orgy of mutual destruction, were not entirely unaware of their situation. A feeling of foreboding was general, but was not commensurate with the situation, nor specific to the various dangers. Alarms and warnings were frequent, but related to an aspect or part of the situation: these pre-occupied them for a while, and were then forgotten as another crisis arose and seemed overriding. A few Shikastans, and in all countries, understood quite well what was happening.

Shikastans, then, in every country, scurried about like insects when their nest is threatened: a breach has been made, and in that place repairs must be effected. And of course, talking went on continuously and always and everywhere; councils, conferences, meetings, discussions, were held all over the planet, some of these purporting to be in the interests of Shikasta as a whole, but the habit of partisan and sectarian thinking was too ingrained for these to be of use.

None, or few, understood the nature of the intense interest taken in them by various outside localities.

That there was interest, on the part of "beings from space," was suspected, and there was a worldwide belief that heads of states and governments knew factually and specifically about the visits, peaceful or otherwise, from other parts of the galaxy. It was believed that these functionaries and their underlings denied this knowledge out of a fear of the reactions of their populations, who, for their part, because of the innumerable "sightings" and "experiences" of all kinds of unknown spacecraft, believed in "visitors from space," but in a vague and almost mythic way, as they did in religious exemplars and otherworldly beings of a saintly or devilish kind: for there was no part of Shikasta whose myths and legends did not include visits from superior visitors.

Meanwhile, under the noses of the unfortunates, real battles were being fought, real events took place.

First of all, there was our former enemy and uneasy ally Sirius.

Through the long development of Shikasta, Sirius had several times used areas, mostly in the southern hemisphere, and usually with our agreement, for experiments. Some of these animals proved unsatisfactory for Sirian long-term purposes, and were allowed to remain and develop along their own lines, without further modification or interference. Some of the experiments were successful or promising, and more than once Sirian fleets had descended and taken off an entire species, sometimes numbering many thousands, after anything from between five hundred or a thousand, to several thousand, years. These were transferred to other Sirian colonies, to develop along planned and foreseen lines, or to go into service at once according to their specific physiques, their mental development.

Due to the comparative ease of travel in recent times, and the accessibility of all parts of Shikasta to the others, a great deal of racial mixing had taken place.

Sirius was not much involved in the culminating events on Shikasta. One reason was in fact this racial mixing: as soon as travel, due to the developments of technology, had become general, Sirius had wound up certain experiments, and had no further expectations of Shikasta. She always kept us informed, telling us exactly when she withdrew her active participation, placing in our hands details of the experiments she had at various times undertaken, whose results we might have to oversee, or take into account, ourselves. She did send observing spacecraft however, and these were of premier size and quality, the cream of her fleets. This was partly to indicate to us, her ancient rival, that the relinquishing of her power was voluntary, and partly to intimidate Shammat, whose frenzies of mind caused all of us anxiety.

Shammat of Puttiora was now in fact the most powerful planet in that complex, and Puttiora was her puppet, but remained the apparent centre for purposes of Shammat's convenience. Shammat knew that at some time the unfortunate cosmic pattern which had caused the long decline of Shikasta because of the diminishing flow of SOWF was due to end. She knew that Shikasta would again lock into place in the great plan that kept Canopus and her planets and colonies in an always harmoniously interacting whole. At some time, Shammat's influence would end.

But Shammat did not know when. Did not know how complete her overthrow was to be. Did not know what our plans were.

Shammat's disability has always been of the same kind and degree, and can be described in a useful Shikastan saying: it takes one to know one! For Shammat's low level of development has always prevented her from understanding the nature of our interests and intentions.

Shammat's nature has always been that of an exploiter, a drainer, a feeder, a parasite. She has never been able to comprehend that other empires may be based on higher motives.

Shammat, since her rapid rise to a key position in the Puttiora Empire, has been a place of power, highly fortified, always at war, whose citizens, all of a single racial stock, ex-Puttiora, have considered themselves superior, and draw tribute from any other part of the galaxy they might happen to conquer or influence. Shammat sits in the middle of the complex like an ever-open mouth. Shammat is, and always has been, a threat to the overall development of the galaxy. A vast planet, the largest known, it is barren, dry, lacking in resources. Everything has to be imported. And she lacks, completely, any wholesome balancing powers and currents because of her position in the cosmic organisation. Even Puttiora would not develop this dreadful place. Yet by an unfortunate combination of chances, some criminals found their way here, seized it, used its very awfulness to wrench power for themselves from others.

For a short time (in cosmic terms) Shammat was the most luxurious in the galaxy. It overflowed with riches, wealth, the products of a hundred inventive and industrious cultures. The inhabitants lived on a level of self-indulgence and beastliness that has never been equalled, not even during the nastiest episodes on Shikasta.

Power from Shikasta remained always Shammat's main source, and she was not able to find anything to replace it.

More and more power had been drawn from Shikasta. Shammat was taking everything she could, while she could. But she simply was not able to understand what was happening. She did not know how to find out, and flailed about wildly, blindly, in every sort of damaging way, in the hope that "something would work." She knew that we, Canopus, was, is, must always be, her enemy: knew that we were always present, potent, unconquerable—but did not know what to look for, unable to recognise us in our innumerable guises.

Shammat, until the very end, believed that in some extraordinary way or other, it would be possible to maintain "somehow," the link with Shikasta. "Something will happen." "It will all come right." This desperate unclarity was not what characterised Shammat in the days when we observed her accurately foreseeing the weakening of the link Canopus/Shikasta, and what that weakening might offer her in the way of benefits—but Shammat had degenerated. The long history of shameless dependence on others, the selfishness of her attitude towards neighbours in the galaxy, parasitism, her luxury and the weakening of her moral fibre—all had conspired to ruin her. And the emanations from Shikasta itself, in her final phase, were poisonous. The very process that Shammat had set moving—reducing, weakening, enslaving a large part of Shikasta's populations, this had reduced and weakened itself, and caused self-division and civil war.

There were battles fought above Shikasta in those days that had nothing to do with Shikasta! Shammat fought Shammat—wildly, senselessly, self-destructively.

Re: Colonised Planet 5, Shikasta

The skies over Shikasta were in any case filled, crammed, with every sort of mechanical and technical artefact, observing stations, weather stations, relaying stations, some in the service of usefulness, others for war; there were weapons of every kind, of every degree of destructiveness—and these too competed in ways the inhabitants of Shikasta knew nothing about. Shikasta had an outer shell of metal hurtling around it. That this had a weakening effect on the links and meshings of the cosmic forces was of course not a consideration of Shikasta, whose technicians, even at the end when certain facts were becoming obvious, had not yet reached an ability to understand these forces: for several centuries their sciences had been set in a retrograde and backward path of thought which prevented them from thinking usefully along these lines. (They never suspected for instance that certain of their cities, or certain buildings, were built in such a way as inevitably to make their inhabitants mad, or unbalanced at the least.) All around the whirling shell of metal that encased Shikasta battles took place. And others observed these battles. More than once Sirian master-ships appearing on a routine reconnaissance trip put to flight Shammat's craft that had been dogfighting all over the Shikastan skies. More than once Sirian master-craft, and our own, patrolled these skies in protective alliance, keeping away the ugly little Shammat machines, whose almost automatic belligerence only increased the pressures on Shikasta. And the Shikastan moon was hotly contested.

Craft from the Three Planets were also visitors to Shikasta. Their happy balances in the structure of forces had long been affected by the Shikastan descent into barbarism, and to maintain their health had not for a long time been easy. The Twentieth Century War with its evil and deadly emanations, useful only to Shammat, had affected these planets. Their visiting craft were for observation. At all times our servants have been on the best of terms with them, have given them every assistance. They were waiting, as were we all, for the moment when Shikasta's long night would end, and be succeeded by a slow return to the light.

It will be seen, then, that a large part of the work of the visitors to Shikasta was for monitoring and observation, and was no threat at all to that unhappy planet—on the contrary. But that there were so many different visitors, with so many different types of craft, was not known by them. There was of course and in addition the already mentioned fact that the major powers all had weapons of war kept "secret" from each other, and certainly kept secret from the populace, and since from the point of view of such powerful weapons, the skies of Shikasta were small enough, every part of the globe was visited by craft originating in Shikasta itself.

Nor did Shammat fully understand the nature and extent of these many different craft, many visitors.

How very much did Shammat *not* understand; and what damage she did; and how she did crash about and blunder and spoil!

For instance, in her ignorance, Shammat's agents would often destroy large numbers of people whose proper term on Shikasta had not ended—and whose destruction was no help at all to herself. These we would return to Zone Six and immediately reintroduce into Shikasta for service as soon—sometimes—as they could talk and walk.

For instance again: Shammat's preoccupation was always to weaken and soften the moral fibre of the inhabitants. Ours was always the opposite effort. But Shammat was not always—and increasingly less so, towards the end—able to control her own efforts or to observe and understand ours.

Again: Shammat's agents prowled and lurked, feeding the spirit of hatred, antagonism, unreason, contention: we did the opposite always, but they were never able to observe, let alone understand, the techniques working against them, and this led sometimes to situations quite farcical, where they might be working against themselves, without knowing it.

Again: Shammat's agents, relying on the link between Shikasta and Shammat, often saw this bond where it did not exist, or had been destroyed or weakened by us. People who in fact were free of Shammatan influence, and who had clung to us, understanding—perhaps at first only in an inkling, or the thread of a thought—that salvation lay with us, people who in fact were in our service, and often without knowing it, were trusted by Shammat, who did not have the means to recognise the situation.

All over Shikasta, in those last days, moved our agents, our servants, our friends, and with them went the Signature, imprinted on them, in them, in their substance, just as the sick distortion of Shammat was imprinted on Shammat's kith and kin; and anyone who retained, anywhere, even a vestige of the shadow of the Signature, felt our presence, looked up—recognised—and followed. Or tried to. I am not saying that our struggle was anything but desperate, dire, awful. There were many casualties, failures. But just as, during the last days, in the last phase, Shammat's agents filled Shikasta with horror, and terror, and self-disgust, and destruction, so, too, did the Shadow of the Signature summon everyone who could remember . . . there was a sweetness, a promise, a lightness of heart and of hope in those dreadful last days.

Notes added to the above by JOHOR, TAUFIQ, USSELL, and others

With so large an area of Shikasta due to be laid waste, one of our preoccupations was of course the preservation of adequate representative genetic material. This was partly accomplished by judicious and specific pressures on certain individuals and groups of individuals capable of putting personal concerns aside in the interests of the broad perspective. For when directed to certain places temporarily or comparatively "safe," this was not necessarily with the idea of their personal survival. Certain types of Shikastan were able to respond very well: in fact their capacity to respond made them eligible. But of course our difficulty was that admirable and useful traits were so mixed with the undesirable. Sirius and its colonies, Canopus and its colonies, Shammat—and others too—all were now in the inheritance of Shikasta. And the increasing pressure on the Shikastan stock from local and external radiation; from the increasingly poisoned and adapted atmosphere; from their sustenance itself, full of every sort of chemical and radiation, from, too, the sober knowledge deep within them of the responsibilities of their destiny: all this had the effect of adapting the genetic material even more, causing sports of all kinds. Some of these were—and are—valuable, with potential. But others, alas, not.

We shall mention, as an example, a particular hazard that was overcome by—very—long-term foresight and planning: this because it has formed part of the story in this volume, not because it was more or less important than others of our concerns.

It had long been foreseen that there would be a strong reaction against the white races, whose technology had ruined so much of the world, and so many of its people. There was a real danger that feelings would run so high that there would be a serious depletion of genetic material. The "white race"—or races—were of a very varied genetic mix. Some parts of the globe, even at the end, were still comparatively homogenous, still virtually unmixed: but the central and western areas of the central landmass, particularly the Northwest fringes, had absorbed such a number of different stocks, from other parts of Shikasta and from outside Shikasta, that it was undesirable this "race" should be lost. A great deal of effort, some of it apparently even bizarre, went into making sure that enough of these animals survived to carry on their genes into the future: these efforts were continuous and energetic everywhere over the northern hemisphere. Or almost everywhere: the Isolated Northern Continent, originally uniformly populated by a fairly homogenous genetic stock, indigenous, adapted to the surroundings, was supplanted by a conquering people, mostly from the Northwest fringes and the central landmass with nothing in the way of genes that was not already receiving our attention.

On the whole, the morale of the white "race" in the northern hemisphere did not assist our efforts. Their partial overrunning by the "yellow" races, their continuous and systematic starvation by the "coloured" races anterior to this conquest, out of the typically Shikastan (or Shammatan!) desire for revenge for past humiliations and deprivations, their slow acceptance of the rest of the globe's view of themselves, which caused a sharp painful readjustment and a relinquishing of assumption of superiority which had sustained them for centuries—all this lowered the tone, and stamina, in the Northwest fringes particularly, to the point where it was affecting not only their own will to live, but also the emanations from these areas: and good strong emanations were essential to our task of trying to prevent unnecessary suffering and bloodshed. The failure of morale swung so far that large numbers of—first of all—the youth, and then the older people, were unable to sustain in themselves any pride in their past at all. All they had accomplished in the way of technical advances, energetic experimentation in patterns of society, justice—fine in concept if not always a success in practice—these accomplishments of theirs seemed to them to be nothing at all, and they were tending to sink into abasement and sullen withdrawal. In fact, this emotional reaction, seeing themselves entirely as villains, the despoilers of the globe, a view reinforced every moment by a thousand exterior sources of propaganda, was as narrow and self-centred as their previous view—when they saw themselves as God-given benefactors of the rest of Shikasta. Both viewpoints failed to see things in interaction, a meshing of events, the reciprocation of needs, abilities, capacities. The "white races," subjugated, insulted, famished, deprived, with large masses of its population drawn off for cheap labour for the use of the reviving parts of the globe, with nothing of its wealth, and little of its culture left, was as unable to see itself as part of a whole as ever it had been. The Shikastan compartmentalism of mind reigned supreme, almost unchallenged—except by our servants and agents, continually at work trying to restore balances, and to heal these woeful defects of imaginative understanding.

From TAFTA, SUPREME LORD of SHIKASTA,
to SUPREME SUPERVISORY LORD
ZARLEM on SHAMMAT, *Greetings!*

Greetings to the Shammat General Rule!

Obeisance!

Obeisance to Puttiora!

All things obey Puttiora, the All-Magnificent!

Shikasta lies beneath your heel, Shikasta awaits your will!

From Zone to Zone, from Pole to Pole, from end to end, Shikasta subserves you.

How deep and fine the service of Shikasta to Shammat, servant of Puttiora!

From end to end, these disgraceful little animals squirm and writhe under our all-seeingness!

In every land these degraded beasts fight and kill and suffer, the aromas of pain and of blood rising like red smoke above every part of Shikasta, deliciously rise to the nostrils of deserving Shammat.

How strong the nurturing flow from Shikasta to Shammat, stronger every day the flow that feeds Shammat, ever stronger the millennial link that provides power which is the right and the due from Shikasta to Shammat, earned by our tutelage, our Overlordship, our Superiority in the Scales of the Galaxy!

Oh Shikasta, bleeding little animal, how we praise you in your willing squalidness, how we applaud you in your subservience, how we succour you, our other self, our sac of blood, our source of strength!

Day and night, and from moment to moment, roll in your Tributes, oh Shikasta, our slavish one, the Vibrations of hatred and dissension feed us, sustain us, make us exalt, Shammat the All-Powerful!

Night and day, oh nasty degraded one, you supply our food to us, the clash of arms, the cries of warriors, the roar of machines in hostility.

Day and night, planet that is lowest of the Low, you shake and shiver beneath our Rule, Shammat the Glorious, the all-glorious son of Puttiora the Glorious, offering your fat and your substance, the perfumes of your anguish, the aromas of your cruelties, your disgustingness.

How low is Shikasta, the worm in the dust, writhing heaps and pits of worms in corruption, all, all, all feeding us, Shammat, feeding Puttiora. Over your skies, Shikasta, the shine and shimmer of your contentions, your frightful inventions, all feeding us with the fuel of your hatreds. Under your oceans, Shikasta, the grind and clash and vibration of your manoeuvring machines, all feeding and perfuming us, Shammat. In your sick minds, Shikasta, the perverted minds of backward and ignorant animals whose good fortune it has even been to attract our kindly rule, flame the animosities that nurse us, Shammat!

Everywhere move our magnificent ones, ever aware, ever watching, ever guarding our own!

Everywhere our Eyes and Ears, and nothing escapes us!

We observe the pitiful heavings of your attempts at revolt, we note and we *Crush!*

We have watched the movements and machinations of our enemies on Shikasta, and have undone them all—confound their knavish tricks, compound their politicks, writhe and expire, suffer and *die!*

We Shammat, Shammat of Puttiora the glorious, confirm the Flow is extant, the Flow is stronger, the Flow is ever and eternal, the Flow is for all time, the sustenance and food of Us, Lords of the Galaxy, Lords of the Worlds. . . .

NOTE ATTACHED to ABOVE:

Hey, Zarl!

I request sick leave. There is some goddamned new virus. We are going down all over the goddamned place. Or if it isn't a virus then it's Treachery. Why aren't I in the new Government? What sort of shitting gratitude is that? There are going to be some changes made, I'll simmer them in their own filthy blood, see if I don't.

LYNDA COLDRIDGE *to* BENJAMIN SHERBAN
(No. 17. *"Various Individuals."*)

Your brother told me to write to you. He says to me that he has told you he is in contact with me. I hope he has done this. Otherwise why should you trust me. It is a hard thing to ask these days. You must trust me for the sake of these people who are coming to you. Otherwise they will be dead. When you think things can't get worse, they can. I've known about all this happening for a long time. But when it does, then it is still a shock. George says these people must come to you. He says you are in Marseilles. That must be a difficult place to be in. These people are trustworthy. All from the hospitals I have been in. They are mostly patients. But some doctors and nurses. So these will be useful. We are not sending you the people who have been so ill they may be a nuisance. Doctor Hebert has helped choose the people. He knows all about these things. Doctor Hebert and I have been working together. I forget how long. I want him to go to you with the others but he won't. He says he is old and due to die. I do not agree with this. He knows so much about useful things, and he is not ever Mad, like me. I hope you know what I mean when I say that about Useful Things. I asked your brother about Doctor Hebert. Your brother says Doctor Hebert must do as he believes is right. Conscience. The individual. Rights of. I am staying. I am old too. Your brother wants me to stay. He has asked me to. He says it will be useful. There will be people left alive, in spite of the awfulness. They will be few. There are underground places. Most of them for bigwigs. *Friends* of ours have made an underground place. No one knows about it except a few. This is for about twenty people. Most of them have the Capacities of contact. George says you sometimes have them. I have tried to contact you but couldn't. Perhaps we aren't on the same wavelength! (Ha Ha) The twenty people are of all ages. Some are children. They are all ready for what is to come. The Wrath. Sometimes I think that if they knew what is to come they wouldn't be. Ready, I mean. I wish it would all happen, and we could get it over. We are going to take into the underground place more people than it is really made for. That is because I won't live long. And Doctor Hebert won't either. And there are two other old people. Doctor Hebert will be the only doctor with us, apart from a half-trained young one. He can train some more. Also he has quite a lot of Capacity. I know when Doctor Hebert and I will die. By then all the others will be trained in the Capacities. They will all live until the rescue teams come and England is opened up again. I don't know if George has told you all this. George just says this and that according to what is necessary. Then he switches off. I mean, we don't have a proper talk. Not a chat. From this I gather he must be very busy. Well I can see he must be. When I first contacted him, it was by accident. I thought it was my own mind talking to me. I wonder if that will make sense to you. Perhaps it will. I know that one's own mind can say all kinds of things. You think it is someone else but it isn't, it is you. Do you understand this. I am writing too much. It is because it is a funny thing working for years and years to rescue people, and not even knowing if you can. Sometimes it was very difficult. At first no one believed me or Doctor Hebert. And it took such a long time. And then after all that you send them off to someone never met. In Marseilles! It will be an awful journey. We have got all the false papers together. And the uniforms. Everything. I can't help worrying. At any rate, we have done what we planned. We said we would rescue people and we have. Here they are. We won't be having any contact after this. Not unless you get better at the Capacities! So goodbye. If this letter gets to you then the people will have reached you. It is a funny thing, isn't it, having to trust someone in this way. I mean, because of the quality of an instruction "over the air." So good luck. Lynda Coldridge.

DOCTOR HEBERT *to* BENJAMIN SHERBAN

Attached is a list of all the people who are about to leave on the dangerous and difficult journey to you. Mrs. Coldridge says that a short description of each one will be helpful and I believe she is right. The qualifications of the professional people are briefly sketched, and the medical history of those who were patients in various hospitals Mrs. Coldridge and I have worked in. In each we found people who had various Capacities in embryo or in potential and because of a misunderstanding of the phenomena they experienced had been classed as ill and incarcerated temporarily or permanently, but due to good fortune or a stronger than usual constitution their treatment had not damaged them. Of course nothing could or can be done for the victims of more draconian or prolonged treatments. It has been no easy task to persuade these people of their own possibilities, since such arguments fell on ears conditioned to be thinking of these either as unscientific or as so "lunatic fringe" that they could not even be listened to. But patience has worked wonders, and here are the results of many years of efforts, all of them undertaken behind the backs of hospital authorities and in conditions always of difficulty and sometimes even of danger. Mental hospitals have not been the safest places to be, not anywhere in the world! These are all people, too, who because of their experience are inured to hardship, misunderstanding, uncertainty, and a capacity for suspending judgement that is the inevitable reward of having to undergo years of suspending judgement on the workings of their own minds. These are most useful qualities! You can believe that I speak from experience! When I discovered in myself certain Capacities my first reaction was that of one who has found an enemy within the gates. For until I met Mrs. Coldridge and could understand what it was she was saying, and—even more—understood her long and painful history, I did not have the ability to be patient with my own flounderings in a realm so new to me that it seemed at first enemy territory. To sharpen this point: all these people can take weight, responsibility, burdens, difficulties, delays, the loss of hope. As we know, this is essential equipment for these hard times. . . . I write this and marvel at the inadequacies of language! What we all live through is worse than our worst nightmares could have warned us of. Yet we do live through them, and some of us, a few, will survive. And that is all that we—the human race—need. We must look at it this way. I want to say something to you that I regard as a testament, an act of faith! It is that if human beings can stand a lifetime of the sort of subjective experience that it has been Mrs. Coldridge's lot to undergo, if they can patiently and stubbornly suffer assaults on their very bastions, as she has done, if we can face living, day after day after day, through what most people could only describe as "hell" and come out the other end, on some sort of even keel, even if damaged—as Mrs. Coldridge would be the first to agree she is—if we, the human race, have in us such strengths of patience and endurance, then what can we not achieve? Mrs. Coldridge has been the inspiration of my life. When I first encountered her, a bedraggled unfortunate, a mere skeleton with vast frightened blue eyes wandering along the corridors of the Lomax Hospital in a dreadful suburb of one of our ugliest cities, she was just another of the deteriorated wrecks among whom I had spent so much of my life, and whom I certainly never regarded as holding the possibilities of any revelations or lessons—yet it was this lunatic, for she was that when I first met her—who has taught me what courage, what tenacity, is possible in a human being, and therefore in us all. What else is there for any of us but courage? And perhaps even that is only a word for being prepared to go on living at all. I send you my best wishes for the success of your undertakings—hoping that this assembly of tired phrases will in fact convey to you what I feel. And I entrust to you these people who . . . what can I say? I part with them in the same spirit a child uses when he launches a leaf into a torrent of street water. I shall pray for you and for them. This on behalf of myself only, for I fear Mrs. Coldridge is scornful of religion. With her experiences I feel she will be forgiven.

BENJAMIN SHERBAN *to* GEORGE SHERBAN

Well my little brother! Here we all are, present and correct. Five hundred of us. The Pacific is terrific, despite everything, forgive the frivolity in these hard times. To get down to essentials. The *inland* water is clean—well, more or less, the food plentiful, and no natives, for these were taken off twenty years ago to clear the area for H. Bomb tests. Who were they to protest? When their Masters spoke? Anyway, it is an ill wind, for there is now plenty of room for us. So far no casualties. Very little illness, and anyway we have suitable supplies both of medics and medicines. Quite a little township is already up, with all cons if not all mod cons. It is Paradise nowe. But for how long? Aye, there's the rub. If I sound manic, then of course it is because I simply cannot believe that any of us is still alive. Resisting the temptation to despatch this in a corked bottle on the next retreating tide, I am sending it by canoe, then cargo ship, then air to Samoa. And will continue to send reports as long as these amenities continue. Ah, civilisation, to imagine we ever complained of you, complained about any nasty little part of you. . . . Please accept my assurances at all times that I remain, your obedient servant. Benjamin. I assume you do know Suzannah is in Camp 7, Andes, with Kassim and Leila?

GEORGE SHERBAN *to* SHARMA PATEL

Dearest Sharma,

First of all, Greetings! In any style you like. No, I am not laughing at you, I assure you. I am writing this in great haste late at night because I get the impression *very strongly* that you have a change of plan. Yes, I do remember how you laugh at me when I say such things. And I feel sorrowful because I have something of importance to say, but I feel you will not listen to me. But perhaps you will, perhaps you can, just this once, and so I am writing to say this to you: *Please* stick to your plan and please leave at the time you said you would. Please do *not* go down into Encampment 8. I beg of you. And if you are prepared, just this once, to trust me, to believe me, take as many of your staff with you as will go with you. Don't stay where you are and don't go down into Camp 8. How can I reach you? How can I persuade you? Do you have any idea what it feels to know someone as I know you, to hear you say I love you, and with such depth of feeling and such sincerity!—and yet know that I shall not be believed, no matter what I say. You will not do as I ask, I know that. And yet I must try.

Sharma, what can I do to make you listen to me? This once, believe me. If I said to you, leave your position at the head of your Army, leave your honours and your responsibilities, you would lecture me for my lack of understanding of your equality with me, my ignorance about women and their capacities, but you would suddenly, even surprising yourself, leave everything behind you, your powers, your position, as if you had been hypnotised, and you would come with me, like a sleepwalker, presenting yourself to me with a smile that said: Here I am. And from that moment you would never again agree with me in anything, or fall in with anything I wished, or trust me. Your life would be a demonstration of how badly I treated you. Do you know this, Sharma? Is that not a remarkable thing? Perhaps you do not agree that this is exactly what would happen. And no, I am not saying that I want you to do any of these things, no I do not. I am only begging you, begging you—listen to me, and don't go down to Encampment 8. Sharma my love, will you listen to me, please listen to me. . . . (*This letter was not sent.*)

[SEE *History of Shikasta*, VOL. 3015, *The Century of Destruction, Twentieth Century War: 3rd and Final Phase.* SUMMARY CHAPTER.]

From SUZANNAH *in* CAMP 7, *the* ANDES,
to GEORGE SHERBAN

My darling,

It is very cold tonight. It is not easy to get adjusted to this altitude. Kassim and Leila are all right, and that is the main thing. A lot of people are finding it hard. We have a lot of chest troubles. Our doctors are working all the time. Luckily we have plenty of medicines. But I wonder for how long. 63 people came in. They got out from France. They say there is nothing much left of Europe. They are full of all kinds of stories but I said I didn't want to hear. I don't see the point. I think it is morbid. What is done is done. So I came to our hut and left them talking. It would be a good thing if you could get hold of warm clothes for all the children. We have nearly 1,200 children now. I did what you said and put Juanita in charge of the children and she has made her husband work with her. They are a good team. All the children like them. Today a party came in from North America. 94. They want to stay here but I said this camp is full. Well it is. How are we going to feed everybody? That is what is on my mind. I said they could stay some days to rest and then they should go to Camp 4. It is only 200 miles. They can leave the weak ones and the children with us. They say North America is full of troubles but I said I didn't want to listen any longer. I have my work cut out. Can you try and find some shoes for the children? I think it would be a good thing if some more camps got set up, if the refugees are going to come and come like this. I don't see what can be possibly left up there. But I don't want to think about it. Kassim says he wants to come and be with you. I said he is too young but he is fifteen. Leila wants to come too. I said definitely no. I said I would find out what you think about Kassim. And they would have to obey. That is a question.

When you think about winter coming up in the North, it is a good thing for the epidemics I suppose, but it is a bad thing for the people who are left. But I don't want to think morbid thoughts.

Philip came in just now and says he saw you and you are working hard. He says you will be coming next week. When you come we should get married because I am pregnant. I am sure now. I wasn't sure until today. It is all very well these young people saying things like that don't matter in these times, but I think we should set an example.

I am two months and two days pregnant.

I hope it is a boy but with my luck I suppose it will be a girl. I don't really mean that, only partly.

I have got Pedro to mend the roof of this hut. Pedro is very nice and I want to suggest we should adopt him when you come. What I mean is, we should tell him we regard him as our child. He is feeling insecure. I can always tell things like that. It is not good for an eight-year-old boy to have no parents and nothing at all. I think we should have some kind of ceremony. We can always think of something. By the time we have finished I expect we shall have a dozen or more, if this goes on! Many a true word is spoken in jest.

I won't tell Pedro he can be our child until you have agreed.

They have built a big fire in the centre of the camp tonight and there is a big moon and it looks nice. They are telling stories about their escapes from the different places. What happens is, someone steps forward into the place just near where the fire is and then everyone is silent and then this person tells their tale. Then this person goes and sits down and another gets up. Or someone sings a song. Some of the songs are very sad. Some of them romantic. And then someone else steps forward and tells their tale of woe. There will be a lot of babies born soon. We shall have to feed them. The doctors are watching all the babies very carefully.

Everything is being done the way you said.

Re: Colonised Planet 5, Shikasta

I feel very lonely without you, I know you don't like it when I say things like that.

I know it is no good my asking you if you feel lonely without me because I suppose you'll just smile as usual.

Well my dear, I shall see you next week, please God.

Your Suzannah

From KASSIM SHERBAN

Dear Leila, and dear Suzannah. And hello! to Pedro and Philip and Anqui and Quitlan and Shoshona

And a very big kiss for little Rachel which is of course the most important thing of all. Tell her that and say I have a beautiful yellow bird for her.

Hello, hello and hello. I know that you Suzannah are waiting for me to say something about George but I can't, because guess what, when I caught up with him he was off North, and he said I was to manage by myself and gave me things to do and pushed me off. But he gave me your news Suzannah, and that's wonderful, and this time it will be a boy, that's what I think.

This is a completely new town. I got here last week. It is the strangest town. Of course it is all of wood and stones and lacquered paper, but the shapes are not what you'd expect, I haven't figured it all out yet. I came walking down the hill into it, and it was like a dream. And what made it worse was that I was scared. After all I am young, not even my best efforts can disguise that, and I am *still* in the old Youth Army uniform, because I can't find anything else, and after all they were running Youth Army people out of towns before the Third World War, and even killing them. The hunters hunted. Do you remember the song:

The hunters hunted,
The weapons turned—

When the hunters hunted,
The world burned . . .

That's all I can remember of it. I don't want to remember it I suppose. There seemed no place to hide when you heard that. How did we survive all that I wonder?—but I didn't mean to start on all that again. I keep deciding never to think of any of it again but my mind goes back to it.

Anyway, I came down into this town scared witless. I didn't know what to expect. At the very least I thought I would have to persuade them I was harmless. But that didn't happen. The town has a central square and a fountain. It is all done in stone. There were people standing about the square, and as I got into it, full of apprehension, it was the strangest thing, but I was accepted at once. No one expected me to be harmful. Can you imagine what that was like?

There is a guesthouse for travellers and for a week every traveller is given food, if not much, and then if there is work he can do he starts earning the food, and if not, he goes on somewhere else. I did not want to start work, because I was on a "fact-finding survey" so George said. So he *said*, and if you have to get facts, then you have to ask questions. Where better than in the guesthouse, and then the café, and the store, and the square again. It had dawned on me by then that it was the people who I was to meet—*that* was the point of the exercise. The people in the square and everywhere else answered any questions I asked. Facts. There are fewer facts in the world now than there were before the smash-up. A woman from the North, an Argentinian, took me to her house and told me what was happening there, and how the War had affected that area, and she made me meet others. It began to dawn on me *then* . . . all the time I was being reminded of something, I didn't know quite what, and I was lying awake every night trying to remember *what* it was, and even now I can't say much about it, but it is like what the other Rachel, and Olga, and Simon, used to tell me of how the three were taught by people just coming past, and how they learned things without there being actual lessons and timetables most of the time. I keep meeting people, and all of them seem to know at once who I am and what to tell me or where to take me. That is very peculiar. Something peculiar is going on, but I don't know what.

Take a simple thing like the shape of this town. There were no plans. No architect. Yet it grew up symmetrical and on the shape of a six-pointed star. I didn't realise it was a star until I walked up out of the town very early one morning, and when I looked down, trying to see if I could notice anything different, I was able to see the star-shape. But no matter who I ask, no one seems able to say anything about plans or a master plan or anything like that. And there is another thing. When I walked down into this town, I was taking it absolutely for granted, but *absolutely*, that there were going to be different factions and the rulers and the armies and the police and I would have to watch my step and be careful what I said. Do you realise how we have all had to do that? *Do you?* Of course I don't mean the little ones, not little Rachel, but even Philip or Pedro. All the time watching our step. It has been drilled into us. But after a couple of days I felt a great relax all over my body, like yawning and stretching, and then I suddenly understood I wasn't afraid of doing the wrong thing and landing in prison or ending up as butchers' meat. I simply couldn't believe it. I can't believe it even now. I haven't seen anybody fight. I haven't seen a riot or walls being smashed down or stones being thrown or people being dragged off screaming or anything like that at all. There is a very old Indian here, and when I was talking to him I said things like this I've written here, and he said, you are the child of great misfortune and now you must learn differently. Did you know that when the old explorers came here long ago there were Giants here? The old Indian told me that, he had learned it in what he called the White School—does *that* take you back?—but it was true, because his grandfather and his great-grandmother knew all about it. Well, I wouldn't like to be asked what *facts* I have got from being here, but I am leaving tomorrow. I have been hoping that the people who were kind to me in this town would say: In the next town, look up so and so. But they haven't. I am walking with four others. An old Israeli, he was a scientist in Tel Aviv, and a girl from the old United Arab Emirates, and an old woman from Norway—she got here somehow—and another woman with two children from the Urals. They wanted to stay here and find work but there isn't any, but there is news that people are wanted thirty miles off in another new town.

It is a week later. When I came down the hill into this town I was looking to see if it has a shape, you bet, and it has. It is beautiful, a circle, but with scallopped edges. The wavy edges are gardens. It is made like the last one I wrote about. It has the same paved centre, a circle, and a very beautiful fountain, with a basin, round, in a local stone, a yellowish rose colour. The basin is shallow, a couple of inches, and the water trickles into it in patterns, and there are patterns in the stone shining up from under the water, and there are the same patterns in the roofing of the houses and the floor tiles and everywhere. It is the most beautiful place I can remember. Again, no one knows anything about plans or architects, it just grew up, or so it would seem. Again I am in the guesthouse. We are all still together, but the woman with the children has got work in the fields and also in the laboratory, and the scientist has, too. As for the others, no luck so far.

Again people talk to me and tell me things. I just move from one to another. I know all about this area and this town and who is in it and what they do and what they have done before the War and what they think. I have the most peculiar thoughts. They are the most extraordinary and outrageous thoughts, but I *am* having them and so I propose to stand by them. Tomorrow I am moving on with the Arab girl and the old woman from Norway. They haven't got work. Also a new travelling companion, a jaguar who walked into the guesthouse last night and lay down and was still with us in the morning. We thought he was tame but no one knows him. We gave him some maize porridge and some sour milk, and we expected him to turn up his nose but he didn't. Apart from the jaguar there is little Rachel's yellow bird, not a real one, it is made of dried grasses, and a very fine mongrel dog who has taken a fancy to me and he and the jaguar gallop along on all sides of us when we walk abroad.

A week later.

This time the town which we came *up* the hill to is octagonal, but we didn't work that out until we were well inside it. It is composed of six linked hexagons. The hexagons are gardens. The lattice is buildings. Again these buildings are strange considering what we are all used to, of bricks and adobe and dried grass screens and lacquered paper. Everything is very light and airy. The central place is a star, and it has a fountain, making patterns of stone and water that echo each other. There are patterns on the walls and floors—different ones from the patterns in the last town. The old Norwegian woman got work in the kitchen of the guesthouse. The girl from the United Arab Emirates is with a man she met at the fountain. That leaves me and the jaguar and the dog. I have spoken with a lot of people in this town. Now I am going to have to say it. Regardless. This is what I have been thinking about all the way along these roads. We used to believe George was so special, well I am not saying he isn't. Not that I thought all that much about it then. I just went along with everything. But there are a lot like George. Did you realize that, you there, Suzannah and everyone? These people I keep meeting in the towns and the ones that are on the roads and walk with us a little way and then go off into the pampas or the forests again, as if they had expected to meet us and had something to say, well, these people are George-people. They are the same. I know this is impossible, but it is the conclusion I have come to. There are more and more George-people all the time.

It is the same in this town as everywhere else. Now I am getting used to walking into a town with my stomach muscles relaxed and not in a twist and not on my toes all the time in case something comes out at me from some corner, and not having to look out for the local Camps, and not feeling scared to death if I see a group of young people, the way we all were. Yes of course I wasn't exactly old myself. Do you suppose that living in a town has been like this in the past? I mean, people relaxed and easy and things happening the right way without laws and rules and orders and armies? And prisons, prisons, prisons. Do you think that is possible? Well, it is an outrageous thought, but suppose it is true?

It is four months later. I have been to four more towns, all new ones, a triangle, a square, another circle, a hexagon. Do you know something? People are leaving the old towns when they can and making new towns in new places, in this new way. Doesn't that make you think different thoughts? The people talk about the old towns and cities as if they are *hell*. If they are like what our cities used to be then they are hell.

I have had quite a few different travelling companions and heard all kinds of stories. From all parts of the world. Suzannah I think you are right when you don't want to hear talk of the events in Europe, etc. I didn't think you were right and in fact I despised you. I am telling you this Suzannah because you are so kind and you won't mind. I have noticed something. As I go along these roads I am sometimes alone with my faithful jaguar and dog but sometimes with others, and when talk starts about the awfulness, then it is as if people *are not hearing*. Not that they are not listening. Not hearing. They look vaguely at you. Blank. Do you know what I think. *They can't believe it.* Well sometimes I look back and it is such a little time, and I can't believe it. I think that dreadfulness happens somewhere else. I don't know how to say that. I mean, when awful things happen, even to the extent we have all just seen, then our minds don't take them in. Not really. There is a gap between people saying hello, have a glass of water, and then bombs falling or lasar beams scorching the world to cinders. That is why no one seemed able to prevent the dreadfulness. They couldn't take it in.

I have understood that the vague blank look is from the past. It is not what we are now. Do you think it is possible it is not so much we *forget* things that are awful but that we never really believed in them happening.

But have you noticed that everyone is different now? We are all much more lively and alert and don't need to sleep all the time and we are all of a piece and not all at sixes and sevens. Do you know what I mean?

I have lost my faithful jaguar. I was walking up and up, along a quite high narrow path, among grasslands, and there was a shepherd, quite of the old sort, with a dog and a donkey. I was worried about the jaguar. The dog I could order about but not the jaguar. The shepherd, who was a young man with a wife and two small children in a nice little house on the hillside was worried too. But my big dog made friends with his dog. And then the jaguar went and lay down a little apart from the dogs. The woman came out of her house with some milk in a basin and he drank it. I slept the night there and then went on alone because my jaguar decided to stay with the shepherd and the woman, and as I went off I saw him helping the shepherd round up some sheep, with the two dogs.

So I was quite alone for twenty miles or more. And then I saw someone ahead of me, and thought That looks like George. And it was George.

He told me you have had your baby, Suzannah, I am glad, and it is a boy. George said he is going to be called Benjamin so I suppose our Benjamin is dead. Benjamin and Rachel.

For a long time in the guesthouses and walking along by myself I was thinking of questions I wanted to ask George, and I asked him first of all about the towns, and how they came to be like that, and he said they are *functional*.

He said that you over there are building a town and it is like the old Star of David. I said, how did you know what it had to be and where. His reply to that was, wait a little and you will see.

He took me first of all to one of the old towns, not a big one, it was on a branch of the Rio Negro. I hated being in it, I felt sick and uneasy from the moment I got into it. And it is a dying town. People are leaving it. Everywhere buildings are collapsing and not being re-built. All the centre was quite empty.

I said, Why?

He said, the new cities are functional.

I could see he wasn't going to explain, I had to work it out.

We stayed the night in a broken-down hotel. It was awful. People are still suspicious and frightened in these places. I felt ill and I could see George didn't feel good. All the next day we walked around the town quite aimlessly. People noticed George, and they wanted to talk to him. He talked to them. Or they would simply follow him. They all looked so desperate and needful.

In the evening he just walked away from the town and about three hundred people followed us, though he had not said one word about their coming too. It was cold that night, and it was wet and misty, and we were all pretty miserable, but we walked on steadily with George and still not a word had been said about what was happening.

When the sun rose it was cold, cold, cold and we were all hungry.

George was standing on a hillside, a steep rocky one, and there was a plateau above us. The birds were wheeling about overhead as the sun came up and they shone in the sunlight. I have never been so cold.

George *remarked*, in a quite ordinary sort of voice, that it would be a good idea if we made a town there.

People said, Where? Where should we start?

He didn't reply. Meanwhile, we were all dying of hunger. Then there was a flock of sheep and another shepherd, and we bought some sheep and made a fire and cooked some meat, and got ourselves fed.

Then we were roaming about over the hillside and the plateau. There were about twenty of us doing this. Suddenly we all knew quite clearly where the city should be. We knew it all at once. Then we found a spring, in the middle of the place. That was how this city was begun. It is going to be a star city, five points.

We found the right soil for bricks nearby and for adobe. There is everything we can need. We have already started the gardens and the fields.

Some of us go into the decaying town every day to get bread and stuff, to keep us going.

The first houses are already up, and the central circular place is paved, and the basin of the fountain is made. As we build, wonderful patterns appear as if our hands were being taught in a way we know nothing about.

It is high up here, very high, with marvellous tall sky over us, a pale clear crystalline blue, and the great birds circling in it.

George left after a few days. I walked with him a little way. I said to him, What is happening, why are things so different?

So he told me.

George says he is going into Europe with a team. He says that you knew he would be going, but not that he would be going now, and that

I should tell you that when his task in Europe is finished, his work will be finished. I did not understand until he had left that it meant he would die then and we would not see him again.

So here we all are.

I am writing this, sitting on a low white wall that has the patterns on it. People are all around me, working at this and that. We are in tents in the meantime, everything makeshift and even difficult but it doesn't seem so, and everything is happening in this new way, there is no need to argue and argue and discuss and disagree and confer and accuse and fight and then kill. All that is over, it is finished, it is dead.

How did we live then? How did we bear it? We were all stumbling about in a thick dark, a thick ugly hot darkness, full of enemies and dangers, we were blind in a heavy hot weight of suspicion and doubt and fear.

Poor people of the past, poor poor people, so many of them, for long thousands of years, not knowing anything, fumbling and stumbling and longing for something different but not knowing what had happened to them or what they longed for.

I can't stop thinking of them, our ancestors, the poor animal-men, always murdering and destroying because they couldn't help it.

And this will go on for us, as if we were being slowly lifted and filled and washed by a soft singing wind that clears our sad muddled minds and holds us safe and heals us and feeds us with lessons we never imagined.

And here we all are together, here we are. . . .

Students are directed to:

The Shorter History of Canopus
Relations Between Canopus and Sirius
    1. War. 2. Peace.
The History of the Sirian Empire
The History of Puttiora
Shammat the Shameful
The Memoirs of Taufiq
Nasar, Ussell, Taufiq, Johor: Selected Material
The Sirian Experiments on Shikasta
The Penultimate Days
Before the Catastrophe on Shikasta
The Little People: Trade, Art, Metallurgy

Re: Colonised Planet 5, Shikasta

Envoys of the Last Days: A Concise History
Tales of the Three Planets
The Canopean Bond (On Shikasta, "SOWF"); properties of, densities of, variations in effects on different species, complete absence of. (Shammat)   (Physics Section)

A NOTE ON THE TYPE

The text of this book was set in Electra, a Linotype face designed by W. A. Dwiggins (1880–1956). All of the available variations of the font—bold face, oblique, and cursive—were used in setting the different sections. The official Shammat documents were set in Spartan Medium, a sans-serif face first made available in 1940.

Although a great deal of Dwiggins' early work was in advertising and he was the author of the standard volume *Layout in Advertising*, Mr. Dwiggins later devoted his prolific talents to book typography and type design and worked with great distinction in both fields. In addition to his designs for Electra, he created the Metro, Caledonia, and Eldorado series of typefaces, as well as a number of experimental cuttings that have never been issued commercially.

Electra cannot be classified as either modern or old-style. It is not based on any historical model, nor does it echo a particular period or style. It avoids the extreme contrast between thick and thin elements that marks most modern faces and attempts to give a feeling of fluidity, power, and speed.

This book was composed by The Maryland Linotype Composition Co., Baltimore, Maryland. It was printed and bound by American Book–Stratford Press, Saddle Brook, New Jersey.

Typography and binding design by Camilla Filancia.